UQ HOLDER!

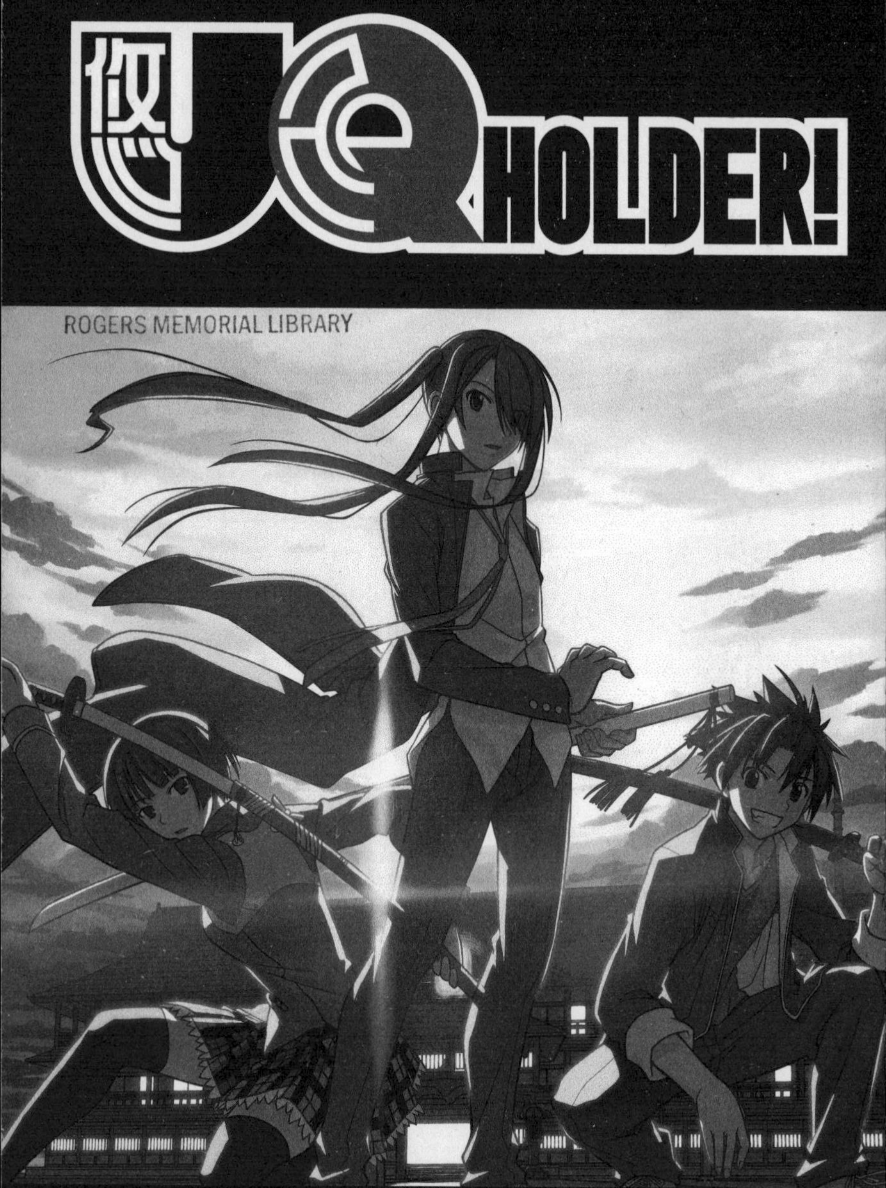

and CHARACTERS

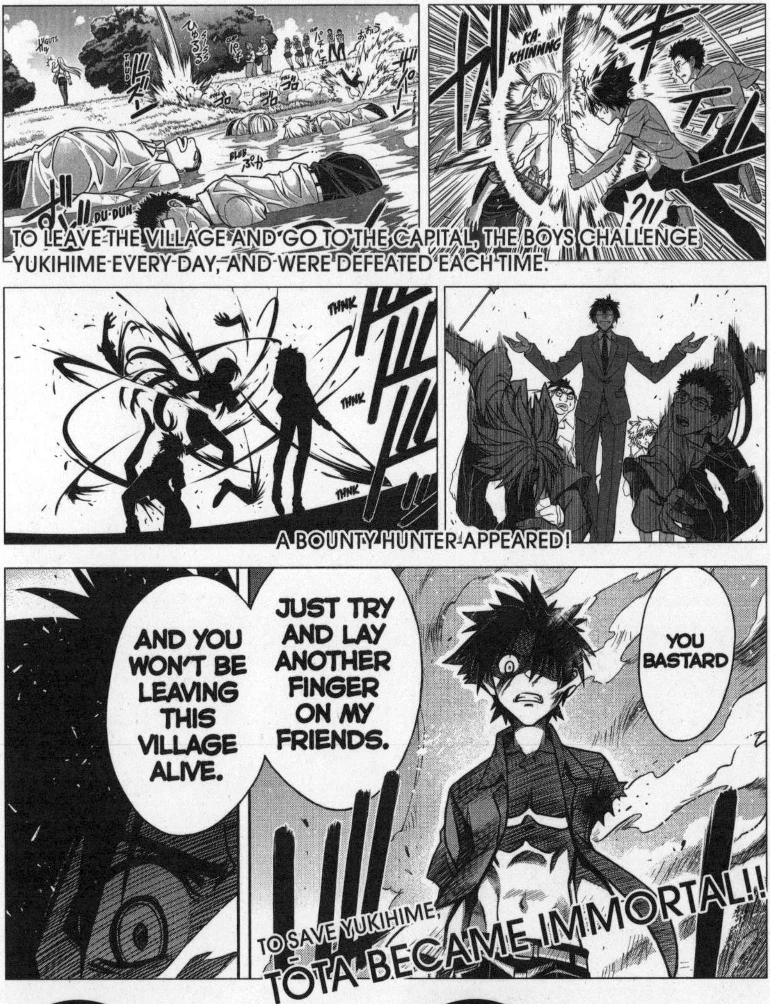
KA-KHINNNG
GUTS
THUD
BLUB
DU-DUN
TO LEAVE THE VILLAGE AND GO TO THE CAPITAL, THE BOYS CHALLENGE YUKIHIME EVERY DAY, AND WERE DEFEATED EACH TIME.
THNK
THNK
THNK
A BOUNTY HUNTER APPEARED!
YOU BASTARD
JUST TRY AND LAY ANOTHER FINGER ON MY FRIENDS.
AND YOU WON'T BE LEAVING THIS VILLAGE ALIVE.
TO SAVE YUKIHIME,
TŌTA BECAME IMMORTAL!!

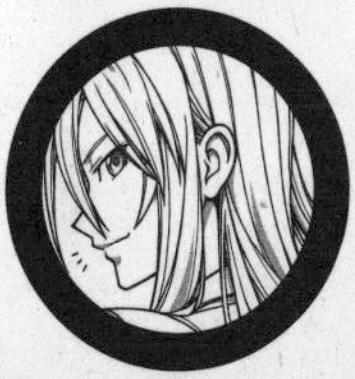

YUKIHIME
FOSTER PARENT TO TŌTA AND POWERFUL MAGIC USER. SHE IS ACTUALLY A 700 YEAR OLD VAMPIRE NAMED EVANGELINE.

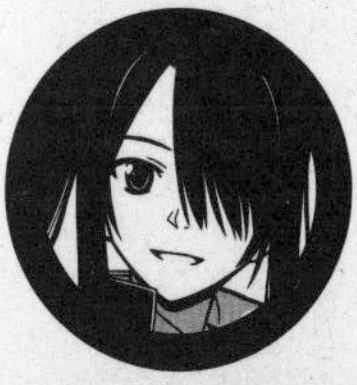

KURŌMARU TOKISAKA
IS ON A MISSION TO HUNT IMMORTALS. IS IMMORTAL HIMSELF.

UQ HOLDER! STORY

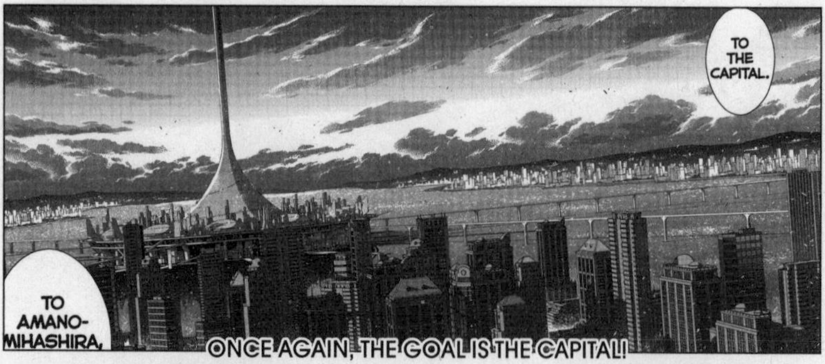
TO THE CAPITAL.
TO AMANO-MIHASHIRA,
ONCE AGAIN, THE GOAL IS THE CAPITAL!

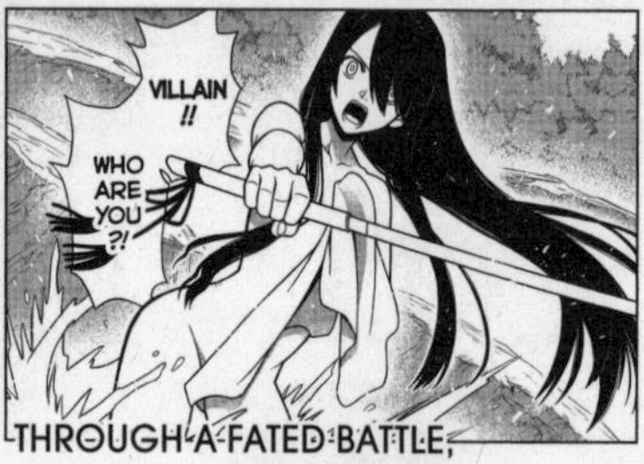
VILLAIN !!
WHO ARE YOU ?!
THROUGH A FATED BATTLE,

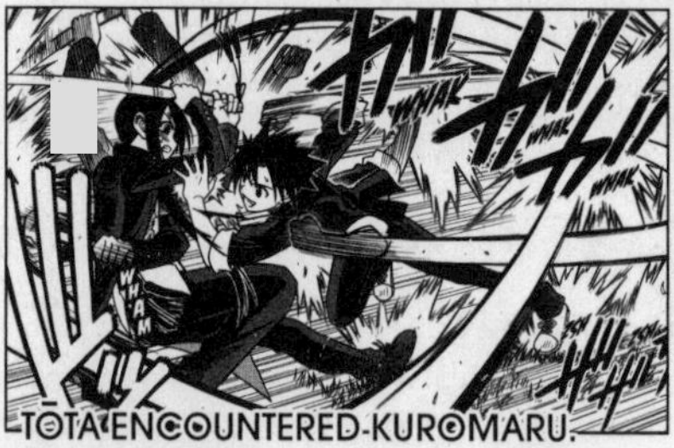
WHAK
WHAK
WHAK
WHAM
TŌTA ENCOUNTERED KUROMARU.

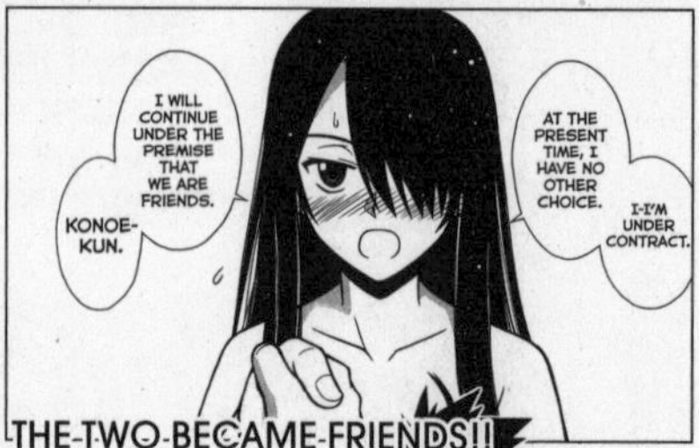
AT THE PRESENT TIME, I HAVE NO OTHER CHOICE.
I-I'M UNDER CONTRACT.
I WILL CONTINUE UNDER THE PREMISE THAT WE ARE FRIENDS.
KONOE-KUN.
THE TWO BECAME FRIENDS!!

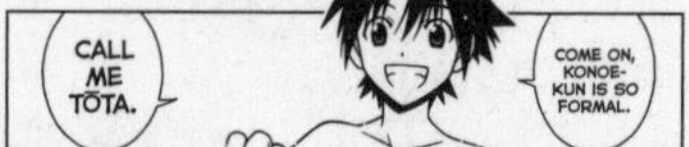
COME ON, KONOE-KUN IS SO FORMAL.
CALL ME TŌTA.

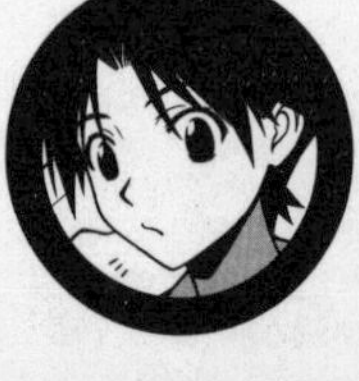

TŌTA KONOE
HIS BODY IS IMMORTAL. HIS DREAM IS TO GO TO THE CAPITAL AND MAKE A NAME FOR HIMSELF.

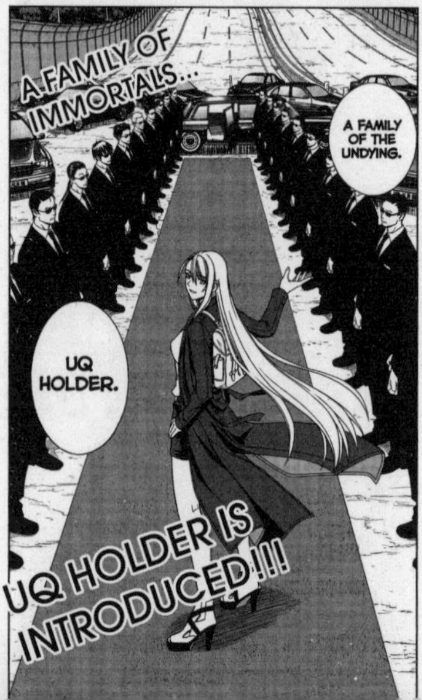
A FAMILY OF THE UNDYING.
A FAMILY OF IMMORTALS...
UQ HOLDER.
UQ HOLDER IS INTRODUCED!!!

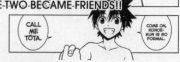

CONTENTS

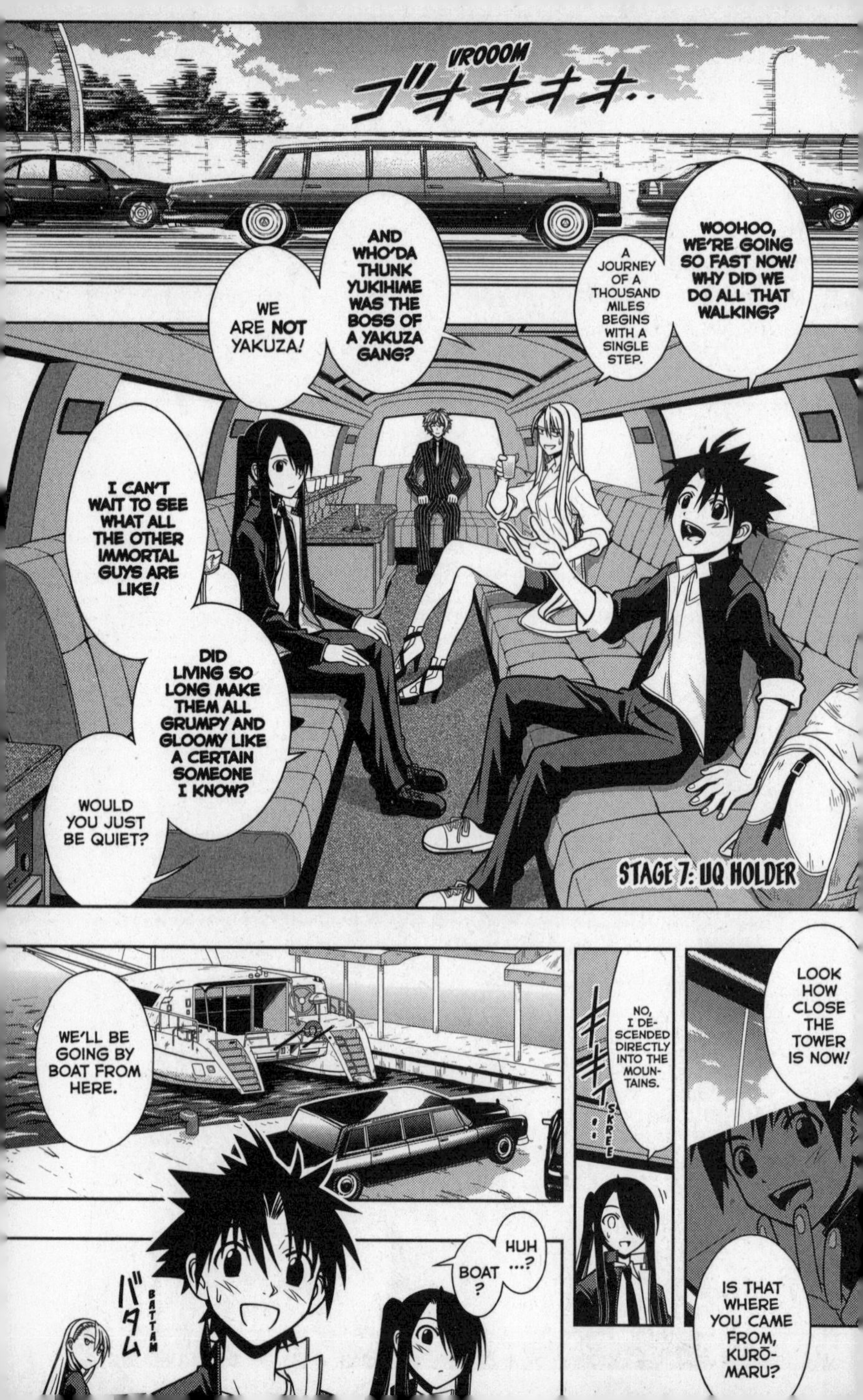
VROOOM
ゴオオオオ‥
WOOHOO, WE'RE GOING SO FAST NOW! WHY DID WE DO ALL THAT WALKING?
A JOURNEY OF A THOUSAND MILES BEGINS WITH A SINGLE STEP.
AND WHO'DA THUNK YUKIHIME WAS THE BOSS OF A YAKUZA GANG?
WE ARE NOT YAKUZA!
I CAN'T WAIT TO SEE WHAT ALL THE OTHER IMMORTAL GUYS ARE LIKE!
DID LIVING SO LONG MAKE THEM ALL GRUMPY AND GLOOMY LIKE A CERTAIN SOMEONE I KNOW?
WOULD YOU JUST BE QUIET?
STAGE 7: UQ HOLDER
LOOK HOW CLOSE THE TOWER IS NOW!
IS THAT WHERE YOU CAME FROM, KURŌ-MARU?
NO, I DE-SCENDED DIRECTLY INTO THE MOUN-TAINS.
SKREE
WE'LL BE GOING BY BOAT FROM HERE.
HUH...?
BOAT?
バタム
BATTAM

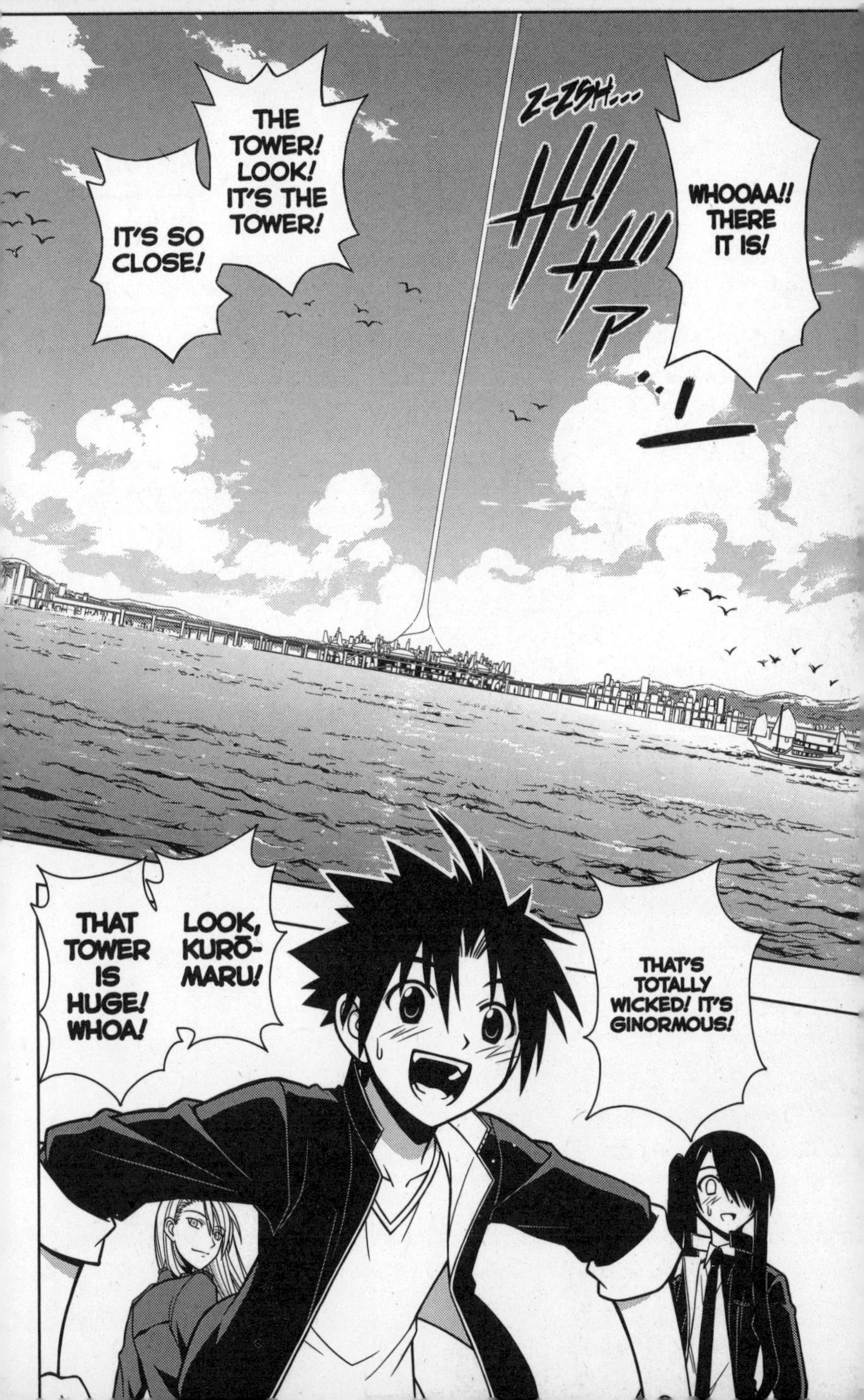
WHOOAA!! THERE IT IS!
Z-ZSH...
THE TOWER! LOOK! IT'S THE TOWER!
IT'S SO CLOSE!
THAT'S TOTALLY WICKED! IT'S GINORMOUS!
LOOK, KURŌ-MARU! THAT TOWER IS HUGE! WHOA!

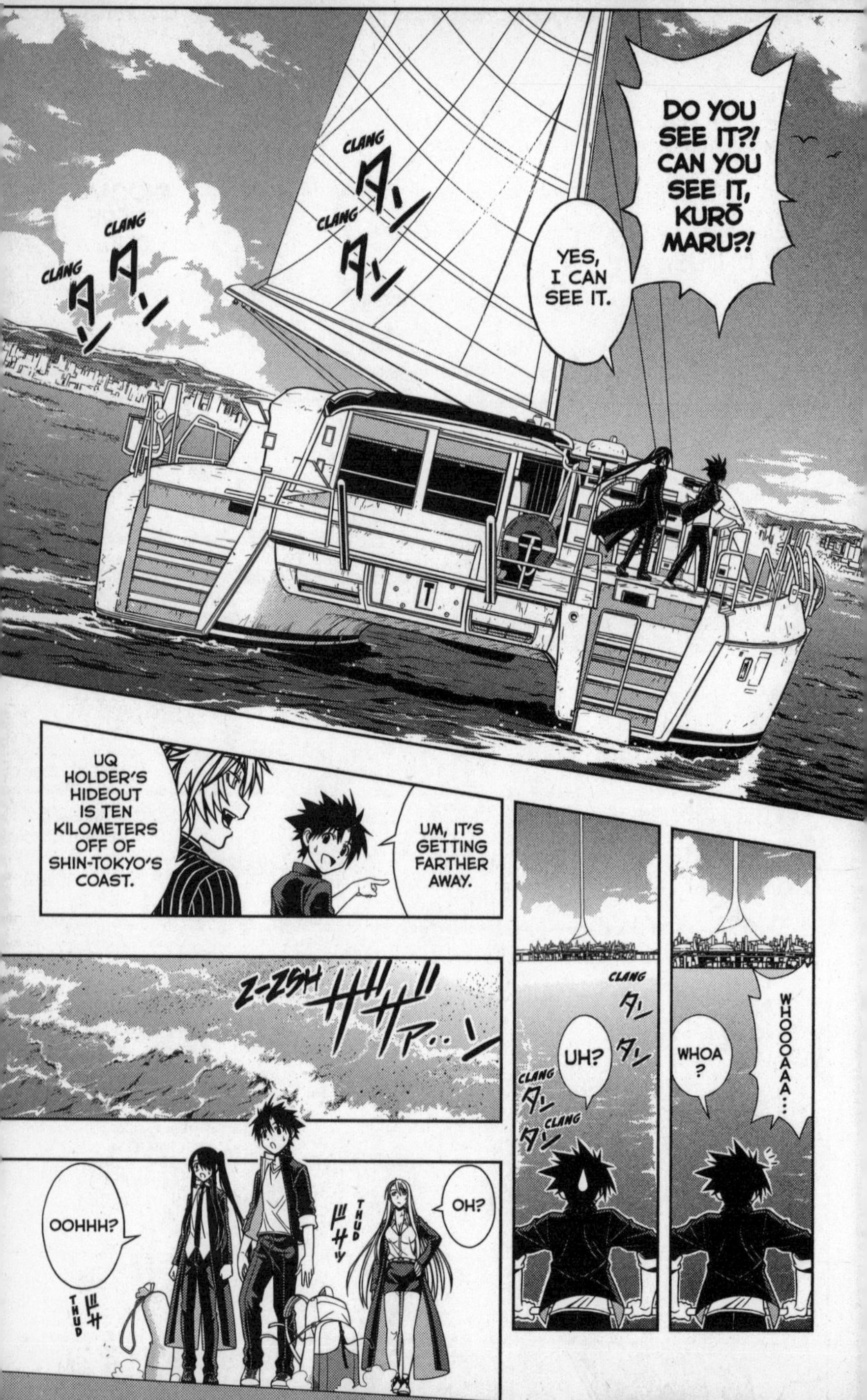
DO YOU SEE IT?! CAN YOU SEE IT, KURŌ MARU?!
YES, I CAN SEE IT.
CLANG
タン
CLANG
タン
CLANG
タン
CLANG
タン
WHOOOOAAA...
WHOA ?
UH?
CLANG
タン
タン
CLANG
タン
CLANG
タン
UM, IT'S GETTING FARTHER AWAY.
UQ HOLDER'S HIDEOUT IS TEN KILOMETERS OFF OF SHIN-TOKYO'S COAST.
Z-ZSH
ザザァ...ン
OH?
THUD
ドサッ
OOHHH?
THUD
ドサ

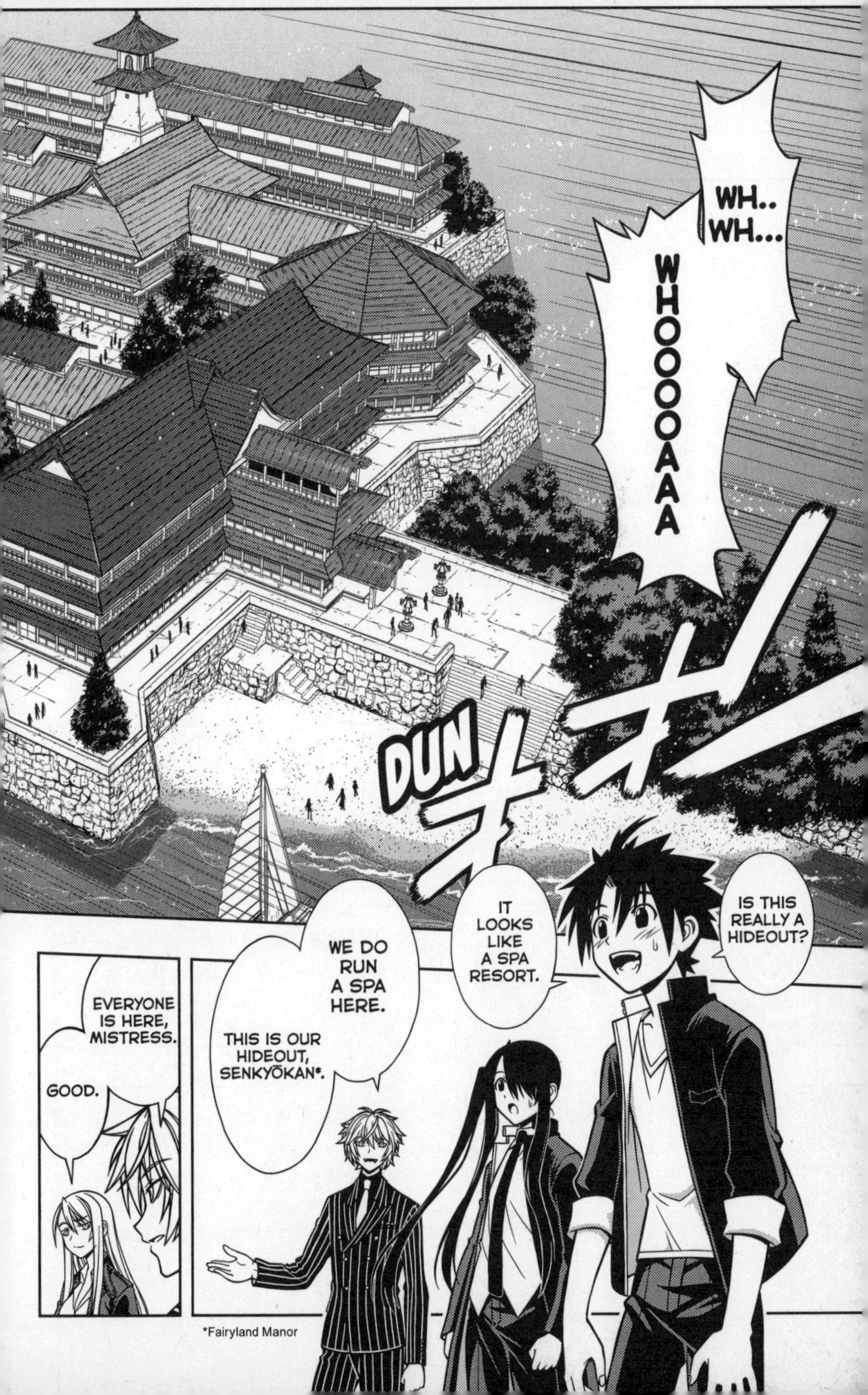
WH.. WH... WHOOOOAAA
DUN
IS THIS REALLY A HIDEOUT?
IT LOOKS LIKE A SPA RESORT.
WE DO RUN A SPA HERE.
THIS IS OUR HIDEOUT, SENKYŌKAN*.
EVERYONE IS HERE, MISTRESS.
GOOD.

*Fairyland Manor

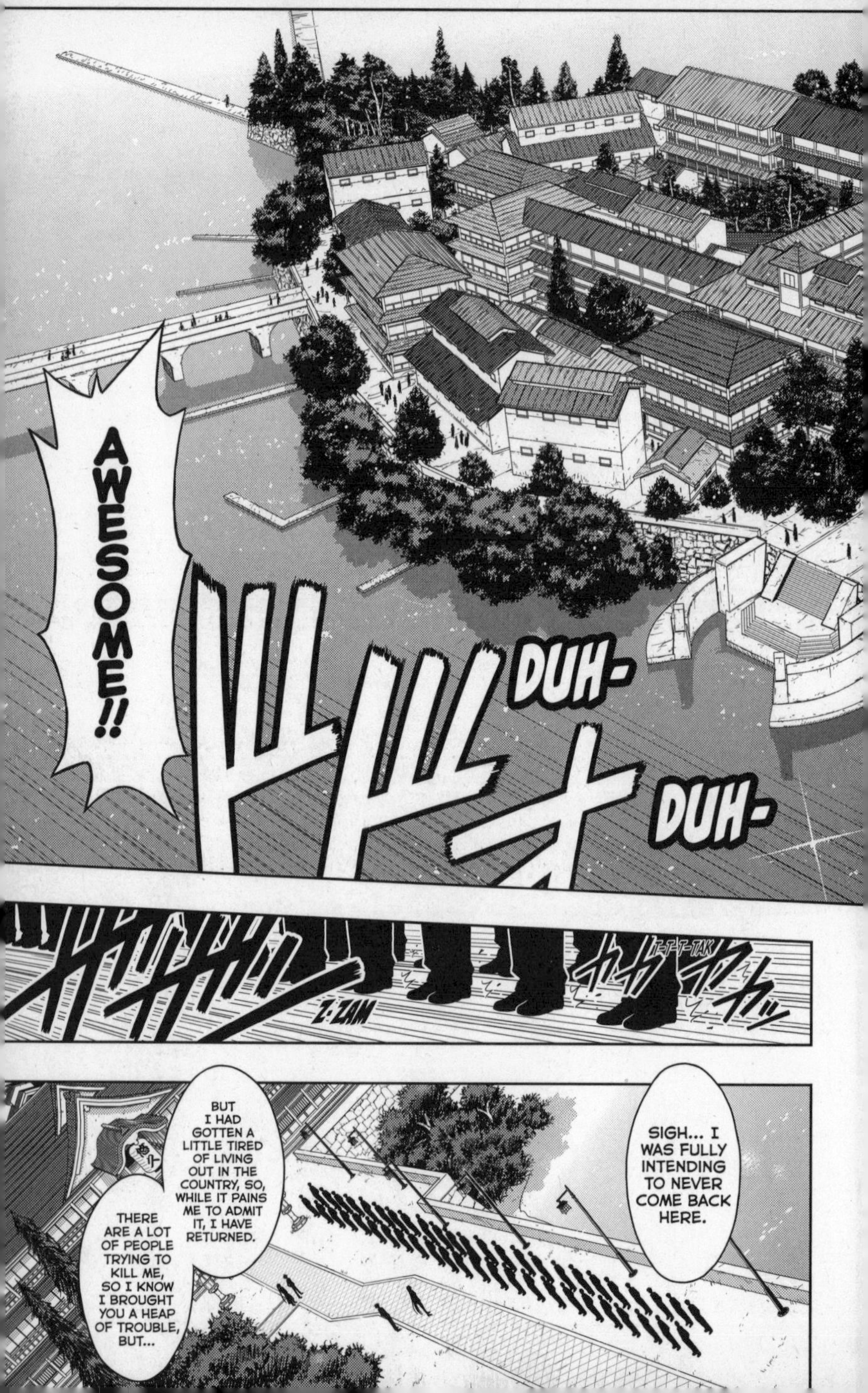
DUH-
DUH-
AWESOME!!
T-T-T-TAK
Z-ZAM
SIGH... I WAS FULLY INTENDING TO NEVER COME BACK HERE.
BUT I HAD GOTTEN A LITTLE TIRED OF LIVING OUT IN THE COUNTRY, SO, WHILE IT PAINS ME TO ADMIT IT, I HAVE RETURNED.
THERE ARE A LOT OF PEOPLE TRYING TO KILL ME, SO I KNOW I BROUGHT YOU A HEAP OF TROUBLE, BUT...

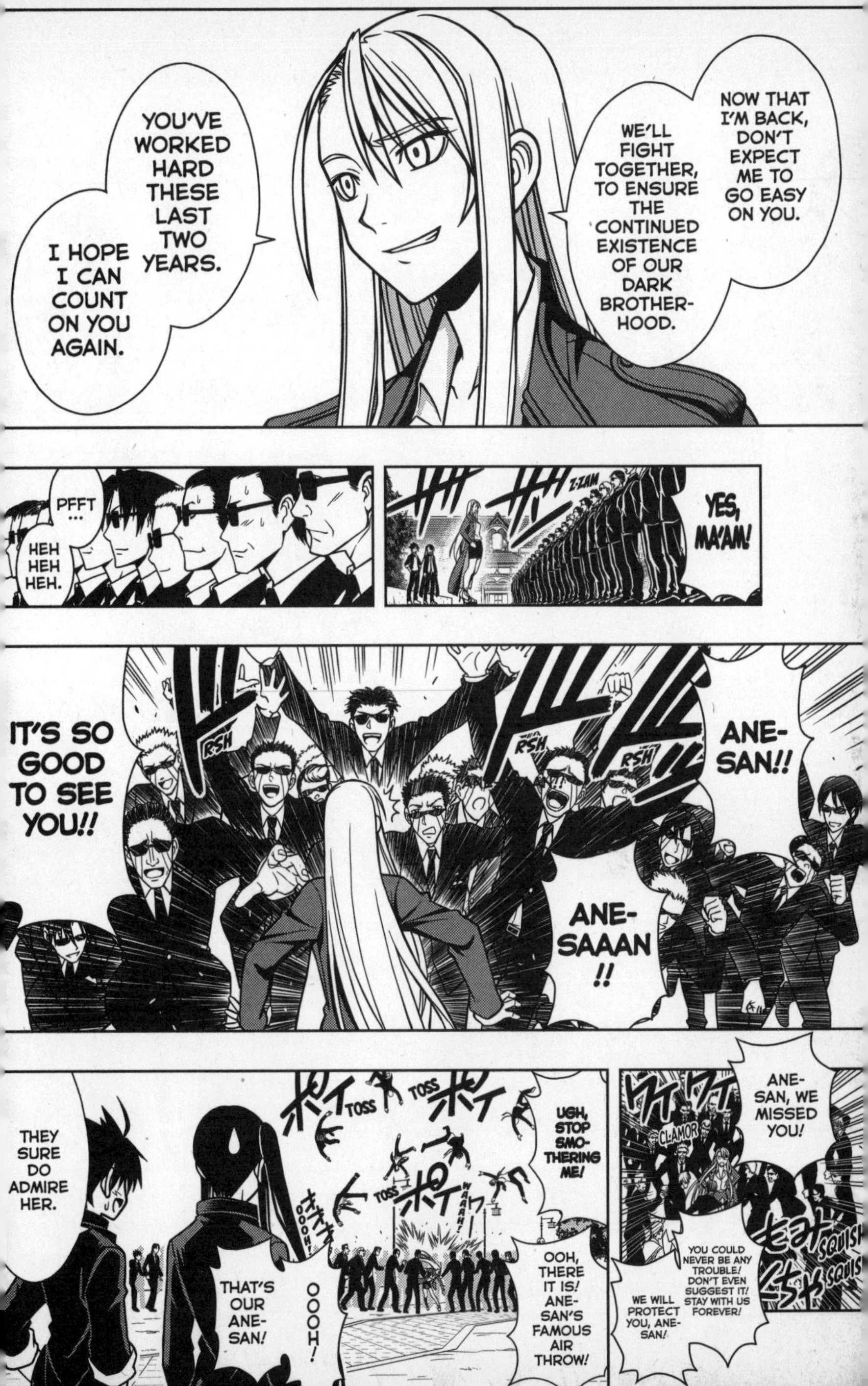
NOW THAT I'M BACK, DON'T EXPECT ME TO GO EASY ON YOU.
WE'LL FIGHT TOGETHER, TO ENSURE THE CONTINUED EXISTENCE OF OUR DARK BROTHER-HOOD.
YOU'VE WORKED HARD THESE LAST TWO YEARS.
I HOPE I CAN COUNT ON YOU AGAIN.
Z-ZAM
YES, MA'AM!
PFFT...
HEH HEH HEH.
ANE-SAN!!
RSH
RSH
ANE-SAAAN!!
RSH
IT'S SO GOOD TO SEE YOU!!
ANE-SAN, WE MISSED YOU!
CLAMOR
SQUISH
SQUISH
YOU COULD NEVER BE ANY TROUBLE! DON'T EVEN SUGGEST IT! STAY WITH US FOREVER!
WE WILL PROTECT YOU, ANE-SAN!
UGH, STOP SMOTHERING ME!
TOSS
TOSS
TOSS
WAAAH!
OOOOH!
OOH, THERE IT IS! ANE-SAN'S FAMOUS AIR THROW!
OOOH!
THAT'S OUR ANE-SAN!
THEY SURE DO ADMIRE HER.

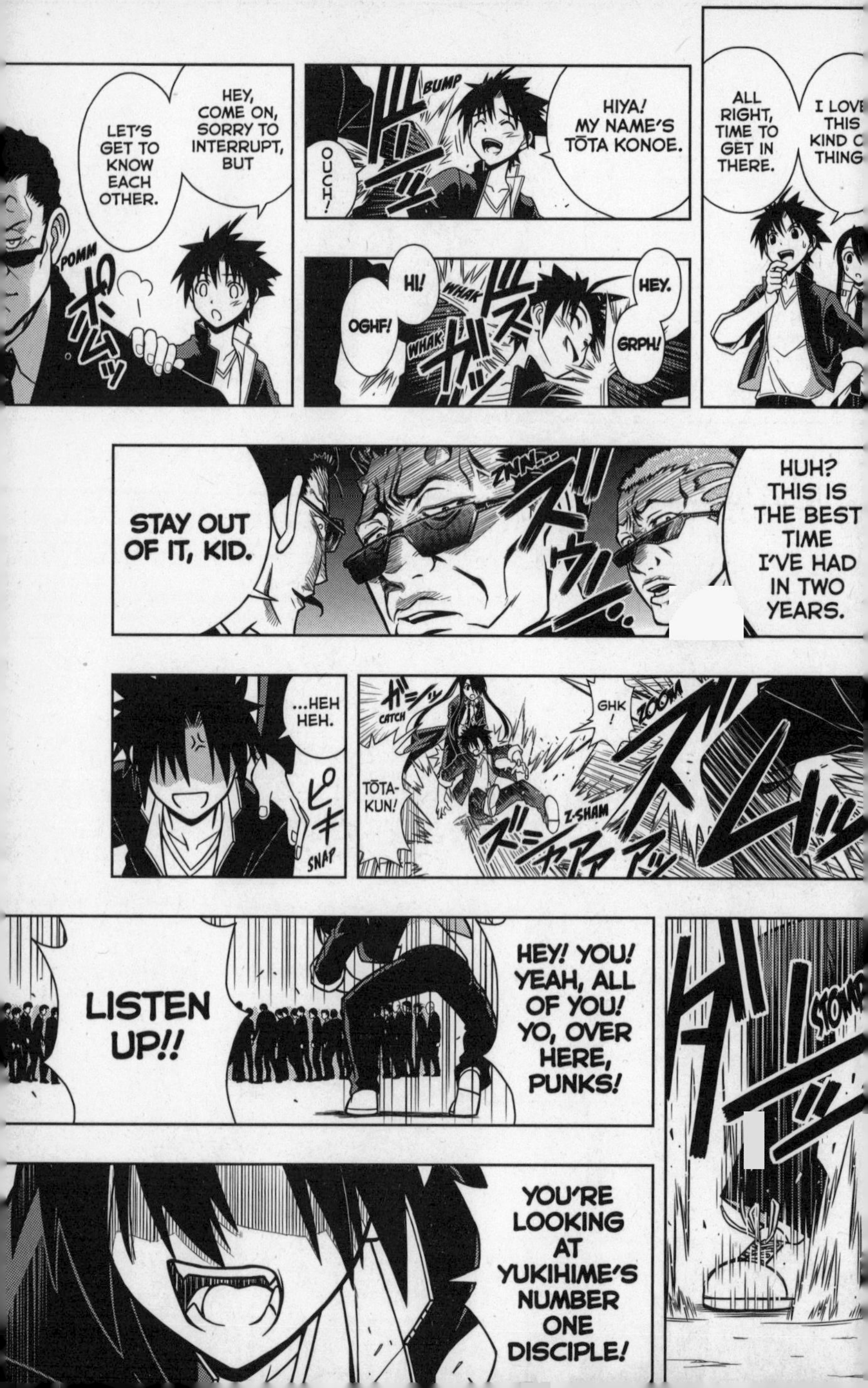
I LOV THIS KIND O THING
ALL RIGHT, TIME TO GET IN THERE.
HIYA! MY NAME'S TŌTA KONOE.
BUMP
OUCH!
HEY.
GRPH!
WHAK
HI!
OGHF!
WHAK
HEY, COME ON, SORRY TO INTERRUPT, BUT
LET'S GET TO KNOW EACH OTHER.
POMM
HUH? THIS IS THE BEST TIME I'VE HAD IN TWO YEARS.
ZNN...
STAY OUT OF IT, KID.
ZOOM
GHK!
CATCH
TŌTA-KUN!
Z-SHAM
...HEH HEH.
SNAP
HEY! YOU! YEAH, ALL OF YOU! YO, OVER HERE, PUNKS!
LISTEN UP!!
YOU'RE LOOKING AT YUKIHIME'S NUMBER ONE DISCIPLE!

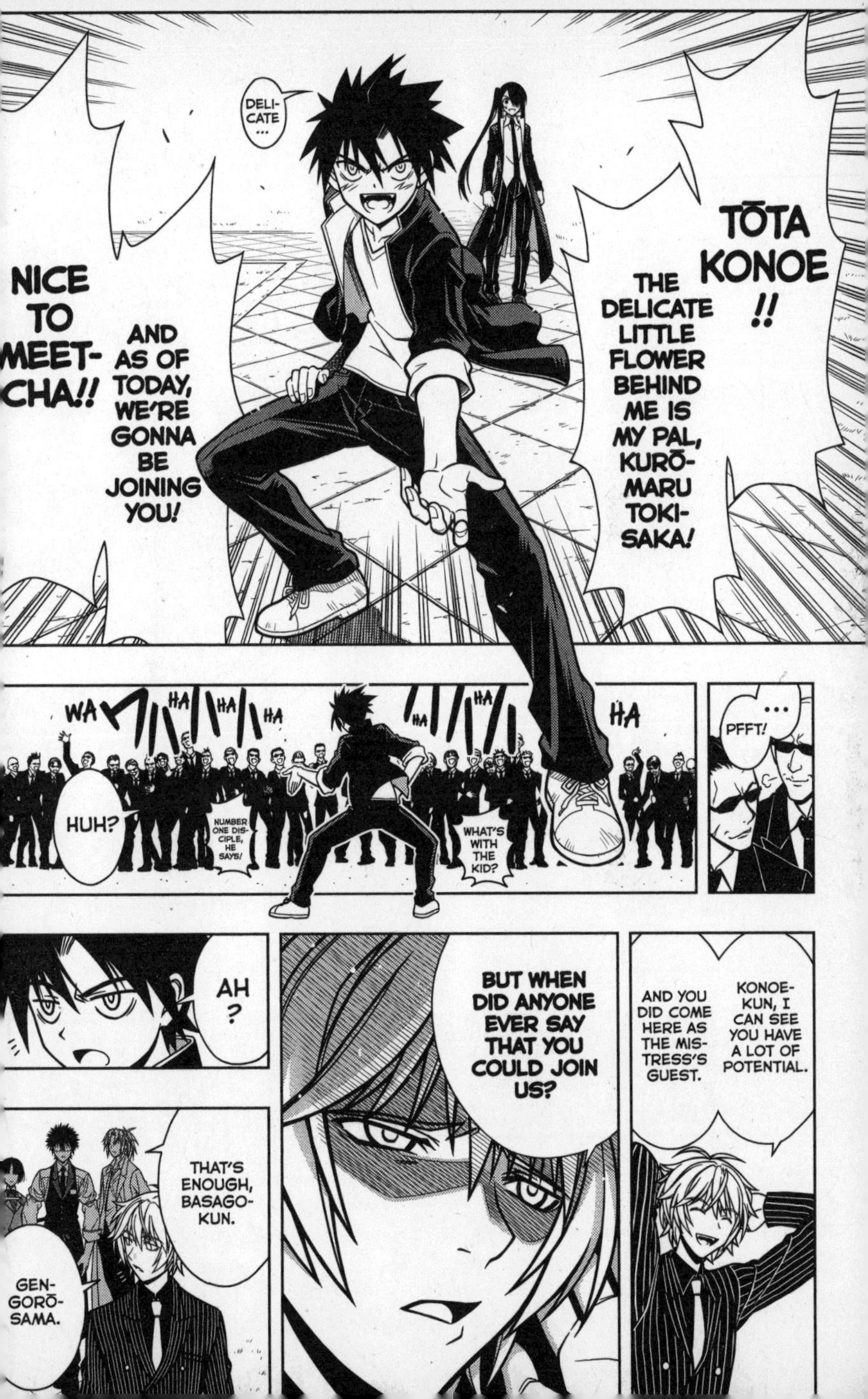
TŌTA KONOE!!
THE DELICATE LITTLE FLOWER BEHIND ME IS MY PAL, KURŌ-MARU TOKI-SAKA!
DELI-CATE...
AND AS OF TODAY, WE'RE GONNA BE JOINING YOU!
NICE TO MEET-CHA!!
...
PFFT!
WA HA HA HA HA HA HA
WHAT'S WITH THE KID?
NUMBER ONE DIS-CIPLE, HE SAYS!
HUH?
KONOE-KUN, I CAN SEE YOU HAVE A LOT OF POTENTIAL.
AND YOU DID COME HERE AS THE MIS-TRESS'S GUEST.
BUT WHEN DID ANYONE EVER SAY THAT YOU COULD JOIN US?
AH?
THAT'S ENOUGH, BASAGO-KUN.
GEN-GORŌ-SAMA.

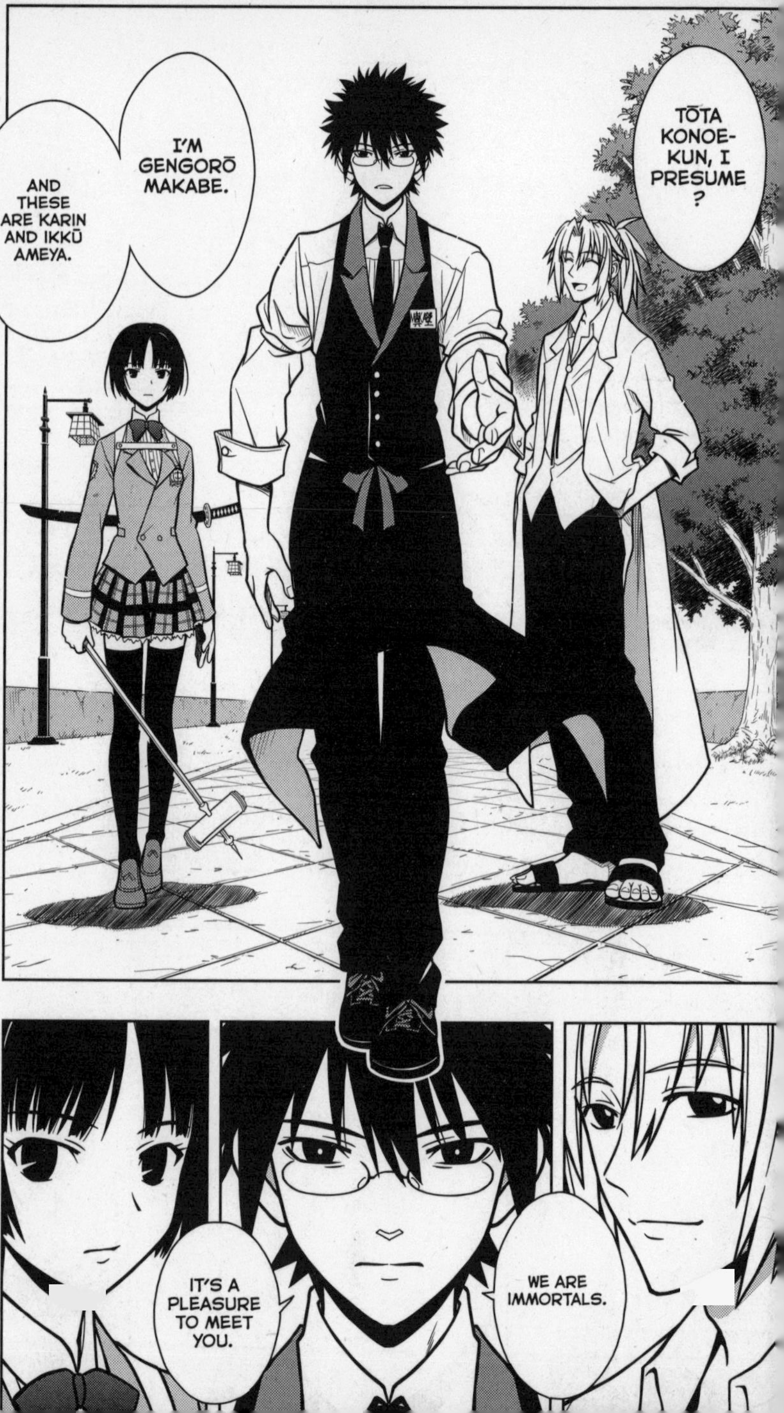
TŌTA KONOE-KUN, I PRESUME?
I'M GENGORŌ MAKABE.
AND THESE ARE KARIN AND IKKŪ AMEYA.
WE ARE IMMORTALS.
IT'S A PLEASURE TO MEET YOU.

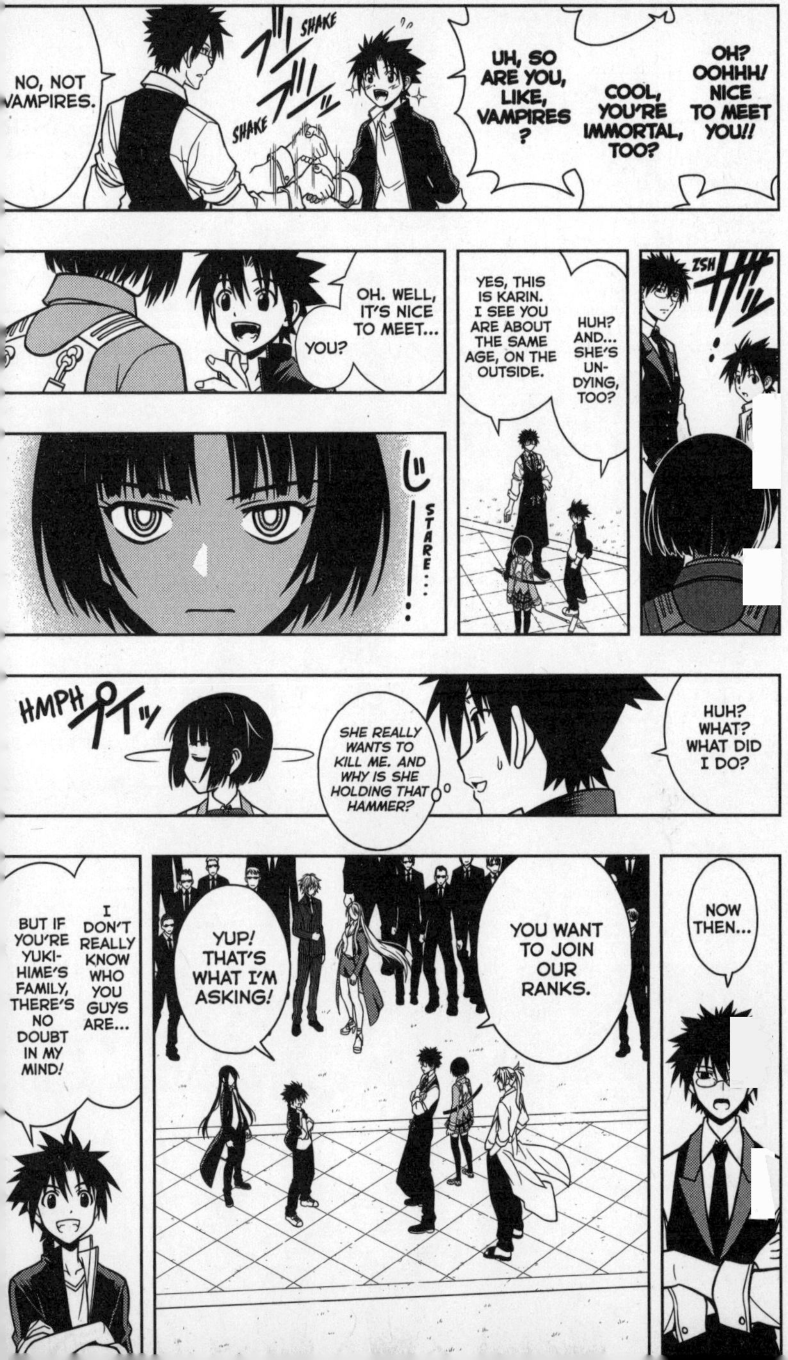
OH? OOHHH! NICE TO MEET YOU!!
COOL, YOU'RE IMMORTAL, TOO?
UH, SO ARE YOU, LIKE, VAMPIRES?
SHAKE
SHAKE
NO, NOT VAMPIRES.
ZSH
YES, THIS IS KARIN. I SEE YOU ARE ABOUT THE SAME AGE, ON THE OUTSIDE.
HUH? AND... SHE'S UN-DYING, TOO?
OH. WELL, IT'S NICE TO MEET...
YOU?
STARE...
HUH? WHAT? WHAT DID I DO?
SHE REALLY WANTS TO KILL ME. AND WHY IS SHE HOLDING THAT HAMMER?
HMPH
NOW THEN...
YOU WANT TO JOIN OUR RANKS.
YUP! THAT'S WHAT I'M ASKING!
I DON'T REALLY KNOW WHO YOU GUYS ARE...
BUT IF YOU'RE YUKI-HIME'S FAMILY, THERE'S NO DOUBT IN MY MIND!

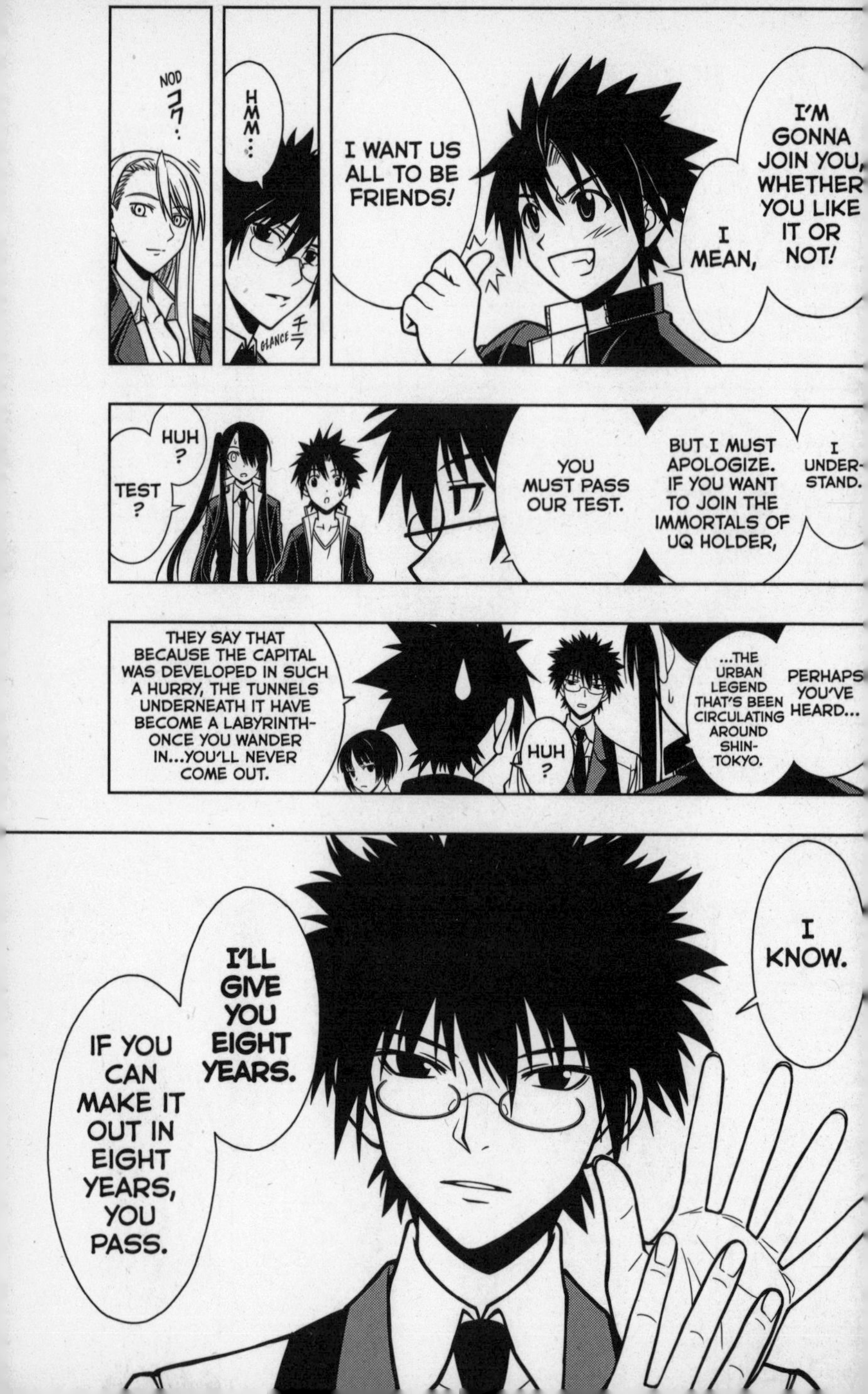
I MEAN, I'M GONNA JOIN YOU, WHETHER YOU LIKE IT OR NOT!
I WANT US ALL TO BE FRIENDS!
HMM...
GLANCE チラ
NOD コク..
I UNDERSTAND.
BUT I MUST APOLOGIZE. IF YOU WANT TO JOIN THE IMMORTALS OF UQ HOLDER,
YOU MUST PASS OUR TEST.
HUH?
TEST?
PERHAPS YOU'VE HEARD...
...THE URBAN LEGEND THAT'S BEEN CIRCULATING AROUND SHIN-TOKYO.
HUH?
THEY SAY THAT BECAUSE THE CAPITAL WAS DEVELOPED IN SUCH A HURRY, THE TUNNELS UNDERNEATH IT HAVE BECOME A LABYRINTH-ONCE YOU WANDER IN...YOU'LL NEVER COME OUT.
I KNOW.
I'LL GIVE YOU EIGHT YEARS.
IF YOU CAN MAKE IT OUT IN EIGHT YEARS, YOU PASS.

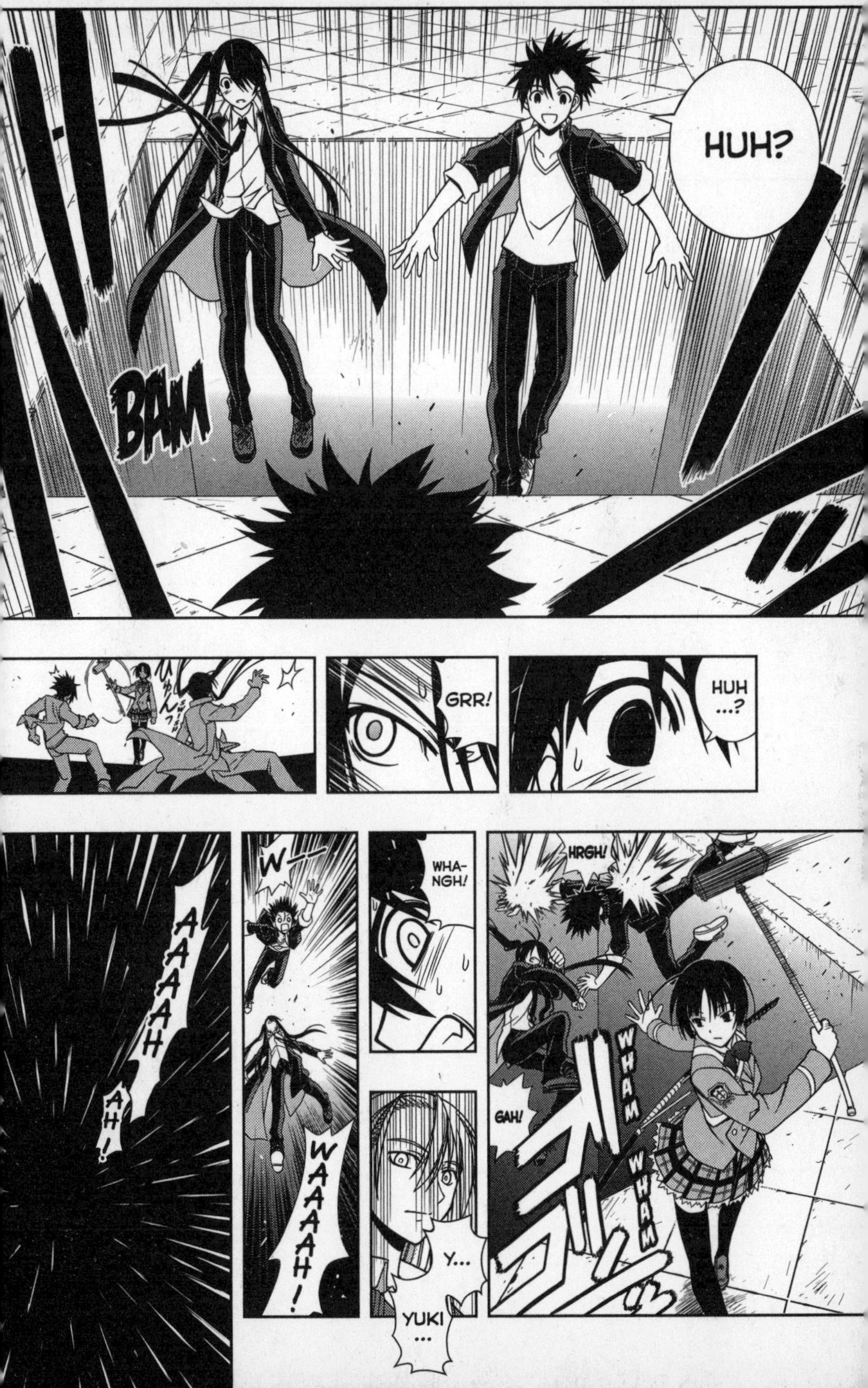
HUH?
BAM
HUH ...?
GRR!
HRGH!
WHAM
WHAM
WHAM
GAH!
WHA-NGH!
Y...
YUKI ...
W—
WAAAAAH!
AAAAAH
AH!

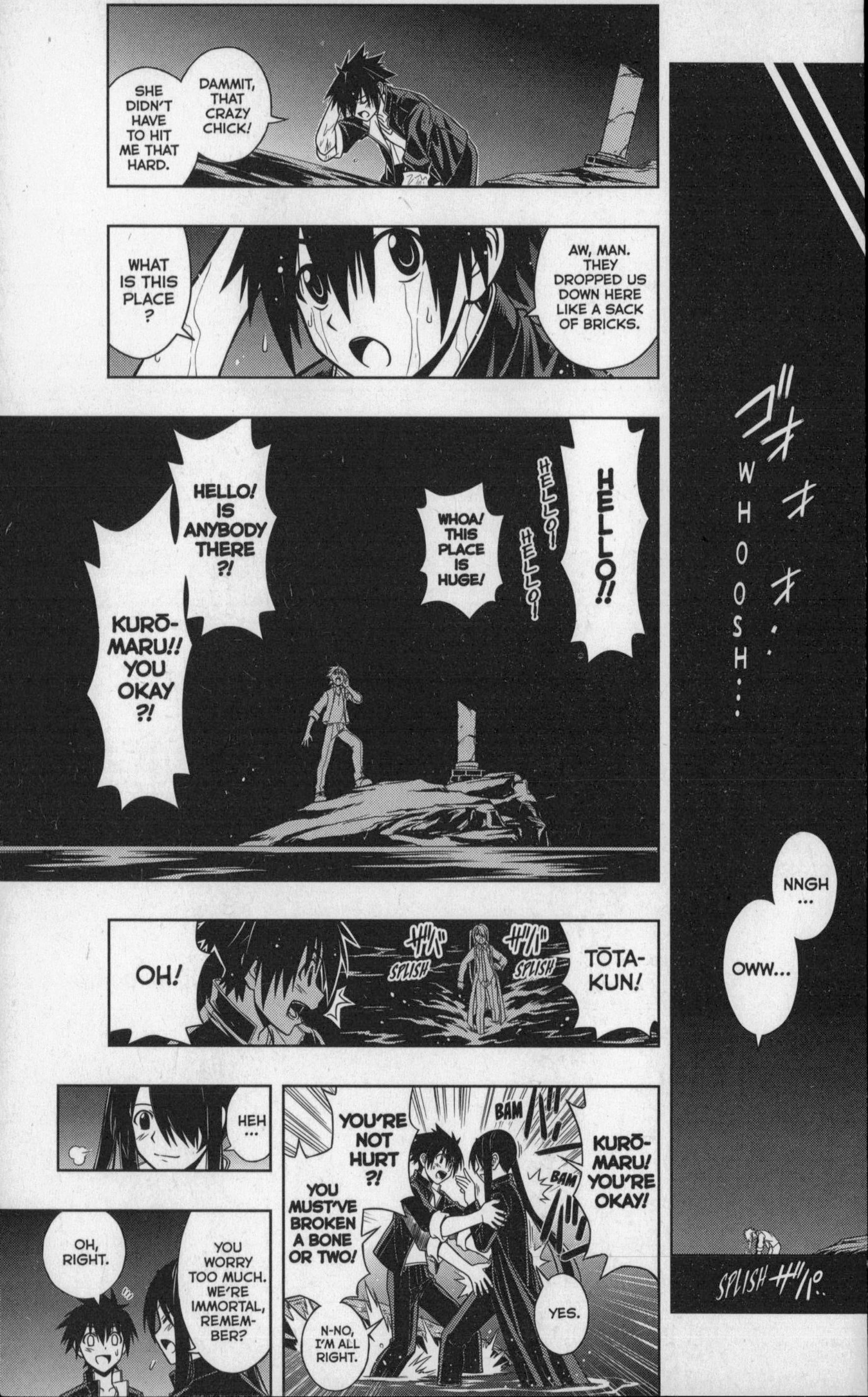
WHOOSH...
NNGH...
OWW...
SPLISH
DAMMIT, THAT CRAZY CHICK!
SHE DIDN'T HAVE TO HIT ME THAT HARD.
AW, MAN. THEY DROPPED US DOWN HERE LIKE A SACK OF BRICKS.
WHAT IS THIS PLACE?
HELLO!!
HELLO! HELLO!
WHOA! THIS PLACE IS HUGE!
HELLO! IS ANYBODY THERE?!
KURŌ-MARU!! YOU OKAY?!
TŌTA-KUN!
SPLISH
SPLISH
OH!
KURŌ-MARU! YOU'RE OKAY!
BAM
BAM
YOU'RE NOT HURT?!
YOU MUST'VE BROKEN A BONE OR TWO!
YES.
N-NO, I'M ALL RIGHT.
HEH...
YOU WORRY TOO MUCH. WE'RE IMMORTAL, REMEMBER?
OH, RIGHT.

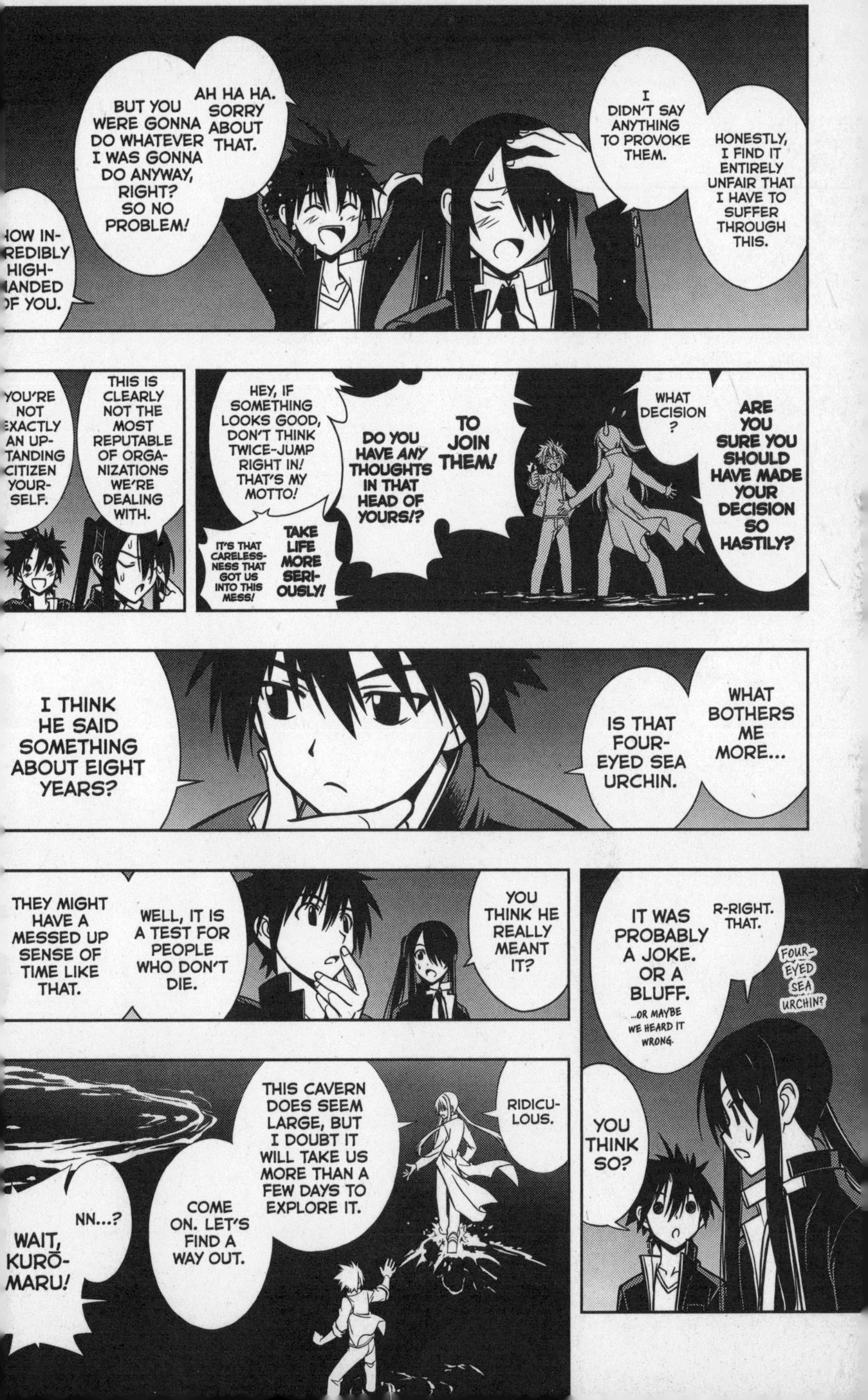
HONESTLY, I FIND IT ENTIRELY UNFAIR THAT I HAVE TO SUFFER THROUGH THIS.
I DIDN'T SAY ANYTHING TO PROVOKE THEM.
AH HA HA. SORRY ABOUT THAT.
BUT YOU WERE GONNA DO WHATEVER I WAS GONNA DO ANYWAY, RIGHT? SO NO PROBLEM!
HOW IN-REDIBLY HIGH-ANDED OF YOU.
ARE YOU SURE YOU SHOULD HAVE MADE YOUR DECISION SO HASTILY?
WHAT DECISION?
TO JOIN THEM!
DO YOU HAVE ANY THOUGHTS IN THAT HEAD OF YOURS!?
HEY, IF SOMETHING LOOKS GOOD, DON'T THINK TWICE-JUMP RIGHT IN! THAT'S MY MOTTO!
TAKE LIFE MORE SERIOUSLY!
IT'S THAT CARELESSNESS THAT GOT US INTO THIS MESS!
THIS IS CLEARLY NOT THE MOST REPUTABLE OF ORGANIZATIONS WE'RE DEALING WITH.
YOU'RE NOT EXACTLY AN UP-TANDING CITIZEN YOURSELF.
WHAT BOTHERS ME MORE...
IS THAT FOUR-EYED SEA URCHIN.
I THINK HE SAID SOMETHING ABOUT EIGHT YEARS?
R-RIGHT. THAT.
FOUR-EYED SEA URCHIN?
IT WAS PROBABLY A JOKE. OR A BLUFF.
...OR MAYBE WE HEARD IT WRONG.
YOU THINK SO?
YOU THINK HE REALLY MEANT IT?
WELL, IT IS A TEST FOR PEOPLE WHO DON'T DIE.
THEY MIGHT HAVE A MESSED UP SENSE OF TIME LIKE THAT.
RIDICULOUS.
THIS CAVERN DOES SEEM LARGE, BUT I DOUBT IT WILL TAKE US MORE THAN A FEW DAYS TO EXPLORE IT.
COME ON. LET'S FIND A WAY OUT.
NN...?
WAIT, KURŌMARU!

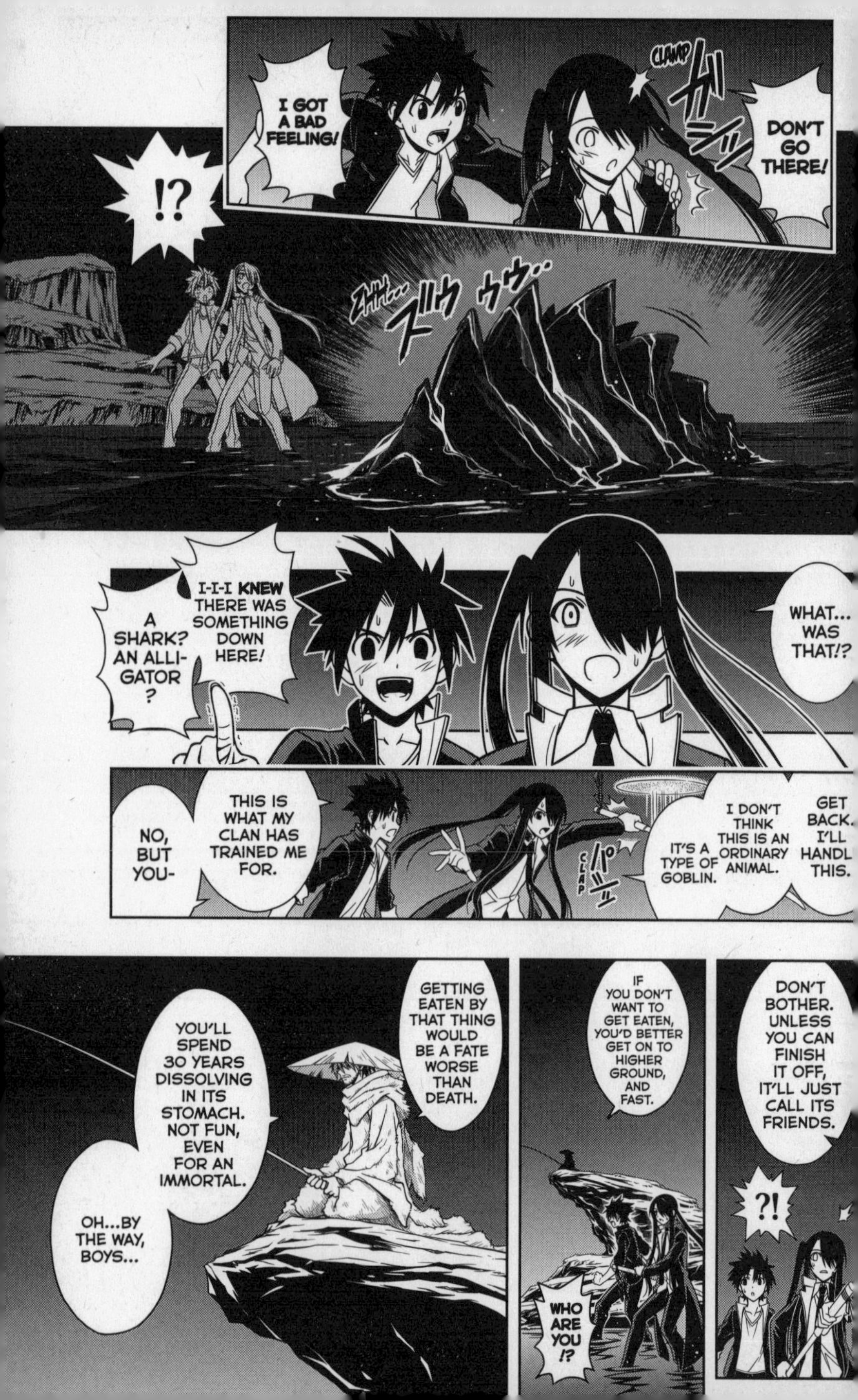
DON'T GO THERE!
CLAMP
I GOT A BAD FEELING!
!?
WHAT... WAS THAT!?
I-I-I KNEW THERE WAS SOMETHING DOWN HERE!
A SHARK? AN ALLIGATOR?
GET BACK. I'LL HANDL THIS.
I DON'T THINK THIS IS AN ORDINARY ANIMAL.
IT'S A TYPE OF GOBLIN.
CLAP
THIS IS WHAT MY CLAN HAS TRAINED ME FOR.
NO, BUT YOU-
DON'T BOTHER. UNLESS YOU CAN FINISH IT OFF, IT'LL JUST CALL ITS FRIENDS.
?!
IF YOU DON'T WANT TO GET EATEN, YOU'D BETTER GET ON TO HIGHER GROUND, AND FAST.
WHO ARE YOU!?
GETTING EATEN BY THAT THING WOULD BE A FATE WORSE THAN DEATH.
YOU'LL SPEND 30 YEARS DISSOLVING IN ITS STOMACH. NOT FUN, EVEN FOR AN IMMORTAL.
OH...BY THE WAY, BOYS...

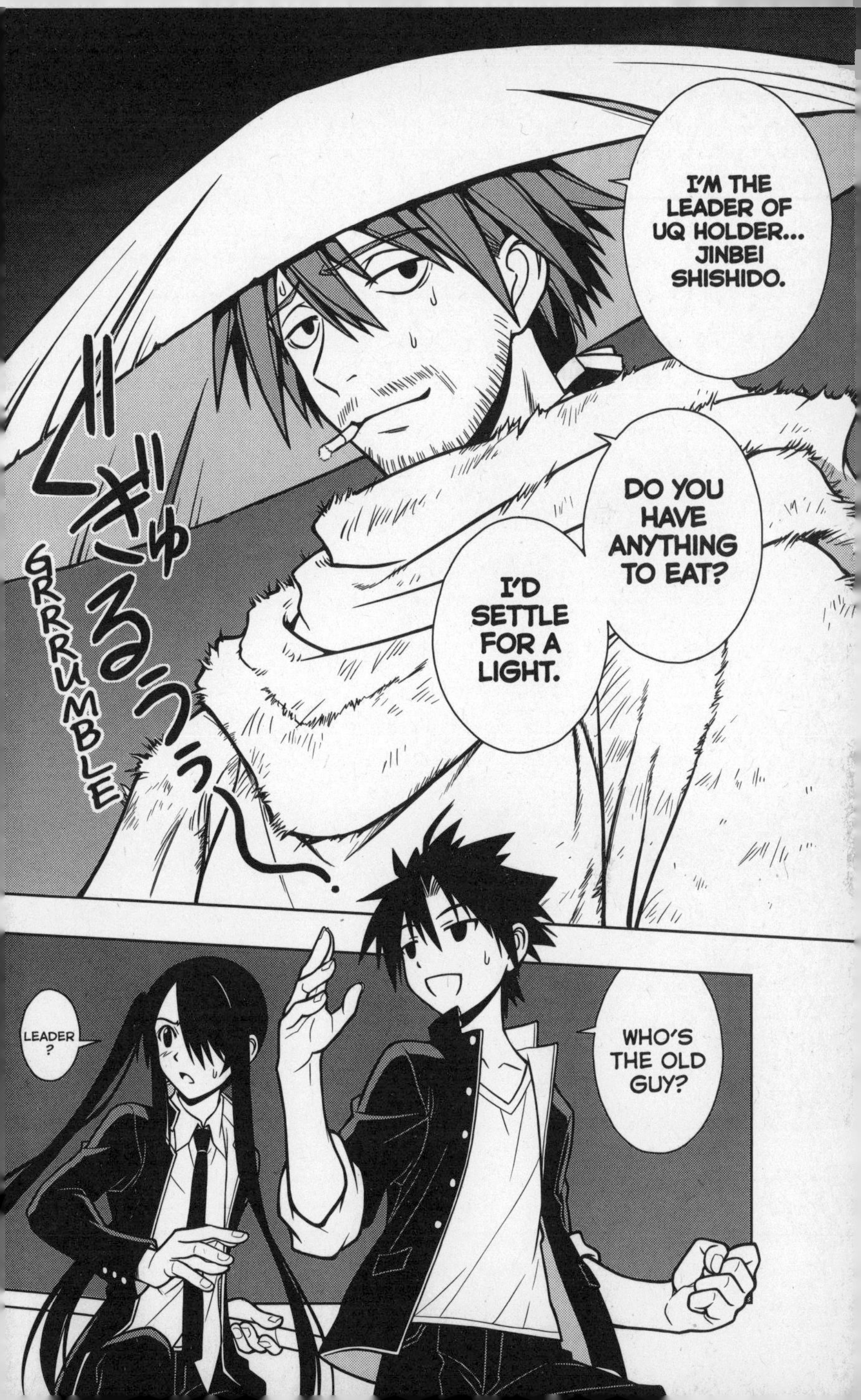
I'M THE LEADER OF UQ HOLDER... JINBEI SHISHIDO.
DO YOU HAVE ANYTHING TO EAT?
I'D SETTLE FOR A LIGHT.
ぎゅるるうぅ～
GRRRUMBLE
WHO'S THE OLD GUY?
LEADER?

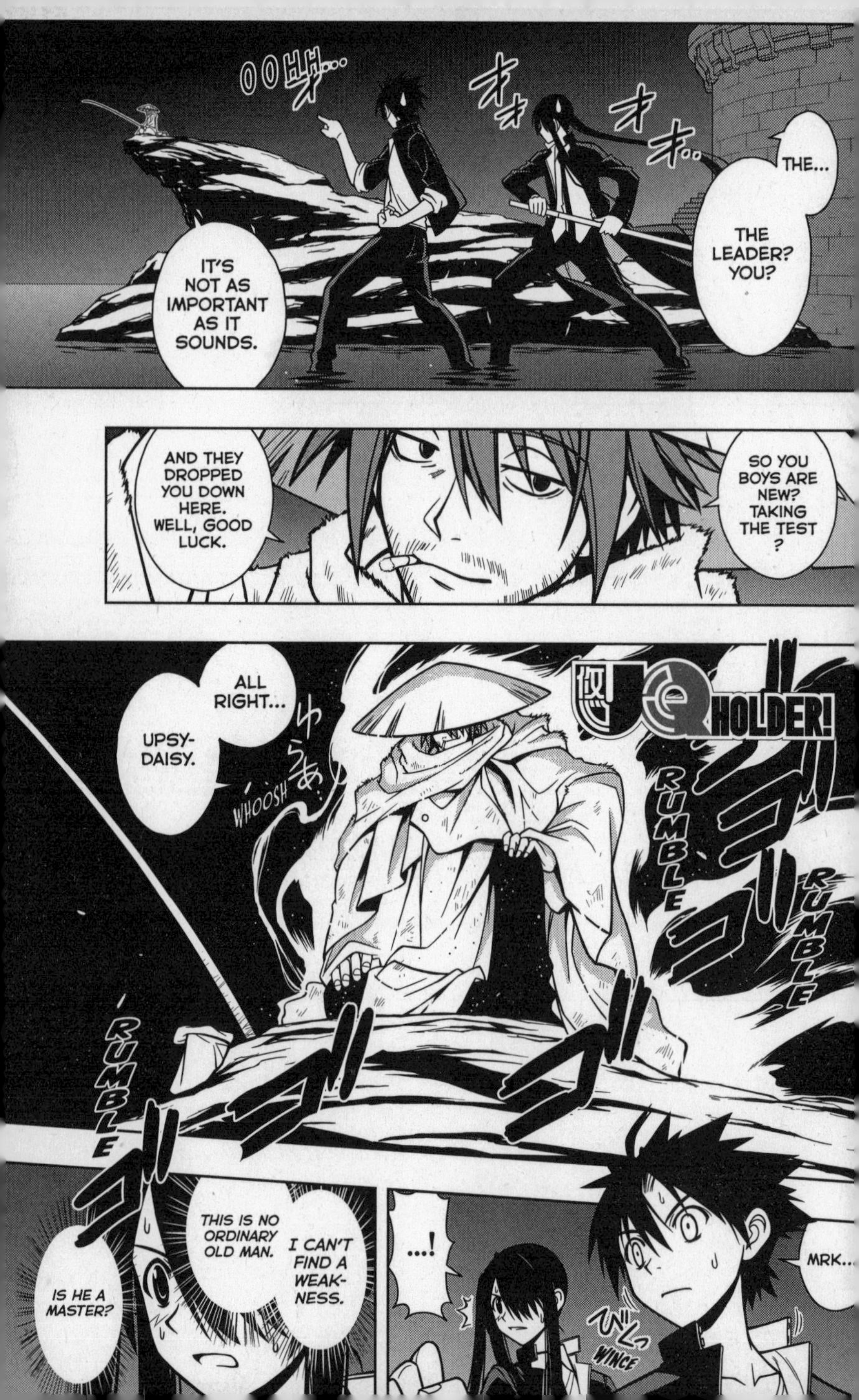
THE...
THE LEADER? YOU?
OOHH...
IT'S NOT AS IMPORTANT AS IT SOUNDS.
SO YOU BOYS ARE NEW? TAKING THE TEST?
AND THEY DROPPED YOU DOWN HERE. WELL, GOOD LUCK.
HOLDER!
RUMBLE
RUMBLE
ALL RIGHT...
UPSY-DAISY.
WHOOSH
RUMBLE
MRK...
WINCE
...!
THIS IS NO ORDINARY OLD MAN.
I CAN'T FIND A WEAKNESS.
IS HE A MASTER?

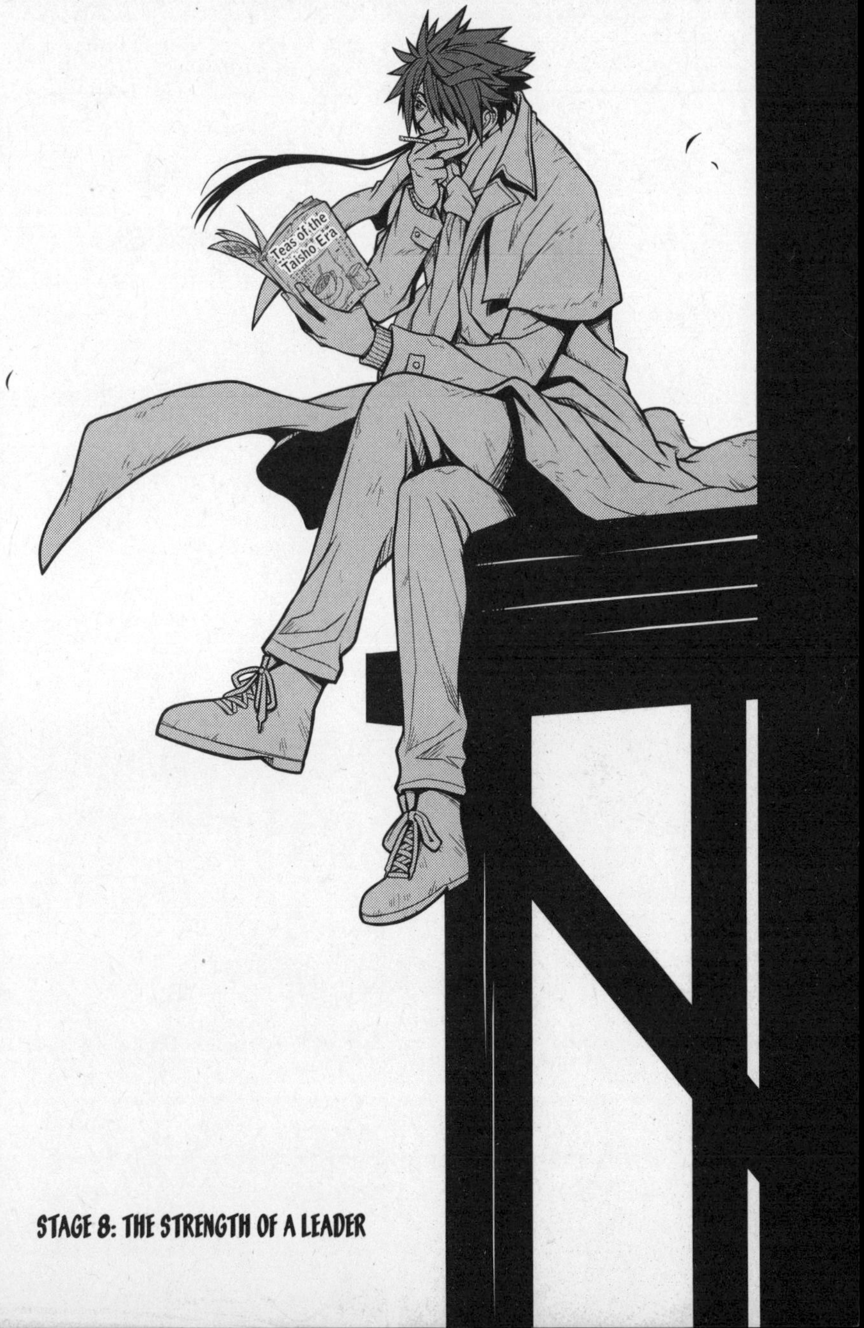
Teas of the Taisho Era

STAGE 8: THE STRENGTH OF A LEADER

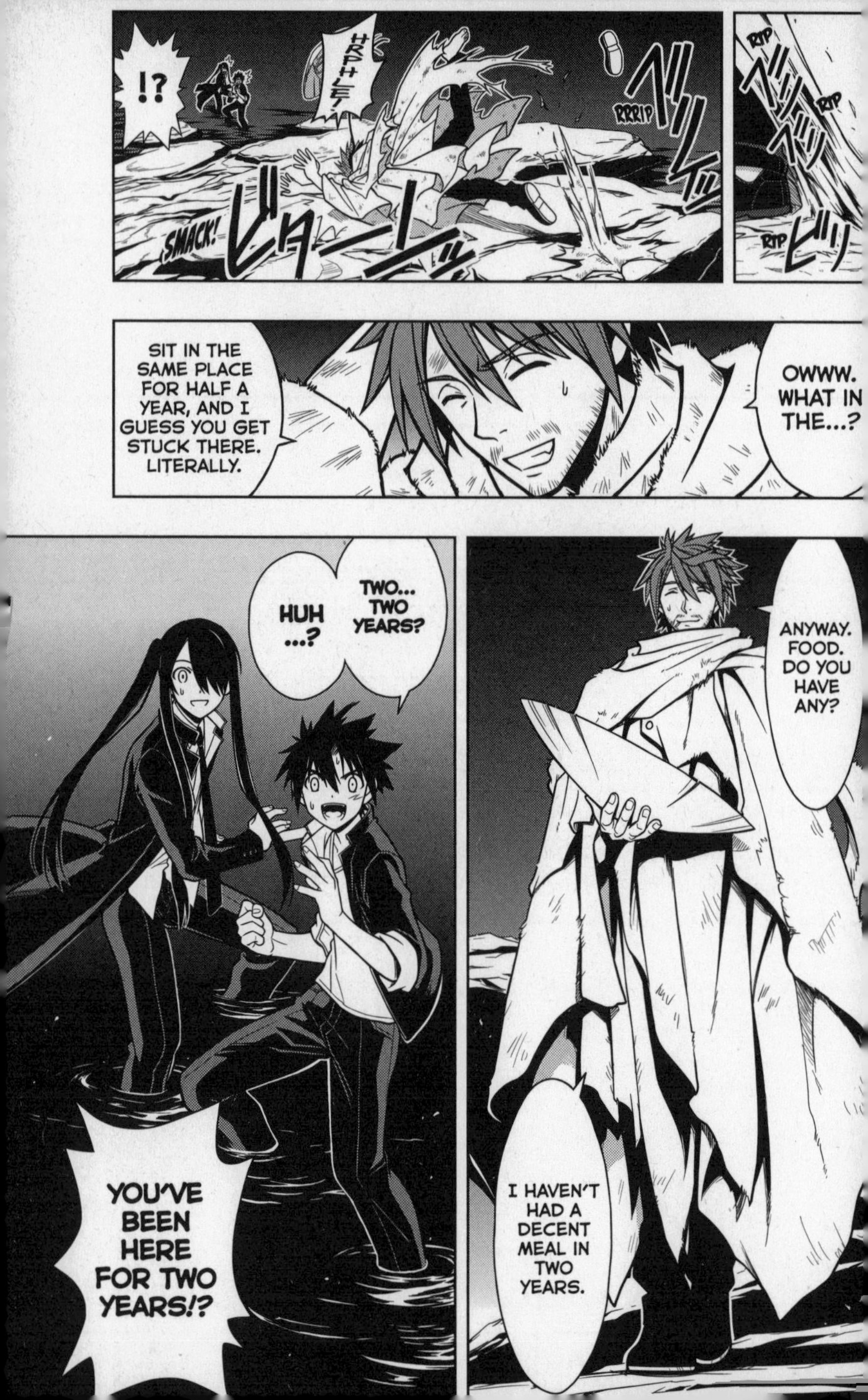
RIP
RIP
RIP
!?
HRPHLE!
RRRIP
SMACK!
OWWW. WHAT IN THE...?
SIT IN THE SAME PLACE FOR HALF A YEAR, AND I GUESS YOU GET STUCK THERE. LITERALLY.
ANYWAY. FOOD. DO YOU HAVE ANY?
I HAVEN'T HAD A DECENT MEAL IN TWO YEARS.
TWO... TWO YEARS?
HUH ...?
YOU'VE BEEN HERE FOR TWO YEARS!?

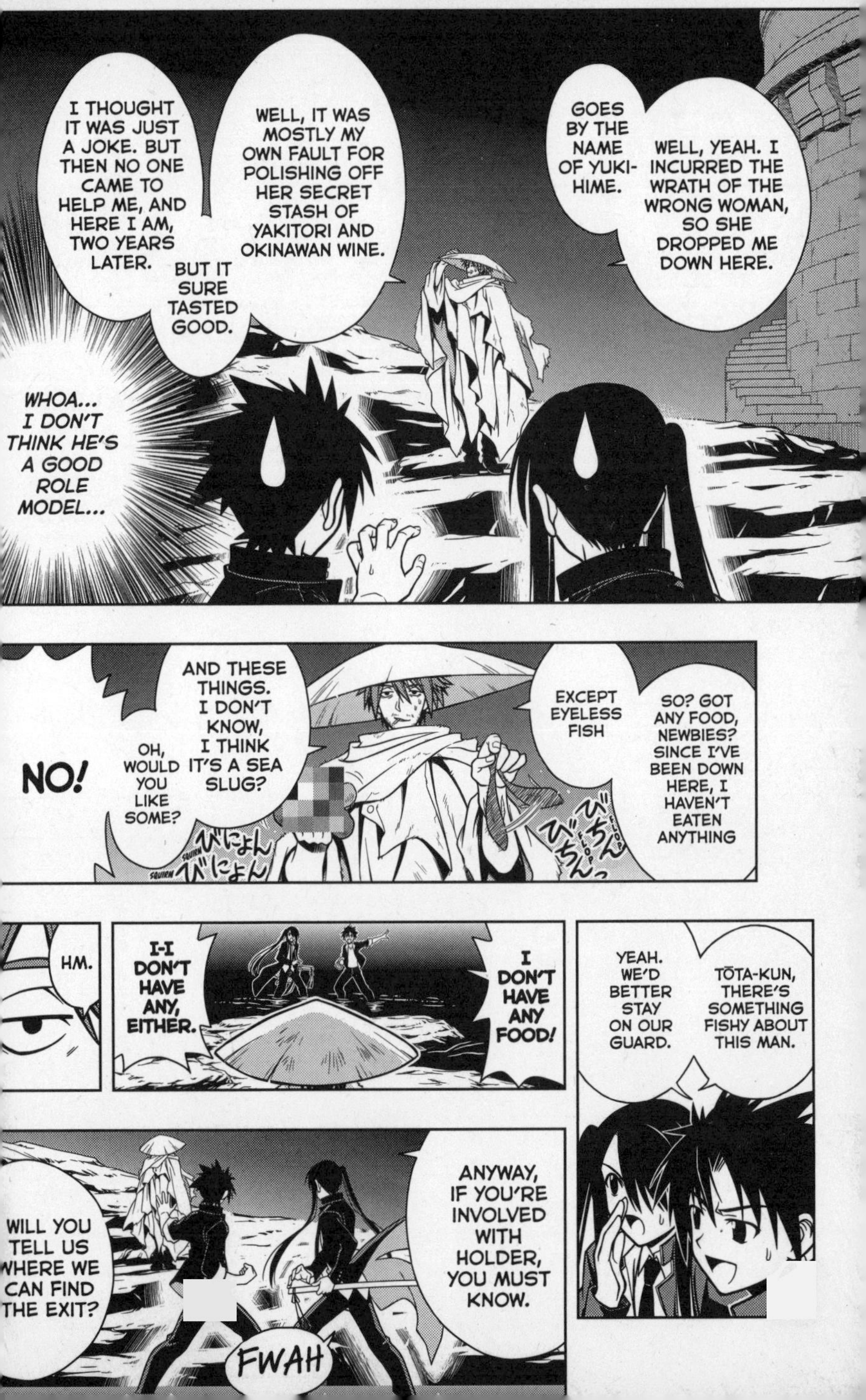
WELL, YEAH. I INCURRED THE WRATH OF THE WRONG WOMAN, SO SHE DROPPED ME DOWN HERE.
GOES BY THE NAME OF YUKI-HIME.
WELL, IT WAS MOSTLY MY OWN FAULT FOR POLISHING OFF HER SECRET STASH OF YAKITORI AND OKINAWAN WINE.
BUT IT SURE TASTED GOOD.
I THOUGHT IT WAS JUST A JOKE. BUT THEN NO ONE CAME TO HELP ME, AND HERE I AM, TWO YEARS LATER.
WHOA... I DON'T THINK HE'S A GOOD ROLE MODEL...
SO? GOT ANY FOOD, NEWBIES? SINCE I'VE BEEN DOWN HERE, I HAVEN'T EATEN ANYTHING
EXCEPT EYELESS FISH
ぴちん ぴちん
FLOP FLOP
AND THESE THINGS. I DON'T KNOW, I THINK IT'S A SEA SLUG?
OH, WOULD YOU LIKE SOME?
びにょん びにょん
SQUIRM SQUIRM
NO!
TŌTA-KUN, THERE'S SOMETHING FISHY ABOUT THIS MAN.
YEAH. WE'D BETTER STAY ON OUR GUARD.
I DON'T HAVE ANY FOOD!
I-I DON'T HAVE ANY, EITHER.
HM.
ANYWAY, IF YOU'RE INVOLVED WITH HOLDER, YOU MUST KNOW.
WILL YOU TELL US WHERE WE CAN FIND THE EXIT?
FWAH

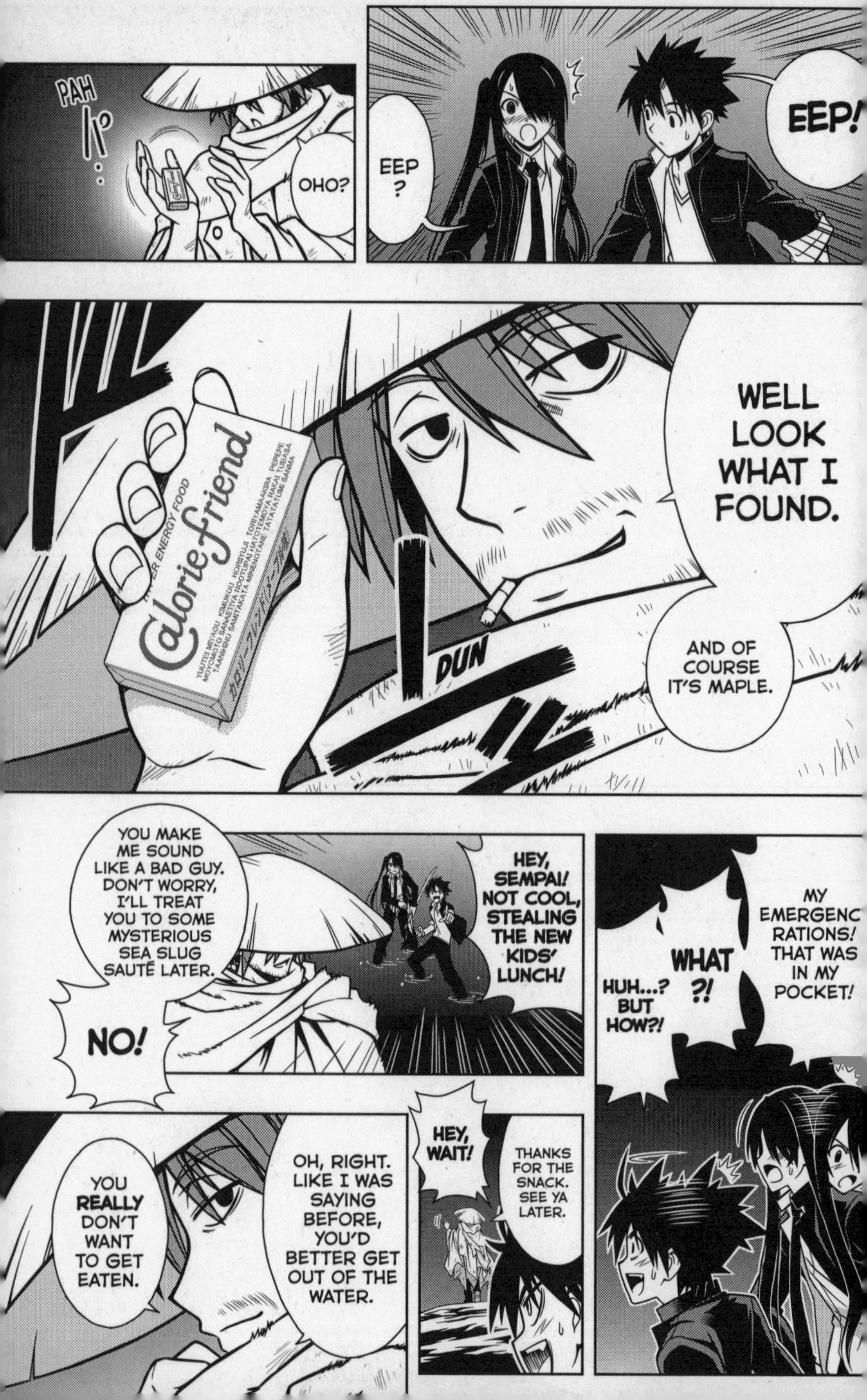
EEP!
EEP ?
OHO?
PAH
WELL LOOK WHAT I FOUND.
AND OF COURSE IT'S MAPLE.
DUN
Calorie friend
MY EMERGENC RATIONS! THAT WAS IN MY POCKET!
WHAT ?!
HUH...? BUT HOW?!
HEY, SEMPAI! NOT COOL, STEALING THE NEW KIDS' LUNCH!
YOU MAKE ME SOUND LIKE A BAD GUY. DON'T WORRY, I'LL TREAT YOU TO SOME MYSTERIOUS SEA SLUG SAUTÉ LATER.
NO!
THANKS FOR THE SNACK. SEE YA LATER.
HEY, WAIT!
OH, RIGHT. LIKE I WAS SAYING BEFORE, YOU'D BETTER GET OUT OF THE WATER.
YOU REALLY DON'T WANT TO GET EATEN.

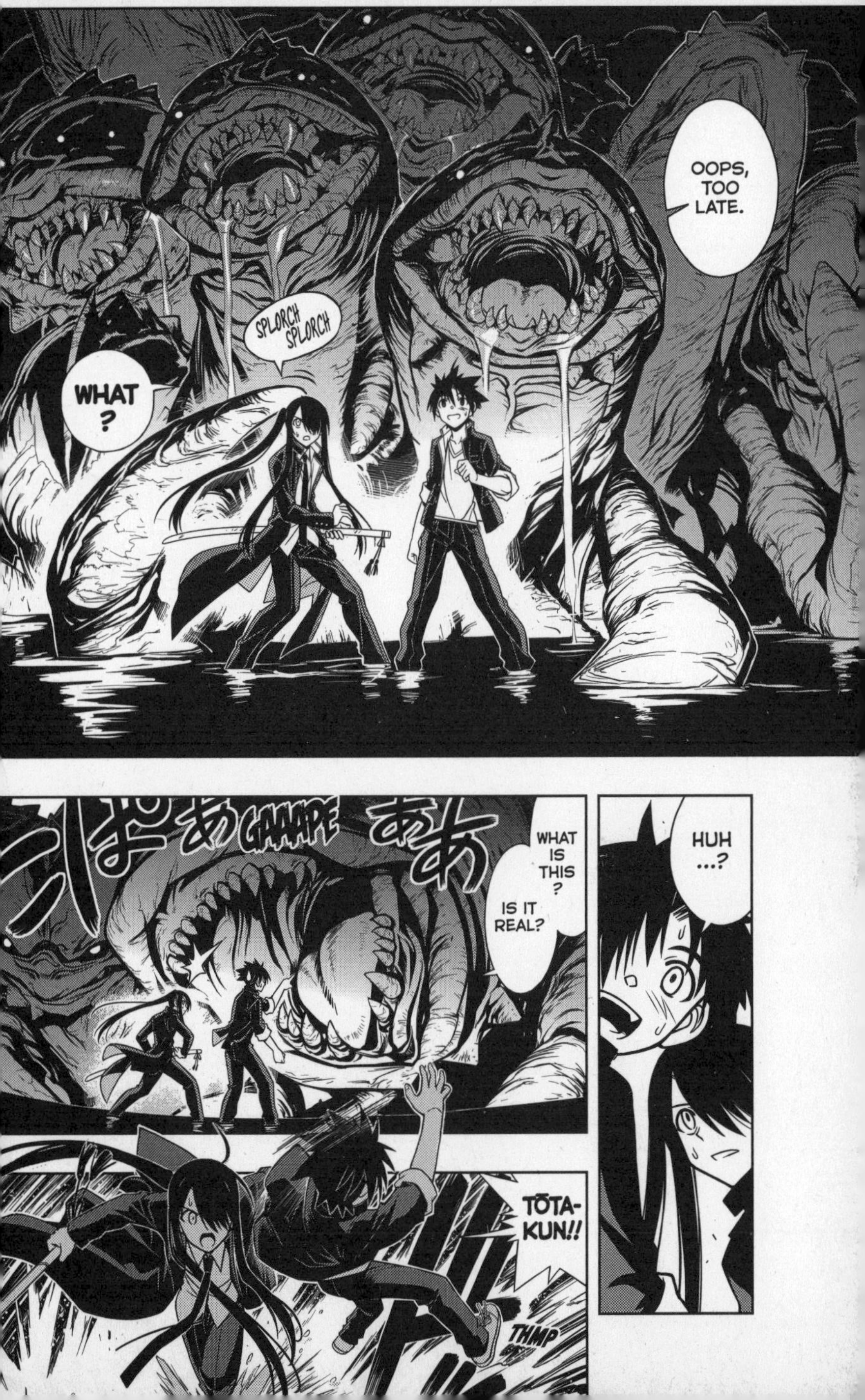
OOPS, TOO LATE.
SPLORCH SPLORCH
WHAT?
HUH...?
GAAAPE
WHAT IS THIS?
IS IT REAL?
TŌTA-KUN!!
THMP

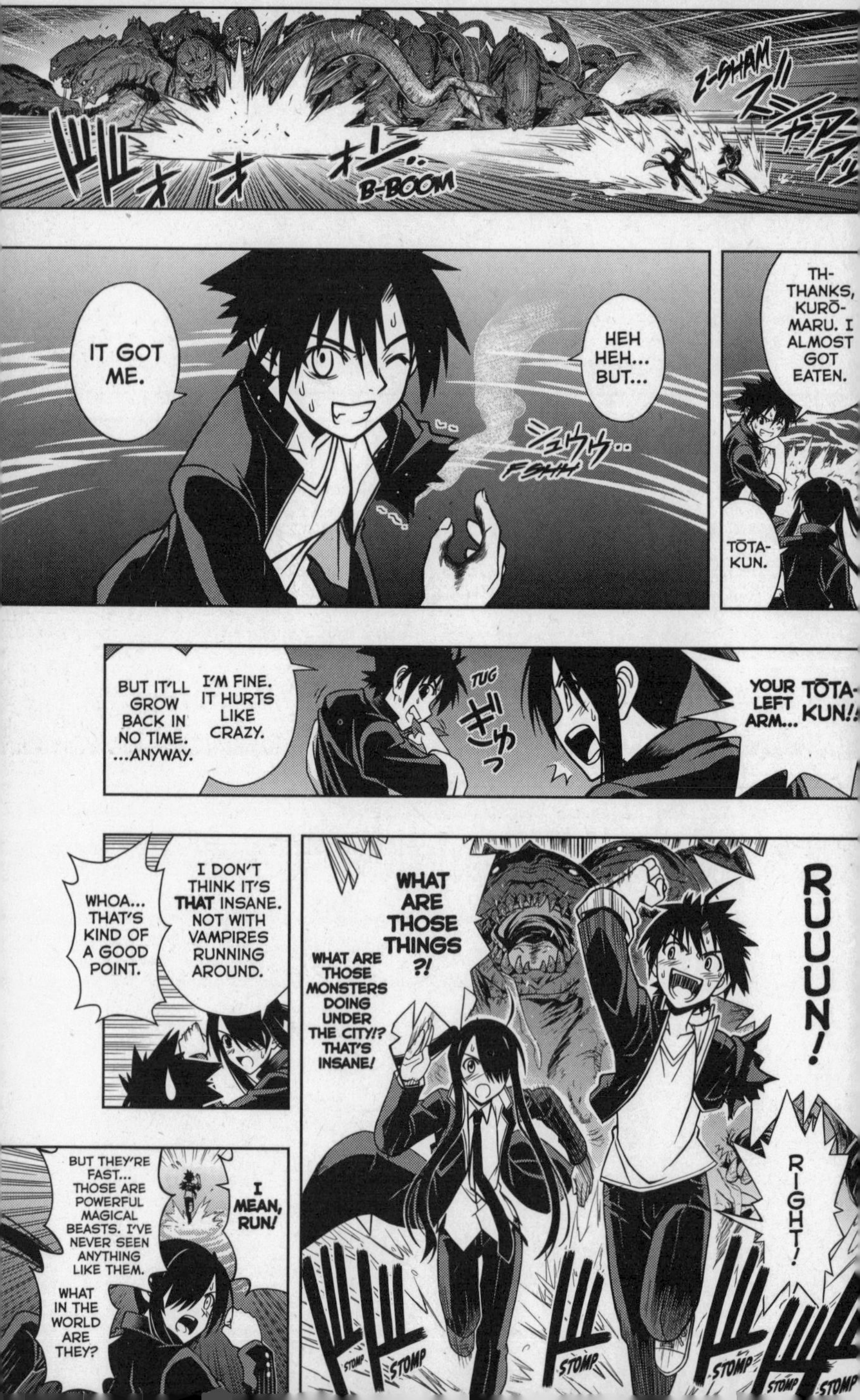
Z-SHAM
ズシャアッ
ドドォオオオン..
B-BOOM
TH-THANKS, KURŌMARU. I ALMOST GOT EATEN.
TŌTA-KUN.
HEH HEH... BUT...
シュウウ..
FSHH
IT GOT ME.
TŌTA-KUN!!
YOUR LEFT ARM...
TUG
ぎゅっ
I'M FINE. IT HURTS LIKE CRAZY.
BUT IT'LL GROW BACK IN NO TIME. ...ANYWAY.
RUUUN!
WHAT ARE THOSE THINGS?!
WHAT ARE THOSE MONSTERS DOING UNDER THE CITY!? THAT'S INSANE!
RIGHT!
STOMP
STOMP
STOMP
STOMP
STOMP
STOMP
I DON'T THINK IT'S THAT INSANE. NOT WITH VAMPIRES RUNNING AROUND.
WHOA... THAT'S KIND OF A GOOD POINT.
I MEAN, RUN!
BUT THEY'RE FAST... THOSE ARE POWERFUL MAGICAL BEASTS. I'VE NEVER SEEN ANYTHING LIKE THEM.
WHAT IN THE WORLD ARE THEY?

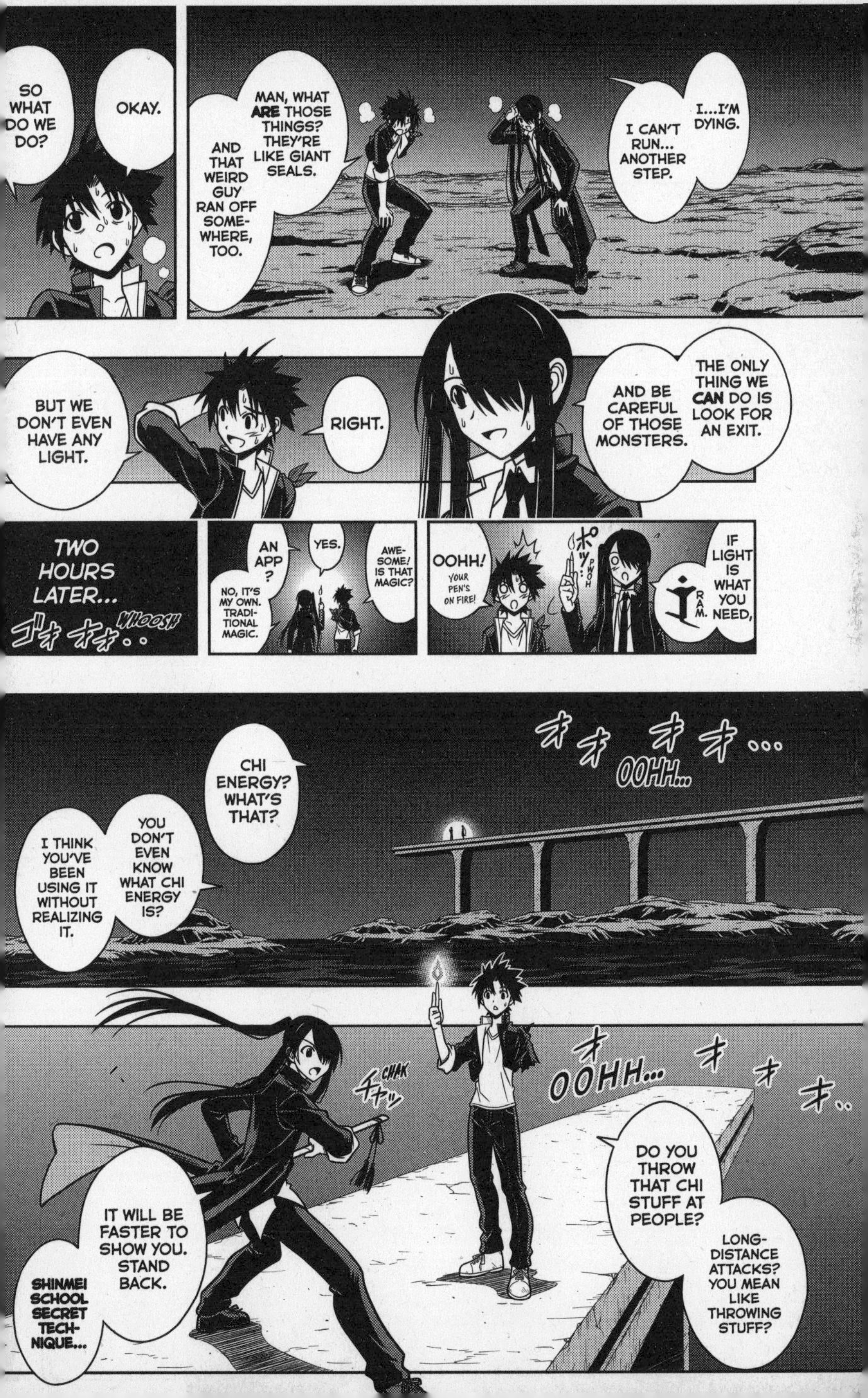
I...I'M DYING.
I CAN'T RUN... ANOTHER STEP.
MAN, WHAT ARE THOSE THINGS? THEY'RE LIKE GIANT SEALS.
AND THAT WEIRD GUY RAN OFF SOMEWHERE, TOO.
OKAY.
SO WHAT DO WE DO?
THE ONLY THING WE CAN DO IS LOOK FOR AN EXIT.
AND BE CAREFUL OF THOSE MONSTERS.
RIGHT.
BUT WE DON'T EVEN HAVE ANY LIGHT.
IF LIGHT IS WHAT YOU NEED,
RAM.
ポッ PWOH
OOHH!
YOUR PEN'S ON FIRE!
AWESOME! IS THAT MAGIC?
YES.
AN APP?
NO, IT'S MY OWN. TRADITIONAL MAGIC.
TWO HOURS LATER...
ゴォォォ.. WHOOSH
オォオォ... OOHH...
CHI ENERGY? WHAT'S THAT?
YOU DON'T EVEN KNOW WHAT CHI ENERGY IS?
I THINK YOU'VE BEEN USING IT WITHOUT REALIZING IT.
オォ OOHH... オォ..
LONG-DISTANCE ATTACKS? YOU MEAN LIKE THROWING STUFF?
DO YOU THROW THAT CHI STUFF AT PEOPLE?
チャッ CHAK
IT WILL BE FASTER TO SHOW YOU. STAND BACK.
SHINMEI SCHOOL SECRET TECHNIQUE...

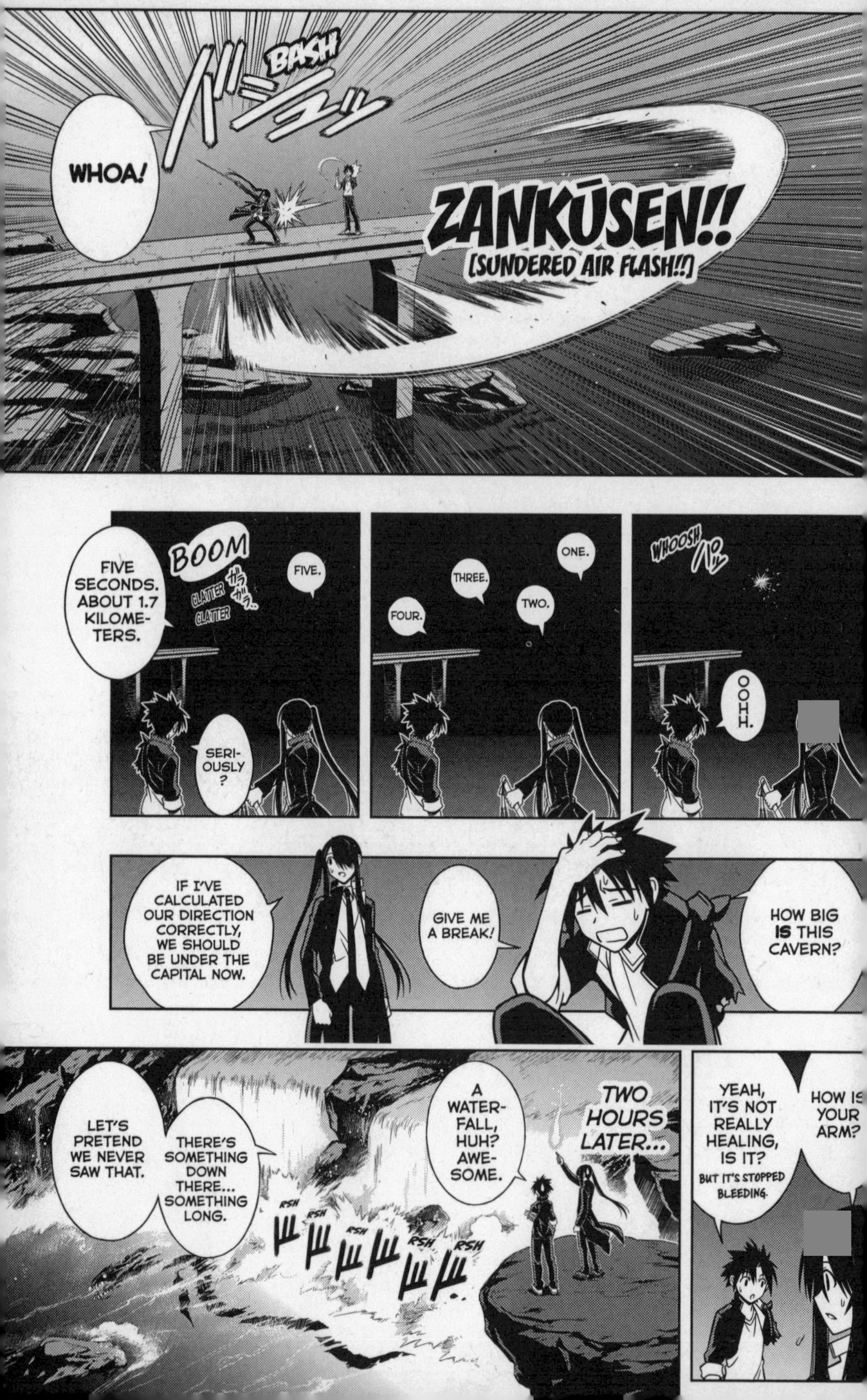
BASH
ZANKŪSEN!!
[SUNDERED AIR FLASH!!]
WHOA!
WHOOSH
OOHH.
FOUR.
THREE.
TWO.
ONE.
FIVE.
BOOM
CLATTER CLATTER
FIVE SECONDS. ABOUT 1.7 KILOMETERS.
SERIOUSLY?
HOW BIG IS THIS CAVERN?
GIVE ME A BREAK!
IF I'VE CALCULATED OUR DIRECTION CORRECTLY, WE SHOULD BE UNDER THE CAPITAL NOW.
HOW IS YOUR ARM?
YEAH, IT'S NOT REALLY HEALING, IS IT?
BUT IT'S STOPPED BLEEDING.
TWO HOURS LATER...
A WATERFALL, HUH? AWESOME.
RSH RSH RSH RSH RSH
THERE'S SOMETHING DOWN THERE... SOMETHING LONG.
LET'S PRETEND WE NEVER SAW THAT.

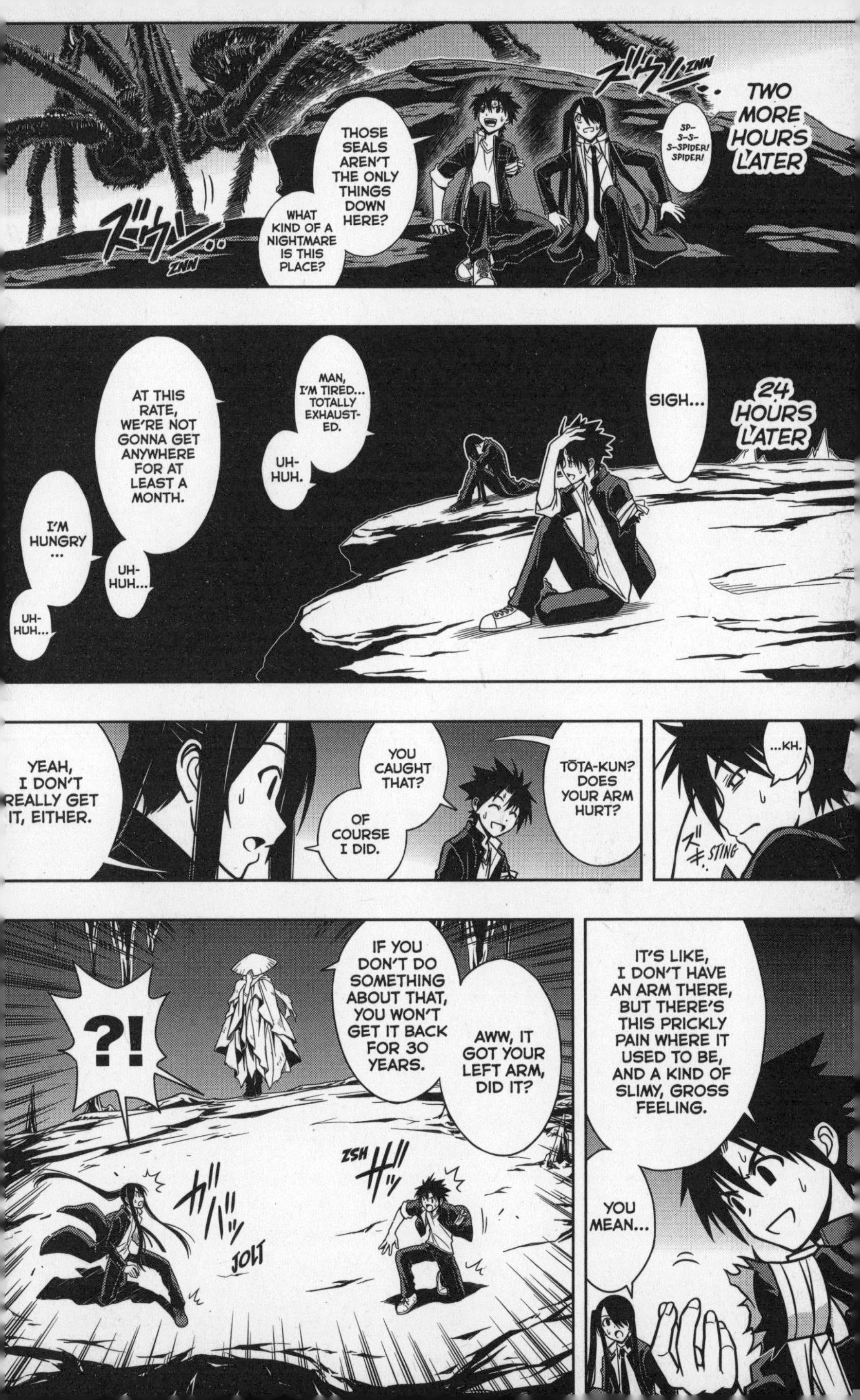
TWO MORE HOURS LATER
ZNN
SP-S-S-SPIDER! SPIDER!
THOSE SEALS AREN'T THE ONLY THINGS DOWN HERE?
WHAT KIND OF A NIGHTMARE IS THIS PLACE?
ZNN
24 HOURS LATER
SIGH...
MAN, I'M TIRED... TOTALLY EXHAUST-ED.
UH-HUH.
AT THIS RATE, WE'RE NOT GONNA GET ANYWHERE FOR AT LEAST A MONTH.
UH-HUH...
I'M HUNGRY ...
UH-HUH...
...KH.
STING
TŌTA-KUN? DOES YOUR ARM HURT?
YOU CAUGHT THAT?
OF COURSE I DID.
YEAH, I DON'T REALLY GET IT, EITHER.
IT'S LIKE, I DON'T HAVE AN ARM THERE, BUT THERE'S THIS PRICKLY PAIN WHERE IT USED TO BE, AND A KIND OF SLIMY, GROSS FEELING.
YOU MEAN...
AWW, IT GOT YOUR LEFT ARM, DID IT?
IF YOU DON'T DO SOMETHING ABOUT THAT, YOU WON'T GET IT BACK FOR 30 YEARS.
?!
ZSH
JOLT

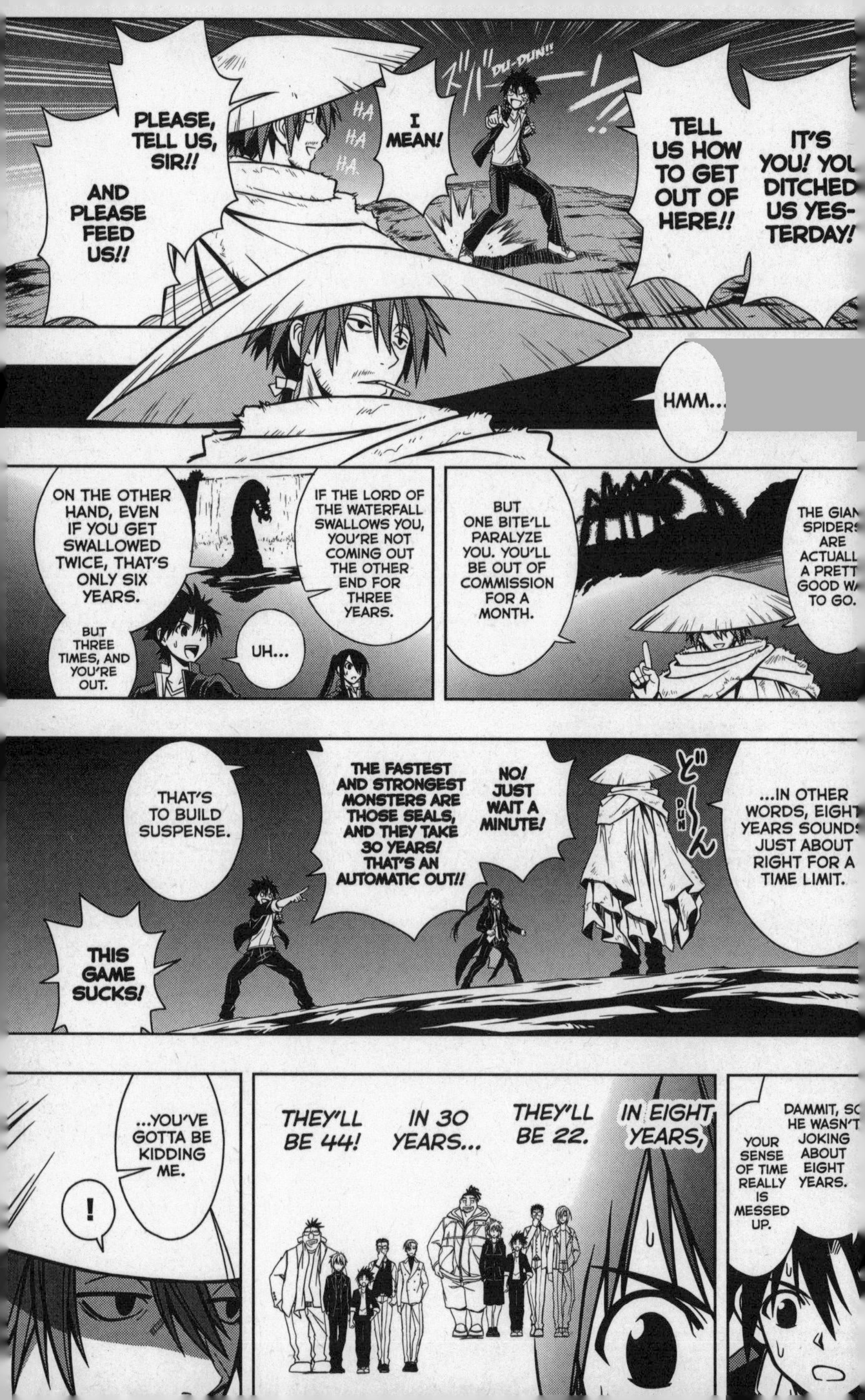
IT'S YOU! YOU DITCHED US YES-TERDAY!
TELL US HOW TO GET OUT OF HERE!!
DU-DUN!!
I MEAN!
HA HA HA HA
PLEASE, TELL US, SIR!!
AND PLEASE FEED US!!
HMM...
THE GIAN SPIDERS ARE ACTUALL A PRETT GOOD WA TO GO.
BUT ONE BITE'LL PARALYZE YOU. YOU'LL BE OUT OF COMMISSION FOR A MONTH.
IF THE LORD OF THE WATERFALL SWALLOWS YOU, YOU'RE NOT COMING OUT THE OTHER END FOR THREE YEARS.
ON THE OTHER HAND, EVEN IF YOU GET SWALLOWED TWICE, THAT'S ONLY SIX YEARS.
UH...
BUT THREE TIMES, AND YOU'RE OUT.
...IN OTHER WORDS, EIGHT YEARS SOUNDS JUST ABOUT RIGHT FOR A TIME LIMIT.
どーん
DUN
NO! JUST WAIT A MINUTE!
THE FASTEST AND STRONGEST MONSTERS ARE THOSE SEALS, AND THEY TAKE 30 YEARS! THAT'S AN AUTOMATIC OUT!!
THAT'S TO BUILD SUSPENSE.
THIS GAME SUCKS!
DAMMIT, SO HE WASN'T JOKING ABOUT EIGHT YEARS.
YOUR SENSE OF TIME REALLY IS MESSED UP.
IN EIGHT YEARS,
THEY'LL BE 22.
IN 30 YEARS...
THEY'LL BE 44!
...YOU'VE GOTTA BE KIDDING ME.
!

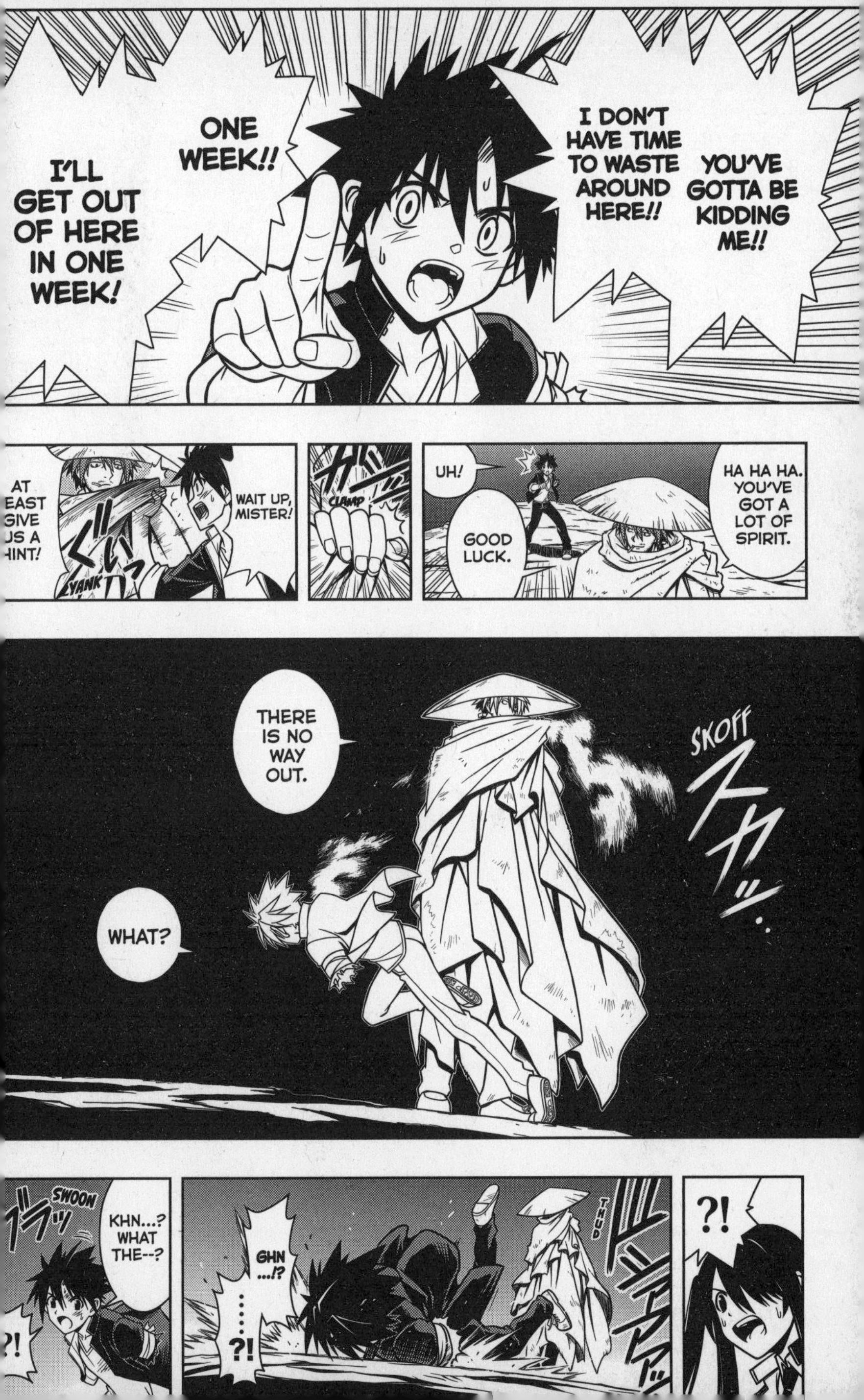
YOU'VE GOTTA BE KIDDING ME!!
I DON'T HAVE TIME TO WASTE AROUND HERE!!
ONE WEEK!!
I'LL GET OUT OF HERE IN ONE WEEK!
HA HA HA. YOU'VE GOT A LOT OF SPIRIT.
UH!
GOOD LUCK.
CLAMP
WAIT UP, MISTER!
AT EAST GIVE US A HINT!
YANK
SKOFF
THERE IS NO WAY OUT.
WHAT?
?!
THUD
GHN ...!?
......?!
SWOON
KHN...? WHAT THE--?
?!

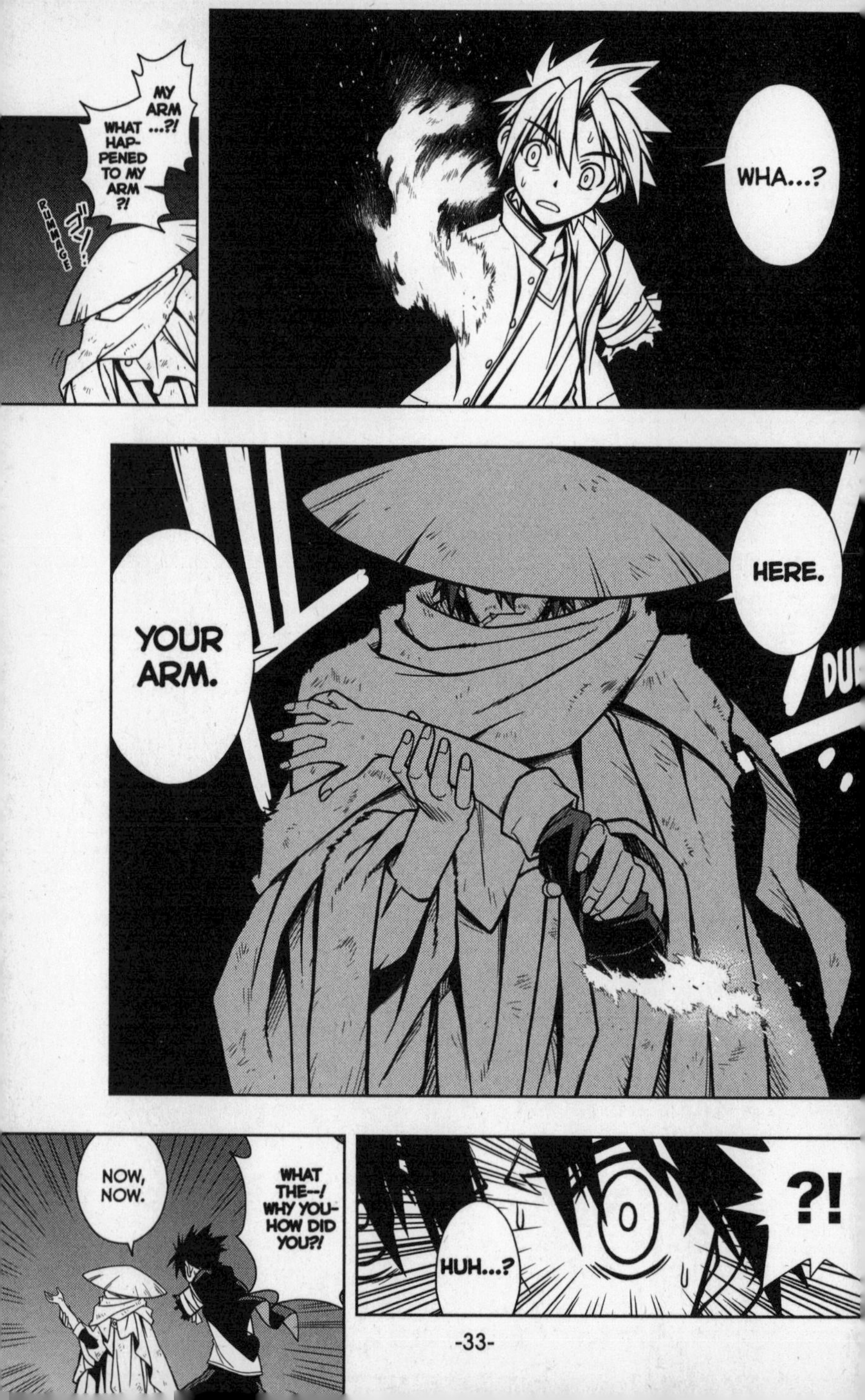
WHA...?
MY ARM ...?!
WHAT HAPPENED TO MY ARM ?!
RUMMAGE
HERE.
YOUR ARM.
?!
HUH...?
WHAT THE--! WHY YOU- HOW DID YOU?!
NOW, NOW.

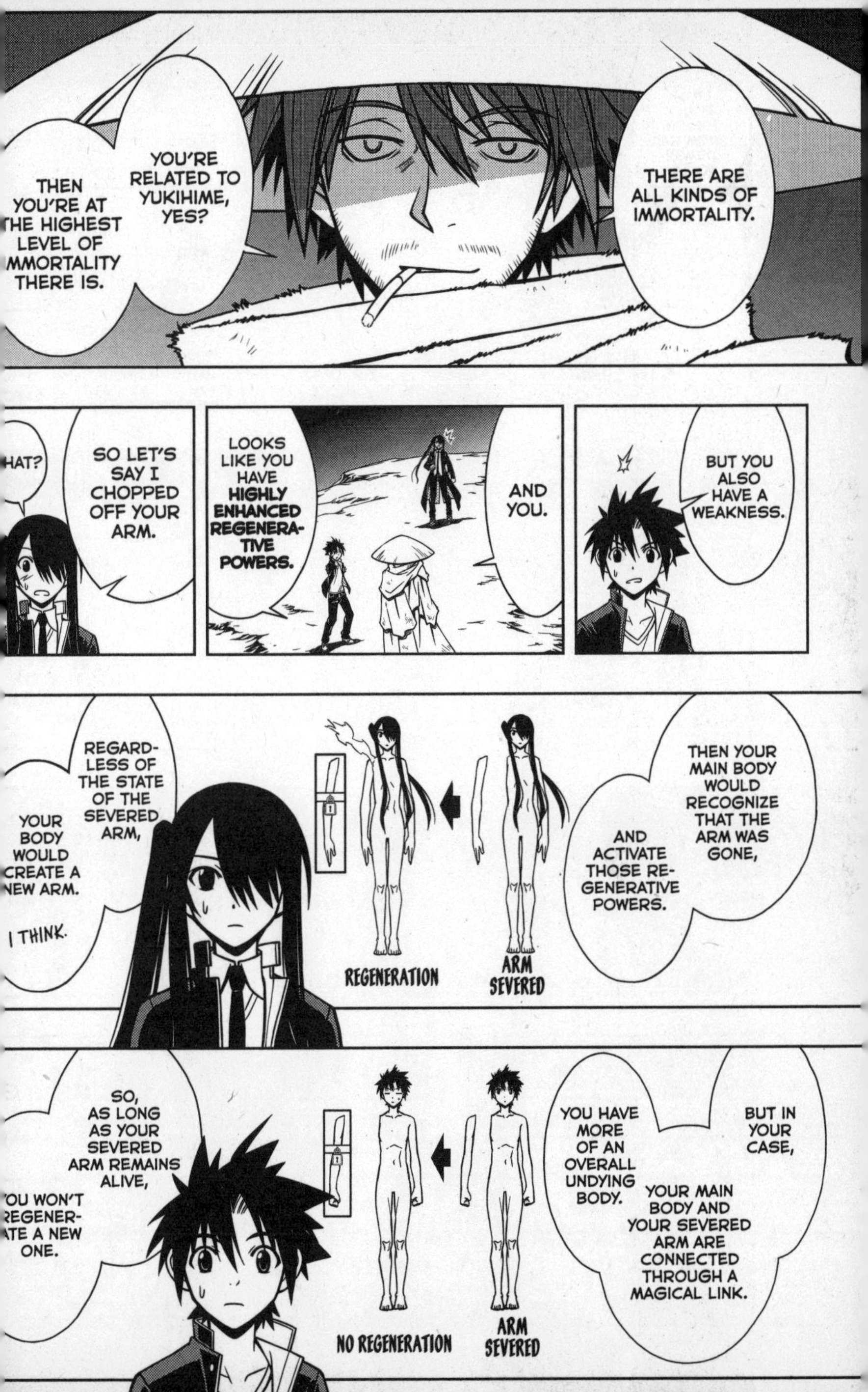
THERE ARE ALL KINDS OF IMMORTALITY.
YOU'RE RELATED TO YUKIHIME, YES?
THEN YOU'RE AT THE HIGHEST LEVEL OF MMORTALITY THERE IS.
BUT YOU ALSO HAVE A WEAKNESS.
AND YOU.
LOOKS LIKE YOU HAVE HIGHLY ENHANCED REGENERATIVE POWERS.
SO LET'S SAY I CHOPPED OFF YOUR ARM.
HAT?
THEN YOUR MAIN BODY WOULD RECOGNIZE THAT THE ARM WAS GONE,
AND ACTIVATE THOSE REGENERATIVE POWERS.
ARM SEVERED
REGENERATION
REGARDLESS OF THE STATE OF THE SEVERED ARM,
YOUR BODY WOULD CREATE A NEW ARM.
I THINK.
BUT IN YOUR CASE,
YOU HAVE MORE OF AN OVERALL UNDYING BODY.
YOUR MAIN BODY AND YOUR SEVERED ARM ARE CONNECTED THROUGH A MAGICAL LINK.
ARM SEVERED
NO REGENERATION
SO, AS LONG AS YOUR SEVERED ARM REMAINS ALIVE,
OU WON'T REGENERATE A NEW ONE.

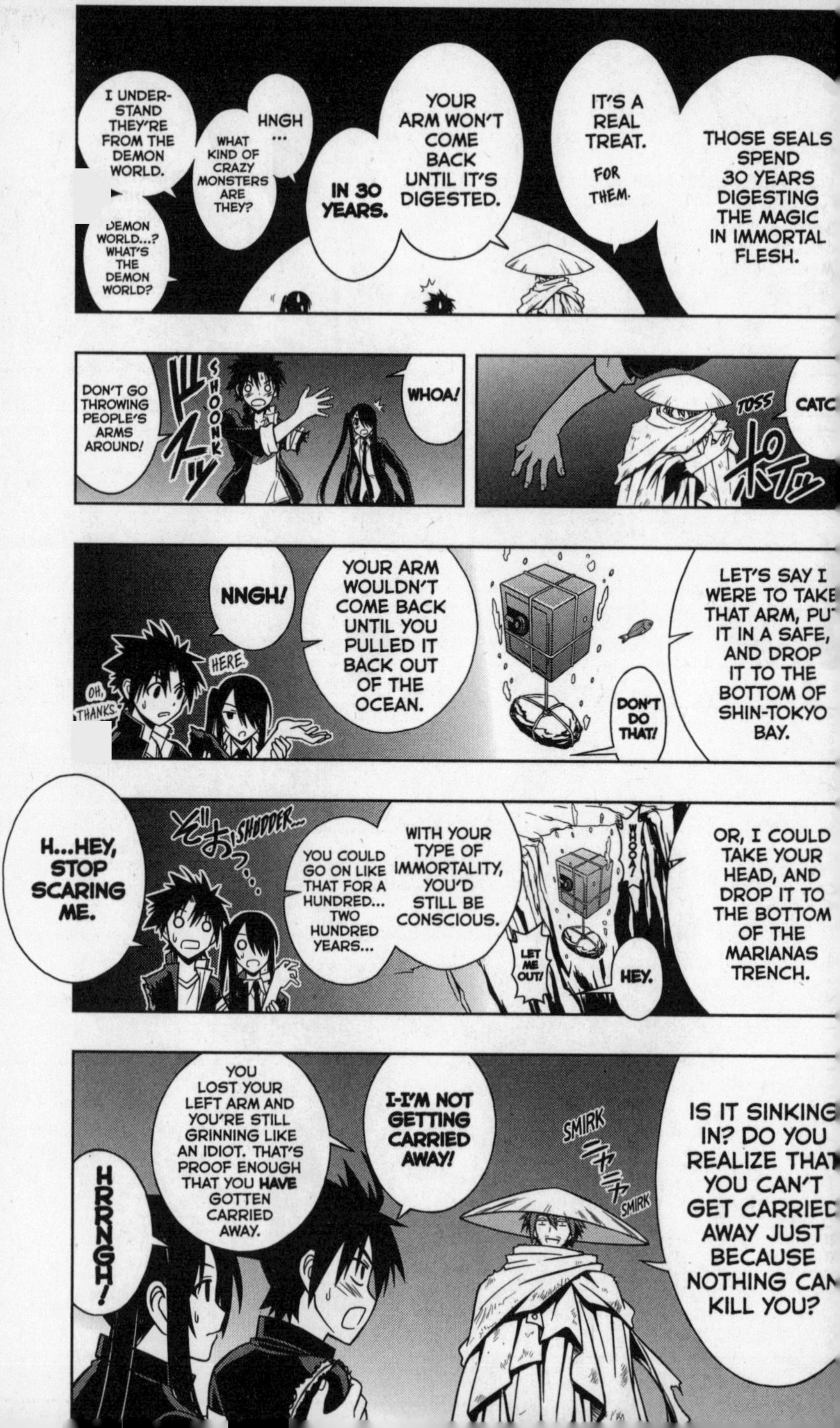
THOSE SEALS SPEND 30 YEARS DIGESTING THE MAGIC IN IMMORTAL FLESH.
IT'S A REAL TREAT.
FOR THEM.
YOUR ARM WON'T COME BACK UNTIL IT'S DIGESTED.
IN 30 YEARS.
HNGH...
WHAT KIND OF CRAZY MONSTERS ARE THEY?
I UNDER-STAND THEY'RE FROM THE DEMON WORLD.
DEMON WORLD...? WHAT'S THE DEMON WORLD?
CATC
TOSS
WHOA!
SHOONK
DON'T GO THROWING PEOPLE'S ARMS AROUND!
LET'S SAY I WERE TO TAKE THAT ARM, PU IT IN A SAFE, AND DROP IT TO THE BOTTOM OF SHIN-TOKYO BAY.
DON'T DO THAT!
YOUR ARM WOULDN'T COME BACK UNTIL YOU PULLED IT BACK OUT OF THE OCEAN.
NNGH!
HERE.
OH, THANKS.
OR, I COULD TAKE YOUR HEAD, AND DROP IT TO THE BOTTOM OF THE MARIANAS TRENCH.
WHOA!?
HEY.
LET ME OUT!
WITH YOUR TYPE OF IMMORTALITY, YOU'D STILL BE CONSCIOUS.
YOU COULD GO ON LIKE THAT FOR A HUNDRED... TWO HUNDRED YEARS...
SHUDDER...
H...HEY, STOP SCARING ME.
IS IT SINKING IN? DO YOU REALIZE THA YOU CAN'T GET CARRIE AWAY JUST BECAUSE NOTHING CA KILL YOU?
SMIRK
SMIRK
I-I'M NOT GETTING CARRIED AWAY!
YOU LOST YOUR LEFT ARM AND YOU'RE STILL GRINNING LIKE AN IDIOT. THAT'S PROOF ENOUGH THAT YOU HAVE GOTTEN CARRIED AWAY.
HRRNGH!

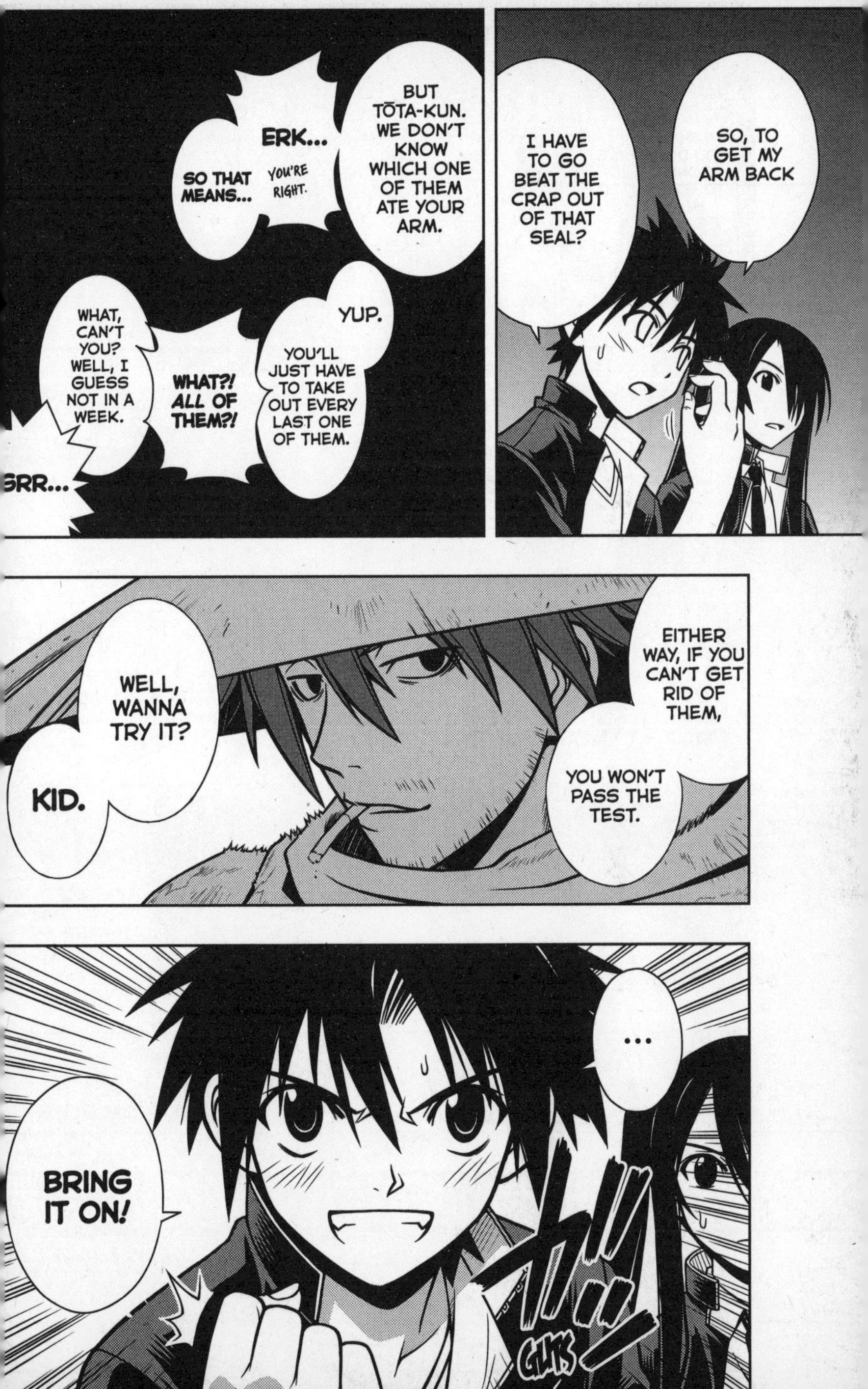
SO, TO GET MY ARM BACK
I HAVE TO GO BEAT THE CRAP OUT OF THAT SEAL?
BUT TŌTA-KUN. WE DON'T KNOW WHICH ONE OF THEM ATE YOUR ARM.
ERK...
YOU'RE RIGHT.
SO THAT MEANS...
YUP.
YOU'LL JUST HAVE TO TAKE OUT EVERY LAST ONE OF THEM.
WHAT?! ALL OF THEM?!
WHAT, CAN'T YOU? WELL, I GUESS NOT IN A WEEK.
GRR...
EITHER WAY, IF YOU CAN'T GET RID OF THEM,
YOU WON'T PASS THE TEST.
WELL, WANNA TRY IT?
KID.
...
BRING IT ON!
GUTS

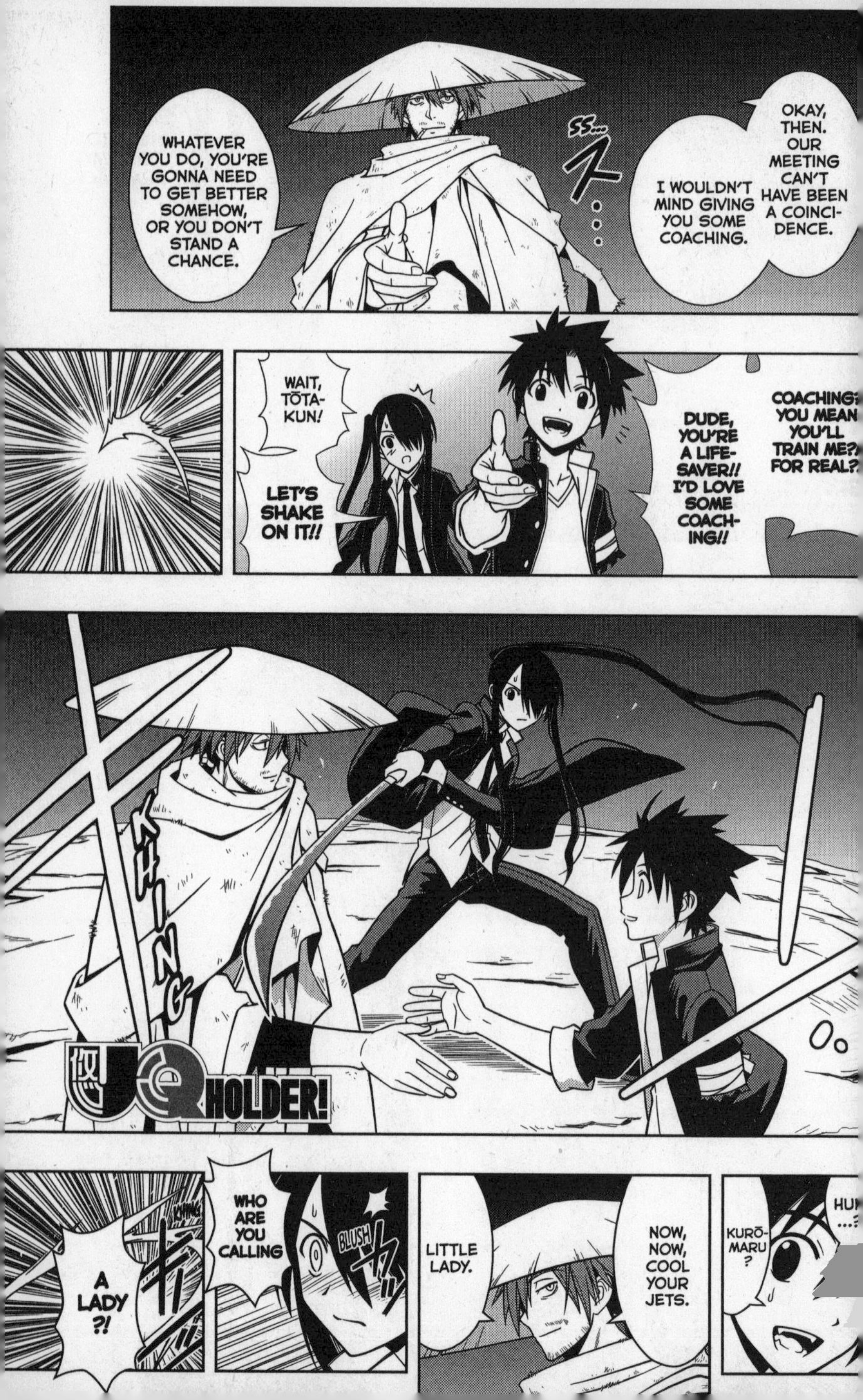
OKAY, THEN. OUR MEETING CAN'T HAVE BEEN A COINCIDENCE.
I WOULDN'T MIND GIVING YOU SOME COACHING.
SS...
WHATEVER YOU DO, YOU'RE GONNA NEED TO GET BETTER SOMEHOW, OR YOU DON'T STAND A CHANCE.
COACHING? YOU MEAN YOU'LL TRAIN ME?! FOR REAL?!
DUDE, YOU'RE A LIFE-SAVER!! I'D LOVE SOME COACH-ING!!
WAIT, TŌTA-KUN!
LET'S SHAKE ON IT!!
Oo
KHING
UQ HOLDER!
HUH...?
KURŌMARU?
NOW, NOW, COOL YOUR JETS.
LITTLE LADY.
WHO ARE YOU CALLING
BLUSH
A LADY?!

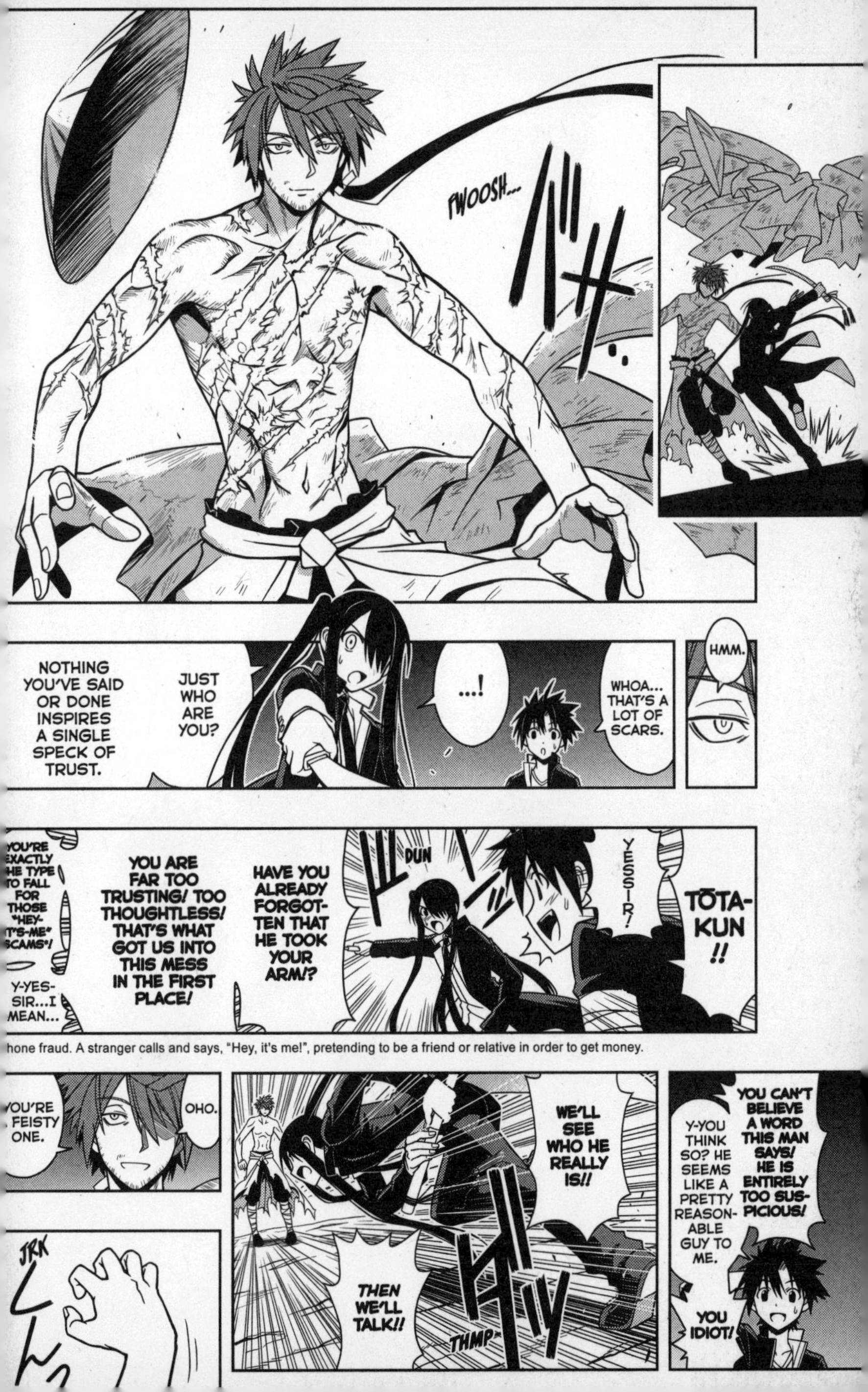
FWOOSH...
HMM.
WHOA... THAT'S A LOT OF SCARS.
...!
JUST WHO ARE YOU?
NOTHING YOU'VE SAID OR DONE INSPIRES A SINGLE SPECK OF TRUST.
TŌTA-KUN!!
YESSIR!
DUN
HAVE YOU ALREADY FORGOT-TEN THAT HE TOOK YOUR ARM!?
YOU ARE FAR TOO TRUSTING! TOO THOUGHTLESS! THAT'S WHAT GOT US INTO THIS MESS IN THE FIRST PLACE!
YOU'RE EXACTLY THE TYPE TO FALL FOR THOSE "HEY-IT'S-ME" SCAMS*!
Y-YES-SIR...I MEAN...
YOU CAN'T BELIEVE A WORD THIS MAN SAYS! HE IS ENTIRELY TOO SUS-PICIOUS!
Y-YOU THINK SO? HE SEEMS LIKE A PRETTY REASON-ABLE GUY TO ME.
YOU IDIOT!
WE'LL SEE WHO HE REALLY IS!!
THEN WE'LL TALK!!
THMP
OHO.
YOU'RE FEISTY ONE.
JRK

hone fraud. A stranger calls and says, "Hey, it's me!", pretending to be a friend or relative in order to get money.

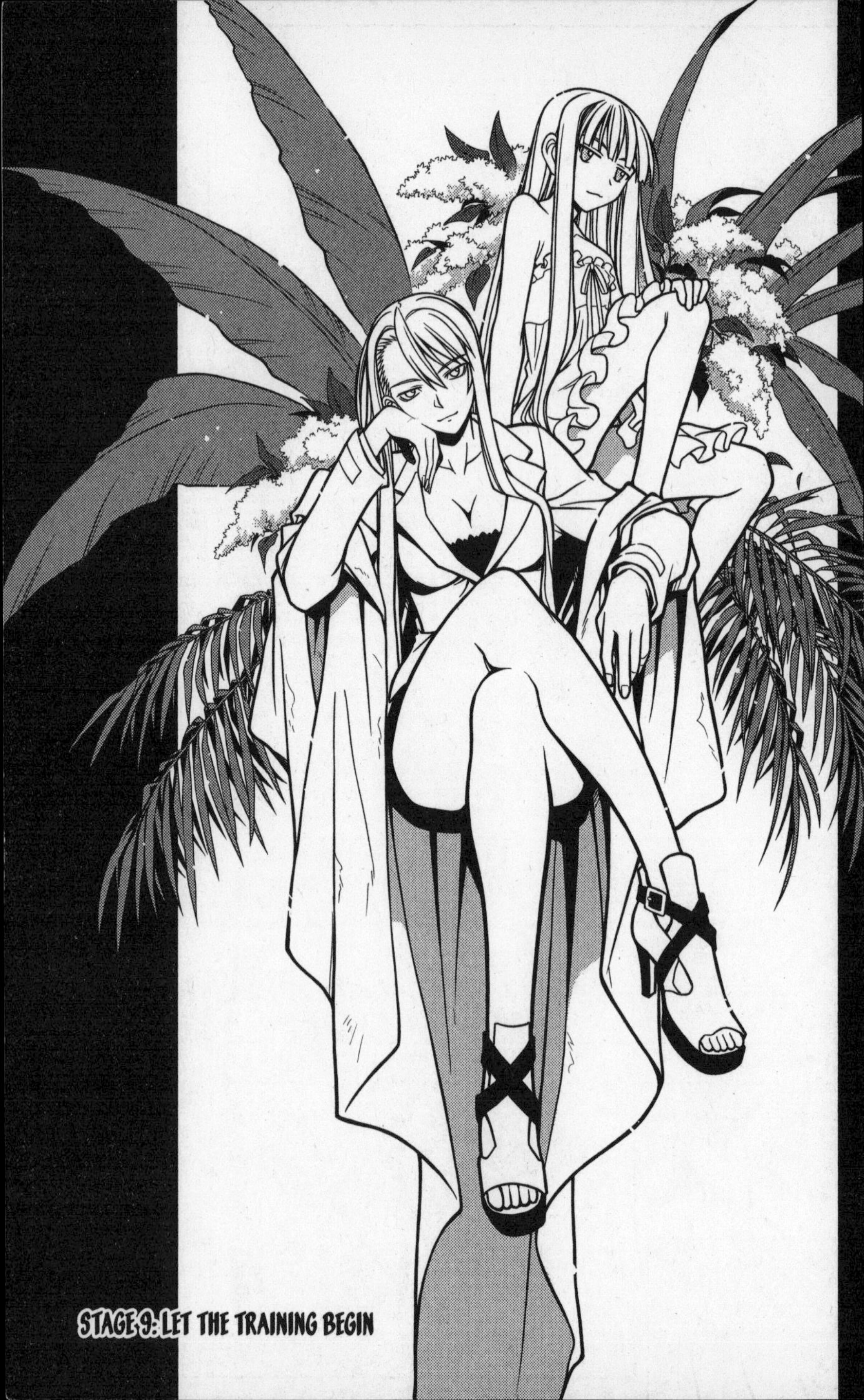

STAGE 9: LET THE TRAINING BEGIN

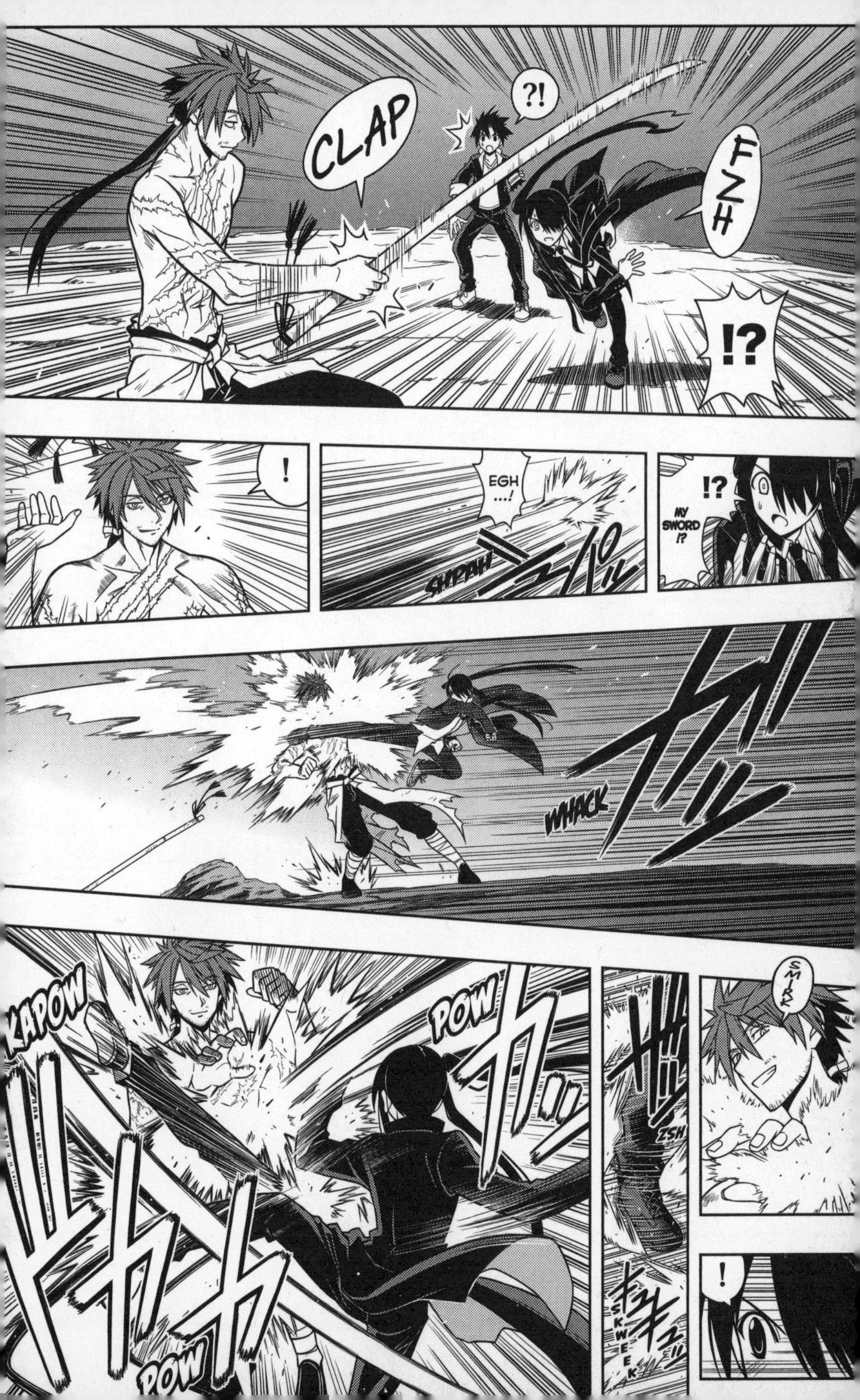
FZH
?!
CLAP
!?
!?
MY SWORD !?
EGH ...!
SHPAH
!
WHACK
SMIRK
!
ZSH
SKWEEK
POW
KAPOW
POW

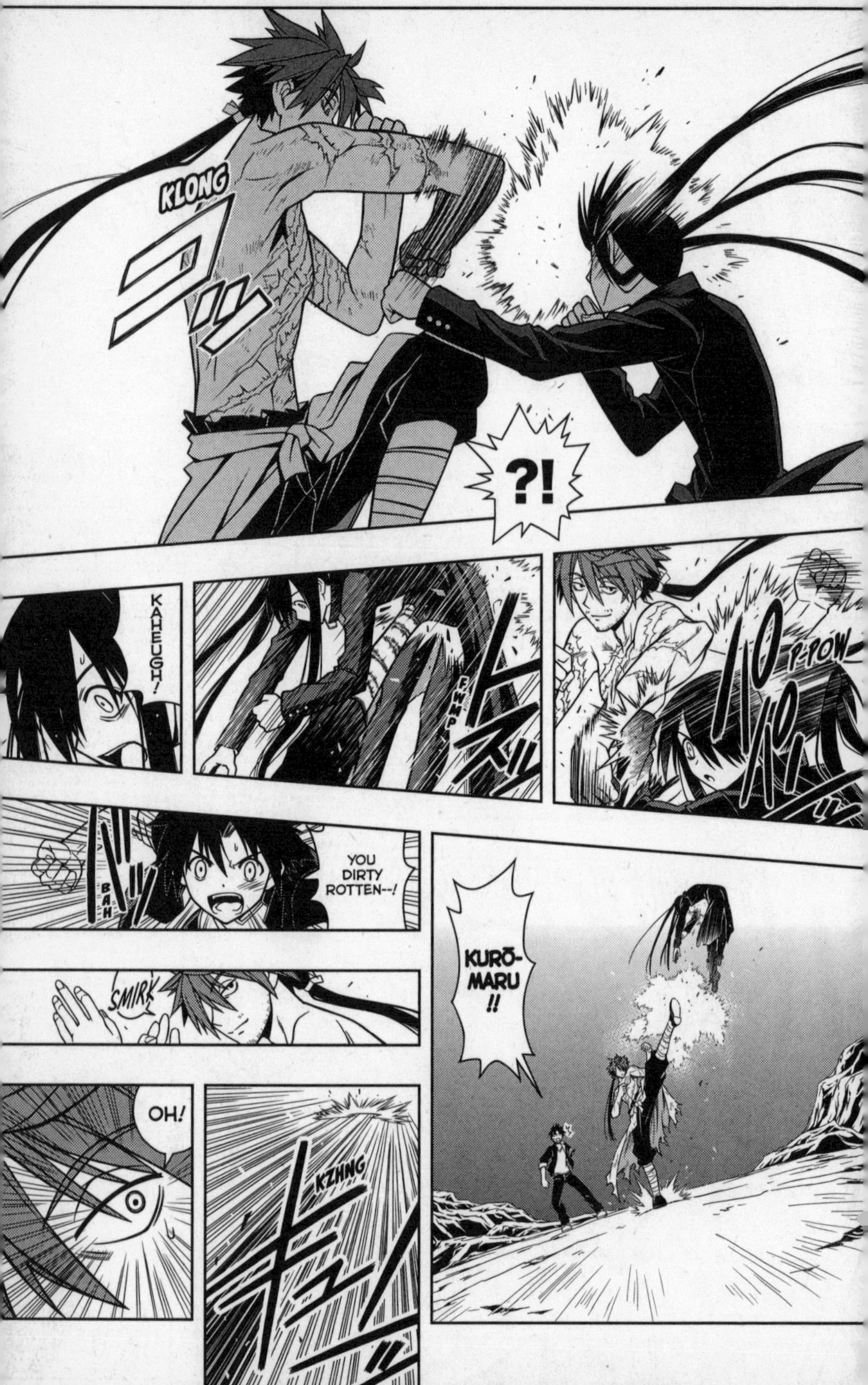
KLONG
?!
P-POW
FWMP
KAHEUGH!
KURŌ-MARU!!
YOU DIRTY ROTTEN--!
BAH
SMIRK
KZHNG
OH!

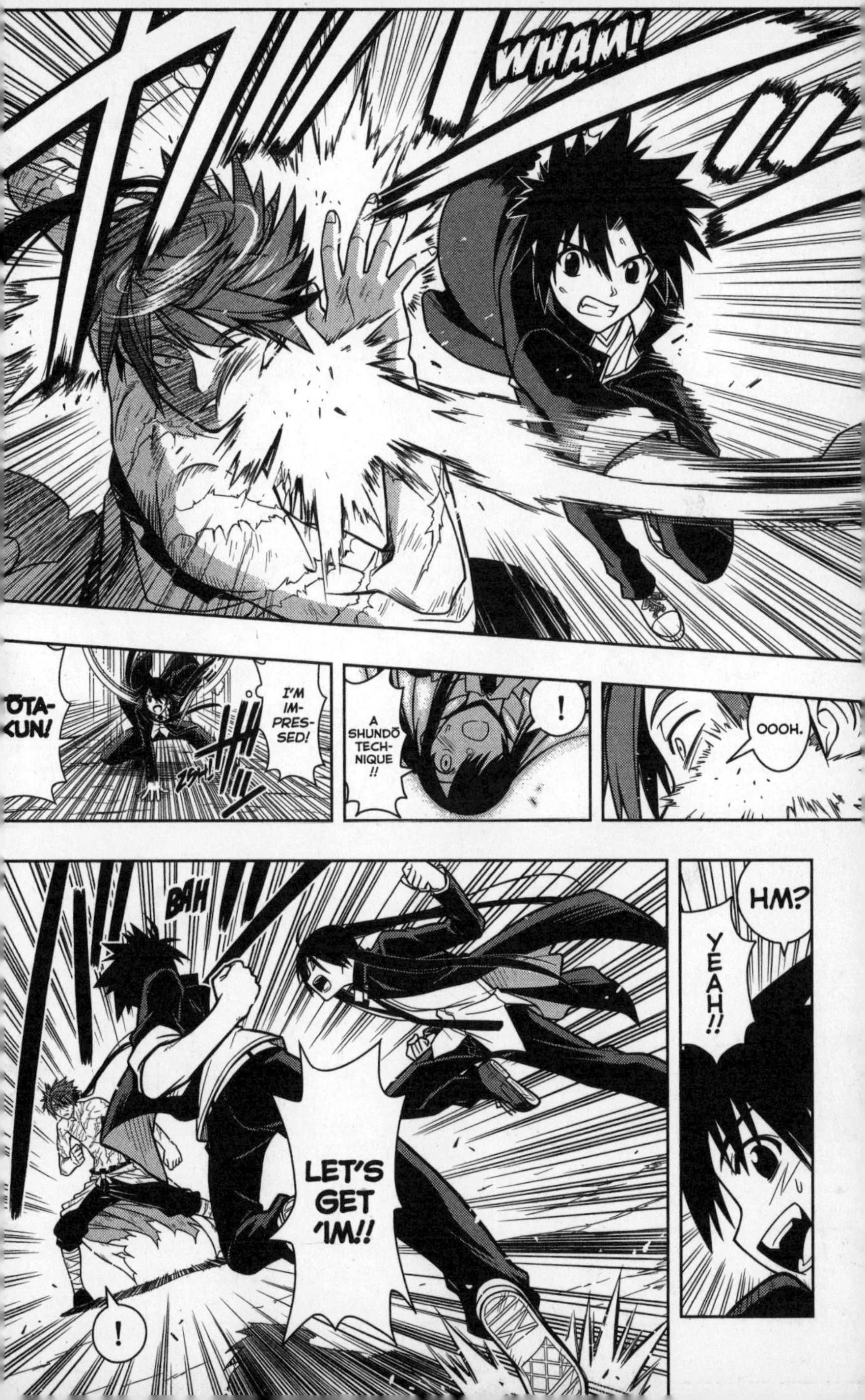
WHAM!
OOOH.
!
A SHUNDŌ TECHNIQUE!!
I'M IMPRESSED!
ŌTA-KUN!
HM?
YEAH!!
BAH
LET'S GET 'IM!!
!

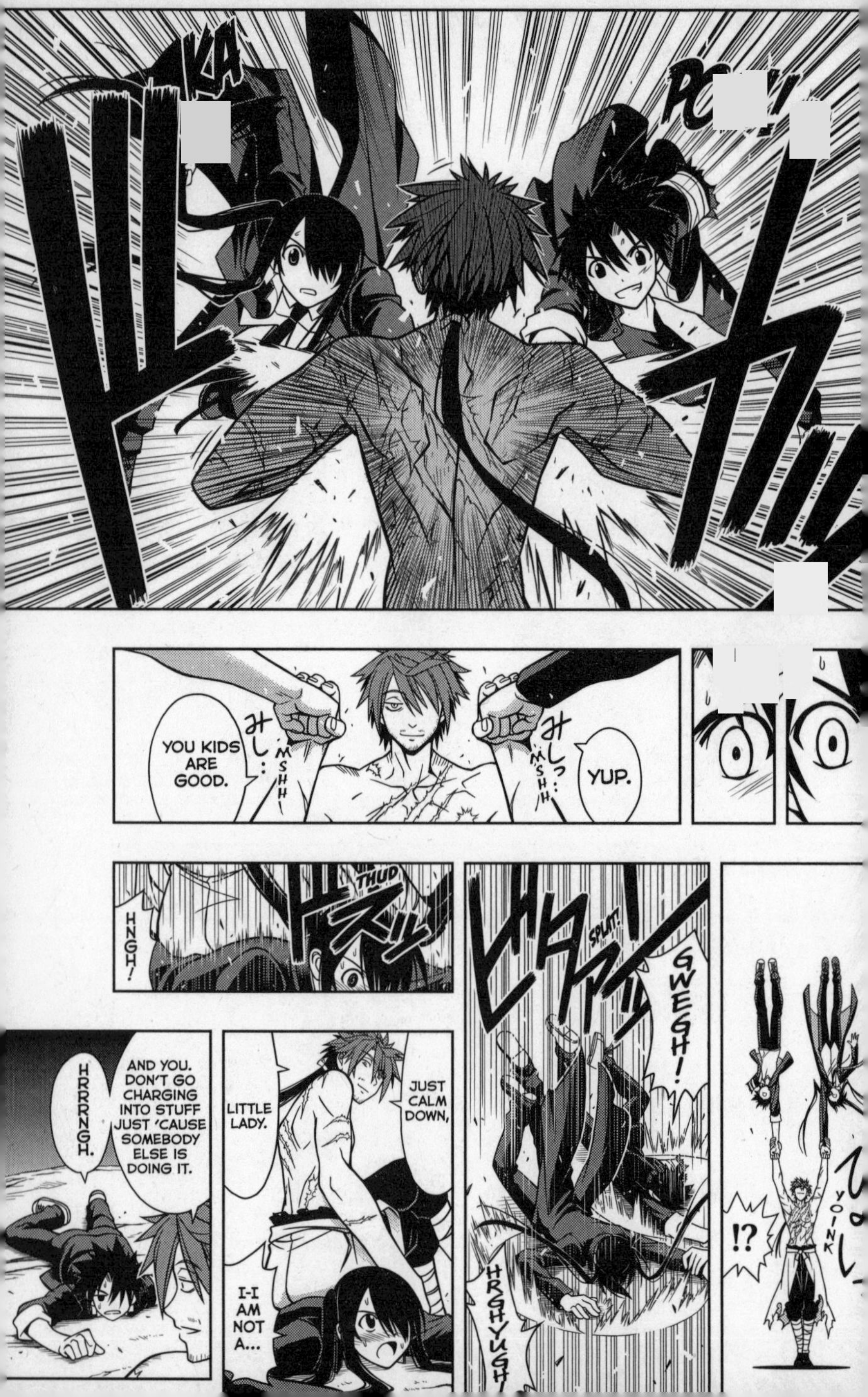

PO
KA
YUP.
みしっ
MSHH
YOU KIDS ARE GOOD.
みし
MSHH
!?
YOINK
SPLAT!
GWEGH!
HRGHYUGH!
THUD
HNGH!
JUST CALM DOWN,
LITTLE LADY.
I-I AM NOT A...
AND YOU. DON'T GO CHARGING INTO STUFF JUST 'CAUSE SOMEBODY ELSE IS DOING IT.
HRRRNGH.

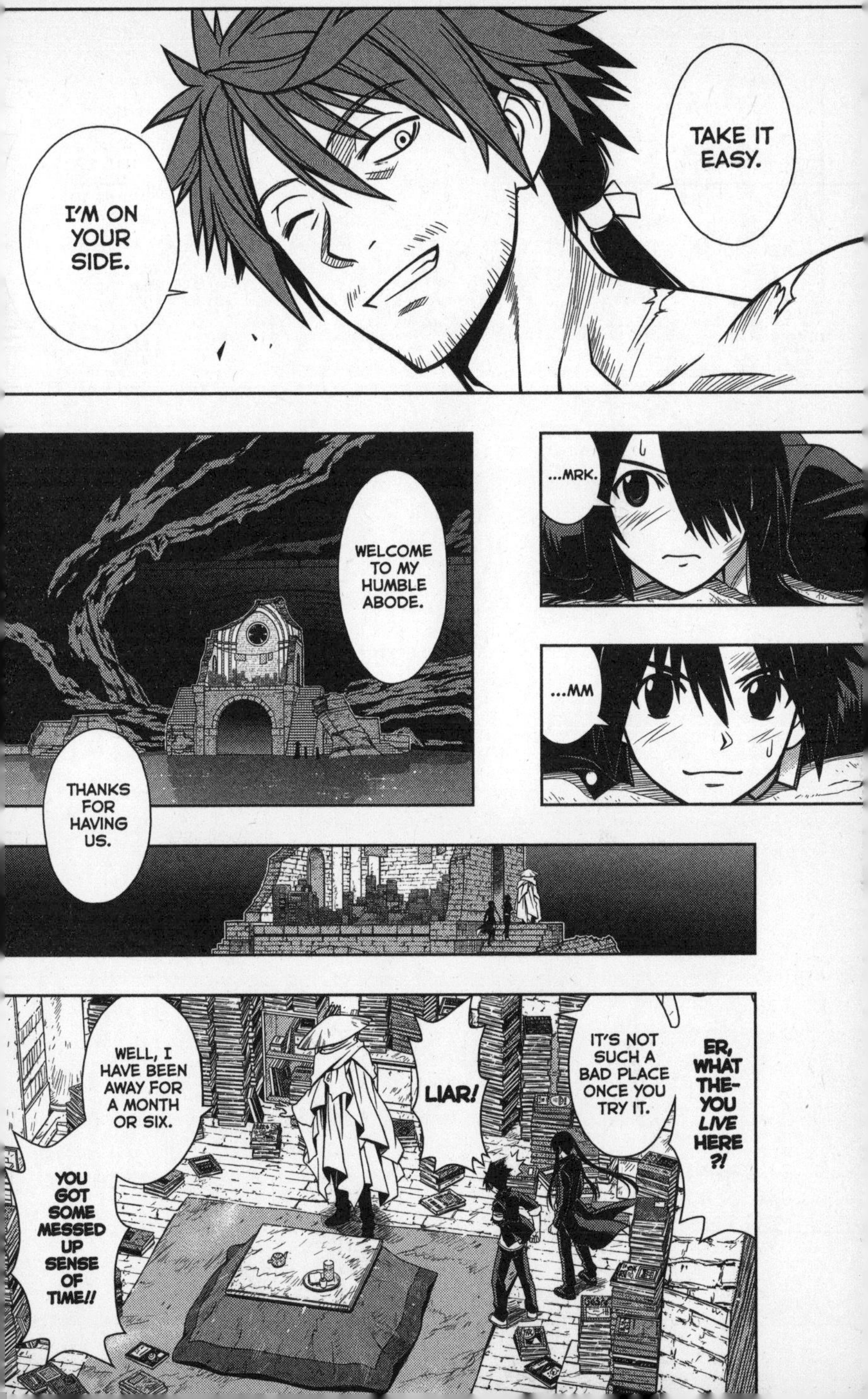
TAKE IT EASY.
I'M ON YOUR SIDE.
...MRK.
...MM
WELCOME TO MY HUMBLE ABODE.
THANKS FOR HAVING US.
ER, WHAT THE- YOU *LIVE* HERE?!
IT'S NOT SUCH A BAD PLACE ONCE YOU TRY IT.
LIAR!
WELL, I HAVE BEEN AWAY FOR A MONTH OR SIX.
YOU GOT SOME MESSED UP SENSE OF TIME!!

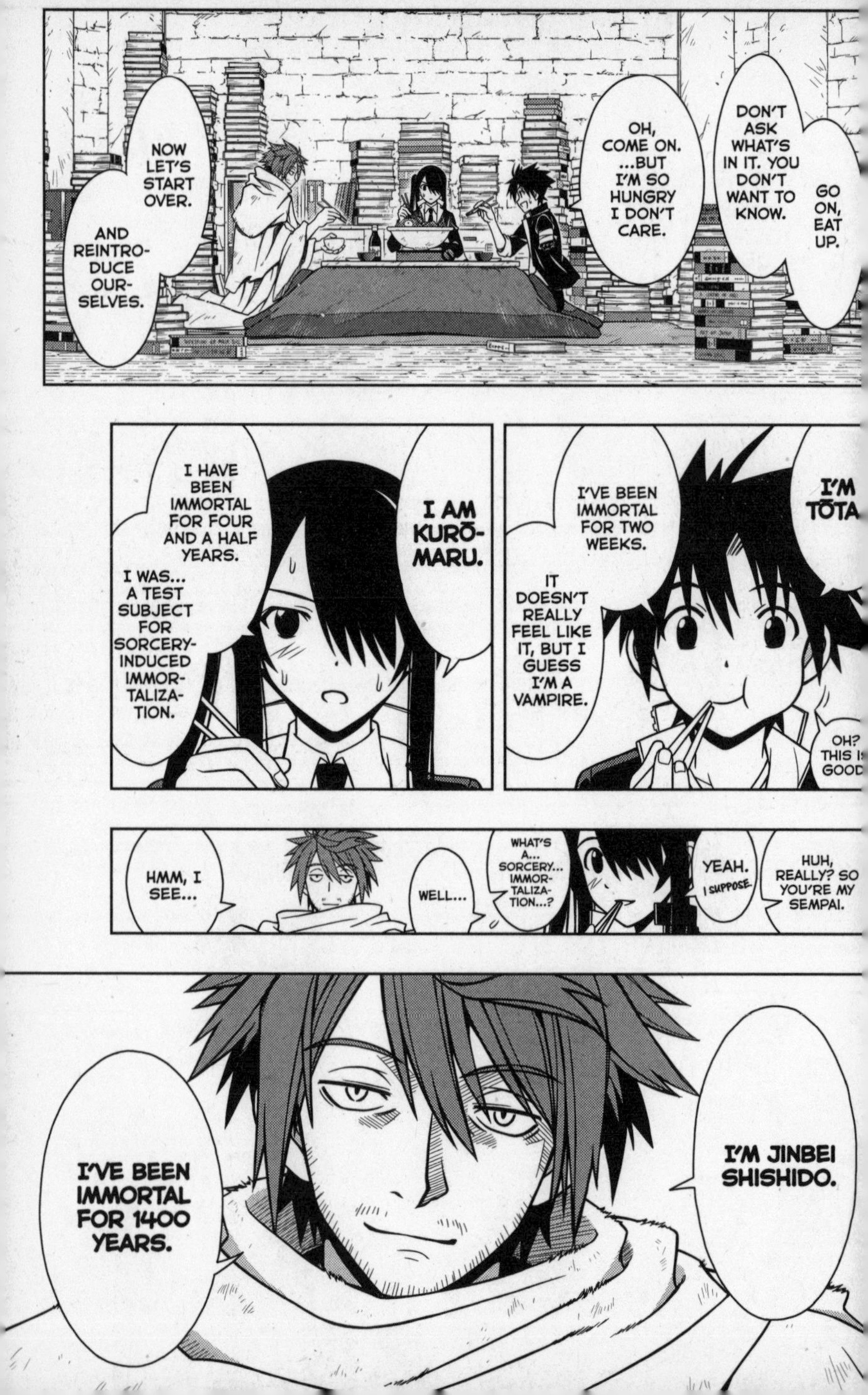
GO ON, EAT UP.
DON'T ASK WHAT'S IN IT. YOU DON'T WANT TO KNOW.
OH, COME ON. ...BUT I'M SO HUNGRY I DON'T CARE.
NOW LET'S START OVER.
AND REINTRODUCE OURSELVES.
I'M TŌTA
I'VE BEEN IMMORTAL FOR TWO WEEKS.
IT DOESN'T REALLY FEEL LIKE IT, BUT I GUESS I'M A VAMPIRE.
OH? THIS I GOOD
I AM KURŌMARU.
I HAVE BEEN IMMORTAL FOR FOUR AND A HALF YEARS.
I WAS... A TEST SUBJECT FOR SORCERY-INDUCED IMMORTALIZATION.
HUH, REALLY? SO YOU'RE MY SEMPAI.
YEAH. I SUPPOSE.
WHAT'S A... SORCERY... IMMORTALIZATION...?
WELL...
HMM, I SEE...
I'M JINBEI SHISHIDO.
I'VE BEEN IMMORTAL FOR 1400 YEARS.

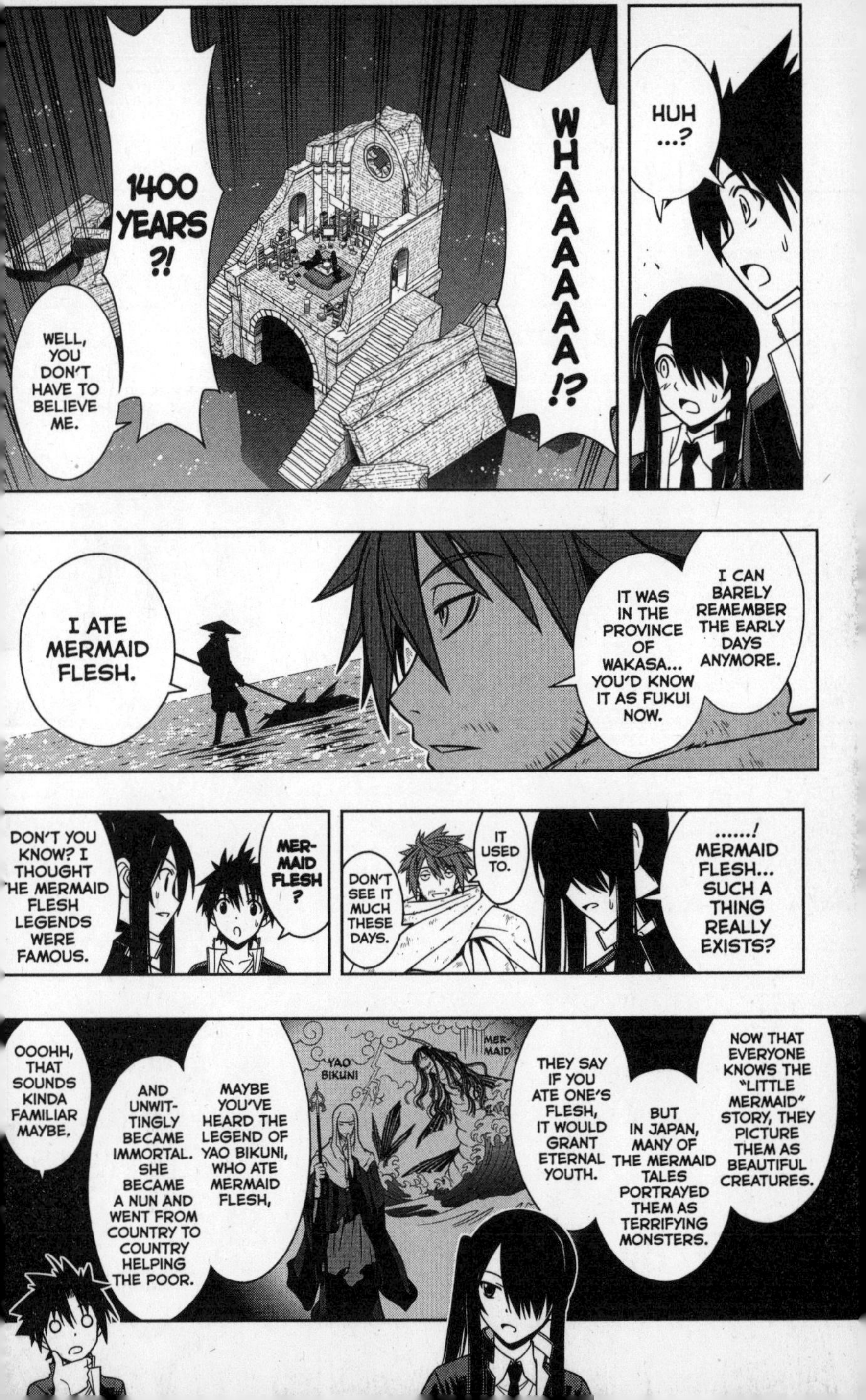
HUH ...?
WHAAAAAAA!?
1400 YEARS ?!
WELL, YOU DON'T HAVE TO BELIEVE ME.
I CAN BARELY REMEMBER THE EARLY DAYS ANYMORE.
IT WAS IN THE PROVINCE OF WAKASA... YOU'D KNOW IT AS FUKUI NOW.
I ATE MERMAID FLESH.
......! MERMAID FLESH... SUCH A THING REALLY EXISTS?
IT USED TO.
DON'T SEE IT MUCH THESE DAYS.
MER-MAID FLESH ?
DON'T YOU KNOW? I THOUGHT THE MERMAID FLESH LEGENDS WERE FAMOUS.
NOW THAT EVERYONE KNOWS THE "LITTLE MERMAID" STORY, THEY PICTURE THEM AS BEAUTIFUL CREATURES.
BUT IN JAPAN, MANY OF THE MERMAID TALES PORTRAYED THEM AS TERRIFYING MONSTERS.
THEY SAY IF YOU ATE ONE'S FLESH, IT WOULD GRANT ETERNAL YOUTH.
MER-MAID
YAO BIKUNI
MAYBE YOU'VE HEARD THE LEGEND OF YAO BIKUNI, WHO ATE MERMAID FLESH,
AND UNWIT-TINGLY BECAME IMMORTAL. SHE BECAME A NUN AND WENT FROM COUNTRY TO COUNTRY HELPING THE POOR.
OOOHH, THAT SOUNDS KINDA FAMILIAR MAYBE.

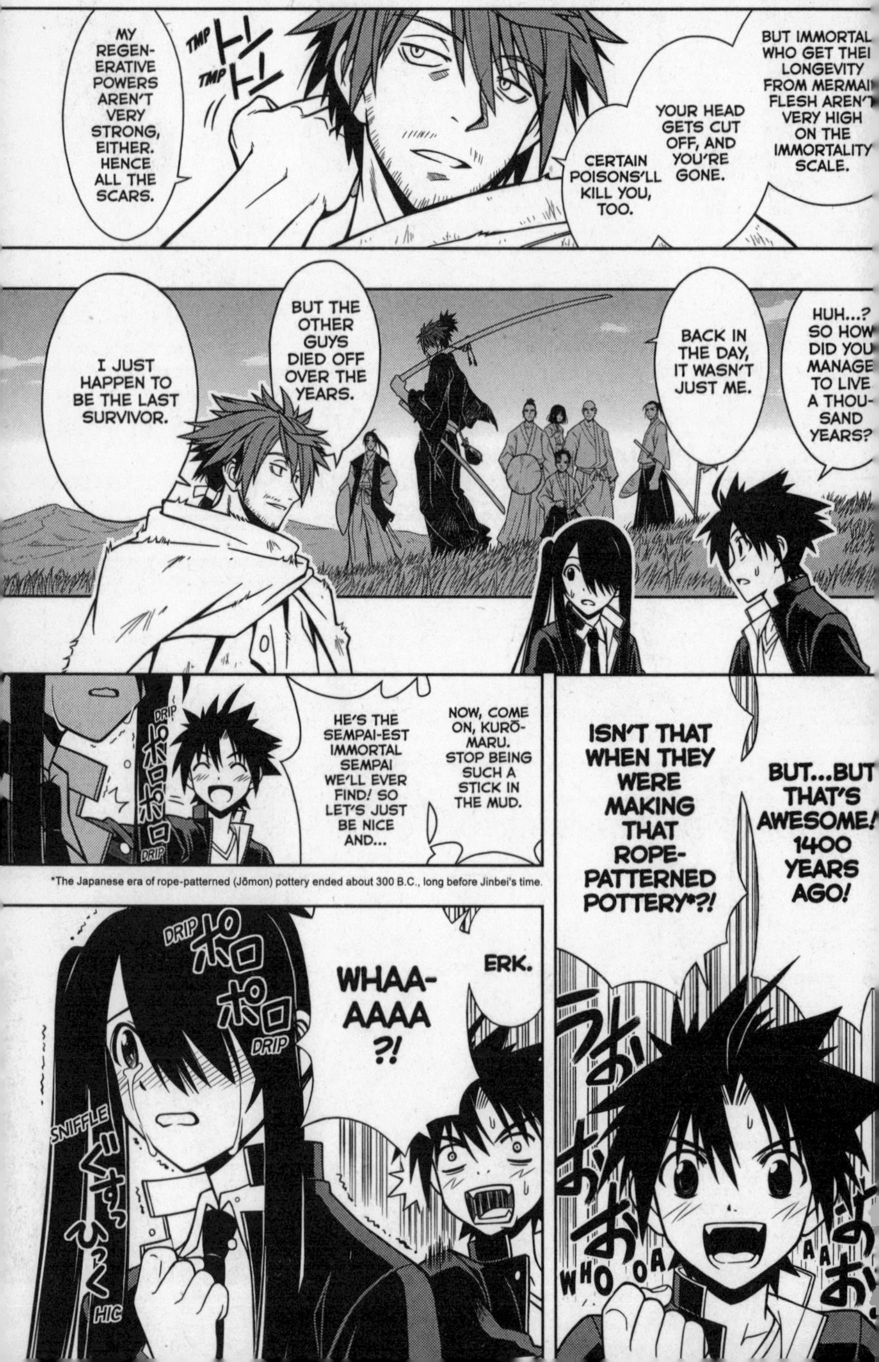
BUT IMMORTAL WHO GET THEI LONGEVITY FROM MERMAI FLESH AREN'T VERY HIGH ON THE IMMORTALITY SCALE.
YOUR HEAD GETS CUT OFF, AND YOU'RE GONE.
CERTAIN POISONS'LL KILL YOU, TOO.
TMP トン
TMP トン
MY REGENERATIVE POWERS AREN'T VERY STRONG, EITHER. HENCE ALL THE SCARS.
HUH...? SO HOW DID YOU MANAGE TO LIVE A THOUSAND YEARS?
BACK IN THE DAY, IT WASN'T JUST ME.
BUT THE OTHER GUYS DIED OFF OVER THE YEARS.
I JUST HAPPEN TO BE THE LAST SURVIVOR.
BUT...BUT THAT'S AWESOME! 1400 YEARS AGO!
ISN'T THAT WHEN THEY WERE MAKING THAT ROPE-PATTERNED POTTERY*?!
うおおお
おおお
WHOOA
AAA
NOW, COME ON, KURŌMARU. STOP BEING SUCH A STICK IN THE MUD.
HE'S THE SEMPAI-EST IMMORTAL SEMPAI WE'LL EVER FIND! SO LET'S JUST BE NICE AND...
DRIP ポロポロ DRIP
ERK.
WHAA-AAAA?!
DRIP ポロポロ DRIP
SNIFFLE ぐすっ
ひっく HIC

*The Japanese era of rope-patterned (Jōmon) pottery ended about 300 B.C., long before Jinbei's time.

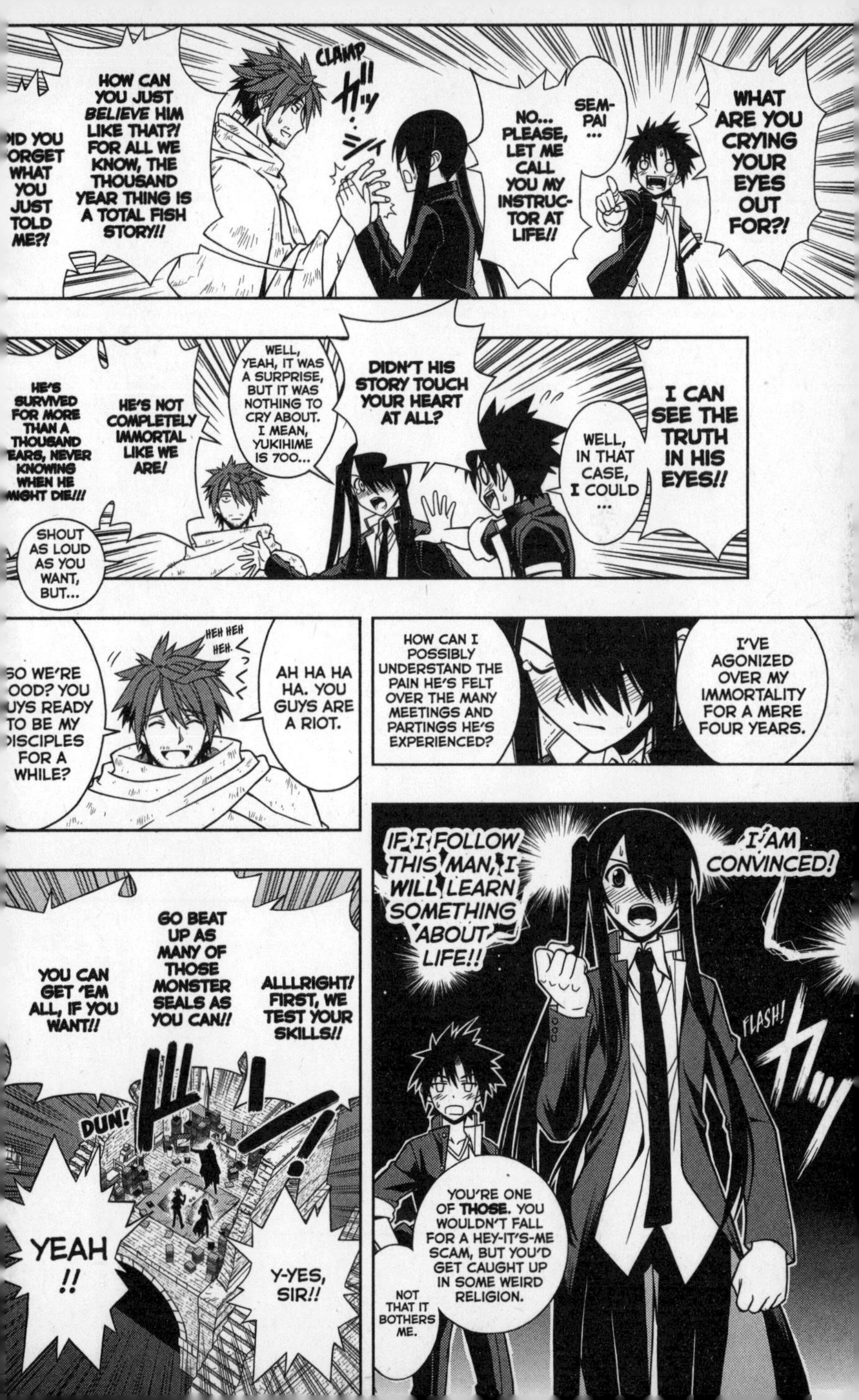
WHAT ARE YOU CRYING YOUR EYES OUT FOR?!
SEM-PAI ...
NO... PLEASE, LET ME CALL YOU MY INSTRUCTOR AT LIFE!!
CLAMP
HOW CAN YOU JUST *BELIEVE* HIM LIKE THAT?! FOR ALL WE KNOW, THE THOUSAND YEAR THING IS A TOTAL FISH STORY!!
ID YOU ORGET WHAT YOU JUST TOLD ME?!
I CAN SEE THE TRUTH IN HIS EYES!!
WELL, IN THAT CASE, I COULD ...
DIDN'T HIS STORY TOUCH YOUR HEART AT ALL?
WELL, YEAH, IT WAS A SURPRISE, BUT IT WAS NOTHING TO CRY ABOUT. I MEAN, YUKIHIME IS 700...
HE'S NOT COMPLETELY IMMORTAL LIKE WE ARE!
HE'S SURVIVED FOR MORE THAN A THOUSAND EARS, NEVER KNOWING WHEN HE MIGHT DIE!!!
SHOUT AS LOUD AS YOU WANT, BUT...
I'VE AGONIZED OVER MY IMMORTALITY FOR A MERE FOUR YEARS.
HOW CAN I POSSIBLY UNDERSTAND THE PAIN HE'S FELT OVER THE MANY MEETINGS AND PARTINGS HE'S EXPERIENCED?
HEH HEH HEH.
AH HA HA HA. YOU GUYS ARE A RIOT.
SO WE'RE OOD? YOU UYS READY TO BE MY ISCIPLES FOR A WHILE?
I AM CONVINCED!
IF I FOLLOW THIS MAN, I WILL LEARN SOMETHING ABOUT LIFE!!
FLASH!
YOU'RE ONE OF **THOSE.** YOU WOULDN'T FALL FOR A HEY-IT'S-ME SCAM, BUT YOU'D GET CAUGHT UP IN SOME WEIRD RELIGION.
NOT THAT IT BOTHERS ME.
ALLLRIGHT! FIRST, WE TEST YOUR SKILLS!!
GO BEAT UP AS MANY OF THOSE MONSTER SEALS AS YOU CAN!!
YOU CAN GET 'EM ALL, IF YOU WANT!!
DUN!
Y-YES, SIR!!
YEAH !!

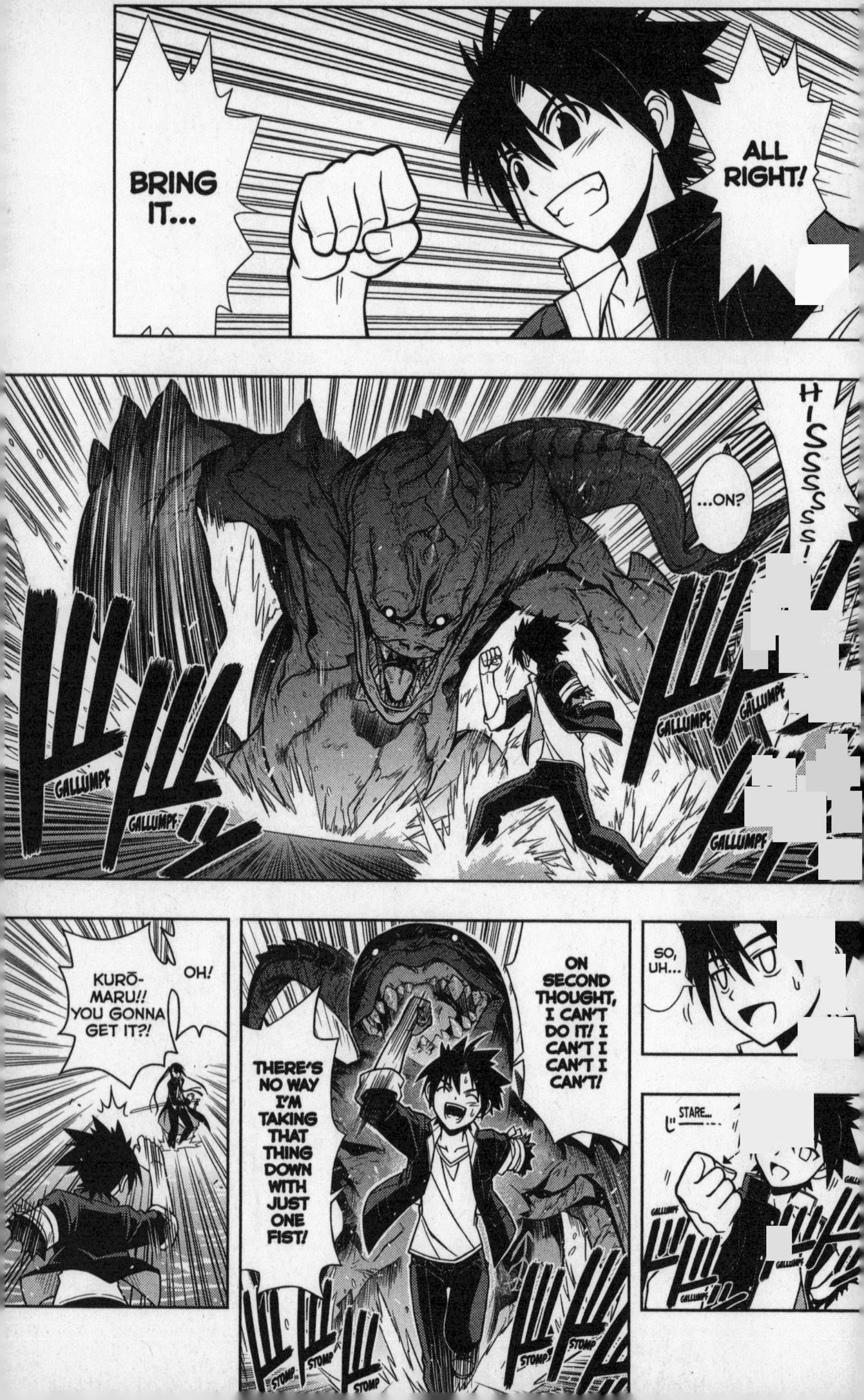
ALL RIGHT!
BRING IT...
HISSSSSS!
...ON?
GALLUMPF
GALLUMPF
GALLUMPF
GALLUMPF
GALLUMPF
SO, UH...
STARE...
GALLUMPF
GALLUMPF
GALLUMPF
ON SECOND THOUGHT, I CAN'T DO IT! I CAN'T I CAN'T I CAN'T!
THERE'S NO WAY I'M TAKING THAT THING DOWN WITH JUST ONE FIST!
STOMP
STOMP
STOMP
STOMP
STOMP
OH!
KURŌ-MARU!! YOU GONNA GET IT?!

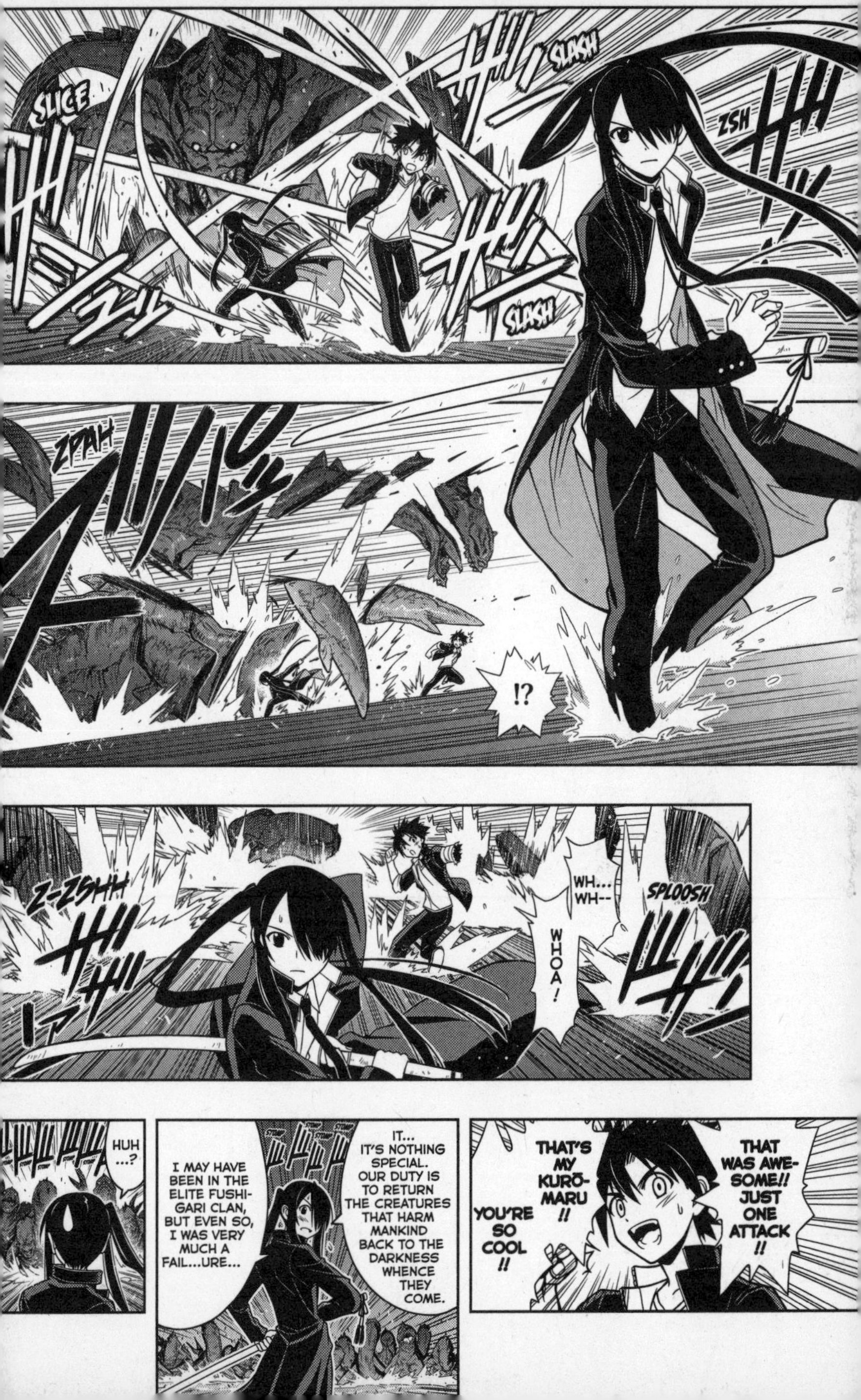
SLASH
ZSH
SLASH
SLICE
ZPAH
!?
SPLOOSH
WH... WH--
WHOA!
Z-ZSHH
THAT WAS AWESOME!! JUST ONE ATTACK!!
THAT'S MY KURŌMARU!!
YOU'RE SO COOL!!
IT... IT'S NOTHING SPECIAL. OUR DUTY IS TO RETURN THE CREATURES THAT HARM MANKIND BACK TO THE DARKNESS WHENCE THEY COME.
I MAY HAVE BEEN IN THE ELITE FUSHIGARI CLAN, BUT EVEN SO, I WAS VERY MUCH A FAIL...URE...
HUH ...?

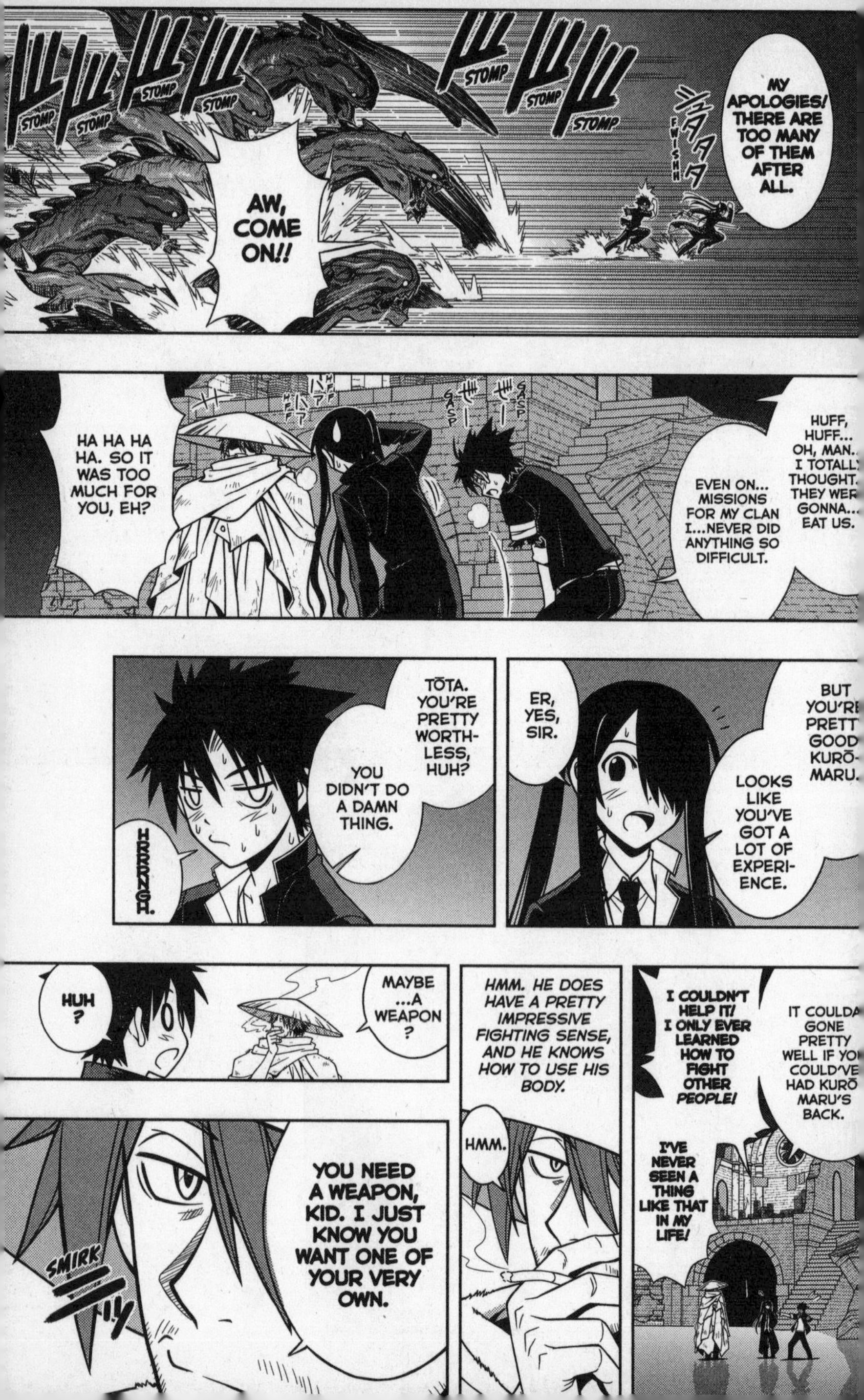
MY APOLOGIES! THERE ARE TOO MANY OF THEM AFTER ALL.
FWISHH
STOMP STOMP STOMP
STOMP STOMP STOMP STOMP
AW, COME ON!!
HUFF, HUFF... OH, MAN.. I TOTALL THOUGHT. THEY WER GONNA... EAT US.
EVEN ON... MISSIONS FOR MY CLAN I...NEVER DID ANYTHING SO DIFFICULT.
GASP
GASP
HA HA HA HA. SO IT WAS TOO MUCH FOR YOU, EH?
BUT YOU'RE PRETT GOOD KURŌMARU.
LOOKS LIKE YOU'VE GOT A LOT OF EXPERIENCE.
ER, YES, SIR.
TŌTA. YOU'RE PRETTY WORTHLESS, HUH?
YOU DIDN'T DO A DAMN THING.
HRRRNGH.
IT COULDA GONE PRETTY WELL IF YO COULD'VE HAD KURŌMARU'S BACK.
I COULDN'T HELP IT! I ONLY EVER LEARNED HOW TO FIGHT OTHER PEOPLE!
I'VE NEVER SEEN A THING LIKE THAT IN MY LIFE!
HMM. HE DOES HAVE A PRETTY IMPRESSIVE FIGHTING SENSE, AND HE KNOWS HOW TO USE HIS BODY.
HMM.
MAYBE ...A WEAPON?
HUH?
YOU NEED A WEAPON, KID. I JUST KNOW YOU WANT ONE OF YOUR VERY OWN.
SMIRK

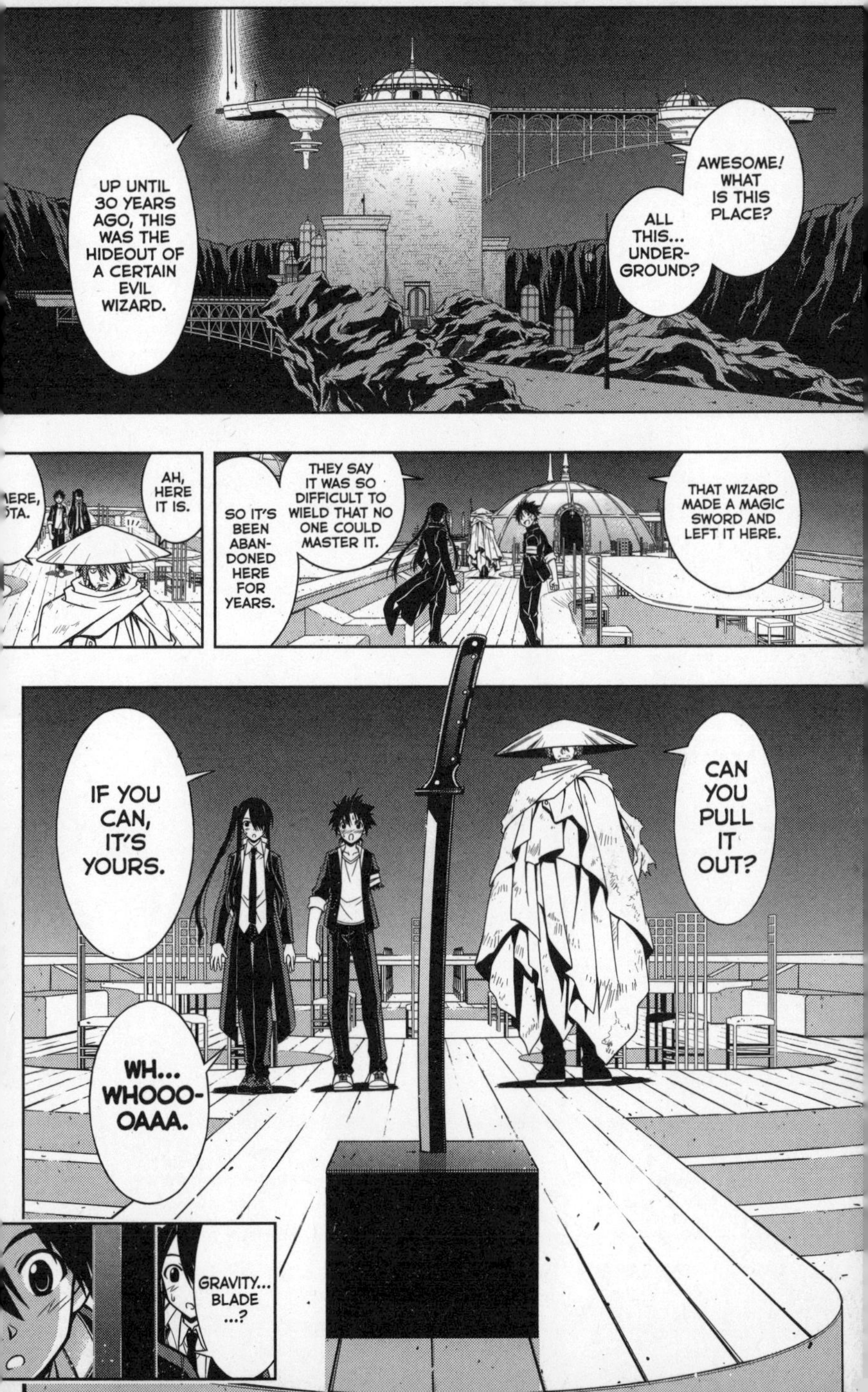
AWESOME! WHAT IS THIS PLACE?
ALL THIS... UNDERGROUND?
UP UNTIL 30 YEARS AGO, THIS WAS THE HIDEOUT OF A CERTAIN EVIL WIZARD.
THAT WIZARD MADE A MAGIC SWORD AND LEFT IT HERE.
THEY SAY IT WAS SO DIFFICULT TO WIELD THAT NO ONE COULD MASTER IT.
SO IT'S BEEN ABANDONED HERE FOR YEARS.
AH, HERE IT IS.
CAN YOU PULL IT OUT?
IF YOU CAN, IT'S YOURS.
WH... WHOOO-OAAA.
GRAVITY... BLADE ...?

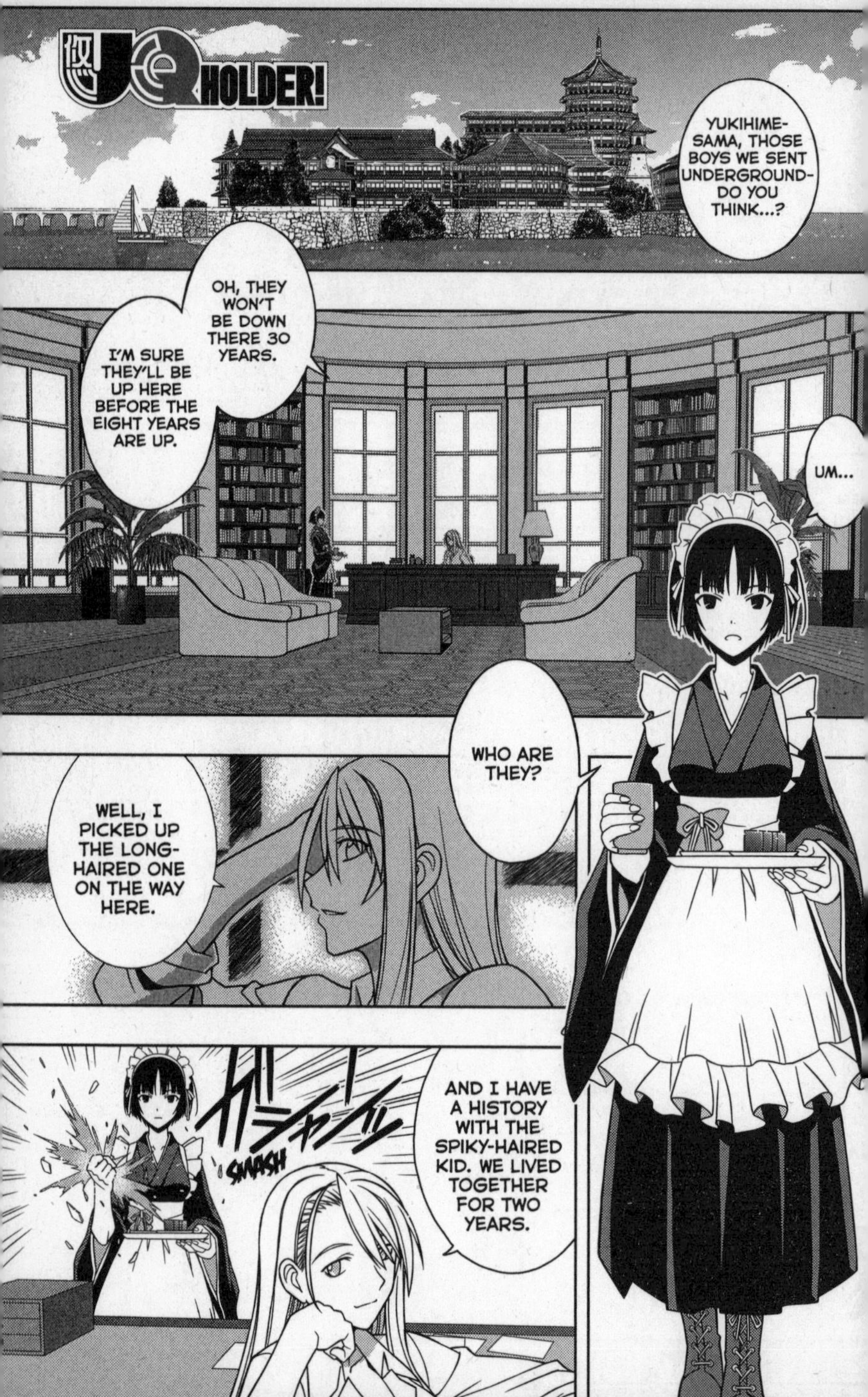
UQ HOLDER!
YUKIHIME-SAMA, THOSE BOYS WE SENT UNDERGROUND- DO YOU THINK...?
UM...
OH, THEY WON'T BE DOWN THERE 30 YEARS.
I'M SURE THEY'LL BE UP HERE BEFORE THE EIGHT YEARS ARE UP.
WHO ARE THEY?
WELL, I PICKED UP THE LONG-HAIRED ONE ON THE WAY HERE.
AND I HAVE A HISTORY WITH THE SPIKY-HAIRED KID. WE LIVED TOGETHER FOR TWO YEARS.
SMASH

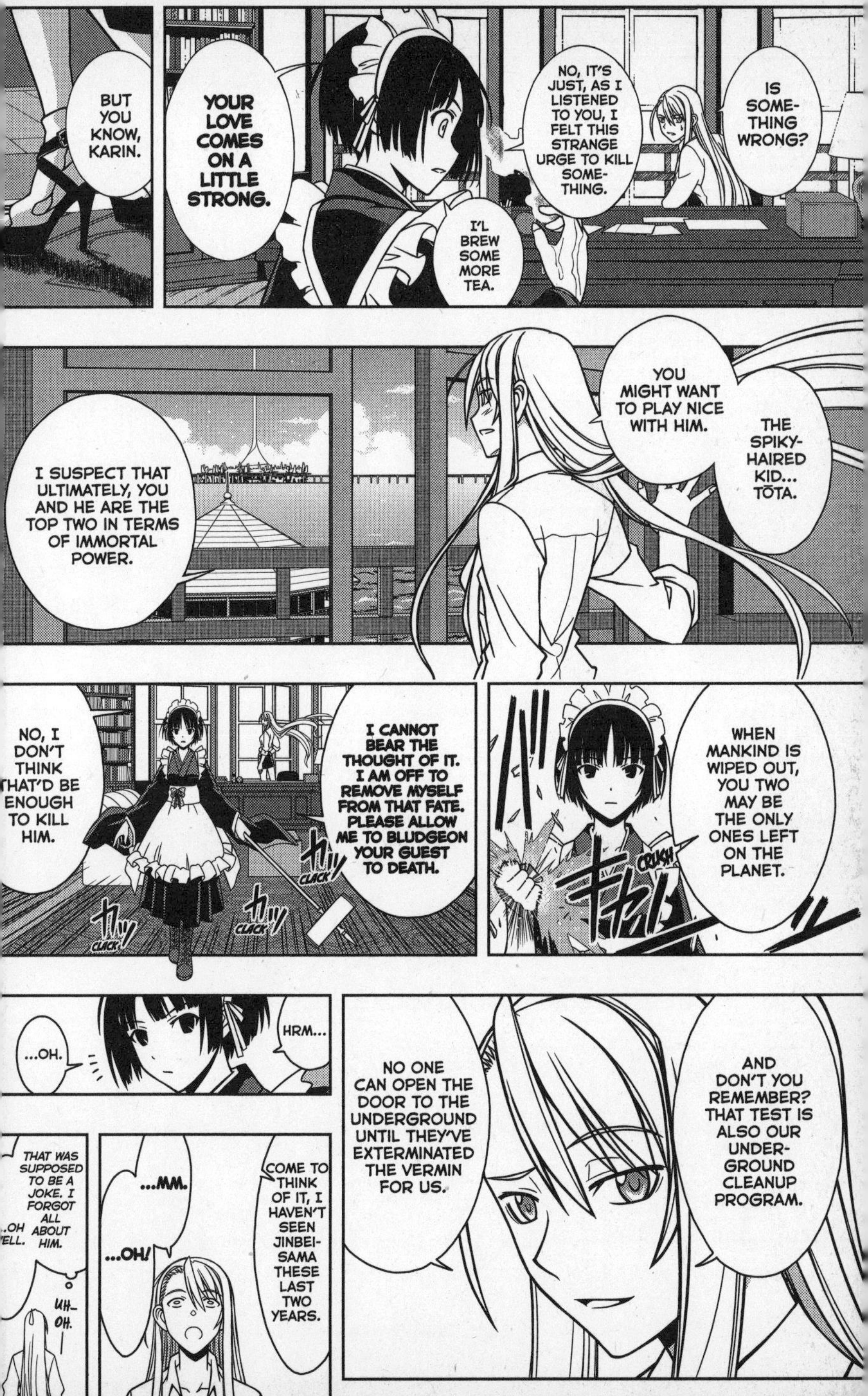
IS SOMETHING WRONG?
NO, IT'S JUST, AS I LISTENED TO YOU, I FELT THIS STRANGE URGE TO KILL SOMETHING.
I'L BREW SOME MORE TEA.
YOUR LOVE COMES ON A LITTLE STRONG.
BUT YOU KNOW, KARIN.
THE SPIKY-HAIRED KID... TŌTA.
YOU MIGHT WANT TO PLAY NICE WITH HIM.
I SUSPECT THAT ULTIMATELY, YOU AND HE ARE THE TOP TWO IN TERMS OF IMMORTAL POWER.
WHEN MANKIND IS WIPED OUT, YOU TWO MAY BE THE ONLY ONES LEFT ON THE PLANET.
CRUSH
I CANNOT BEAR THE THOUGHT OF IT. I AM OFF TO REMOVE MYSELF FROM THAT FATE. PLEASE ALLOW ME TO BLUDGEON YOUR GUEST TO DEATH.
CLACK
CLACK
CLACK
NO, I DON'T THINK THAT'D BE ENOUGH TO KILL HIM.
AND DON'T YOU REMEMBER? THAT TEST IS ALSO OUR UNDERGROUND CLEANUP PROGRAM.
NO ONE CAN OPEN THE DOOR TO THE UNDERGROUND UNTIL THEY'VE EXTERMINATED THE VERMIN FOR US.
HRM...
...OH.
COME TO THINK OF IT, I HAVEN'T SEEN JINBEI-SAMA THESE LAST TWO YEARS.
...MM.
...OH!
THAT WAS SUPPOSED TO BE A JOKE. I FORGOT ALL ABOUT HIM.
..OH ELL.
UH-OH.

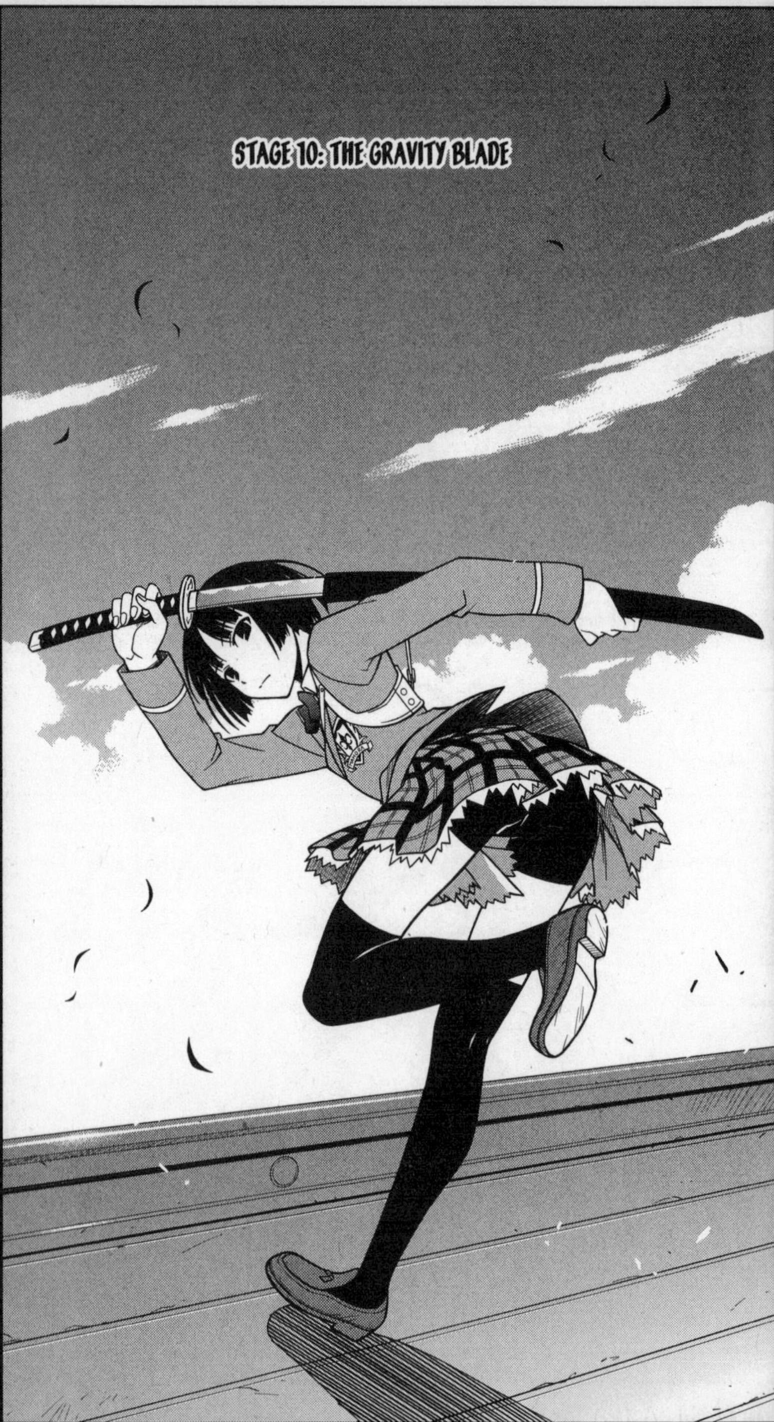
STAGE 10: THE GRAVITY BLADE

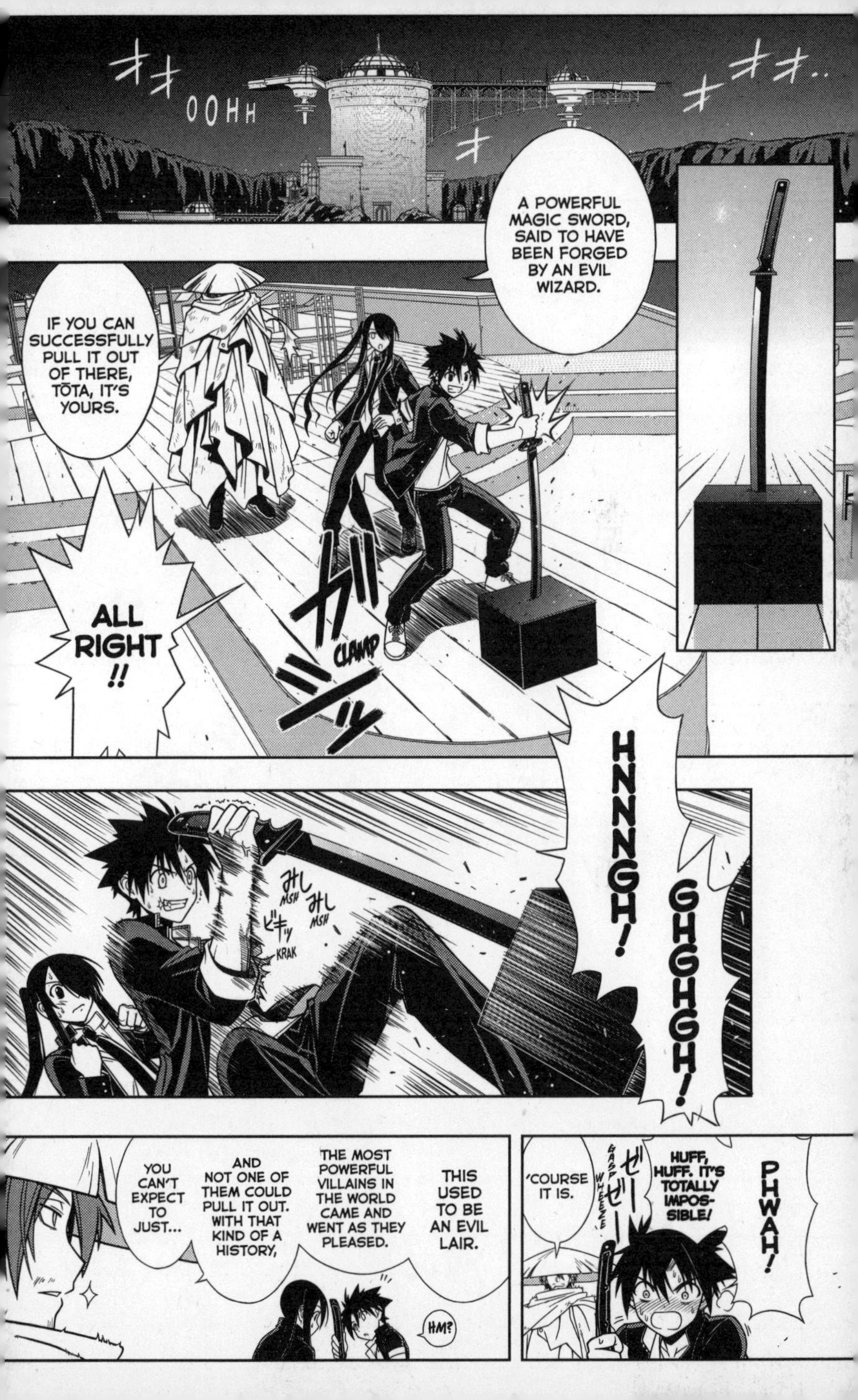

オオ
OOHH
オオオ..
A POWERFUL MAGIC SWORD, SAID TO HAVE BEEN FORGED BY AN EVIL WIZARD.
IF YOU CAN SUCCESSFULLY PULL IT OUT OF THERE, TŌTA, IT'S YOURS.
ALL RIGHT!!
ガシ
CLAMP
HNNNGH!
GHGHGH!
みし
MSH
みし
MSH
ビキッ
KRAK
PHWAH!
HUFF, HUFF. IT'S TOTALLY IMPOSSIBLE!
ゼーゼー
GASP WHEEZE
'COURSE IT IS.
THIS USED TO BE AN EVIL LAIR.
THE MOST POWERFUL VILLAINS IN THE WORLD CAME AND WENT AS THEY PLEASED.
AND NOT ONE OF THEM COULD PULL IT OUT. WITH THAT KIND OF A HISTORY,
YOU CAN'T EXPECT TO JUST...
HM?

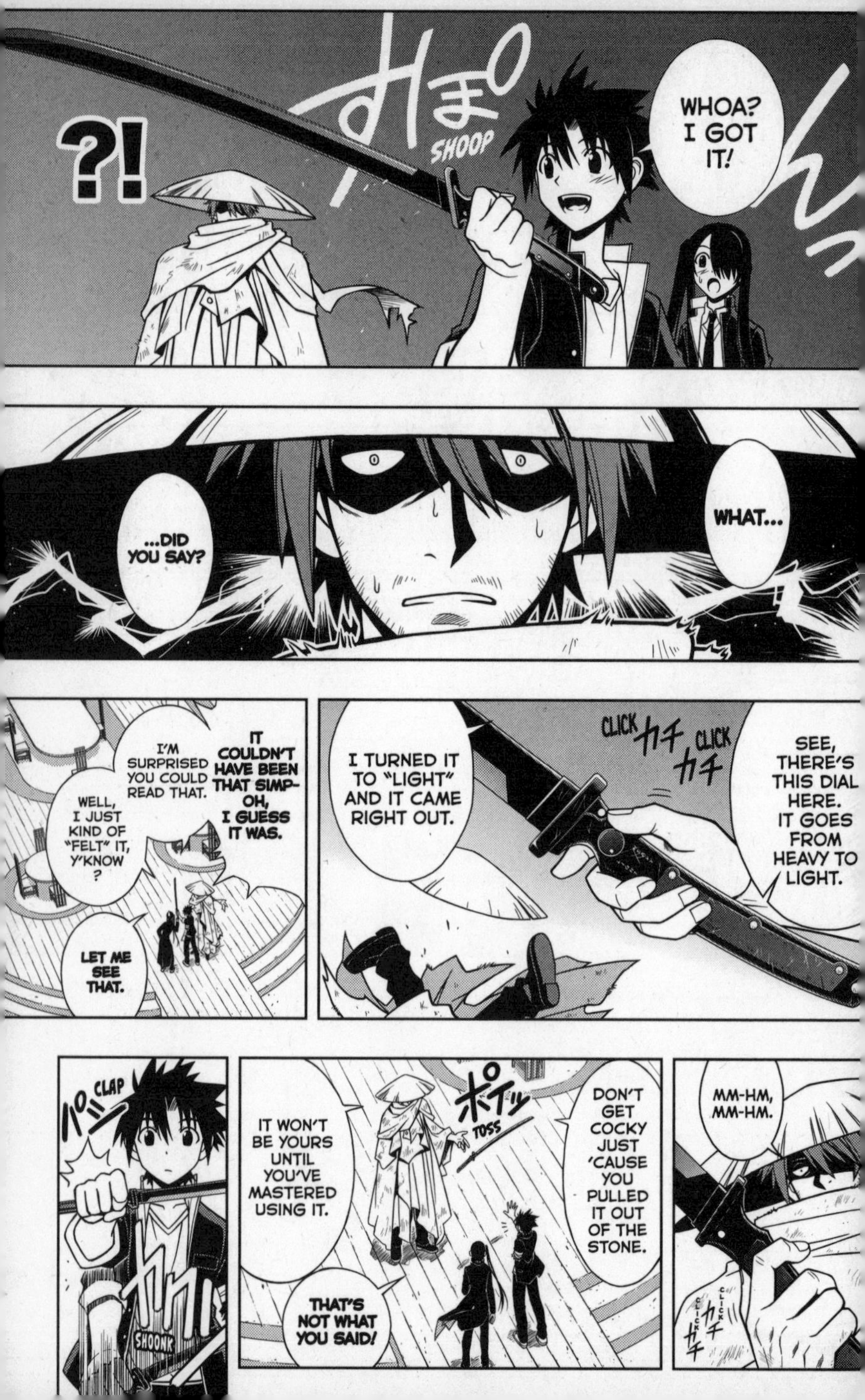
WHOA? I GOT IT!
SHOOP
?!
WHAT...
...DID YOU SAY?
SEE, THERE'S THIS DIAL HERE. IT GOES FROM HEAVY TO LIGHT.
CLICK CLICK
I TURNED IT TO "LIGHT" AND IT CAME RIGHT OUT.
IT COULDN'T HAVE BEEN THAT SIMP- OH, I GUESS IT WAS.
I'M SURPRISED YOU COULD READ THAT.
WELL, I JUST KIND OF "FELT" IT, Y'KNOW?
LET ME SEE THAT.
MM-HM, MM-HM.
CLICK CLICK
DON'T GET COCKY JUST 'CAUSE YOU PULLED IT OUT OF THE STONE.
TOSS
IT WON'T BE YOURS UNTIL YOU'VE MASTERED USING IT.
THAT'S NOT WHAT YOU SAID!
CLAP
SHOONK

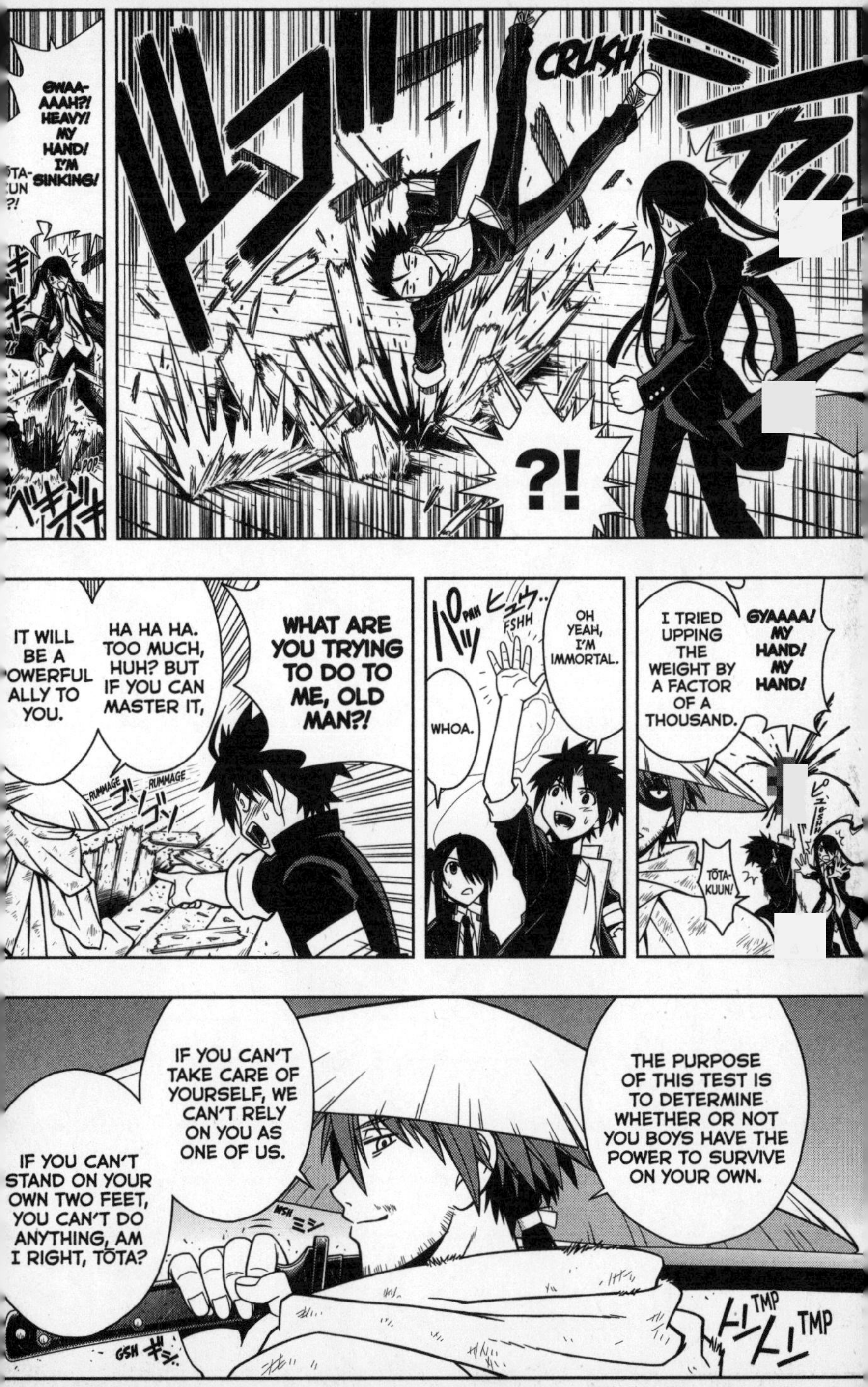
CRUSH
?!
GWAA-AAAH?! HEAVY! MY HAND! I'M SINKING!
TŌTA-UN ?!
POP
GYAAAA! MY HAND! MY HAND!
I TRIED UPPING THE WEIGHT BY A FACTOR OF A THOUSAND.
FSHH
TŌTA-KUUN!
PAH
FSHH
OH YEAH, I'M IMMORTAL.
WHOA.
WHAT ARE YOU TRYING TO DO TO ME, OLD MAN?!
HA HA HA. TOO MUCH, HUH? BUT IF YOU CAN MASTER IT,
IT WILL BE A OWERFUL ALLY TO YOU.
RUMMAGE
RUMMAGE
THE PURPOSE OF THIS TEST IS TO DETERMINE WHETHER OR NOT YOU BOYS HAVE THE POWER TO SURVIVE ON YOUR OWN.
IF YOU CAN'T TAKE CARE OF YOURSELF, WE CAN'T RELY ON YOU AS ONE OF US.
IF YOU CAN'T STAND ON YOUR OWN TWO FEET, YOU CAN'T DO ANYTHING, AM I RIGHT, TŌTA?
WSH
TMP
TMP
GSH

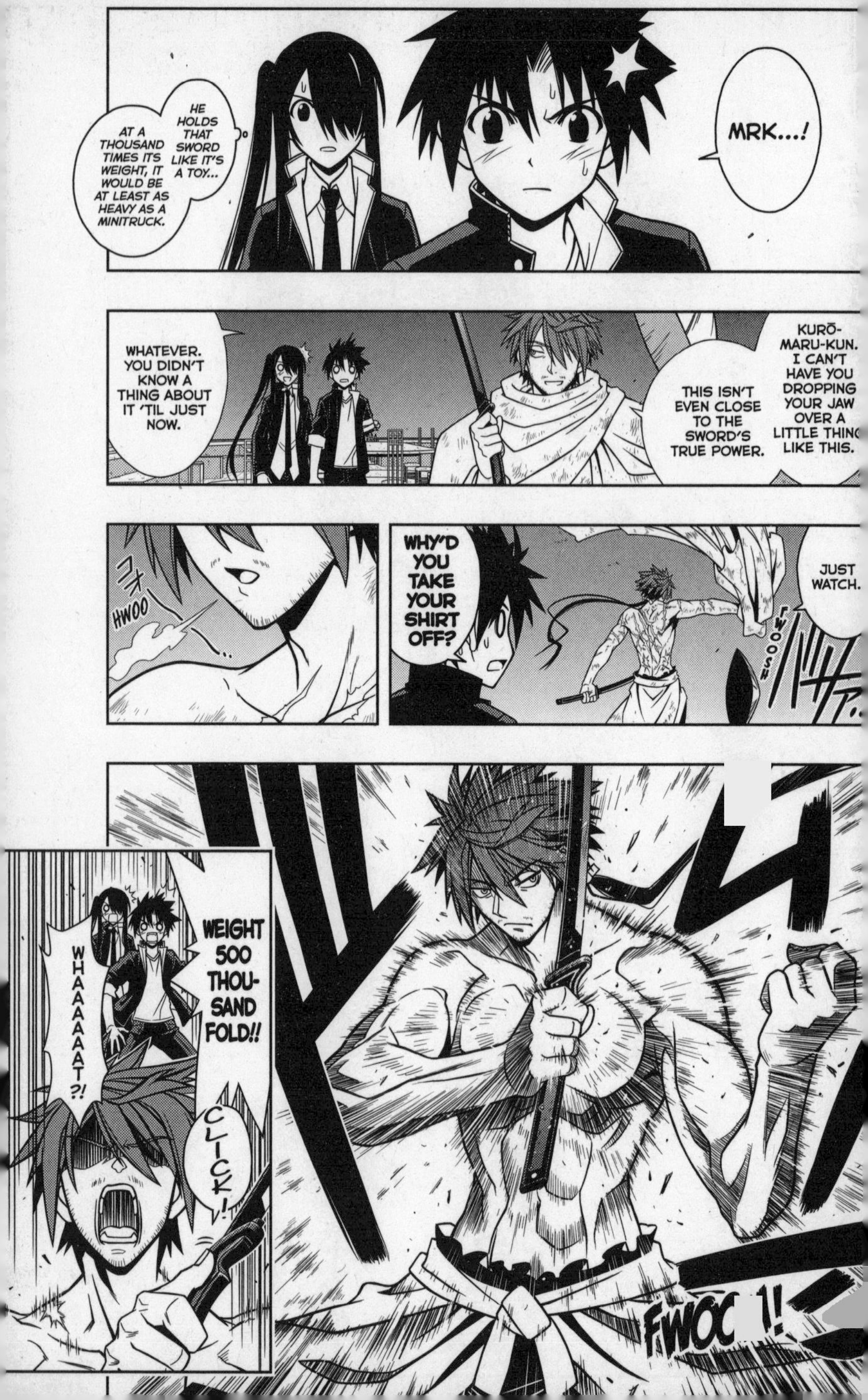
MRK...!
HE HOLDS THAT SWORD LIKE IT'S A TOY...
AT A THOUSAND TIMES ITS WEIGHT, IT WOULD BE AT LEAST AS HEAVY AS A MINITRUCK.
KURŌ-MARU-KUN. I CAN'T HAVE YOU DROPPING YOUR JAW OVER A LITTLE THING LIKE THIS.
THIS ISN'T EVEN CLOSE TO THE SWORD'S TRUE POWER.
WHATEVER. YOU DIDN'T KNOW A THING ABOUT IT 'TIL JUST NOW.
JUST WATCH.
FWOOSH
WHY'D YOU TAKE YOUR SHIRT OFF?
HWOO
WEIGHT 500 THOUSAND FOLD!!
CLICK!
WHAAAAAAT?!

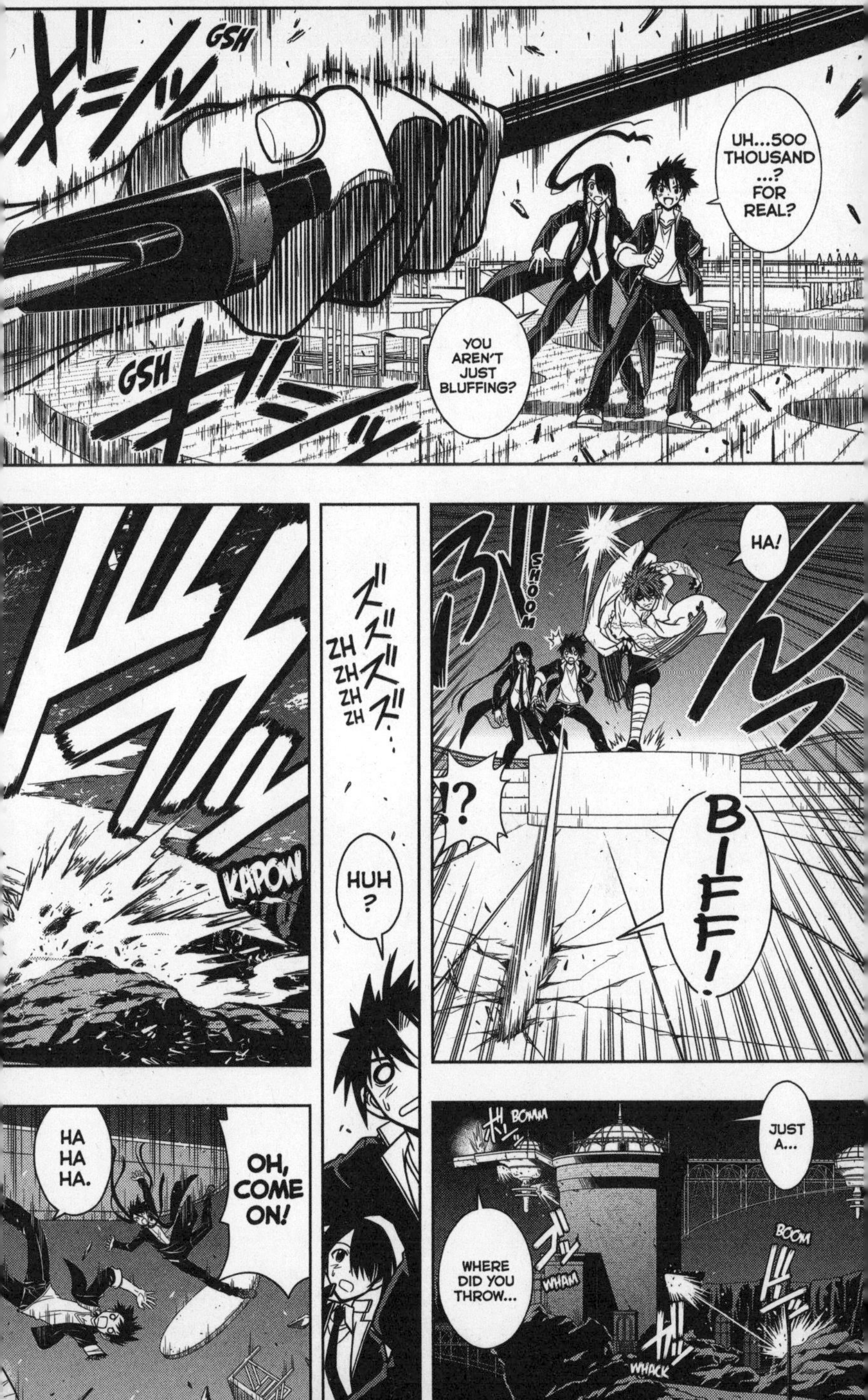

GSH
UH...500 THOUSAND ...? FOR REAL?
YOU AREN'T JUST BLUFFING?
GSH
HA!
SHOOM
!?
BIFF!
JUST A...
BOMM
WHERE DID YOU THROW...
WHAM
BOOM
WHACK
ZH ZH ZH ZH
HUH?
KAPOW
OH, COME ON!
HA HA HA.

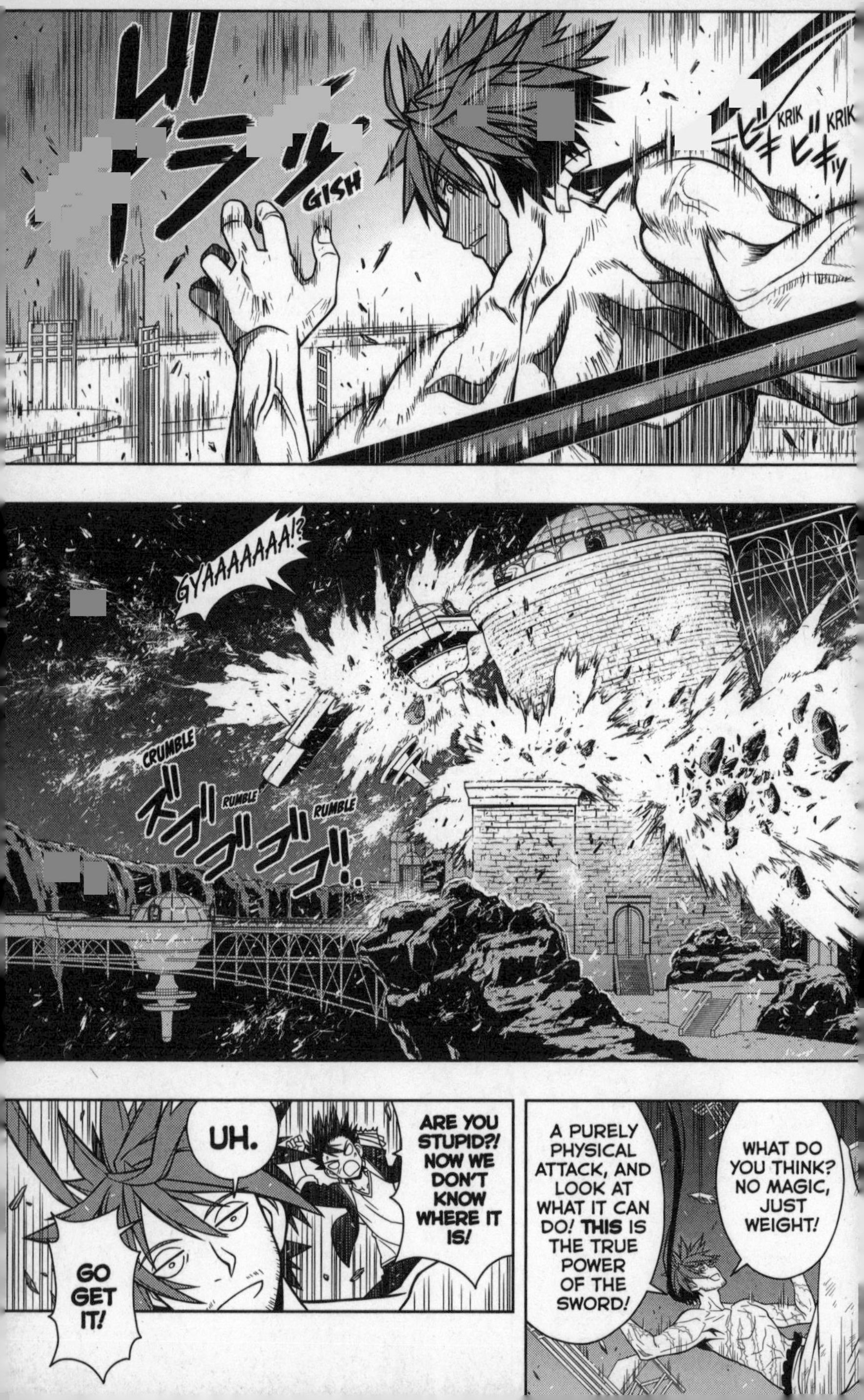
KRIK
KRIK
GISH
GYAAAAAAA!?
CRUMBLE
RUMBLE
RUMBLE
WHAT DO YOU THINK? NO MAGIC, JUST WEIGHT!
A PURELY PHYSICAL ATTACK, AND LOOK AT WHAT IT CAN DO! THIS IS THE TRUE POWER OF THE SWORD!
ARE YOU STUPID?! NOW WE DON'T KNOW WHERE IT IS!
UH.
GO GET IT!

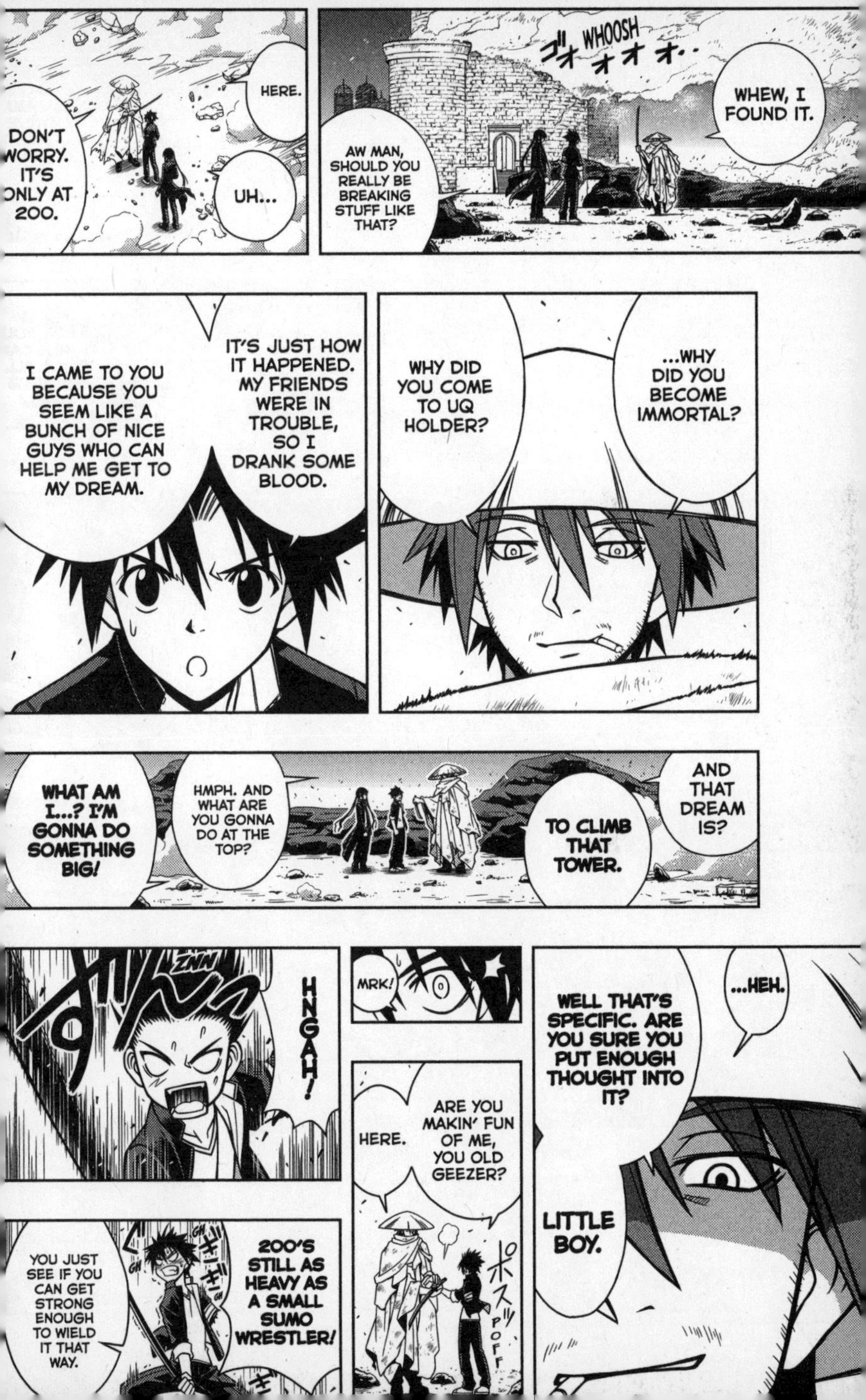
WHOOSH
WHEW, I FOUND IT.
AW MAN, SHOULD YOU REALLY BE BREAKING STUFF LIKE THAT?
HERE.
UH...
DON'T WORRY. IT'S ONLY AT 200.
...WHY DID YOU BECOME IMMORTAL?
WHY DID YOU COME TO UQ HOLDER?
IT'S JUST HOW IT HAPPENED. MY FRIENDS WERE IN TROUBLE, SO I DRANK SOME BLOOD.
I CAME TO YOU BECAUSE YOU SEEM LIKE A BUNCH OF NICE GUYS WHO CAN HELP ME GET TO MY DREAM.
AND THAT DREAM IS?
TO CLIMB THAT TOWER.
HMPH. AND WHAT ARE YOU GONNA DO AT THE TOP?
WHAT AM I...? I'M GONNA DO SOMETHING BIG!
...HEH.
WELL THAT'S SPECIFIC. ARE YOU SURE YOU PUT ENOUGH THOUGHT INTO IT?
LITTLE BOY.
MRK!
ARE YOU MAKIN' FUN OF ME, YOU OLD GEEZER?
HERE.
POFF
HNGAH!
ZNN
200'S STILL AS HEAVY AS A SMALL SUMO WRESTLER!
YOU JUST SEE IF YOU CAN GET STRONG ENOUGH TO WIELD IT THAT WAY.

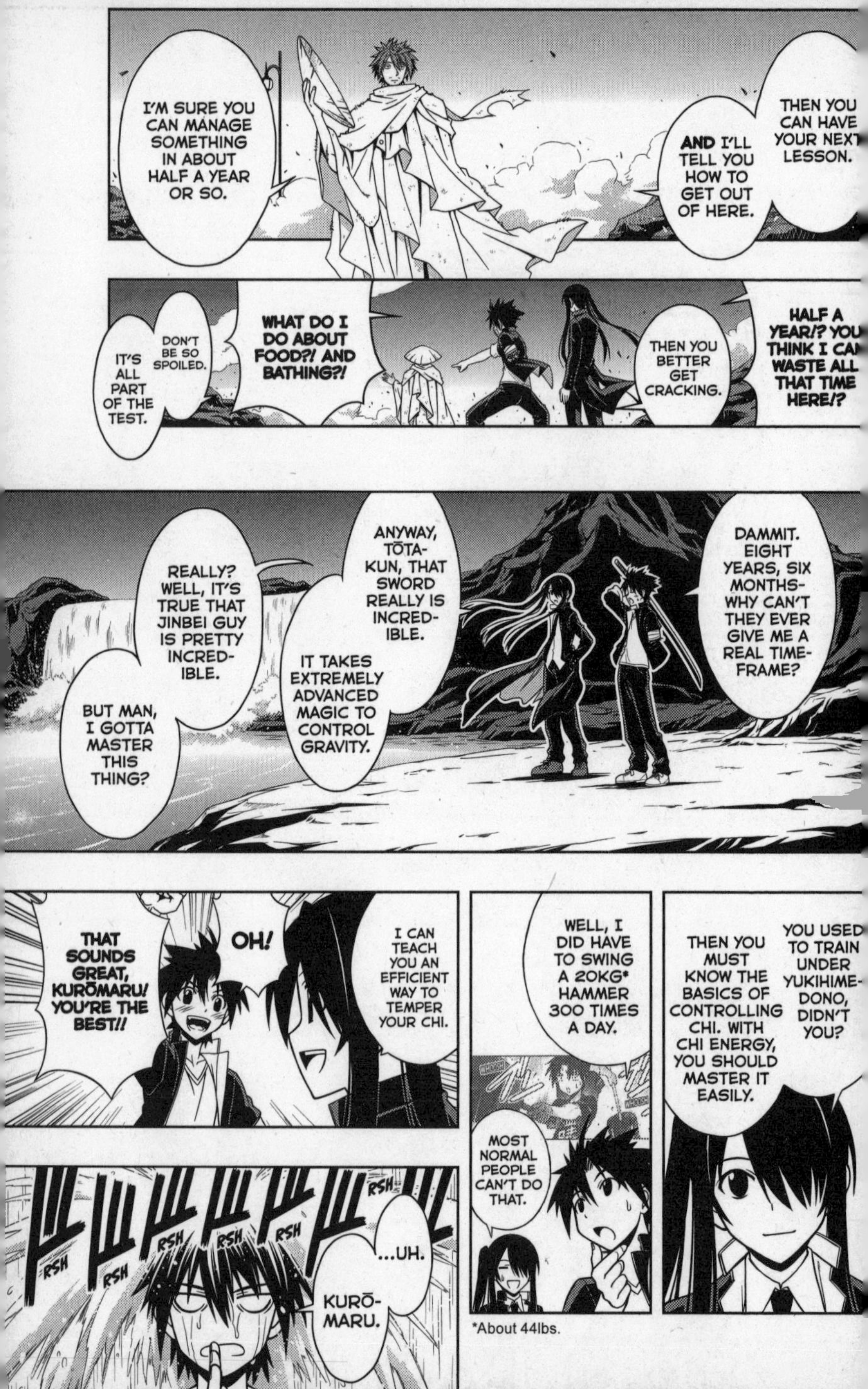
THEN YOU CAN HAVE YOUR NEXT LESSON.
AND I'LL TELL YOU HOW TO GET OUT OF HERE.
I'M SURE YOU CAN MANAGE SOMETHING IN ABOUT HALF A YEAR OR SO.
HALF A YEAR!? YOU THINK I CA WASTE ALL THAT TIME HERE!?
THEN YOU BETTER GET CRACKING.
WHAT DO I DO ABOUT FOOD?! AND BATHING?!
DON'T BE SO SPOILED.
IT'S ALL PART OF THE TEST.
DAMMIT. EIGHT YEARS, SIX MONTHS-WHY CAN'T THEY EVER GIVE ME A REAL TIME-FRAME?
ANYWAY, TŌTA-KUN, THAT SWORD REALLY IS INCRED-IBLE.
IT TAKES EXTREMELY ADVANCED MAGIC TO CONTROL GRAVITY.
REALLY? WELL, IT'S TRUE THAT JINBEI GUY IS PRETTY INCRED-IBLE.
BUT MAN, I GOTTA MASTER THIS THING?
YOU USED TO TRAIN UNDER YUKIHIME-DONO, DIDN'T YOU?
THEN YOU MUST KNOW THE BASICS OF CONTROLLING CHI. WITH CHI ENERGY, YOU SHOULD MASTER IT EASILY.
WELL, I DID HAVE TO SWING A 20KG* HAMMER 300 TIMES A DAY.
MOST NORMAL PEOPLE CAN'T DO THAT.
I CAN TEACH YOU AN EFFICIENT WAY TO TEMPER YOUR CHI.
OH!
THAT SOUNDS GREAT, KURŌMARU! YOU'RE THE BEST!!
RSH RSH RSH RSH RSH RSH
...UH.
KURŌ-MARU.
*About 44lbs.

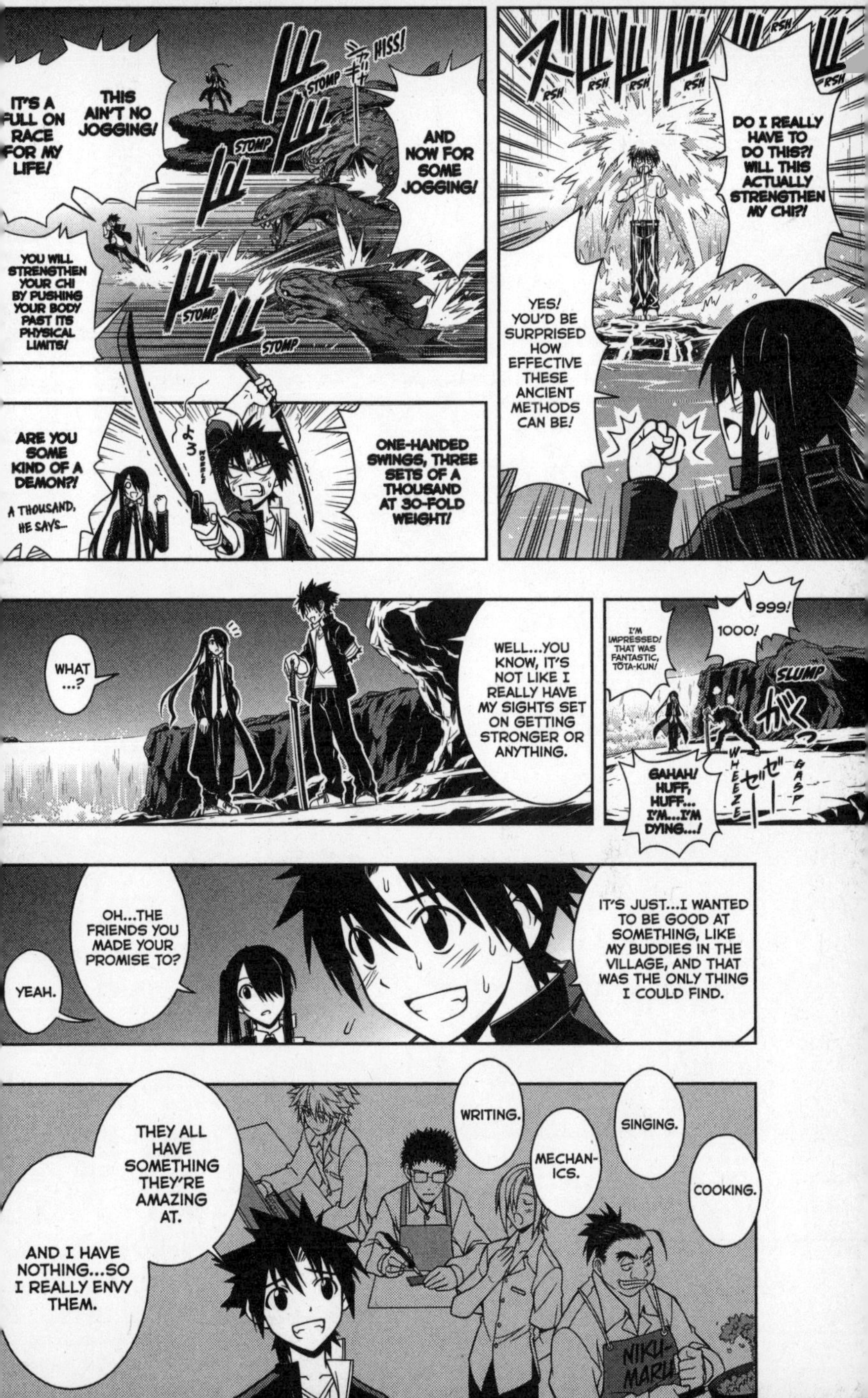
RSH
DO I REALLY HAVE TO DO THIS?! WILL THIS ACTUALLY STRENGTHEN MY CHI?!
YES! YOU'D BE SURPRISED HOW EFFECTIVE THESE ANCIENT METHODS CAN BE!
HISS!
STOMP
AND NOW FOR SOME JOGGING!
THIS AIN'T NO JOGGING!
IT'S A FULL ON RACE FOR MY LIFE!
YOU WILL STRENGTHEN YOUR CHI BY PUSHING YOUR BODY PAST ITS PHYSICAL LIMITS!
ONE-HANDED SWINGS, THREE SETS OF A THOUSAND AT 30-FOLD WEIGHT!
WOBBLE
ARE YOU SOME KIND OF A DEMON?!
A THOUSAND, HE SAYS...
999!
1000!
I'M IMPRESSED! THAT WAS FANTASTIC, TOTA-KUN!
SLUMP
GAHAH! HUFF, HUFF... I'M...I'M DYING...!
WHEEZE
GASP
WELL...YOU KNOW, IT'S NOT LIKE I REALLY HAVE MY SIGHTS SET ON GETTING STRONGER OR ANYTHING.
WHAT ...?
IT'S JUST...I WANTED TO BE GOOD AT SOMETHING, LIKE MY BUDDIES IN THE VILLAGE, AND THAT WAS THE ONLY THING I COULD FIND.
OH...THE FRIENDS YOU MADE YOUR PROMISE TO?
YEAH.
COOKING.
SINGING.
MECHAN-ICS.
WRITING.
THEY ALL HAVE SOMETHING THEY'RE AMAZING AT.
AND I HAVE NOTHING...SO I REALLY ENVY THEM.
NIKU-MARU

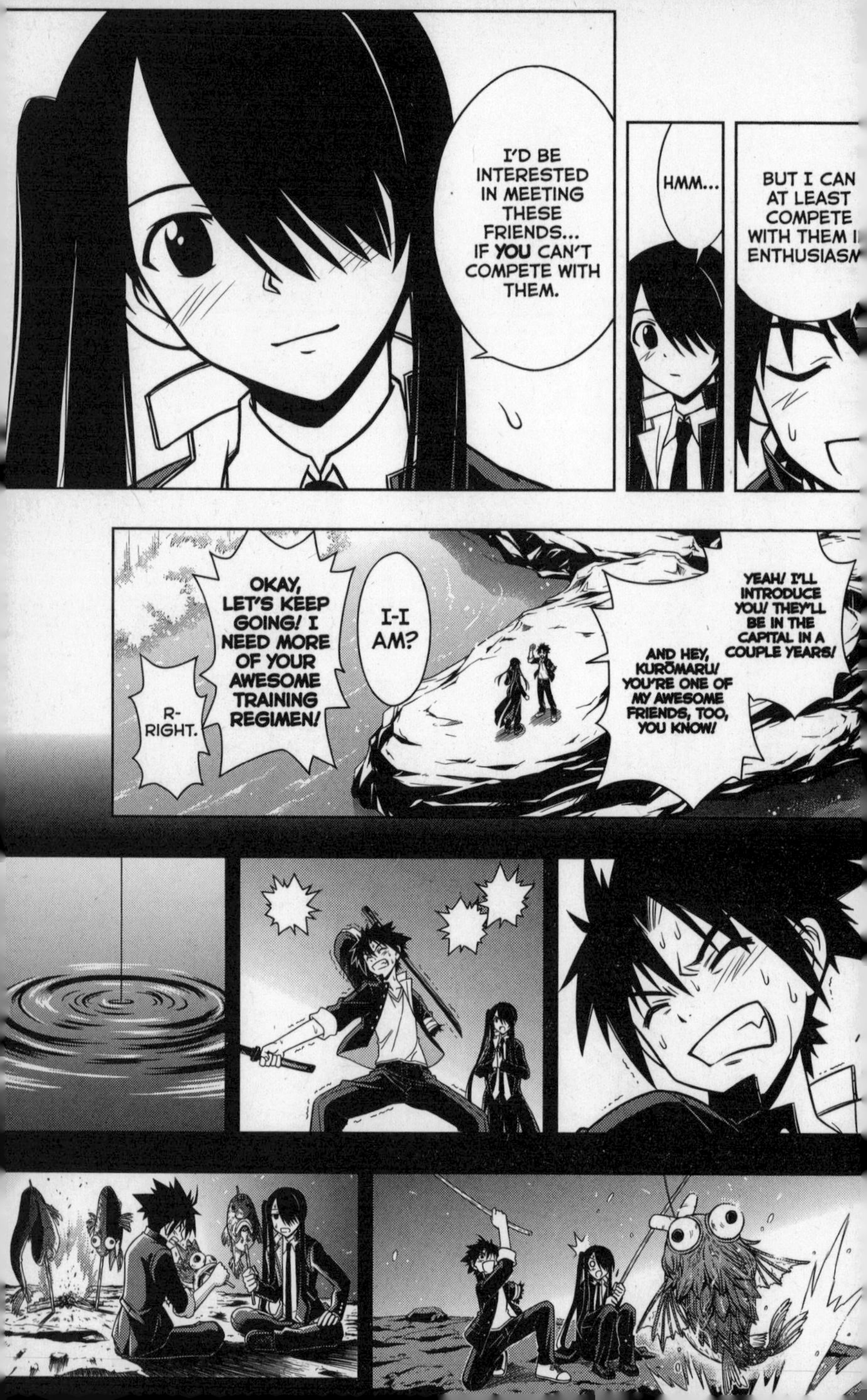
BUT I CAN AT LEAST COMPETE WITH THEM I ENTHUSIASM
HMM...
I'D BE INTERESTED IN MEETING THESE FRIENDS... IF YOU CAN'T COMPETE WITH THEM.
YEAH! I'LL INTRODUCE YOU! THEY'LL BE IN THE CAPITAL IN A COUPLE YEARS!
AND HEY, KURŌMARU! YOU'RE ONE OF MY AWESOME FRIENDS, TOO, YOU KNOW!
I-I AM?
OKAY, LET'S KEEP GOING! I NEED MORE OF YOUR AWESOME TRAINING REGIMEN!
R-RIGHT.

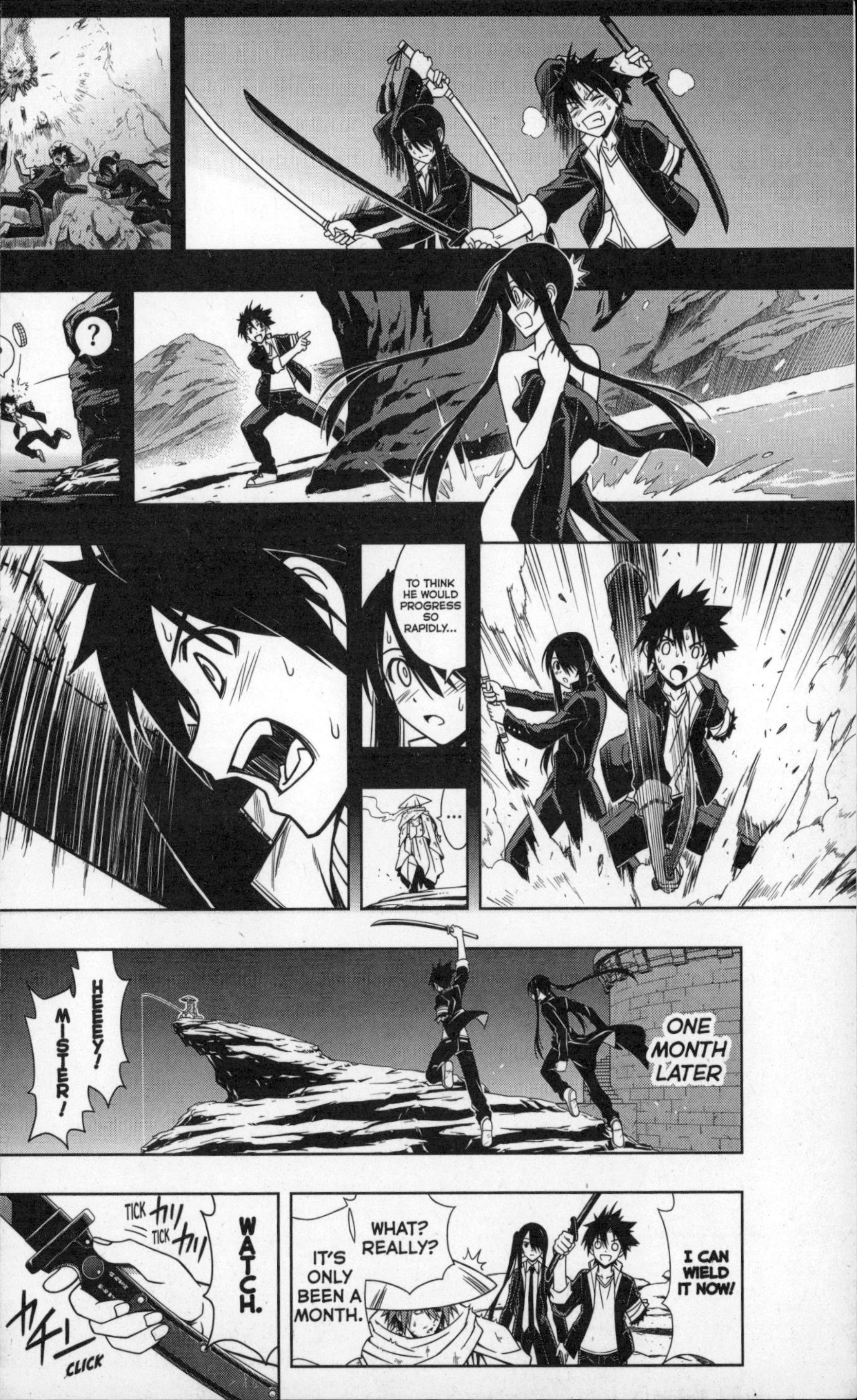
?
TO THINK HE WOULD PROGRESS SO RAPIDLY...
...
ONE MONTH LATER
HEEEY! MISTER!
I CAN WIELD IT NOW!
WHAT? REALLY?
IT'S ONLY BEEN A MONTH.
WATCH.
TICK TICK
CLICK

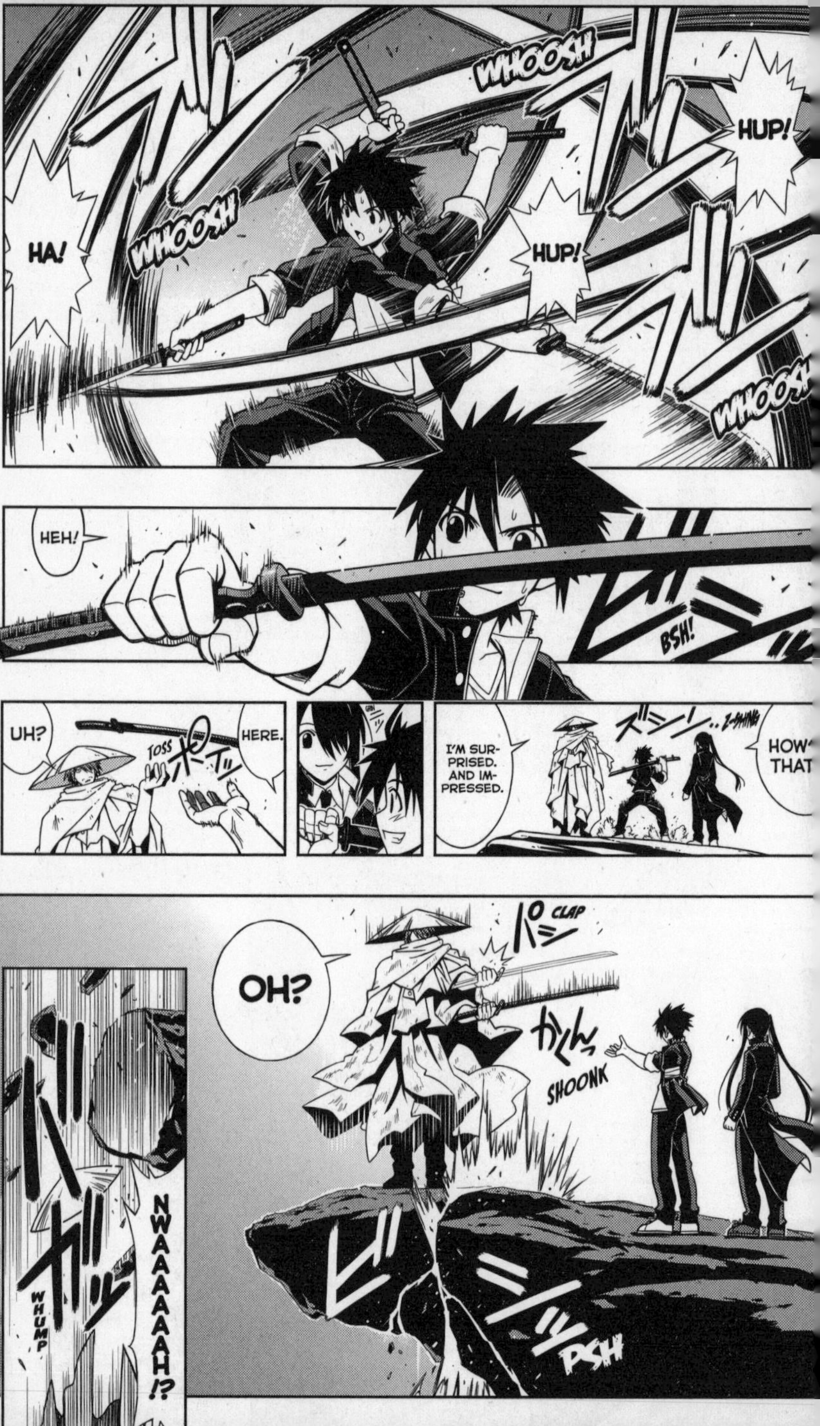

HUP!
WHOOSH
HUP!
WHOOS
WHOOSH
HA!
BSH!
HEH!
HOW
THAT
I'M SURPRISED. AND IMPRESSED.
HERE.
TOSS
UH?
CLAP
OH?
SHOONK
PSH
NWAAAAAAAAH!?
WHUMP

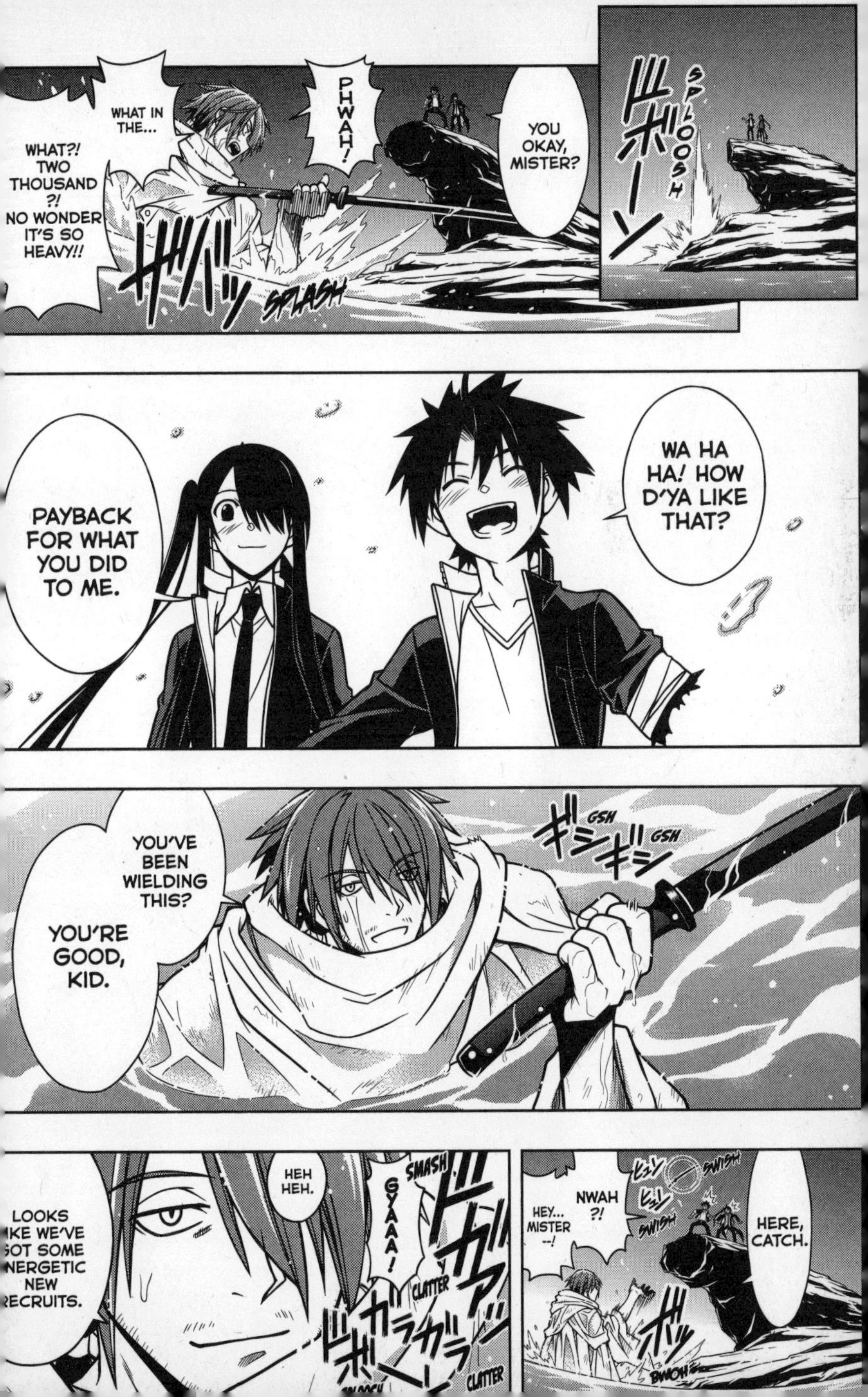

ドボーン
SPLOOSH
YOU OKAY, MISTER?
PHWAH!
WHAT IN THE...
WHAT?! TWO THOUSAND ?! NO WONDER IT'S SO HEAVY!!
ザバッ
SPLASH
WA HA HA! HOW D'YA LIKE THAT?
PAYBACK FOR WHAT YOU DID TO ME.
ギシギシ
GSH GSH
YOU'VE BEEN WIELDING THIS?
YOU'RE GOOD, KID.
HERE, CATCH.
ヒュッ SWISH
ヒュッ SWISH
NWAH ?!
HEY... MISTER --!
ボッ
BWOH
GYAAA!
ドガァ
SMASH
ドボ
ガラガラ
CLATTER
CLATTER
HEH HEH.
LOOKS IKE WE'VE OT SOME NERGETIC NEW RECRUITS.

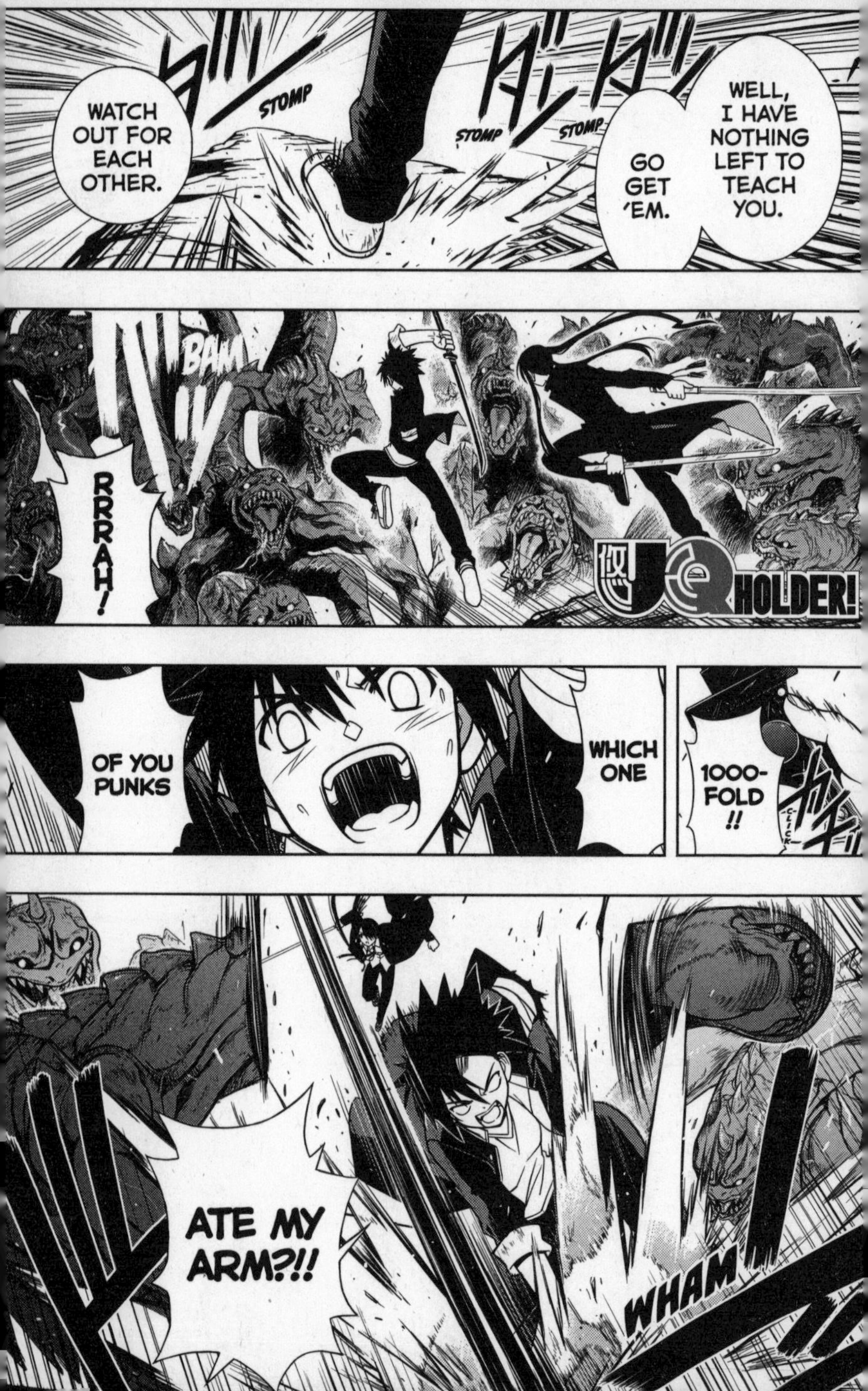
WELL, I HAVE NOTHING LEFT TO TEACH YOU.
GO GET 'EM.
STOMP
STOMP
STOMP
WATCH OUT FOR EACH OTHER.
BAM
RRRAH!
1000-FOLD !!
CLICK
WHICH ONE
OF YOU PUNKS
ATE MY ARM?!!
WHAM

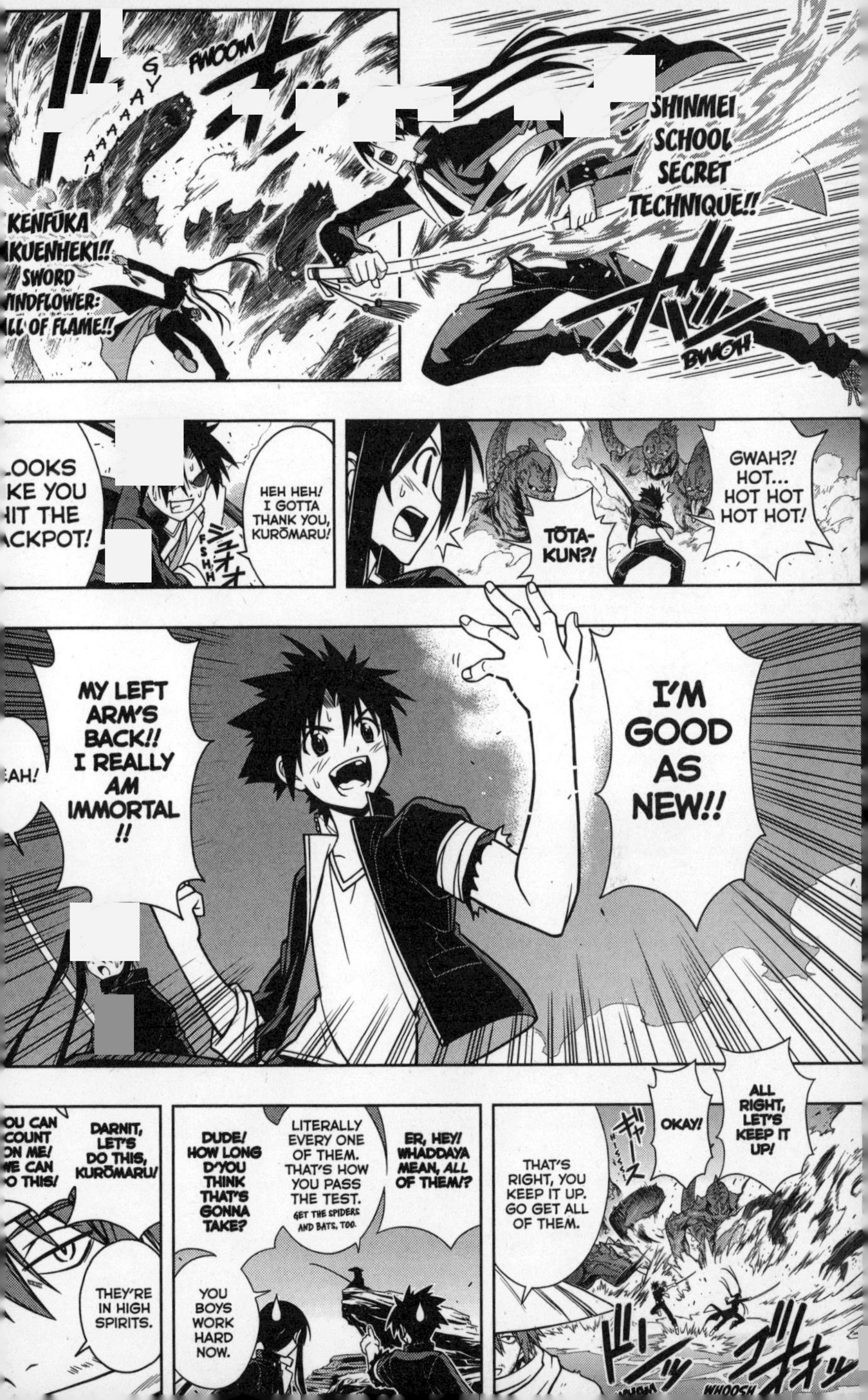

SHINMEI SCHOOL SECRET TECHNIQUE!!
BWOH
FWOOM
GYAAAAAA
KENFŪKA KUENHEKI!! SWORD WINDFLOWER: LL OF FLAME!!
GWAH?! HOT... HOT HOT HOT HOT!
TŌTA-KUN?!
HEH HEH! I GOTTA THANK YOU, KURŌMARU!
LOOKS KE YOU HIT THE ACKPOT!
FSHH
I'M GOOD AS NEW!!
MY LEFT ARM'S BACK!! I REALLY AM IMMORTAL!!
EAH!
ALL RIGHT, LET'S KEEP IT UP!
OKAY!
THAT'S RIGHT, YOU KEEP IT UP. GO GET ALL OF THEM.
HISSS
WHOOSH
ER, HEY! WHADDAYA MEAN, ALL OF THEM!?
LITERALLY EVERY ONE OF THEM. THAT'S HOW YOU PASS THE TEST. GET THE SPIDERS AND BATS, TOO.
DUDE! HOW LONG D'YOU THINK THAT'S GONNA TAKE?
YOU BOYS WORK HARD NOW.
DARNIT, LET'S DO THIS, KURŌMARU!
OU CAN COUNT ON ME! WE CAN O THIS!
THEY'RE IN HIGH SPIRITS.

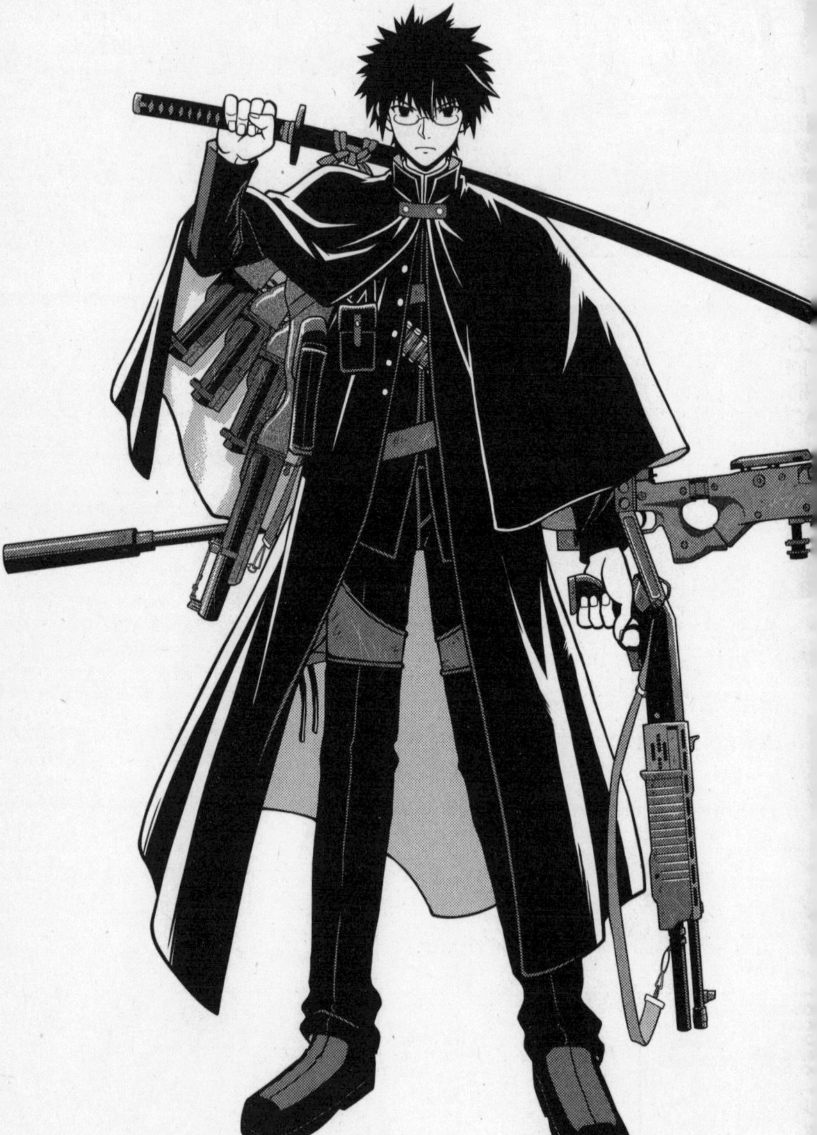

STAGE 11: BEAST EXTERMINATORS

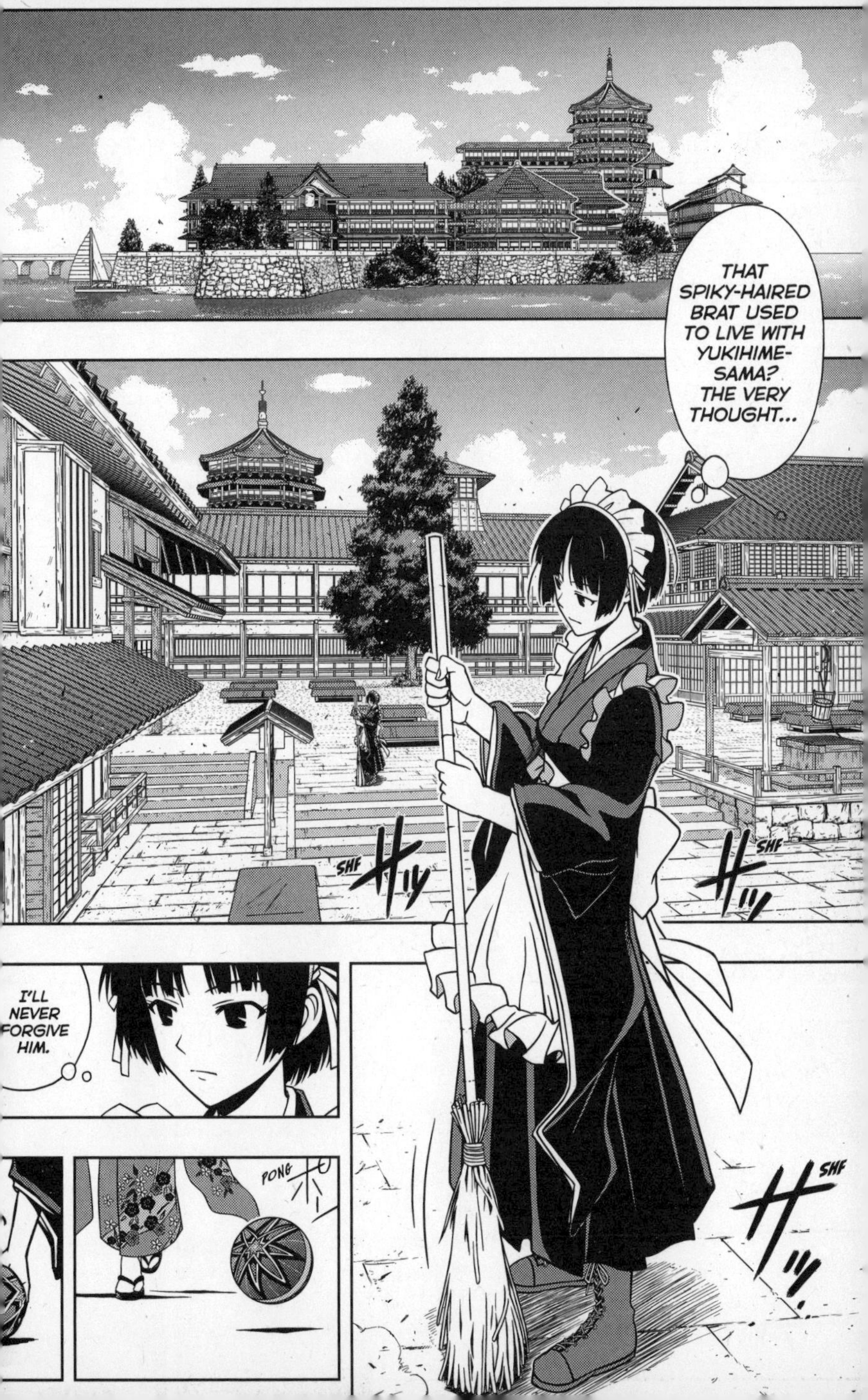
THAT SPIKY-HAIRED BRAT USED TO LIVE WITH YUKIHIME-SAMA? THE VERY THOUGHT...
SHF
SHF
SHF
I'LL NEVER FORGIVE HIM.
PONG

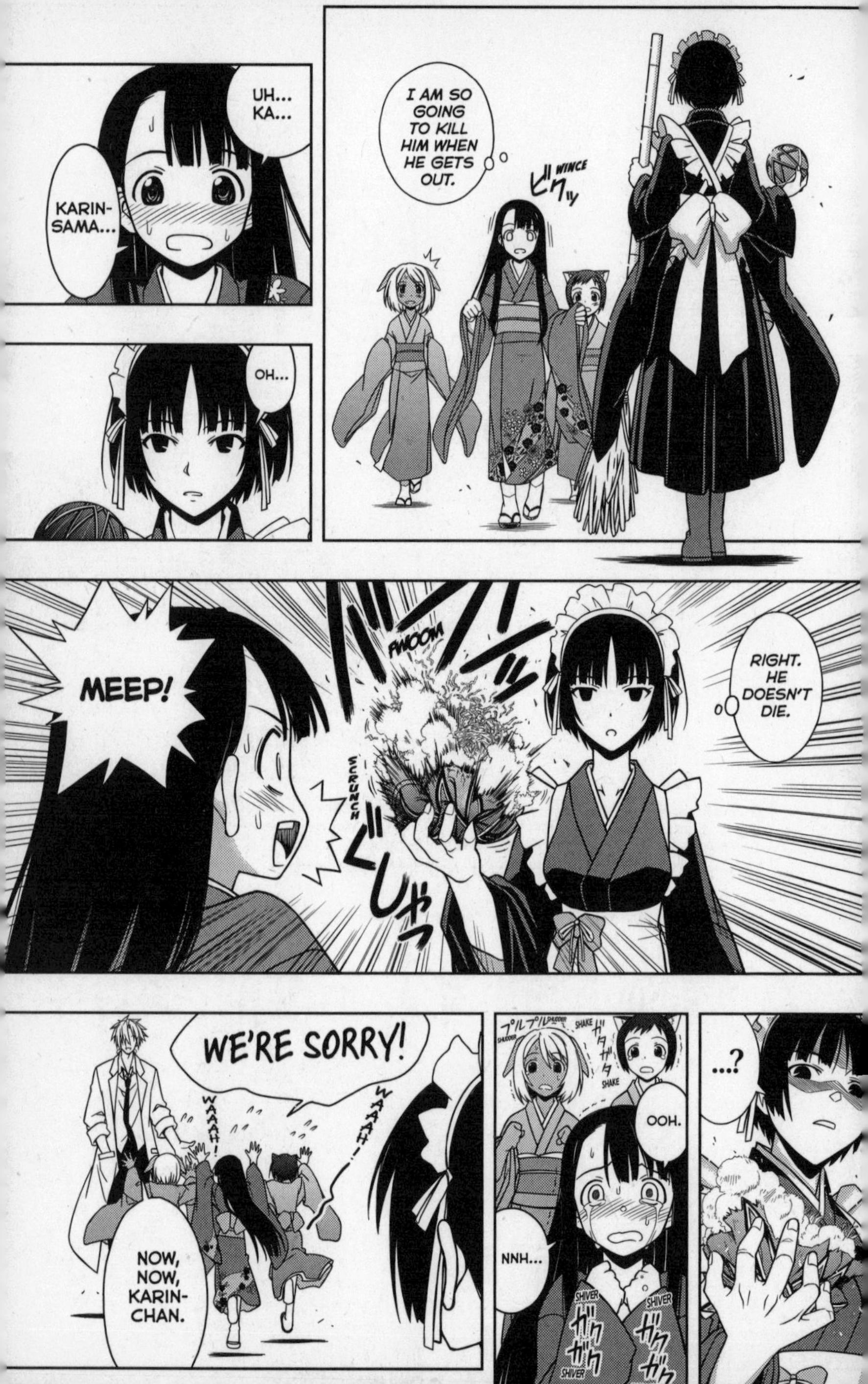

I AM SO GOING TO KILL HIM WHEN HE GETS OUT.
WINCE
UH... KA...
KARIN-SAMA...
OH...
RIGHT. HE DOESN'T DIE.
FWOOM
SCRUNCH
MEEP!
...?
SHUDDER
SHAKE
SHAKE
OOH.
NNH...
SHIVER
SHIVER
SHIVER
WE'RE SORRY!
WAAAH!
WAAAH!
NOW, NOW, KARIN-CHAN.

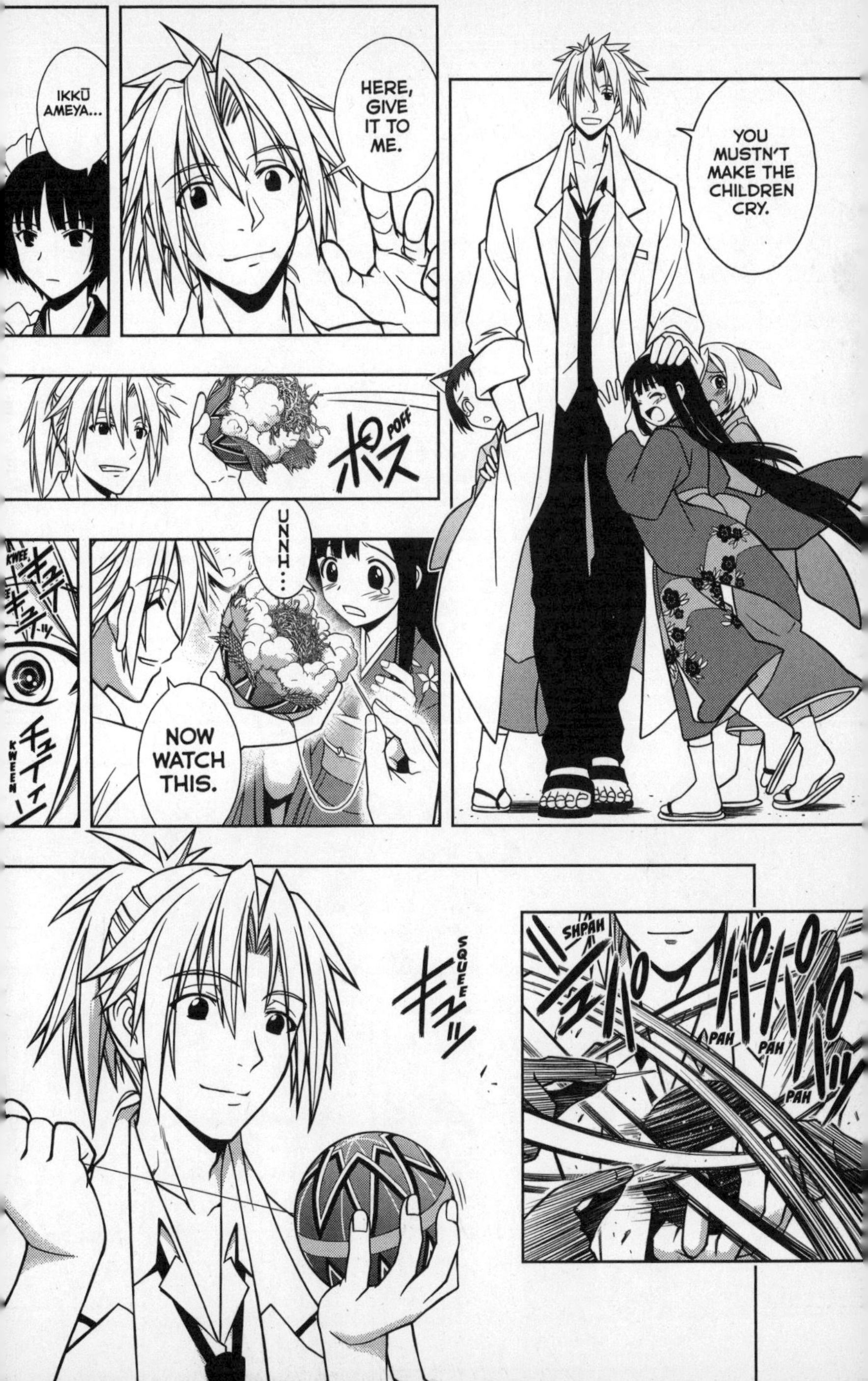
YOU MUSTN'T MAKE THE CHILDREN CRY.
HERE, GIVE IT TO ME.
IKKŪ AMEYA...
ポス
POFF
UNNH...
NOW WATCH THIS.
KWEE
KWEEN
SHPAH
PAH
PAH
PAH
SQUEE

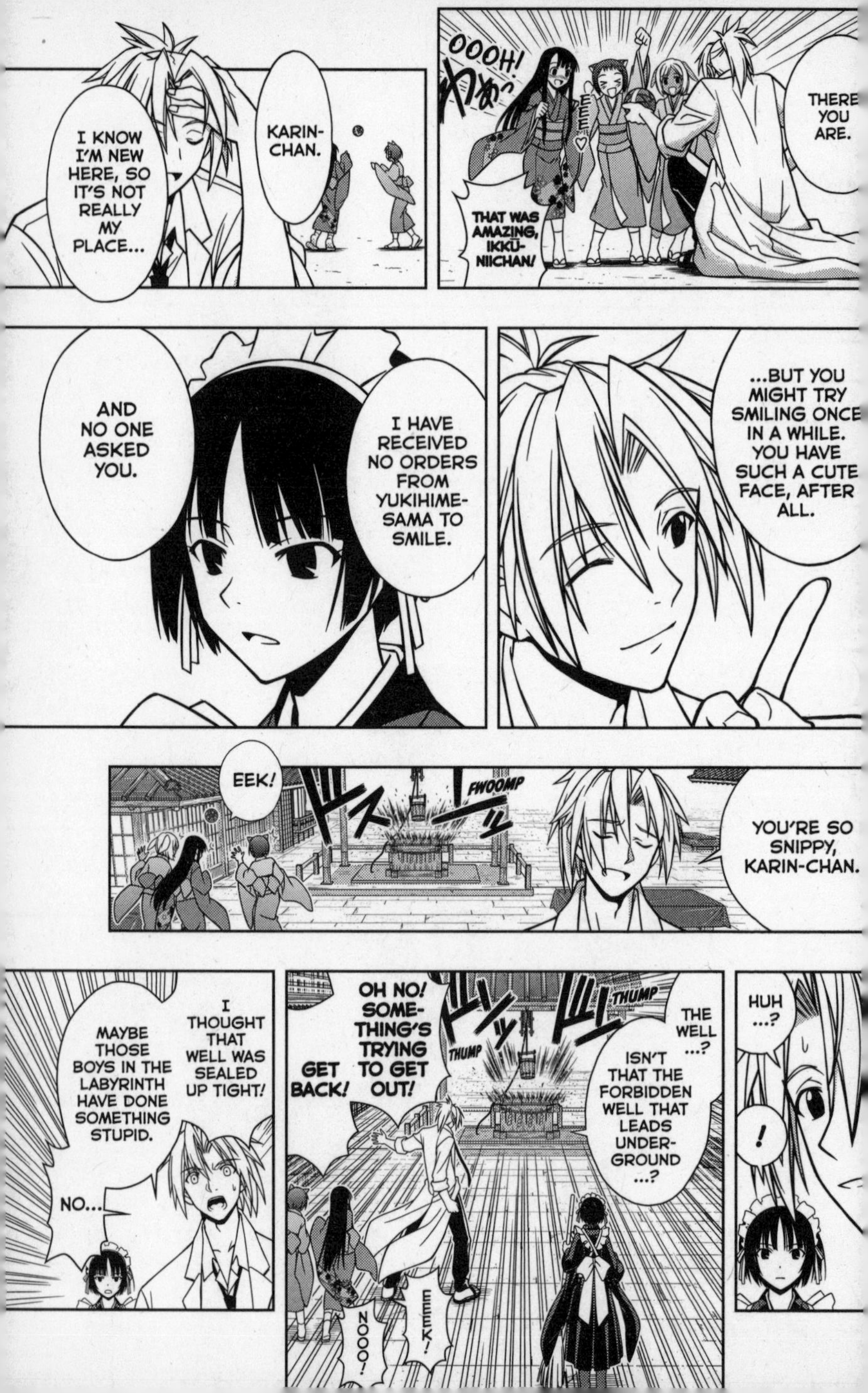
THERE YOU ARE.
OOOH!
EEE♡
THAT WAS AMAZING, IKKŪ-NIICHAN!
KARIN-CHAN.
I KNOW I'M NEW HERE, SO IT'S NOT REALLY MY PLACE...
...BUT YOU MIGHT TRY SMILING ONCE IN A WHILE. YOU HAVE SUCH A CUTE FACE, AFTER ALL.
I HAVE RECEIVED NO ORDERS FROM YUKIHIME-SAMA TO SMILE.
AND NO ONE ASKED YOU.
YOU'RE SO SNIPPY, KARIN-CHAN.
FWOOMP
EEK!
HUH ...?
!
THE WELL ...?
ISN'T THAT THE FORBIDDEN WELL THAT LEADS UNDERGROUND ...?
THUMP
THUMP
OH NO! SOMETHING'S TRYING TO GET OUT!
GET BACK!
EEEK!
NOOO!
I THOUGHT THAT WELL WAS SEALED UP TIGHT!
MAYBE THOSE BOYS IN THE LABYRINTH HAVE DONE SOMETHING STUPID.
NO...

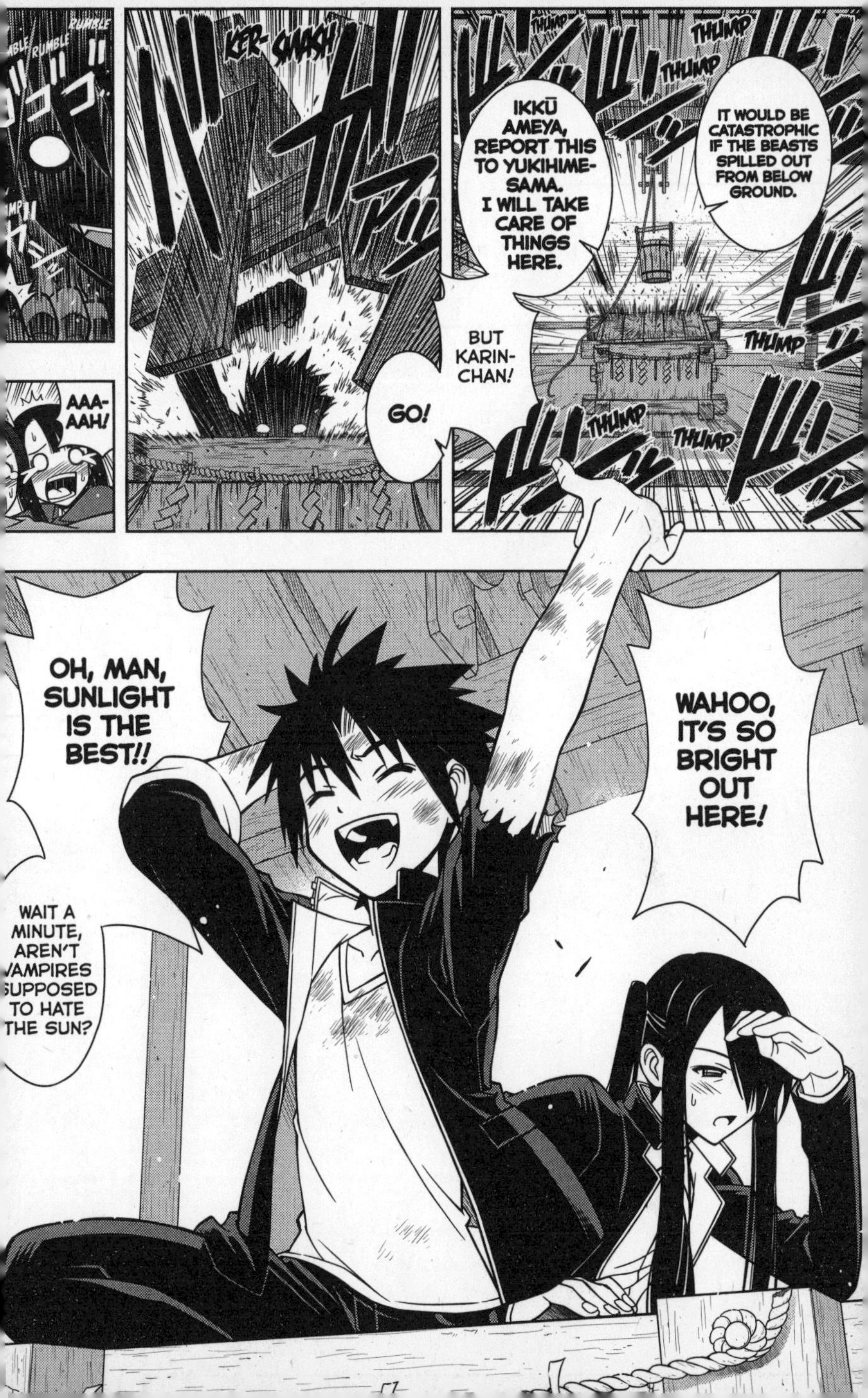
THUMP
THUMP
THUMP
IT WOULD BE CATASTROPHIC IF THE BEASTS SPILLED OUT FROM BELOW GROUND.
IKKŪ AMEYA, REPORT THIS TO YUKIHIME-SAMA. I WILL TAKE CARE OF THINGS HERE.
BUT KARIN-CHAN!
GO!
THUMP
THUMP
THUMP
KER-SMASH
RUMBLE
RUMBLE
AAA-AAH!
WAHOO, IT'S SO BRIGHT OUT HERE!
OH, MAN, SUNLIGHT IS THE BEST!!
WAIT A MINUTE, AREN'T VAMPIRES SUPPOSED TO HATE THE SUN?

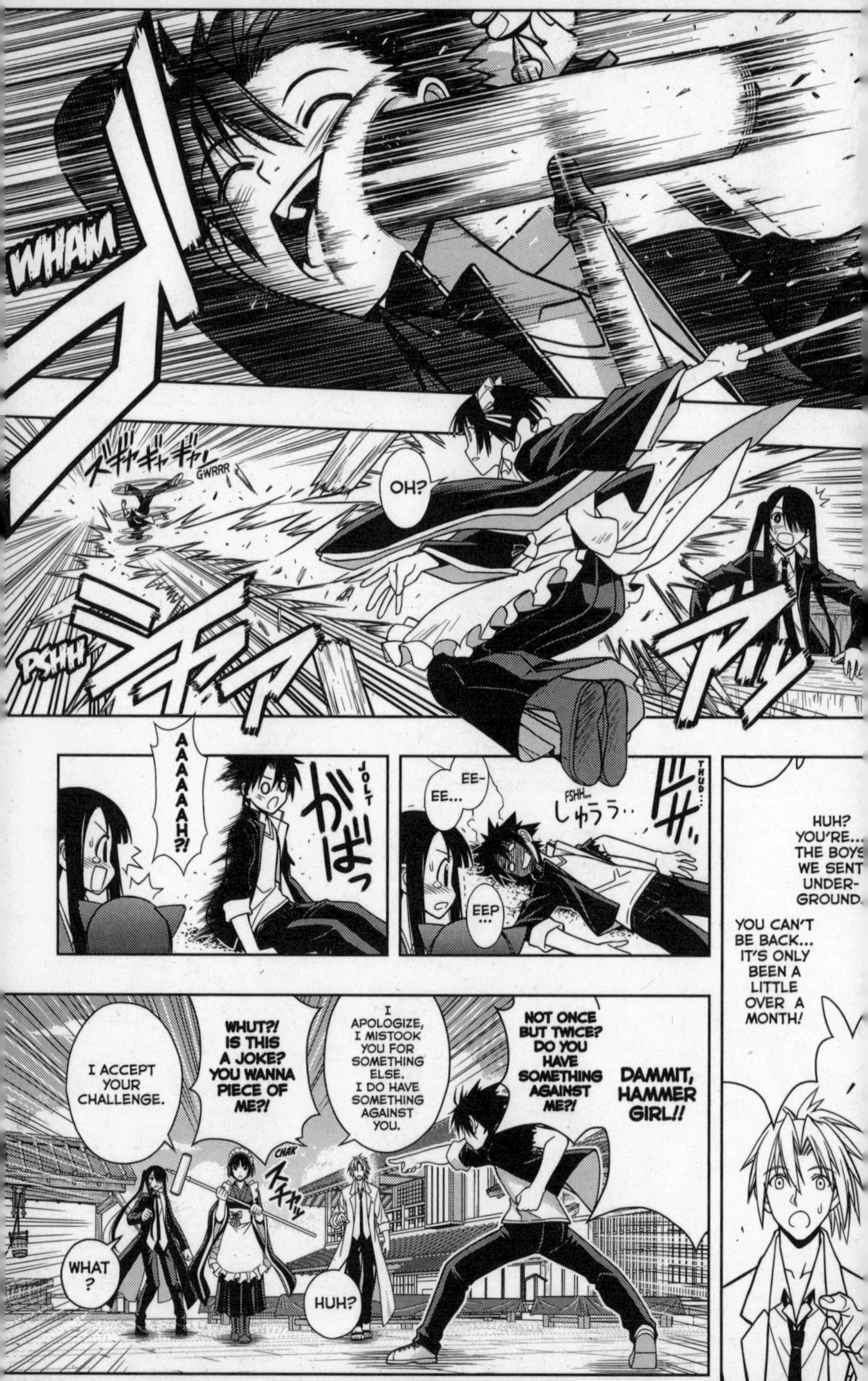
WHAM
GWRRR
OH?
PSHH
HUH? YOU'RE... THE BOYS WE SENT UNDER-GROUND.
YOU CAN'T BE BACK... IT'S ONLY BEEN A LITTLE OVER A MONTH!
THUD...
FSHH...
EE-EE...
EEP...
JOLT
AAAAAAAH?!
DAMMIT, HAMMER GIRL!!
NOT ONCE BUT TWICE? DO YOU HAVE SOMETHING AGAINST ME?!
I APOLOGIZE, I MISTOOK YOU FOR SOMETHING ELSE. I DO HAVE SOMETHING AGAINST YOU.
CHAK
WHUT?! IS THIS A JOKE? YOU WANNA PIECE OF ME?!
I ACCEPT YOUR CHALLENGE.
HUH?
WHAT?

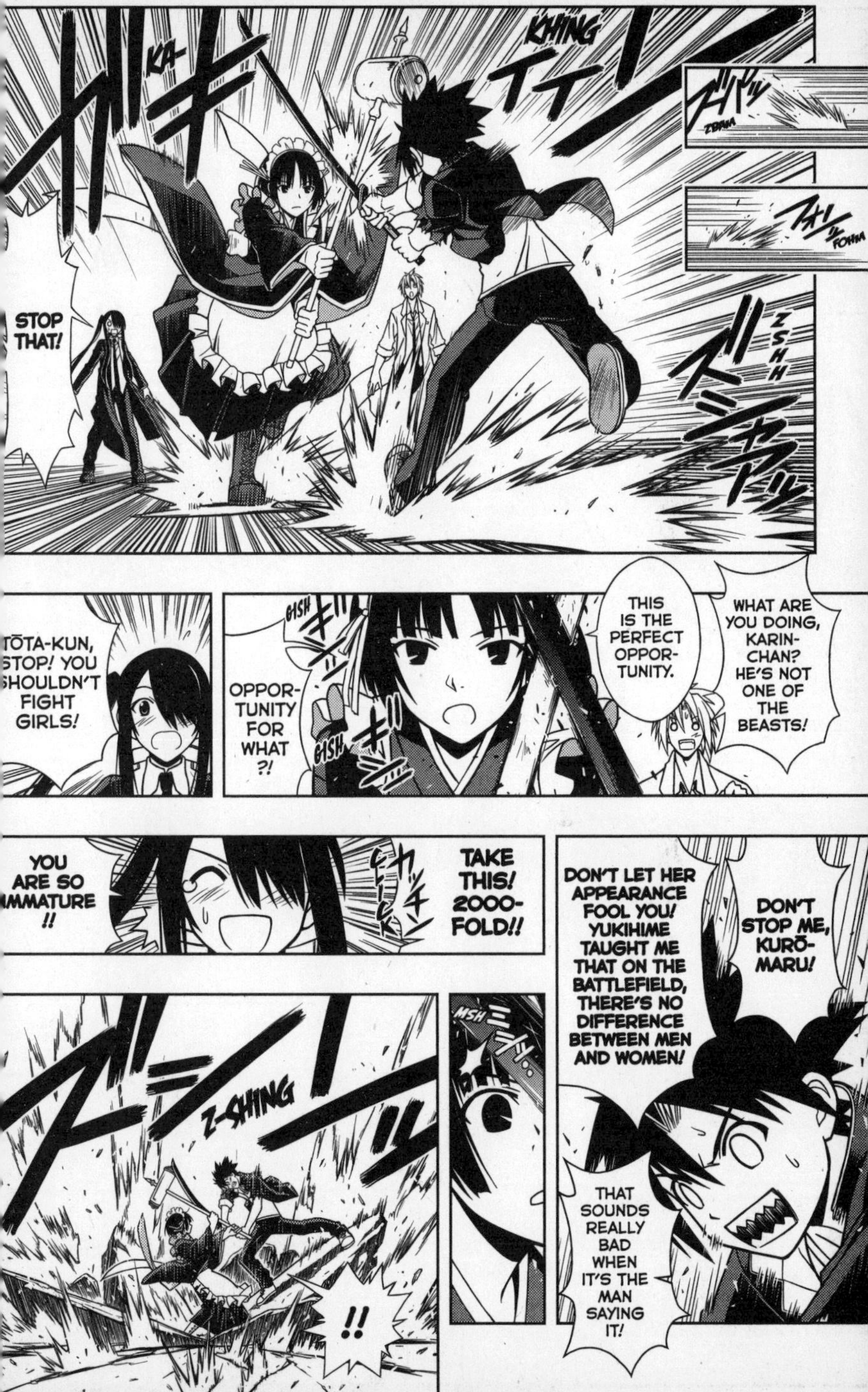
ZBAAA
FOHM
KHING
KA
ZSHH
STOP THAT!
WHAT ARE YOU DOING, KARIN-CHAN? HE'S NOT ONE OF THE BEASTS!
THIS IS THE PERFECT OPPOR-TUNITY.
GISH
OPPOR-TUNITY FOR WHAT?!
GISH
TŌTA-KUN, STOP! YOU SHOULDN'T FIGHT GIRLS!
DON'T STOP ME, KURŌ-MARU!
DON'T LET HER APPEARANCE FOOL YOU! YUKIHIME TAUGHT ME THAT ON THE BATTLEFIELD, THERE'S NO DIFFERENCE BETWEEN MEN AND WOMEN!
THAT SOUNDS REALLY BAD WHEN IT'S THE MAN SAYING IT!
TAKE THIS! 2000-FOLD!!
CLICK
YOU ARE SO IMMATURE!!
MSH
Z-SHING
!!

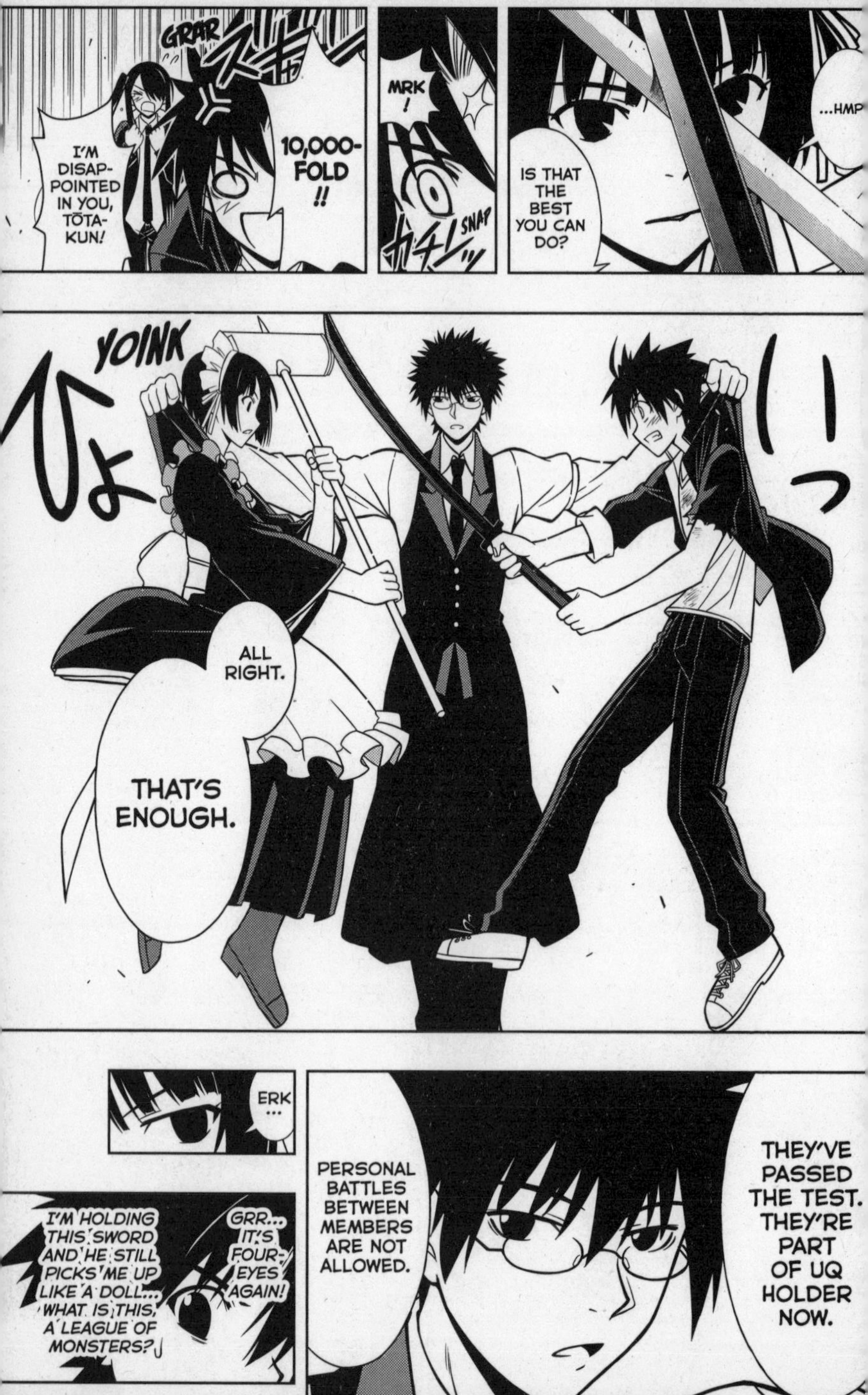
...HMP
IS THAT THE BEST YOU CAN DO?
MRK!
SNAP
GRAR
10,000-FOLD!!
I'M DISAPPOINTED IN YOU, TŌTA-KUN!
YOINK
ALL RIGHT.
THAT'S ENOUGH.
THEY'VE PASSED THE TEST. THEY'RE PART OF UQ HOLDER NOW.
PERSONAL BATTLES BETWEEN MEMBERS ARE NOT ALLOWED.
ERK...
GRR... IT'S FOUR-EYES AGAIN!
I'M HOLDING THIS SWORD AND HE STILL PICKS ME UP LIKE A DOLL... WHAT IS THIS, A LEAGUE OF MONSTERS?

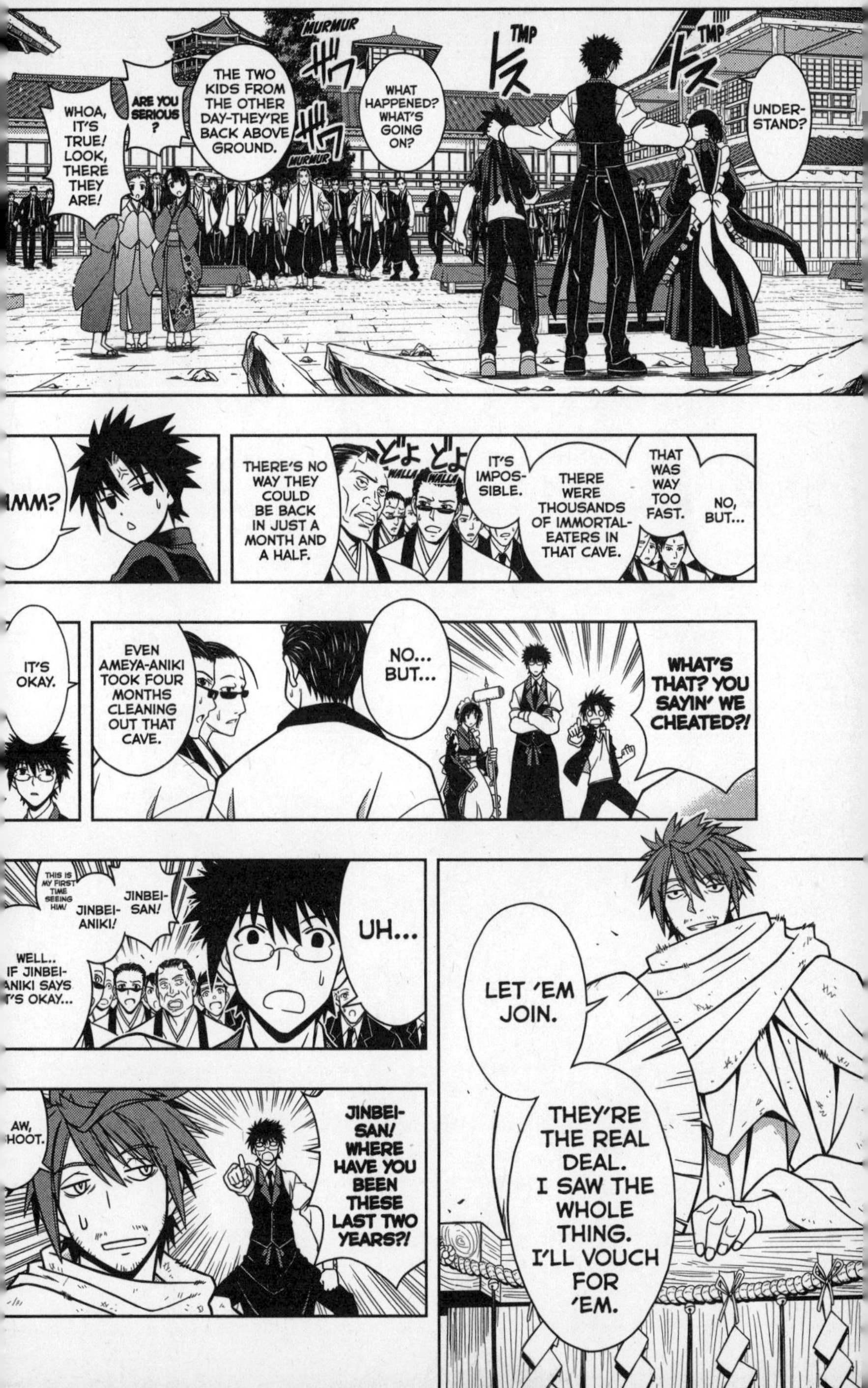
UNDER-STAND?
ドス TMP
ドス TMP
WHAT HAPPENED? WHAT'S GOING ON?
ザワ MURMUR
ザワ MURMUR
THE TWO KIDS FROM THE OTHER DAY-THEY'RE BACK ABOVE GROUND.
ARE YOU SERIOUS?
WHOA, IT'S TRUE! LOOK, THERE THEY ARE!
NO, BUT...
THAT WAS WAY TOO FAST.
THERE WERE THOUSANDS OF IMMORTAL-EATERS IN THAT CAVE.
IT'S IMPOS-SIBLE.
どよ どよ WALLA WALLA
THERE'S NO WAY THEY COULD BE BACK IN JUST A MONTH AND A HALF.
MM?
WHAT'S THAT? YOU SAYIN' WE CHEATED?!
NO... BUT...
EVEN AMEYA-ANIKI TOOK FOUR MONTHS CLEANING OUT THAT CAVE.
IT'S OKAY.
LET 'EM JOIN.
THEY'RE THE REAL DEAL. I SAW THE WHOLE THING. I'LL VOUCH FOR 'EM.
UH...
JINBEI-SAN!
THIS IS MY FIRST TIME SEEING HIM!
JINBEI-ANIKI!
WELL.. IF JINBEI-ANIKI SAYS 'S OKAY...
JINBEI-SAN! WHERE HAVE YOU BEEN THESE LAST TWO YEARS?!
AW, HOOT.

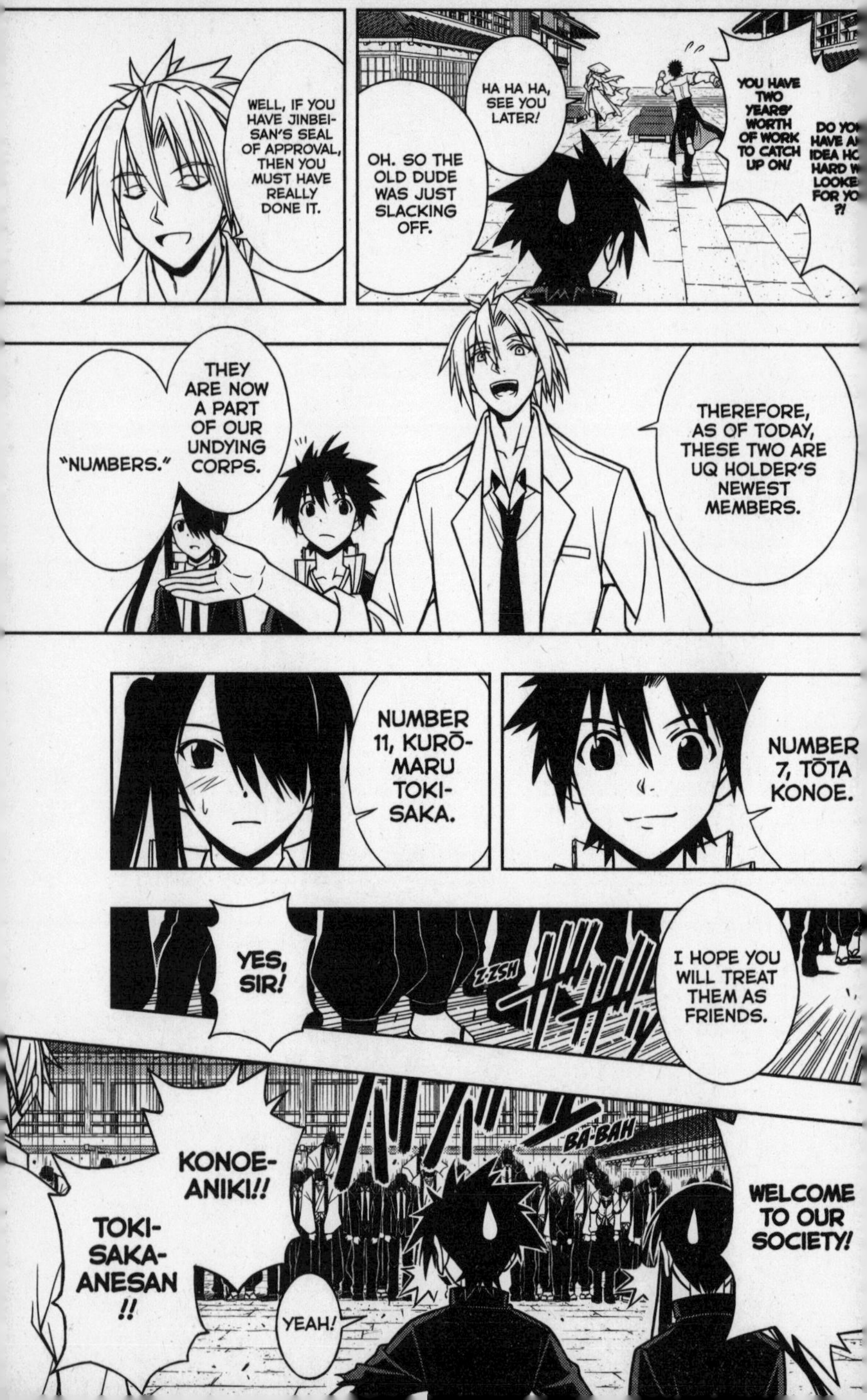
DO YO HAVE A IDEA HO HARD W LOOKE FOR YO ?!
YOU HAVE TWO YEARS' WORTH OF WORK TO CATCH UP ON!
HA HA HA, SEE YOU LATER!
OH. SO THE OLD DUDE WAS JUST SLACKING OFF.
WELL, IF YOU HAVE JINBEI-SAN'S SEAL OF APPROVAL, THEN YOU MUST HAVE REALLY DONE IT.
THEREFORE, AS OF TODAY, THESE TWO ARE UQ HOLDER'S NEWEST MEMBERS.
THEY ARE NOW A PART OF OUR UNDYING CORPS.
"NUMBERS."
NUMBER 7, TŌTA KONOE.
NUMBER 11, KURŌ-MARU TOKI-SAKA.
I HOPE YOU WILL TREAT THEM AS FRIENDS.
Z-ZSH
YES, SIR!
BA-BAH
WELCOME TO OUR SOCIETY!
KONOE-ANIKI!!
TOKI-SAKA-ANESAN !!
YEAH!

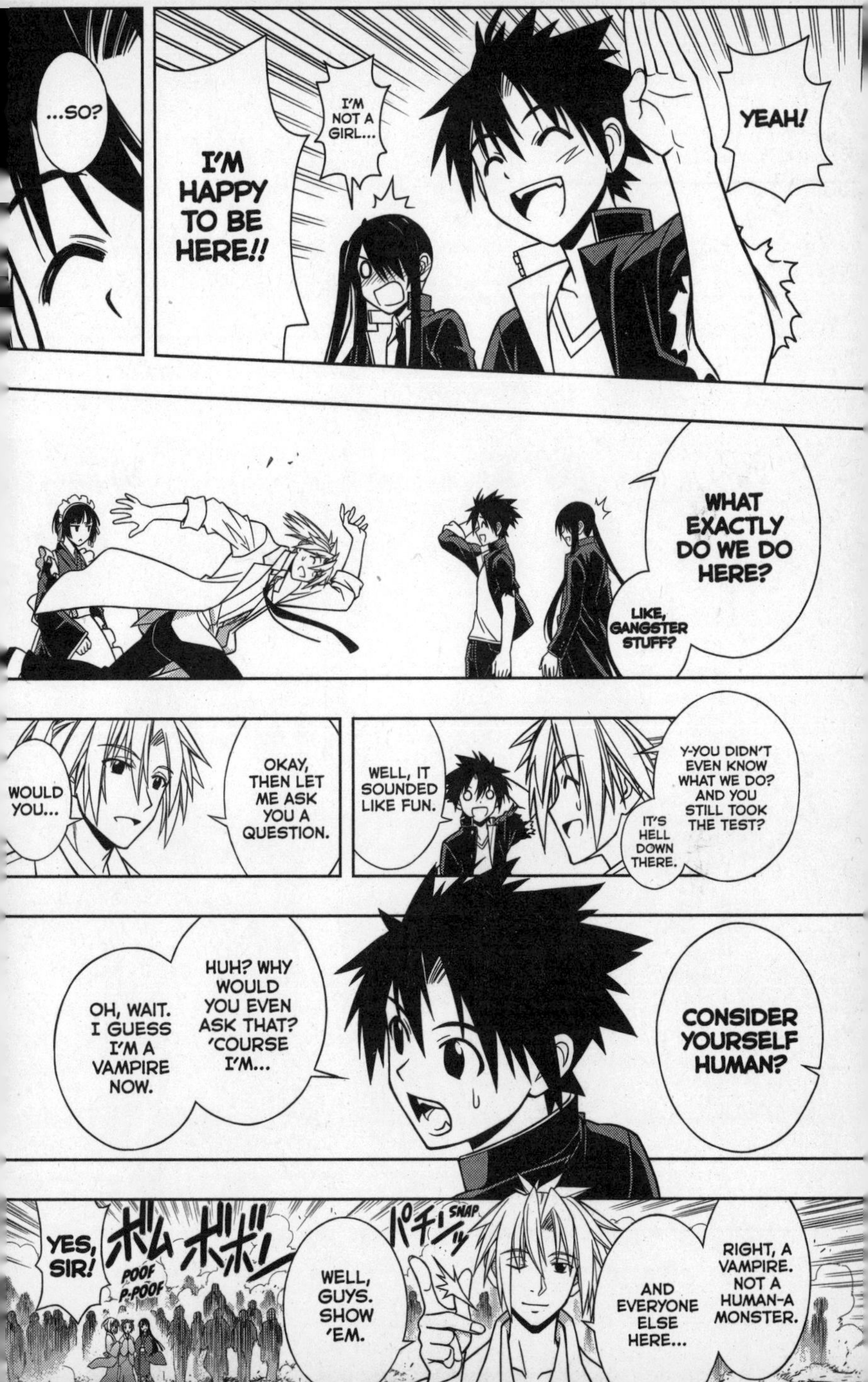
YEAH!
I'M NOT A GIRL...
I'M HAPPY TO BE HERE!!
...SO?
WHAT EXACTLY DO WE DO HERE?
LIKE, GANGSTER STUFF?
Y-YOU DIDN'T EVEN KNOW WHAT WE DO? AND YOU STILL TOOK THE TEST?
IT'S HELL DOWN THERE.
WELL, IT SOUNDED LIKE FUN.
OKAY, THEN LET ME ASK YOU A QUESTION.
WOULD YOU...
CONSIDER YOURSELF HUMAN?
HUH? WHY WOULD YOU EVEN ASK THAT? 'COURSE I'M...
OH, WAIT. I GUESS I'M A VAMPIRE NOW.
RIGHT, A VAMPIRE. NOT A HUMAN-A MONSTER.
AND EVERYONE ELSE HERE...
SNAP
WELL, GUYS. SHOW 'EM.
POOF P-POOF
YES, SIR!

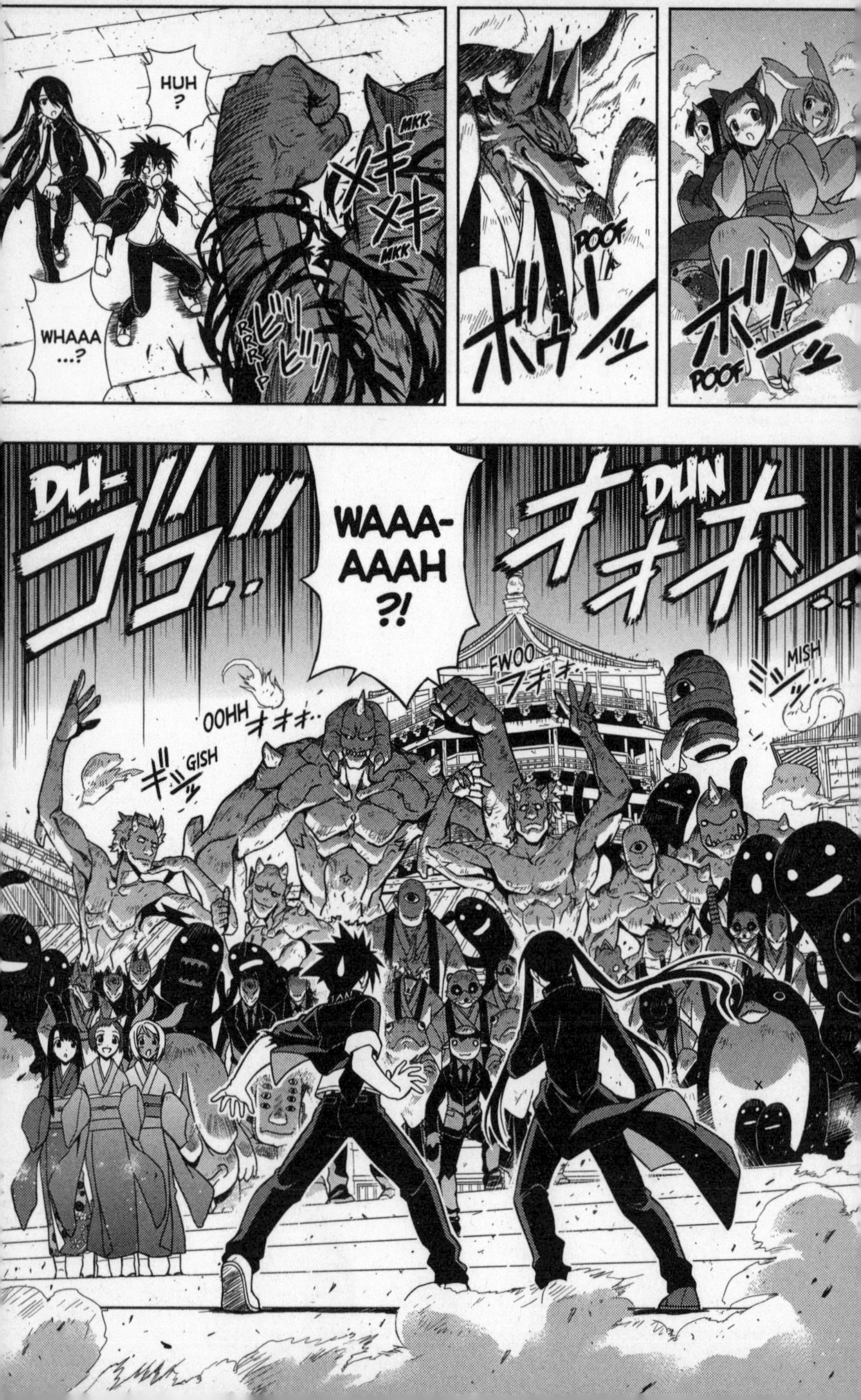
POOF
POOF
MKK
MKK
HUH?
RRRIP
WHAAA...?
DUN
WAAAA-AAAH?!
DU-
MISH
FWOO
OOHH
GISH

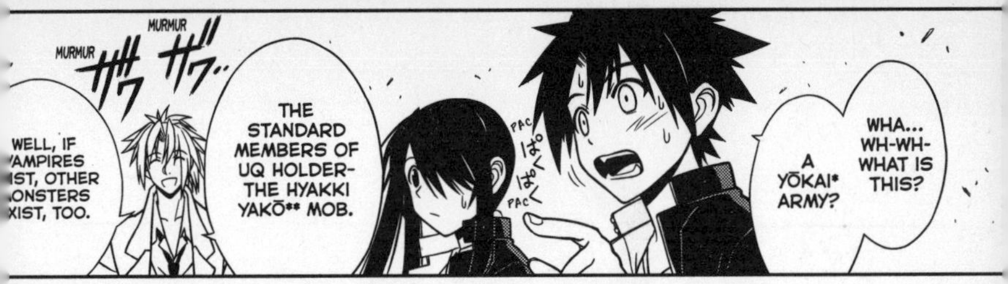
WHA... WH-WH-WHAT IS THIS?
A YŌKAI* ARMY?
PAC ぱく PAC ぱく
THE STANDARD MEMBERS OF UQ HOLDER- THE HYAKKI YAKŌ** MOB.
MURMUR ザワ MURMUR ザワ…
WELL, IF AMPIRES IST, OTHER ONSTERS XIST, TOO.

akki Yakō: a large group of yōkai. * Yōkai: a supernatural being

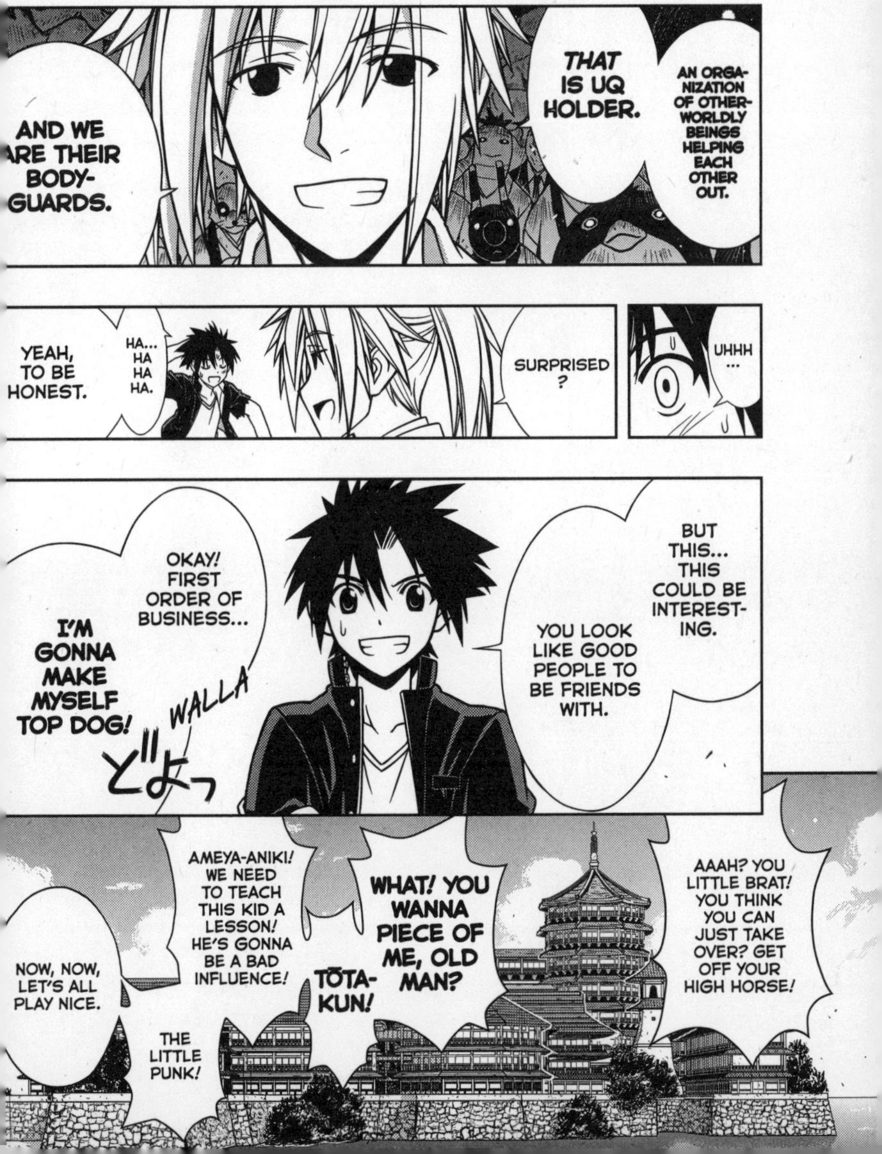
AN ORGANIZATION OF OTHER-WORLDLY BEINGS HELPING EACH OTHER OUT.
THAT IS UQ HOLDER.
AND WE ARE THEIR BODY-GUARDS.
UHHH...
SURPRISED?
HA... HA HA HA.
YEAH, TO BE HONEST.
BUT THIS... THIS COULD BE INTEREST-ING.
YOU LOOK LIKE GOOD PEOPLE TO BE FRIENDS WITH.
OKAY! FIRST ORDER OF BUSINESS...
I'M GONNA MAKE MYSELF TOP DOG!
WALLA どよっ
AAAH? YOU LITTLE BRAT! YOU THINK YOU CAN JUST TAKE OVER? GET OFF YOUR HIGH HORSE!
WHAT! YOU WANNA PIECE OF ME, OLD MAN?
TŌTA-KUN!
AMEYA-ANIKI! WE NEED TO TEACH THIS KID A LESSON! HE'S GONNA BE A BAD INFLUENCE!
THE LITTLE PUNK!
NOW, NOW, LET'S ALL PLAY NICE.

悠久 UQ HOLDER!

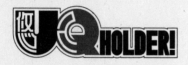

UQ HOLDER!
ユーキューホルダー!

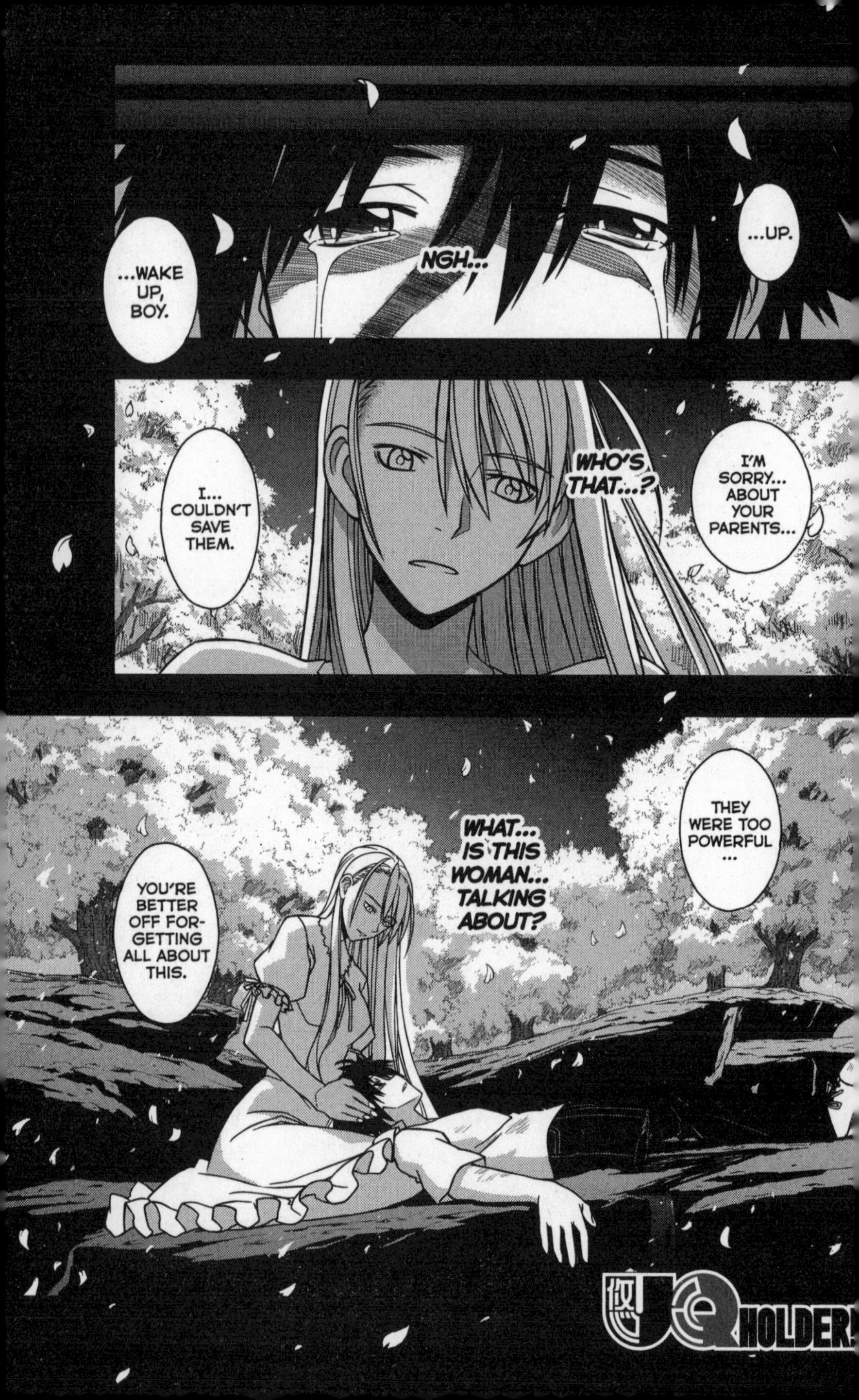
...UP.
NGH...
...WAKE UP, BOY.
I'M SORRY... ABOUT YOUR PARENTS...
WHO'S THAT...?
I... COULDN'T SAVE THEM.
THEY WERE TOO POWERFUL ...
WHAT... IS THIS WOMAN... TALKING ABOUT?
YOU'RE BETTER OFF FOR-GETTING ALL ABOUT THIS.

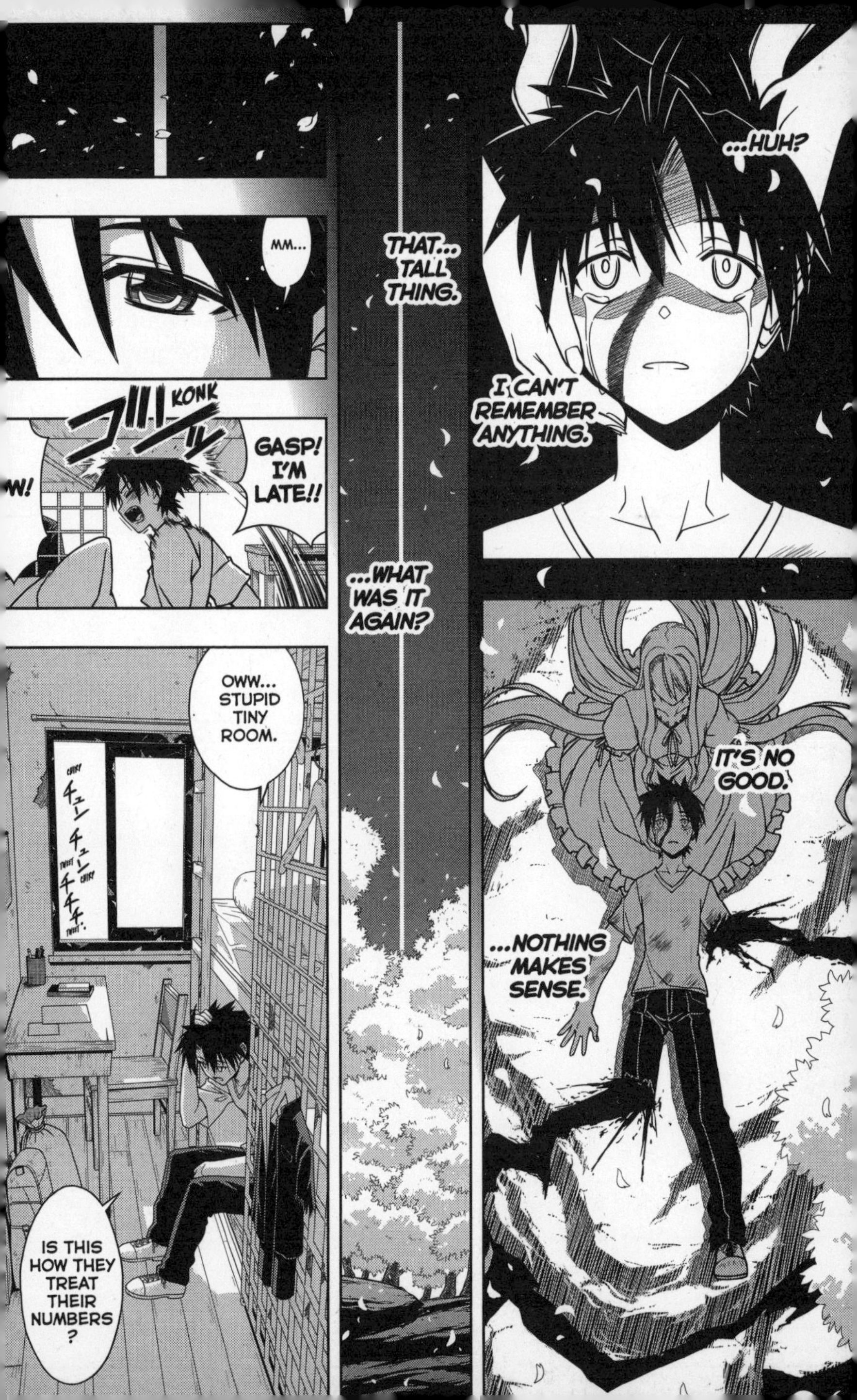
...HUH?
I CAN'T REMEMBER ANYTHING.
IT'S NO GOOD.
...NOTHING MAKES SENSE.
THAT... TALL THING.
...WHAT WAS IT AGAIN?
MM...
KONK
GASP! I'M LATE!!
W!
OWW... STUPID TINY ROOM.
IS THIS HOW THEY TREAT THEIR NUMBERS?

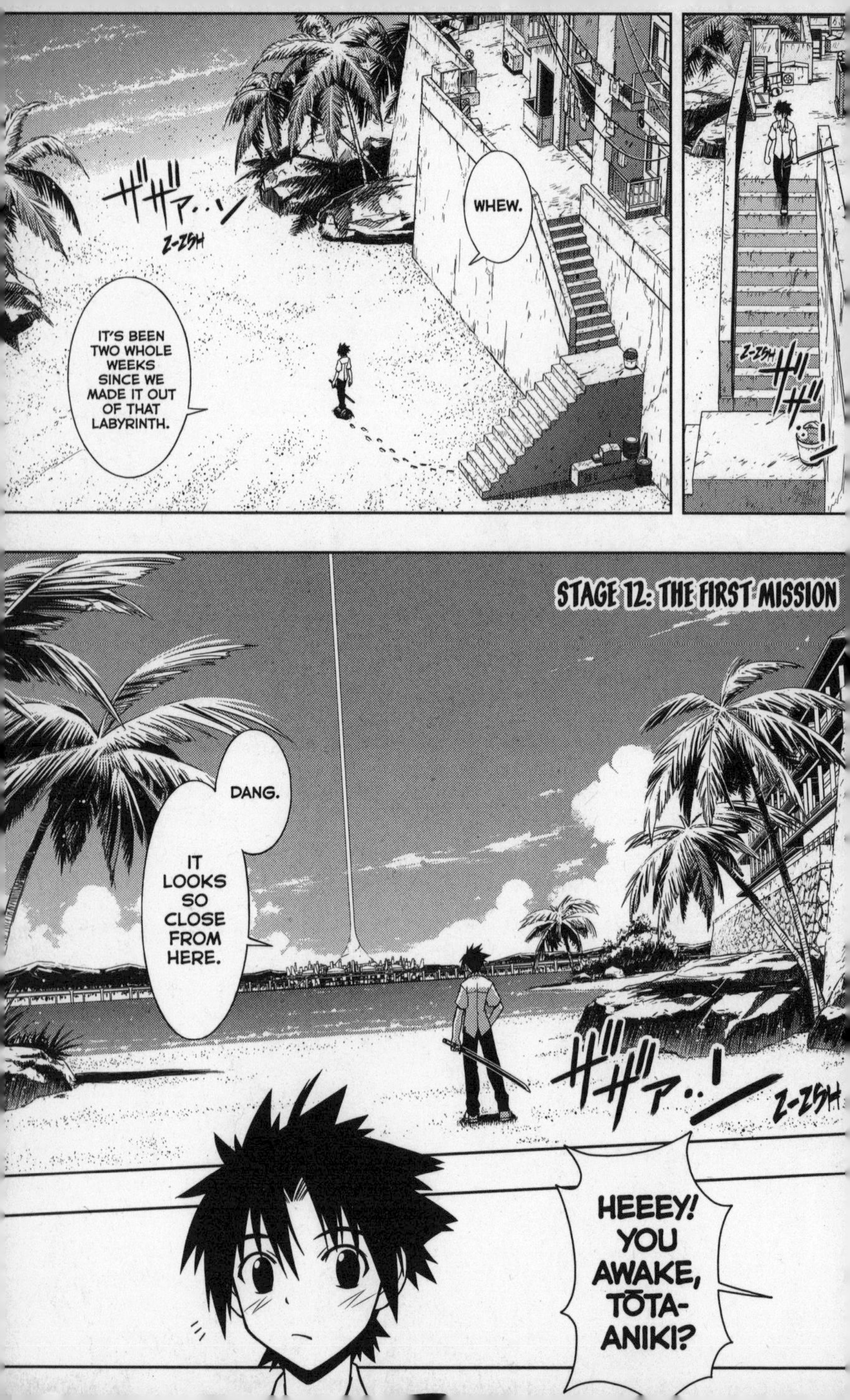
Z-ZSH
ザザ
WHEW.
ザザァ…ッ
Z-ZSH
IT'S BEEN TWO WHOLE WEEKS SINCE WE MADE IT OUT OF THAT LABYRINTH.
STAGE 12: THE FIRST MISSION
DANG.
IT LOOKS SO CLOSE FROM HERE.
ザザァ…ッ
Z-ZSH
HEEEY! YOU AWAKE, TŌTA-ANIKI?

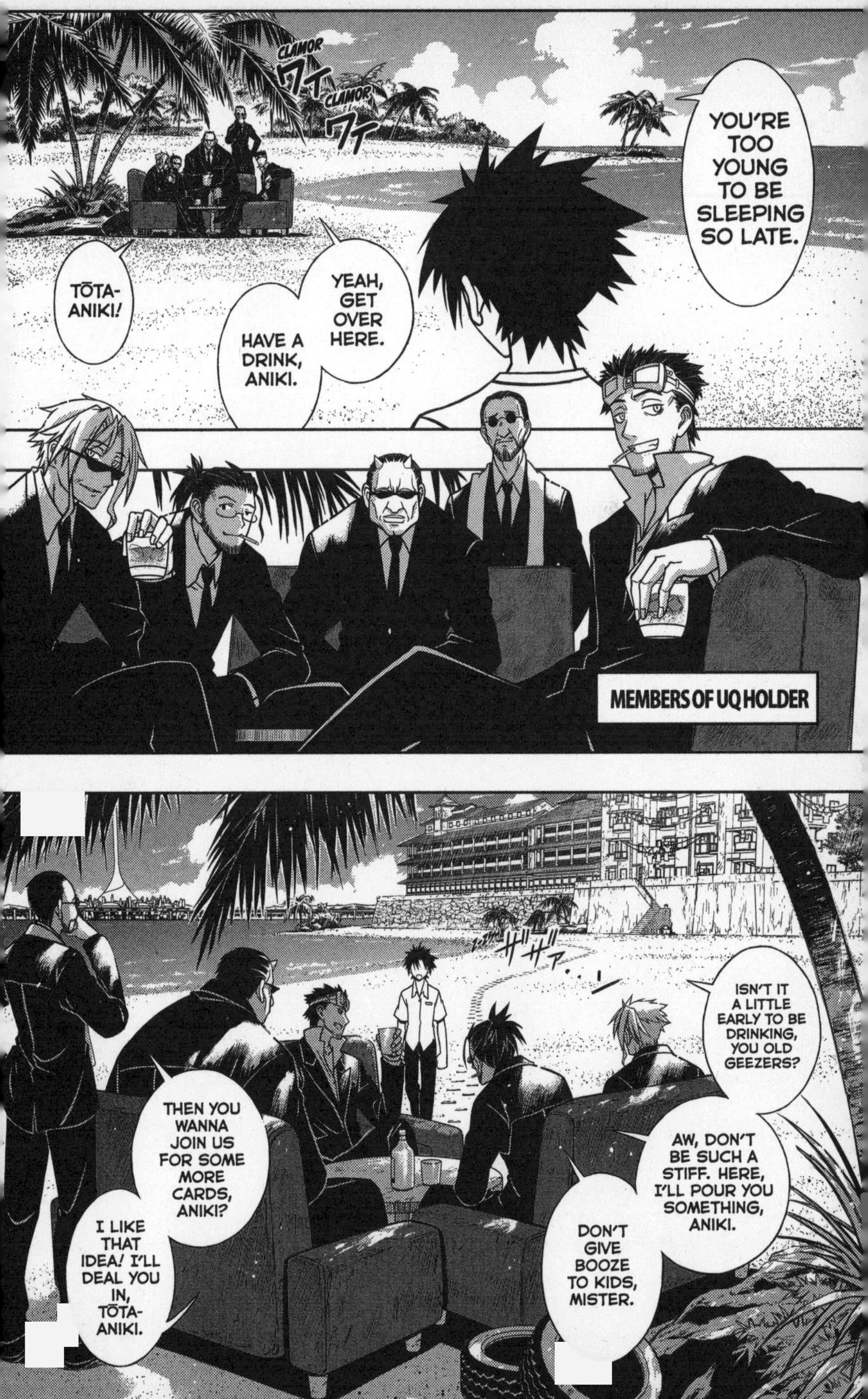
YOU'RE TOO YOUNG TO BE SLEEPING SO LATE.
CLAMOR
ワイ
CLAMOR
ワイ
YEAH, GET OVER HERE.
HAVE A DRINK, ANIKI.
TŌTA-ANIKI!
MEMBERS OF UQ HOLDER
ISN'T IT A LITTLE EARLY TO BE DRINKING, YOU OLD GEEZERS?
ザザァ
AW, DON'T BE SUCH A STIFF. HERE, I'LL POUR YOU SOMETHING, ANIKI.
DON'T GIVE BOOZE TO KIDS, MISTER.
THEN YOU WANNA JOIN US FOR SOME MORE CARDS, ANIKI?
I LIKE THAT IDEA! I'LL DEAL YOU IN, TŌTA-ANIKI.

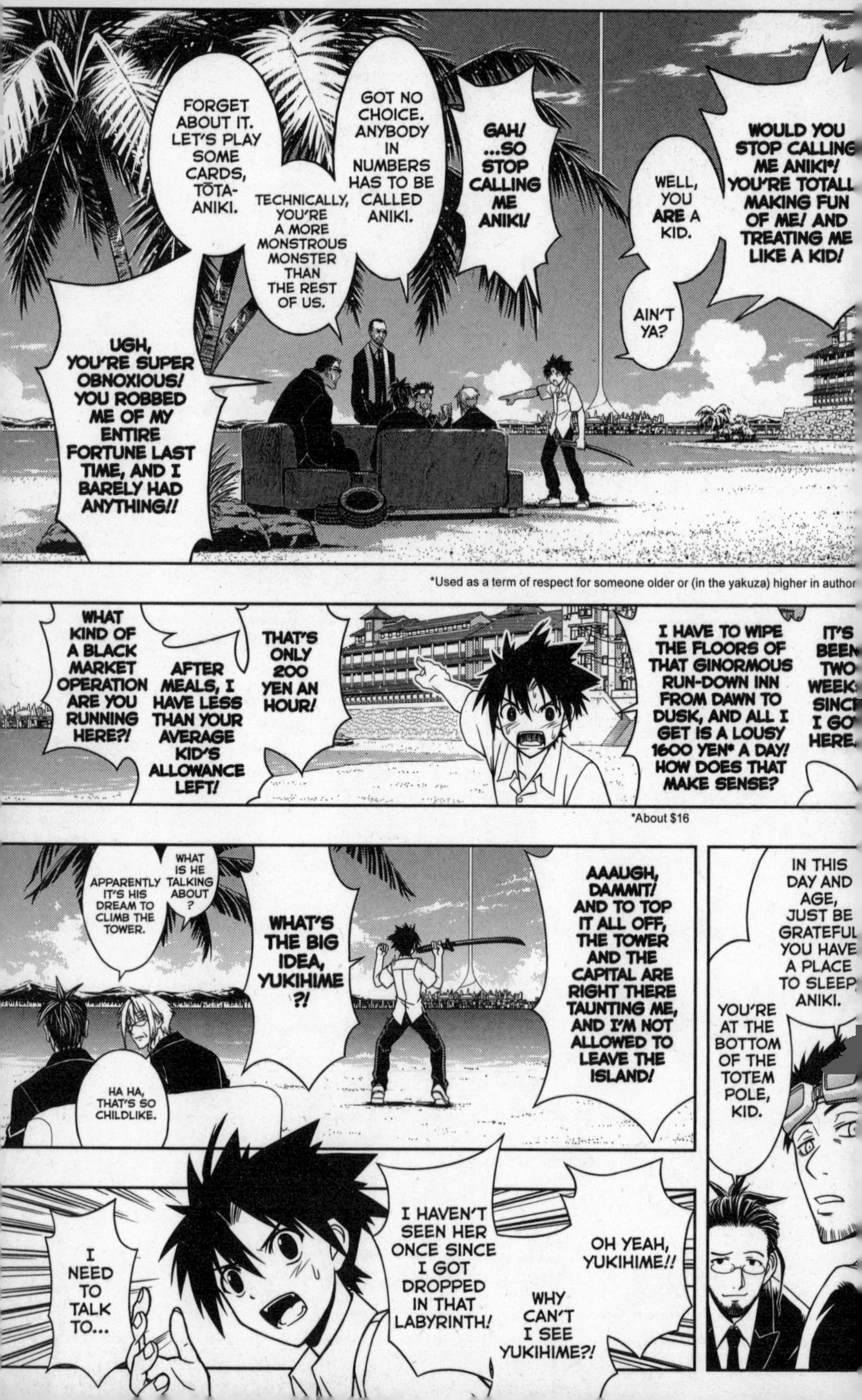
WOULD YOU STOP CALLING ME ANIKI*! YOU'RE TOTALL MAKING FUN OF ME! AND TREATING ME LIKE A KID!
WELL, YOU ARE A KID.
AIN'T YA?
GAH! ...SO STOP CALLING ME ANIKI!
GOT NO CHOICE. ANYBODY IN NUMBERS HAS TO BE CALLED ANIKI.
TECHNICALLY, YOU'RE A MORE MONSTROUS MONSTER THAN THE REST OF US.
FORGET ABOUT IT. LET'S PLAY SOME CARDS, TŌTA-ANIKI.
UGH, YOU'RE SUPER OBNOXIOUS! YOU ROBBED ME OF MY ENTIRE FORTUNE LAST TIME, AND I BARELY HAD ANYTHING!!
IT'S BEEN TWO WEEK SINC I GO HERE.
I HAVE TO WIPE THE FLOORS OF THAT GINORMOUS RUN-DOWN INN FROM DAWN TO DUSK, AND ALL I GET IS A LOUSY 1600 YEN* A DAY! HOW DOES THAT MAKE SENSE?
THAT'S ONLY 200 YEN AN HOUR!
AFTER MEALS, I HAVE LESS THAN YOUR AVERAGE KID'S ALLOWANCE LEFT!
WHAT KIND OF A BLACK MARKET OPERATION ARE YOU RUNNING HERE?!
IN THIS DAY AND AGE, JUST BE GRATEFUL YOU HAVE A PLACE TO SLEEP, ANIKI.
YOU'RE AT THE BOTTOM OF THE TOTEM POLE, KID.
AAAUGH, DAMMIT! AND TO TOP IT ALL OFF, THE TOWER AND THE CAPITAL ARE RIGHT THERE TAUNTING ME, AND I'M NOT ALLOWED TO LEAVE THE ISLAND!
WHAT'S THE BIG IDEA, YUKIHIME?!
WHAT IS HE TALKING ABOUT?
APPARENTLY IT'S HIS DREAM TO CLIMB THE TOWER.
HA HA, THAT'S SO CHILDLIKE.
OH YEAH, YUKIHIME!!
WHY CAN'T I SEE YUKIHIME?!
I HAVEN'T SEEN HER ONCE SINCE I GOT DROPPED IN THAT LABYRINTH!
I NEED TO TALK TO...

*Used as a term of respect for someone older or (in the yakuza) higher in author

*About $16

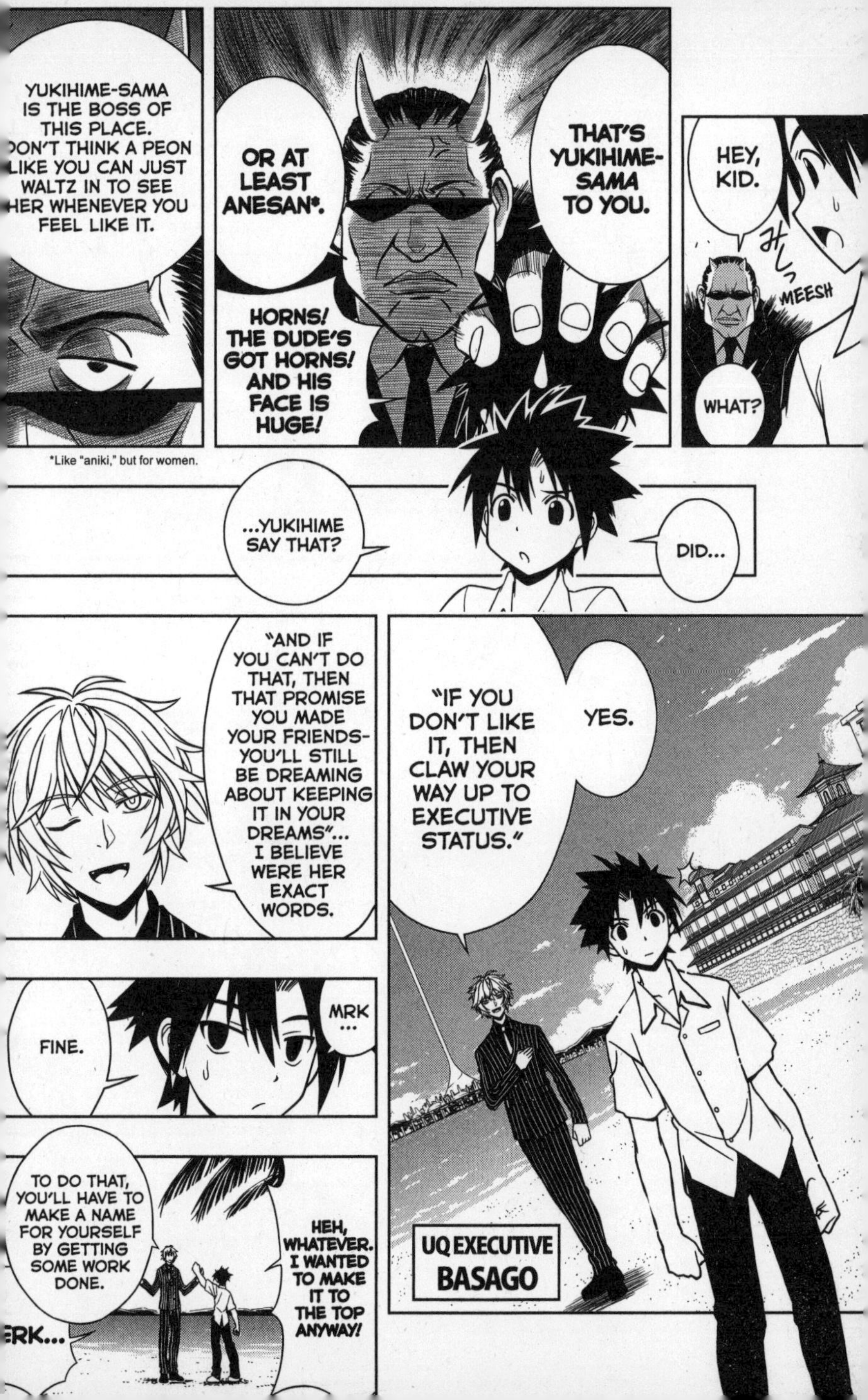
HEY, KID.
みしっ
MEESH
WHAT?
THAT'S YUKIHIME-SAMA TO YOU.
OR AT LEAST ANESAN*.
HORNS! THE DUDE'S GOT HORNS! AND HIS FACE IS HUGE!
YUKIHIME-SAMA IS THE BOSS OF THIS PLACE. ON'T THINK A PEON LIKE YOU CAN JUST WALTZ IN TO SEE HER WHENEVER YOU FEEL LIKE IT.
DID...
...YUKIHIME SAY THAT?
YES.
"IF YOU DON'T LIKE IT, THEN CLAW YOUR WAY UP TO EXECUTIVE STATUS."
UQ EXECUTIVE
BASAGO
"AND IF YOU CAN'T DO THAT, THEN THAT PROMISE YOU MADE YOUR FRIENDS- YOU'LL STILL BE DREAMING ABOUT KEEPING IT IN YOUR DREAMS"... I BELIEVE WERE HER EXACT WORDS.
MRK...
FINE.
HEH, WHATEVER. I WANTED TO MAKE IT TO THE TOP ANYWAY!
TO DO THAT, YOU'LL HAVE TO MAKE A NAME FOR YOURSELF BY GETTING SOME WORK DONE.
RK...

*Like "aniki," but for women.

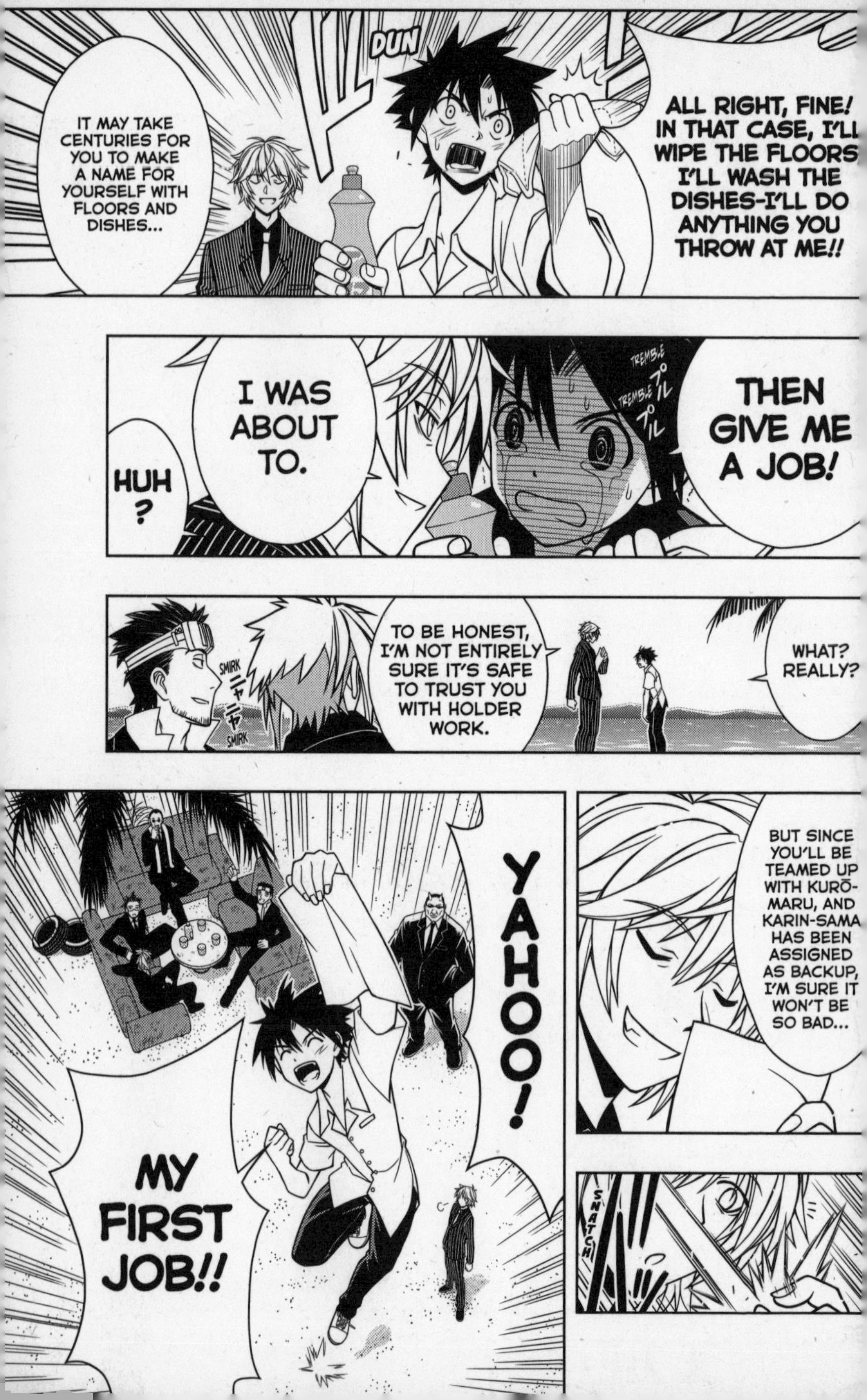
DUN
ALL RIGHT, FINE! IN THAT CASE, I'LL WIPE THE FLOORS, I'LL WASH THE DISHES–I'LL DO ANYTHING YOU THROW AT ME!!
IT MAY TAKE CENTURIES FOR YOU TO MAKE A NAME FOR YOURSELF WITH FLOORS AND DISHES...
THEN GIVE ME A JOB!
TREMBLE プル TREMBLE プル
I WAS ABOUT TO.
HUH?
WHAT? REALLY?
TO BE HONEST, I'M NOT ENTIRELY SURE IT'S SAFE TO TRUST YOU WITH HOLDER WORK.
SMIRK ニヤ SMIRK ニヤ
BUT SINCE YOU'LL BE TEAMED UP WITH KURŌMARU, AND KARIN-SAMA HAS BEEN ASSIGNED AS BACKUP, I'M SURE IT WON'T BE SO BAD...
SNATCH
YAHOO!
MY FIRST JOB!!

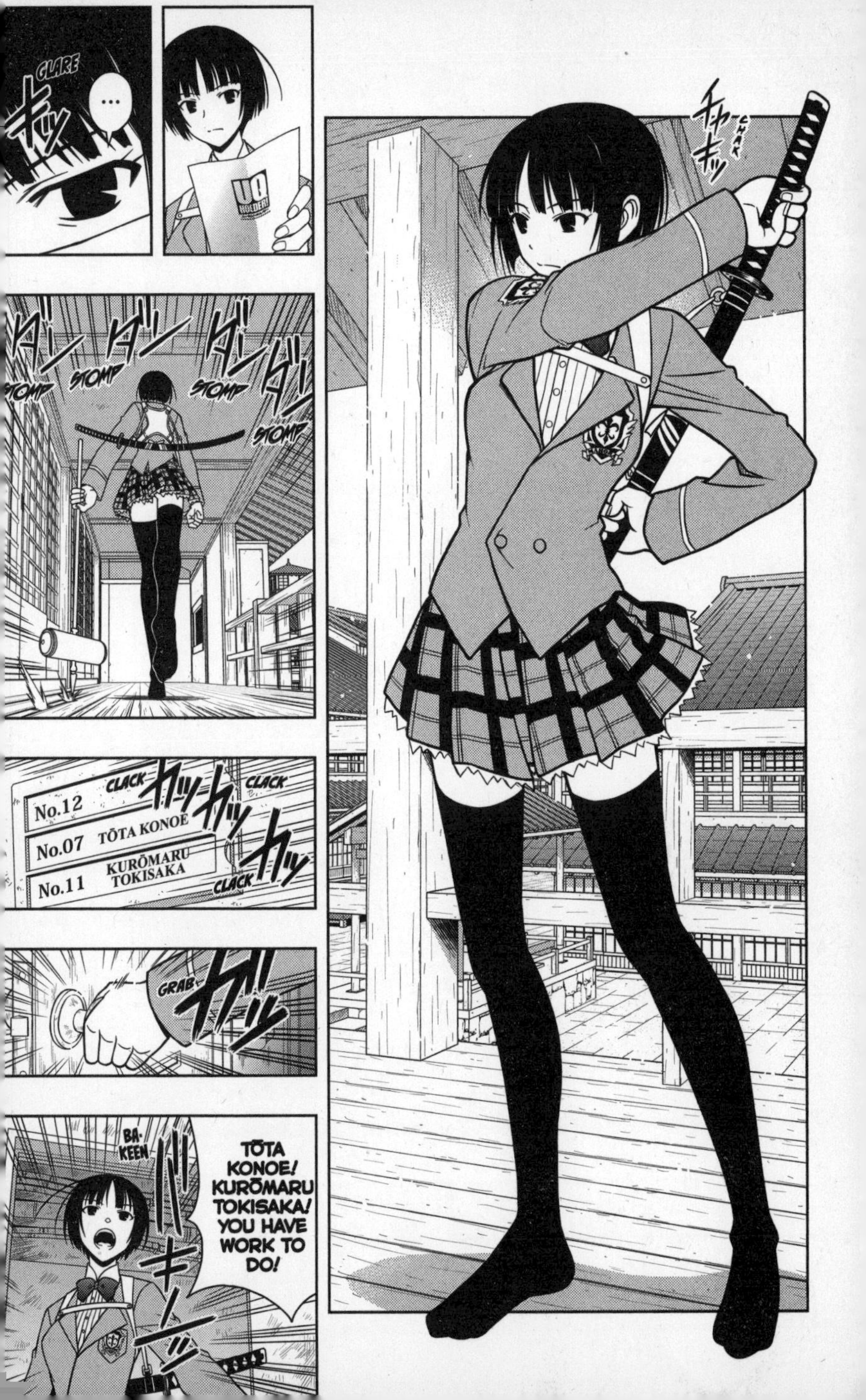
CHAK
GLARE
...
STOMP
STOMP
STOMP
STOMP
CLACK
CLACK
CLACK
No.12
No.07 TŌTA KONOE
No.11 KURŌMARU TOKISAKA
GRAB
BA-KEEN
TŌTA KONOE! KURŌMARU TOKISAKA! YOU HAVE WORK TO DO!

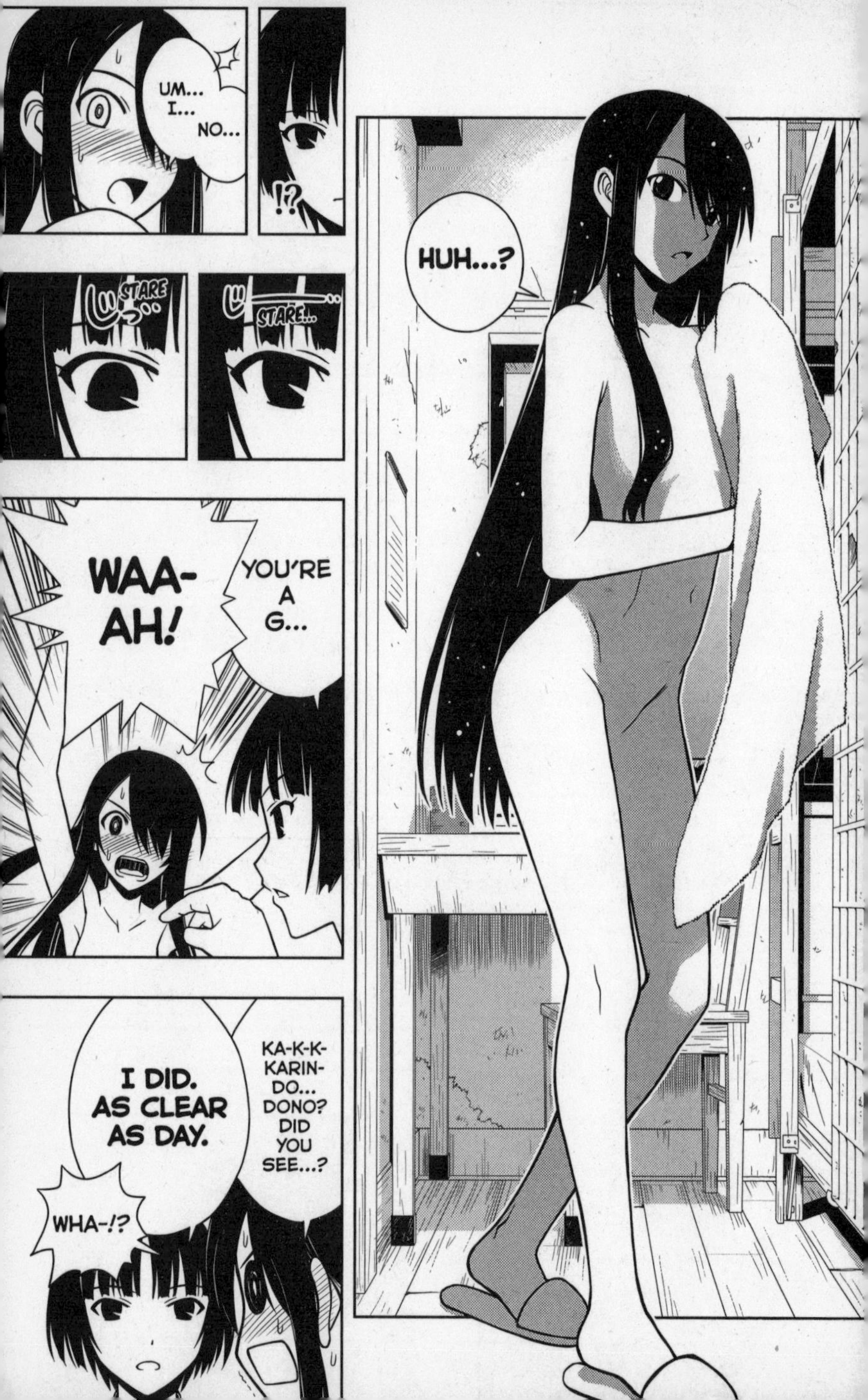
HUH...?
!?
UM... I... NO...
STARE...
STARE
YOU'RE A G...
WAA-AH!
KA-K-K-KARIN-DO... DONO? DID YOU SEE...?
I DID. AS CLEAR AS DAY.
WHA-!?

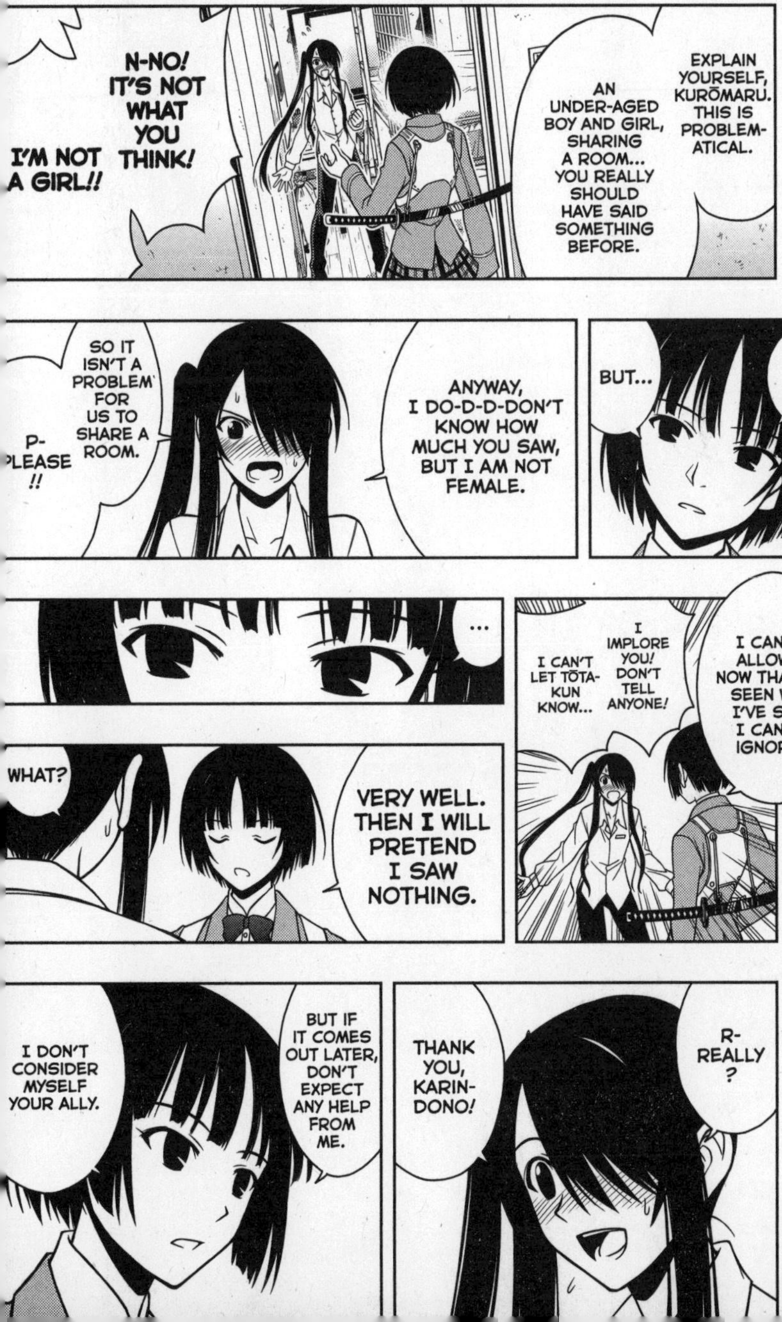
EXPLAIN YOURSELF, KURŌMARU. THIS IS PROBLEMATICAL.
AN UNDER-AGED BOY AND GIRL, SHARING A ROOM... YOU REALLY SHOULD HAVE SAID SOMETHING BEFORE.
N-NO! IT'S NOT WHAT YOU THINK!
I'M NOT A GIRL!!
...?
BUT...
ANYWAY, I DO-D-D-DON'T KNOW HOW MUCH YOU SAW, BUT I AM NOT FEMALE.
SO IT ISN'T A PROBLEM FOR US TO SHARE A ROOM.
P-PLEASE!!
I CANNOT ALLOW IT. NOW THAT I'VE SEEN WHAT I'VE SEEN, I CANNOT IGNORE...
I IMPLORE YOU! DON'T TELL ANYONE!
I CAN'T LET TŌTA-KUN KNOW...
...
VERY WELL. THEN I WILL PRETEND I SAW NOTHING.
WHAT?
R-REALLY?
THANK YOU, KARIN-DONO!
BUT IF IT COMES OUT LATER, DON'T EXPECT ANY HELP FROM ME.
I DON'T CONSIDER MYSELF YOUR ALLY.

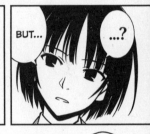

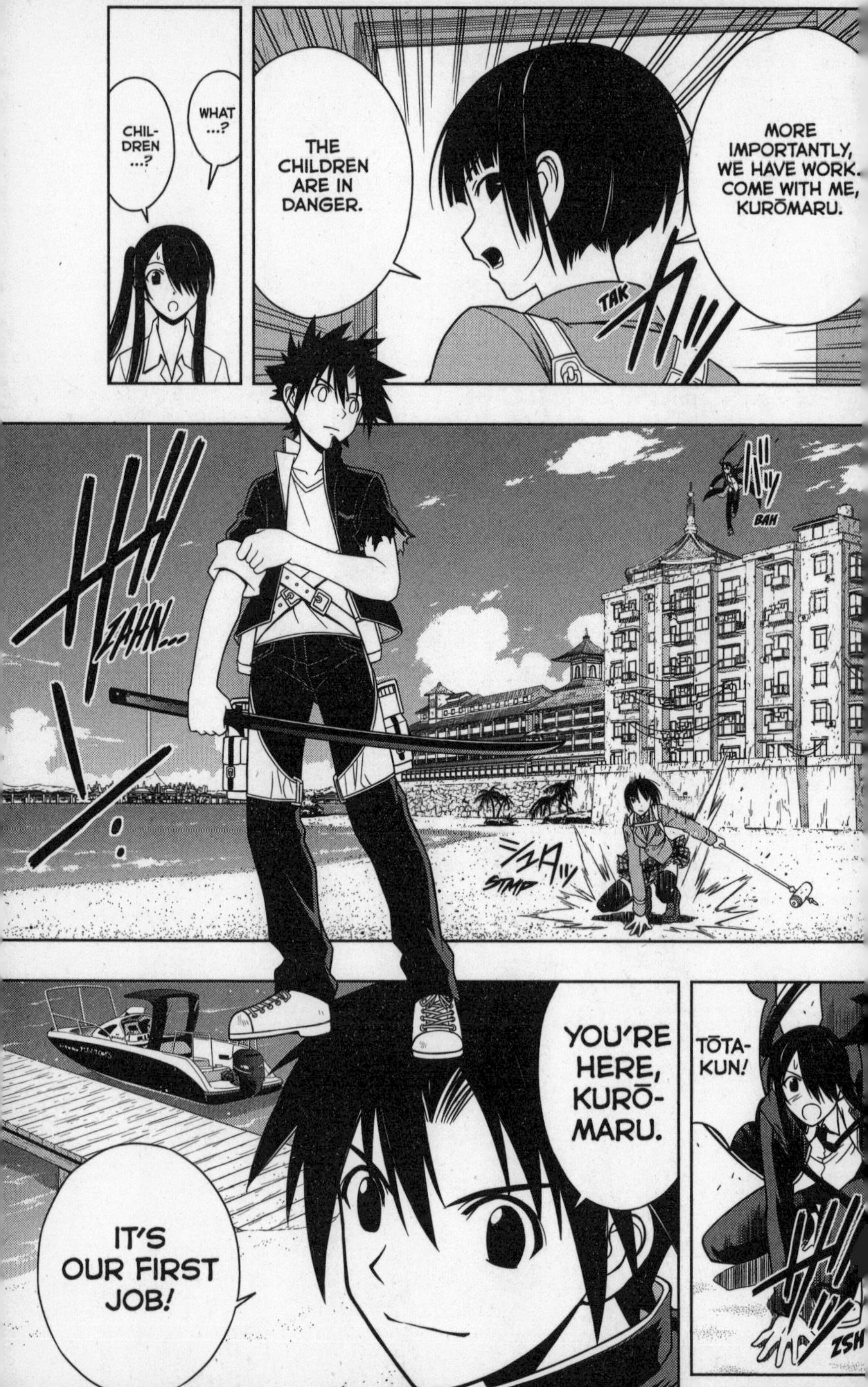

MORE IMPORTANTLY, WE HAVE WORK. COME WITH ME, KURŌMARU.
TAK
THE CHILDREN ARE IN DANGER.
WHAT ...?
CHIL-DREN ...?
BAH
STMP
ZAHN...
TŌTA-KUN!
ZSH
YOU'RE HERE, KURŌ-MARU.
IT'S OUR FIRST JOB!

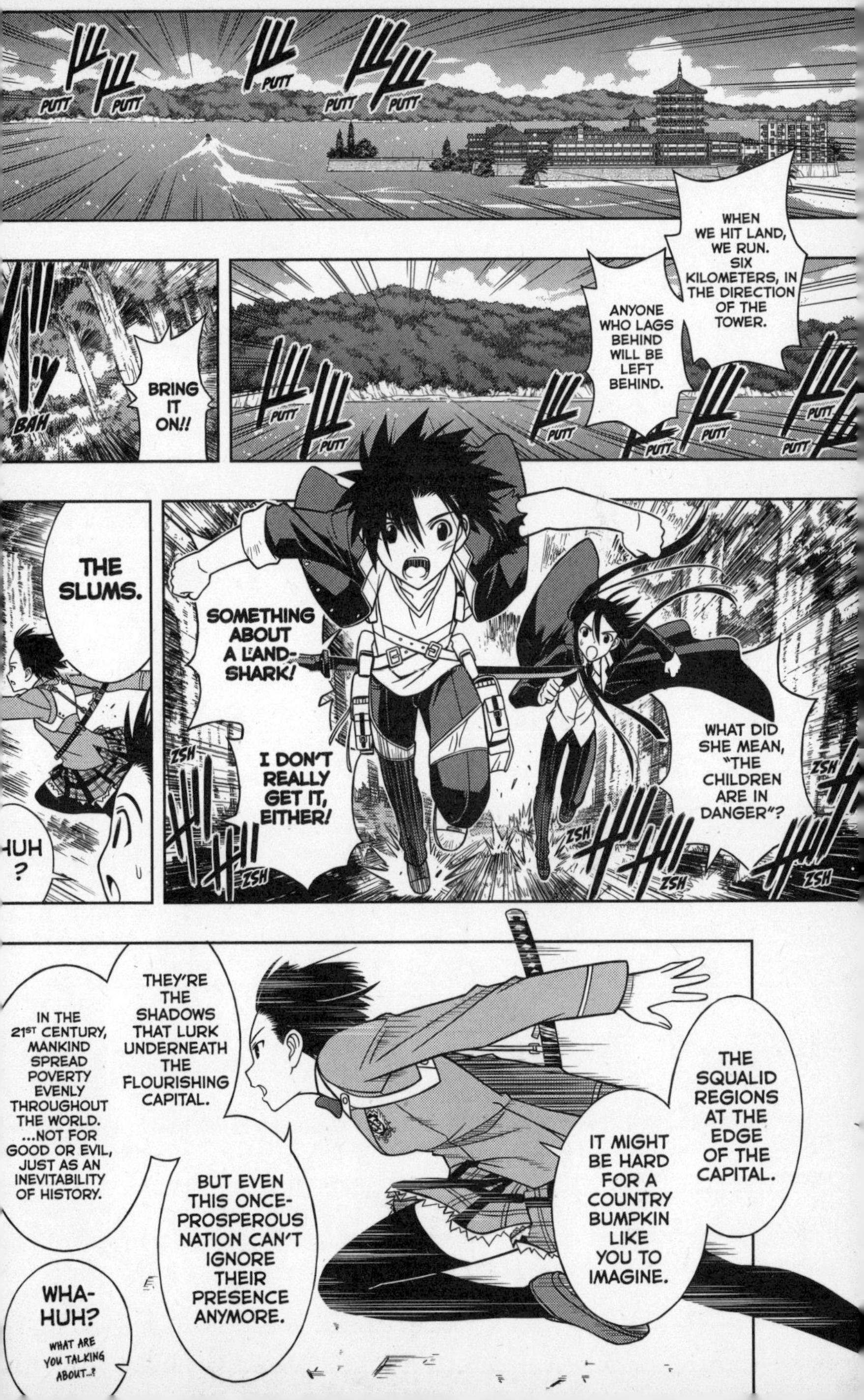
PUTT PUTT
PUTT
PUTT PUTT
WHEN WE HIT LAND, WE RUN. SIX KILOMETERS, IN THE DIRECTION OF THE TOWER.
ANYONE WHO LAGS BEHIND WILL BE LEFT BEHIND.
PUTT PUTT PUTT PUTT PUTT PUTT PUTT
BAH
BRING IT ON!!
WHAT DID SHE MEAN, "THE CHILDREN ARE IN DANGER"?
SOMETHING ABOUT A LAND-SHARK!
I DON'T REALLY GET IT, EITHER!
ZSH ZSH ZSH ZSH ZSH ZSH
THE SLUMS.
HUH?
THE SQUALID REGIONS AT THE EDGE OF THE CAPITAL.
IT MIGHT BE HARD FOR A COUNTRY BUMPKIN LIKE YOU TO IMAGINE.
THEY'RE THE SHADOWS THAT LURK UNDERNEATH THE FLOURISHING CAPITAL.
BUT EVEN THIS ONCE-PROSPEROUS NATION CAN'T IGNORE THEIR PRESENCE ANYMORE.
IN THE 21ST CENTURY, MANKIND SPREAD POVERTY EVENLY THROUGHOUT THE WORLD. ...NOT FOR GOOD OR EVIL, JUST AS AN INEVITABILITY OF HISTORY.
WHA-HUH?
WHAT ARE YOU TALKING ABOUT...!?

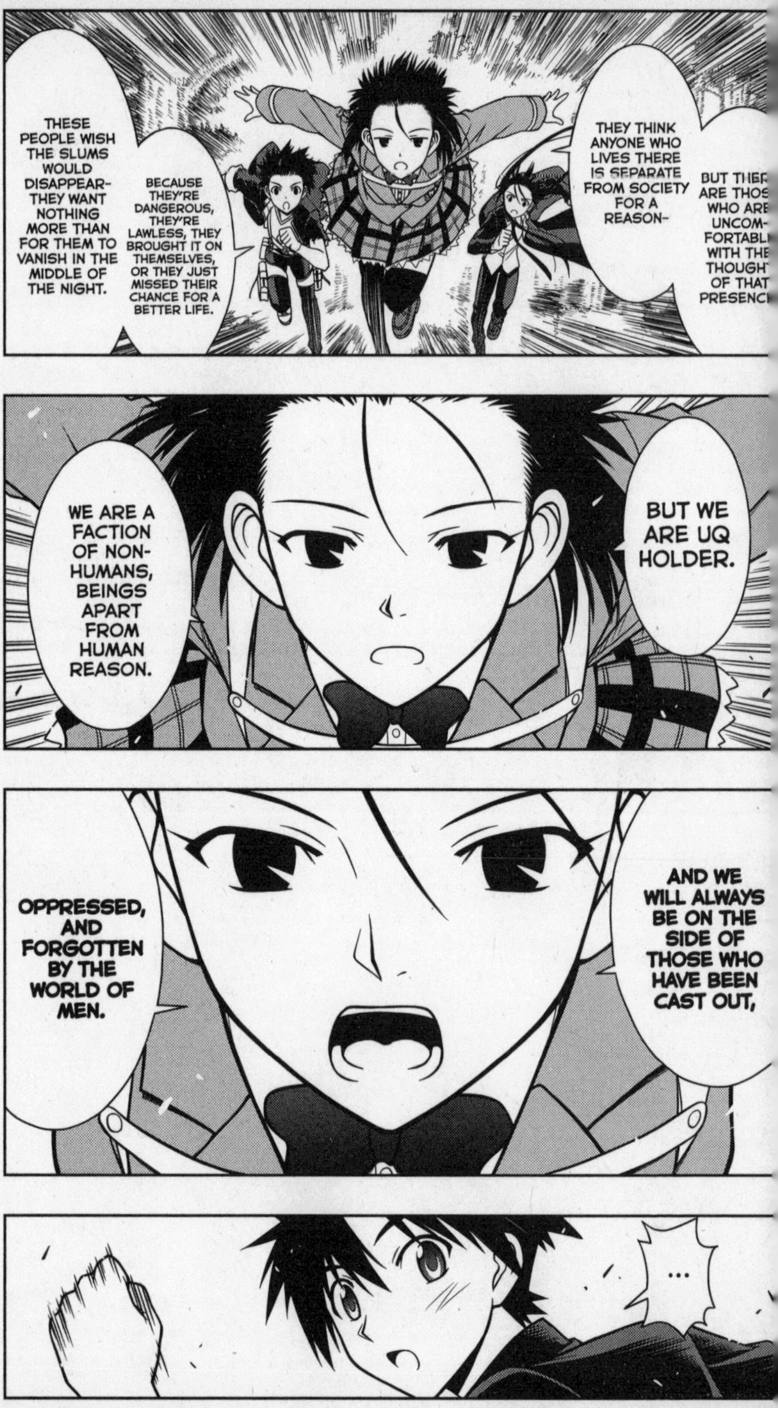
BUT THER ARE THOS WHO ARE UNCOM-FORTABL WITH THE THOUGHT OF THAT PRESENC
THEY THINK ANYONE WHO LIVES THERE IS SEPARATE FROM SOCIETY FOR A REASON-
BECAUSE THEY'RE DANGEROUS, THEY'RE LAWLESS, THEY BROUGHT IT ON THEMSELVES, OR THEY JUST MISSED THEIR CHANCE FOR A BETTER LIFE.
THESE PEOPLE WISH THE SLUMS WOULD DISAPPEAR- THEY WANT NOTHING MORE THAN FOR THEM TO VANISH IN THE MIDDLE OF THE NIGHT.
BUT WE ARE UQ HOLDER.
WE ARE A FACTION OF NON-HUMANS, BEINGS APART FROM HUMAN REASON.
AND WE WILL ALWAYS BE ON THE SIDE OF THOSE WHO HAVE BEEN CAST OUT,
OPPRESSED, AND FORGOTTEN BY THE WORLD OF MEN.
...

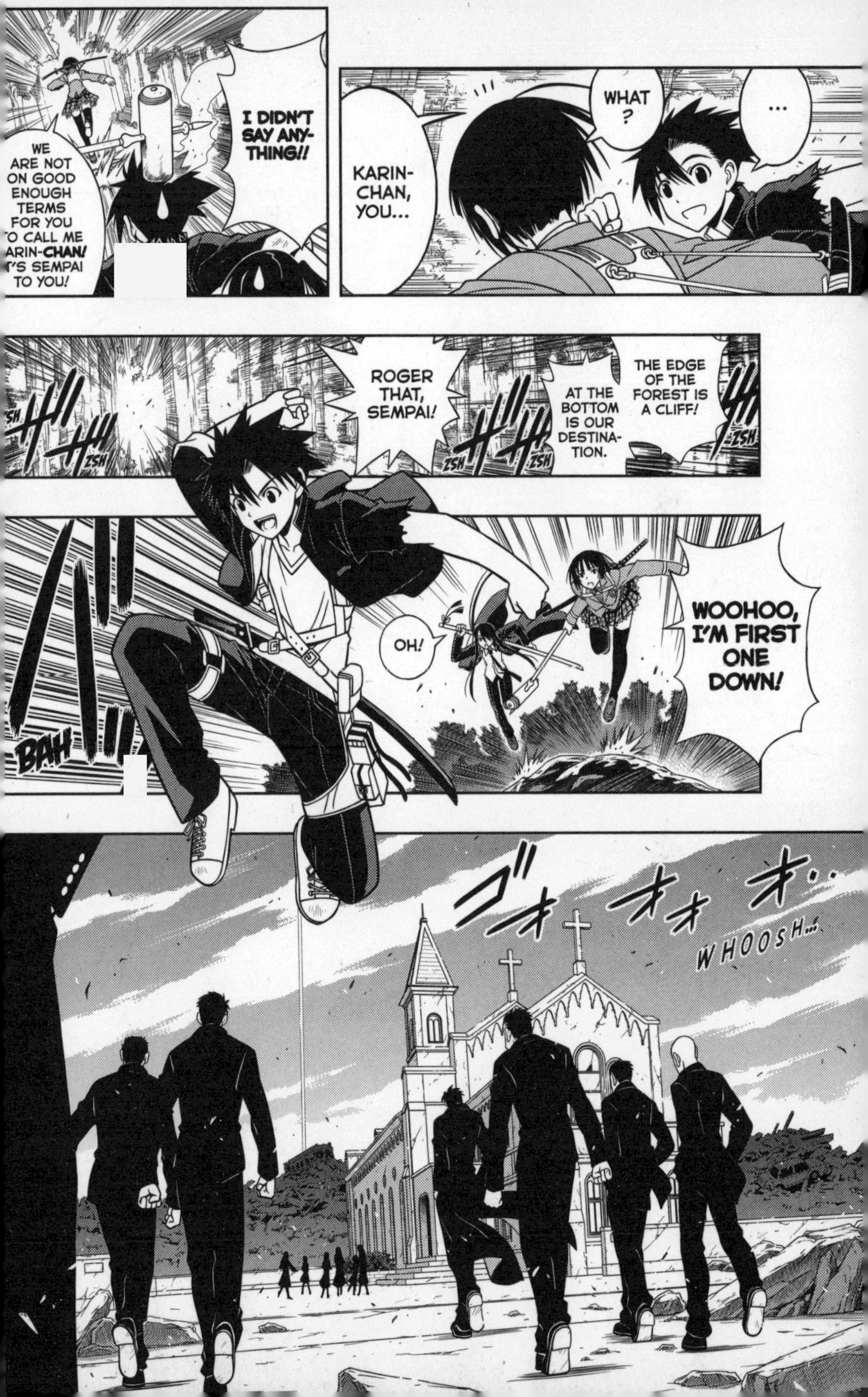
...
WHAT ?
KARIN-CHAN, YOU...
I DIDN'T SAY ANYTHING!!
WE ARE NOT ON GOOD ENOUGH TERMS FOR YOU O CALL ME ARIN-CHAN! 'S SEMPAI TO YOU!
ZSH
THE EDGE OF THE FOREST IS A CLIFF!
AT THE BOTTOM IS OUR DESTINATION.
ZSH
ZSH
ROGER THAT, SEMPAI!
ZSH
ZSH
WOOHOO, I'M FIRST ONE DOWN!
OH!
BAH
ゴォォォ..
WHOOSH...
.....

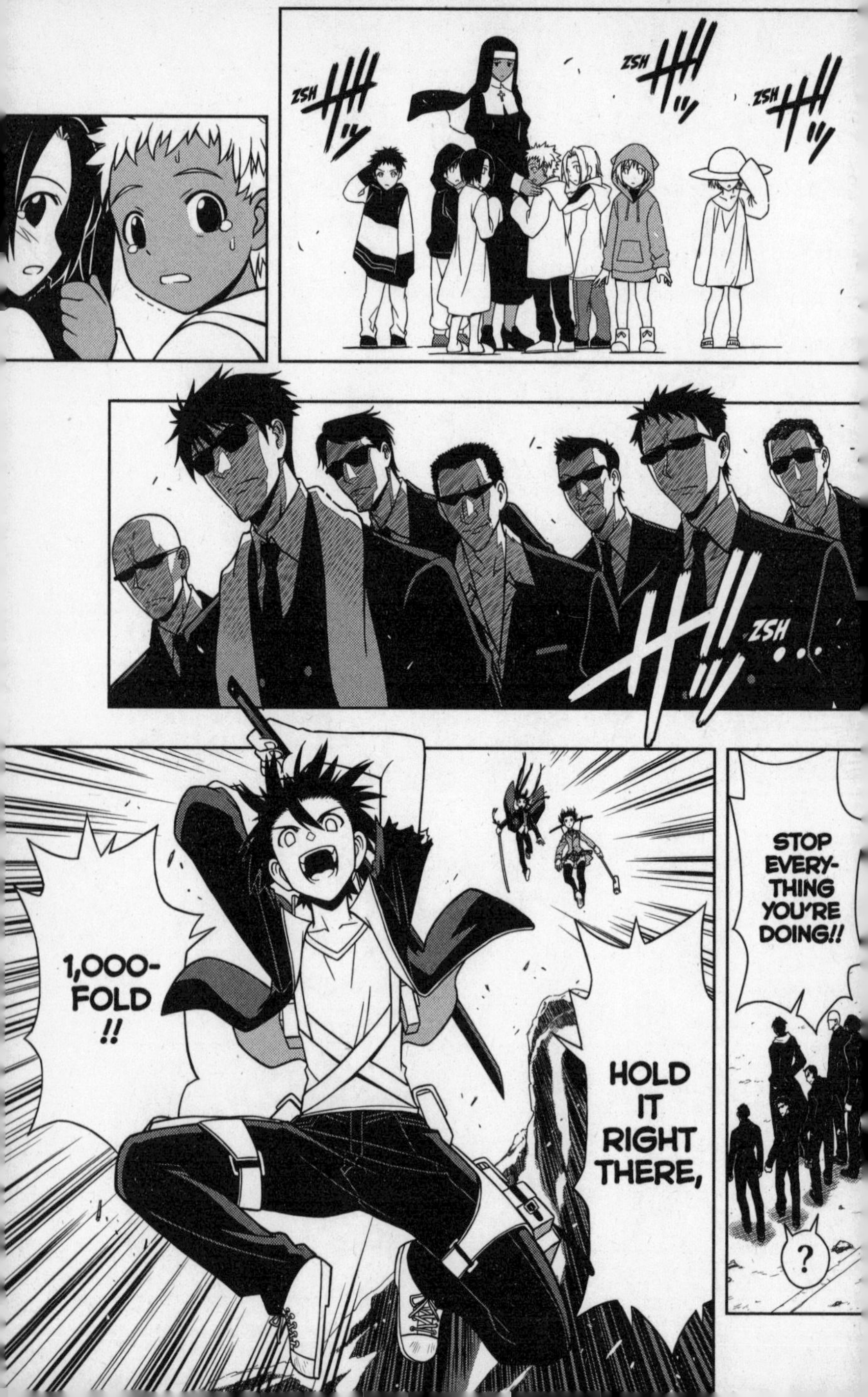
ZSH
ZSH
ZSH
ZSH...
STOP EVERYTHING YOU'RE DOING!!
?
HOLD IT RIGHT THERE,
1,000-FOLD!!

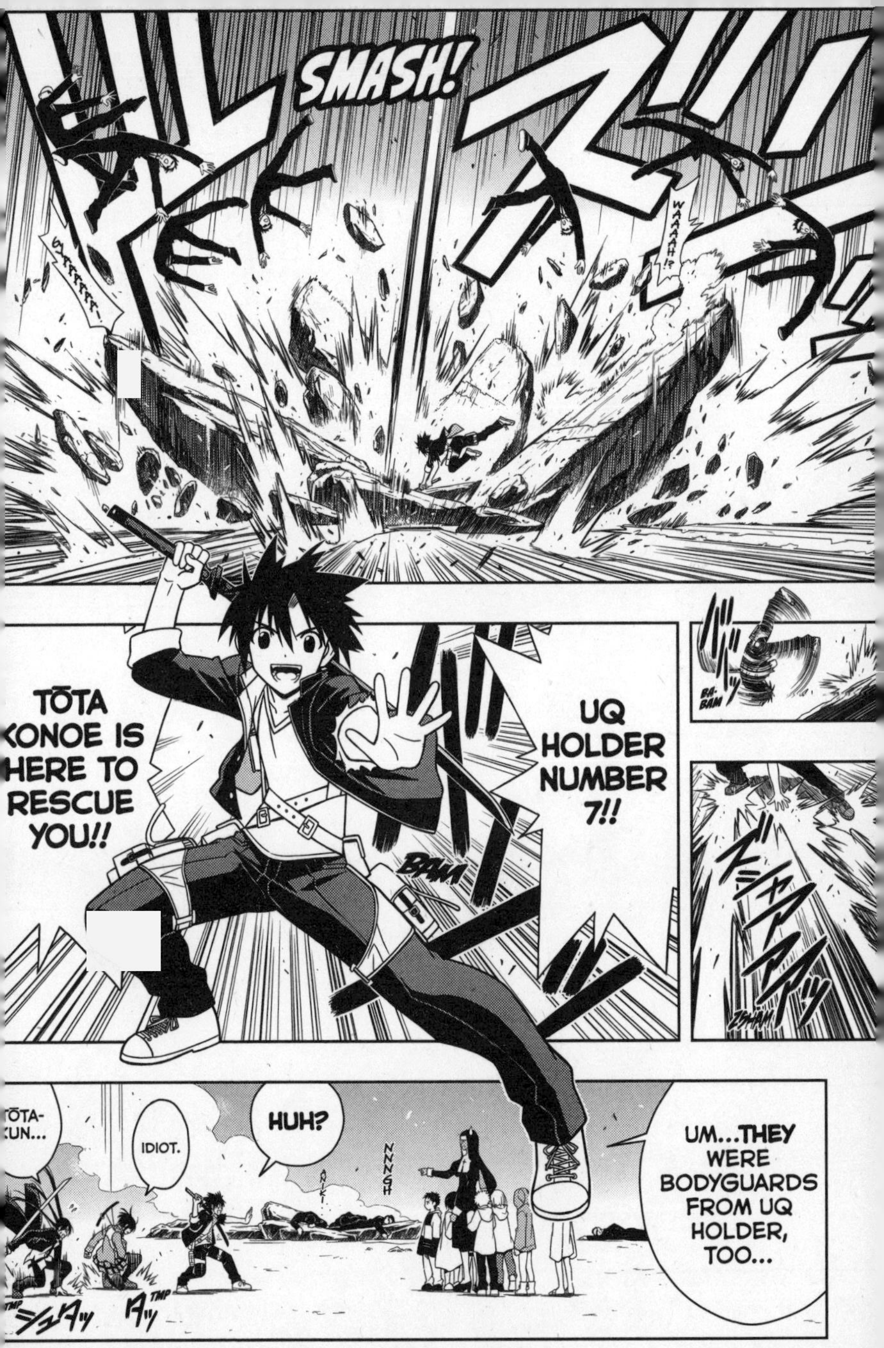
SMASH!
GYAAAAAAA!
WAAAAAH!?
BA-BAM
UQ HOLDER NUMBER 7!!
BAM
TŌTA KONOE IS HERE TO RESCUE YOU!!
UM...THEY WERE BODYGUARDS FROM UQ HOLDER, TOO...
NNNGH
ANIKI
HUH?
IDIOT.
TŌTA-KUN...
TMP
TMP

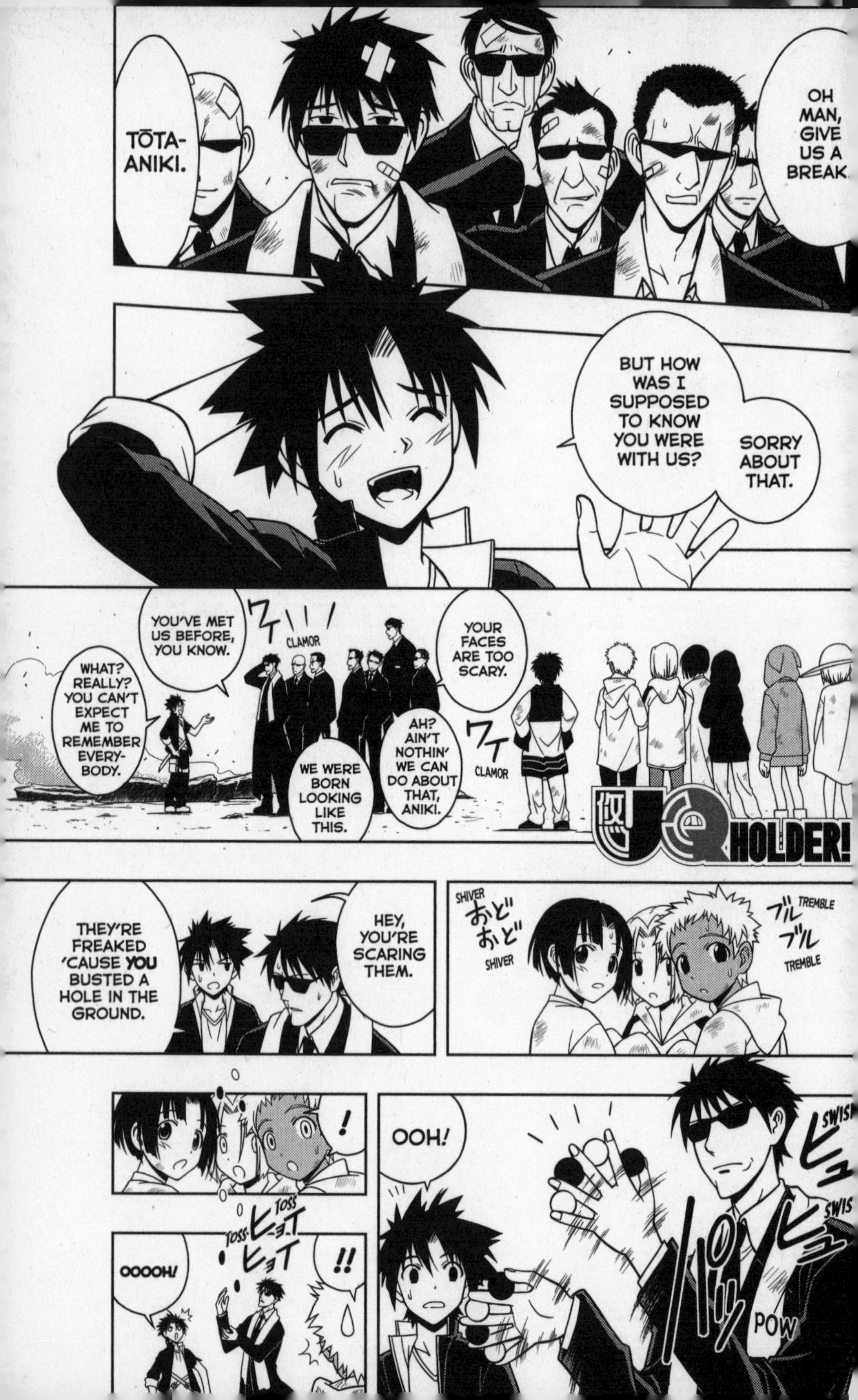
OH MAN, GIVE US A BREAK.
TŌTA-ANIKI.
SORRY ABOUT THAT.
BUT HOW WAS I SUPPOSED TO KNOW YOU WERE WITH US?
YOUR FACES ARE TOO SCARY.
ワイ
CLAMOR
AH? AIN'T NOTHIN' WE CAN DO ABOUT THAT, ANIKI.
WE WERE BORN LOOKING LIKE THIS.
ワイ
CLAMOR
YOU'VE MET US BEFORE, YOU KNOW.
WHAT? REALLY? YOU CAN'T EXPECT ME TO REMEMBER EVERY-BODY.
ブル ブル
TREMBLE
TREMBLE
おど おど
SHIVER
SHIVER
HEY, YOU'RE SCARING THEM.
THEY'RE FREAKED 'CAUSE YOU BUSTED A HOLE IN THE GROUND.
ヒュ
SWIS
ヒュ
SWIS
OOH!
パパ
POW
!
!!
ヒョイ ヒョイ
TOSS
TOSS
OOOOH!

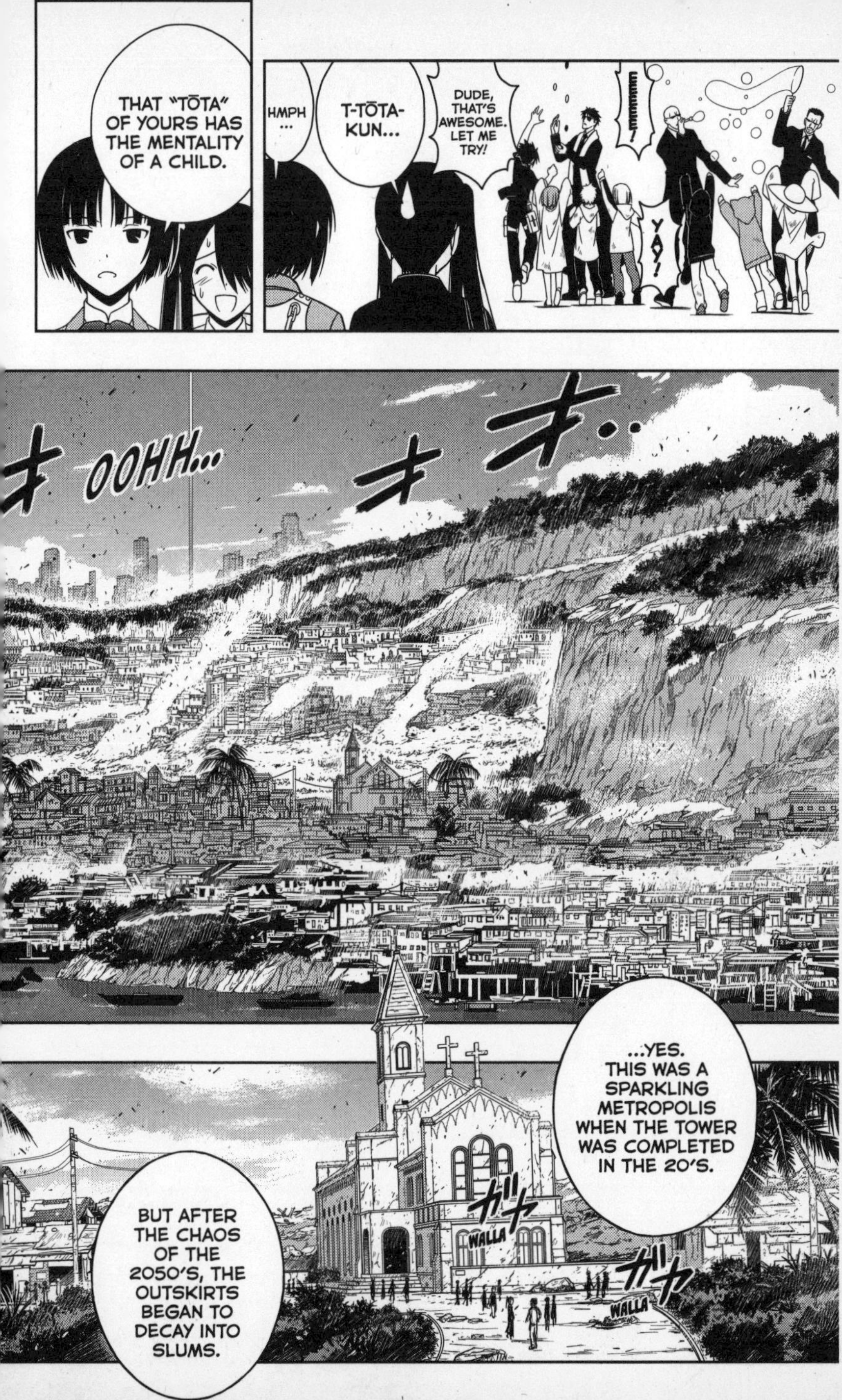
DUDE, THAT'S AWESOME. LET ME TRY!
T-TŌTA-KUN...
HMPH ...
YAY!
THAT "TŌTA" OF YOURS HAS THE MENTALITY OF A CHILD.
OOHH...
...YES. THIS WAS A SPARKLING METROPOLIS WHEN THE TOWER WAS COMPLETED IN THE 20'S.
WALLA
BUT AFTER THE CHAOS OF THE 2050'S, THE OUTSKIRTS BEGAN TO DECAY INTO SLUMS.
WALLA

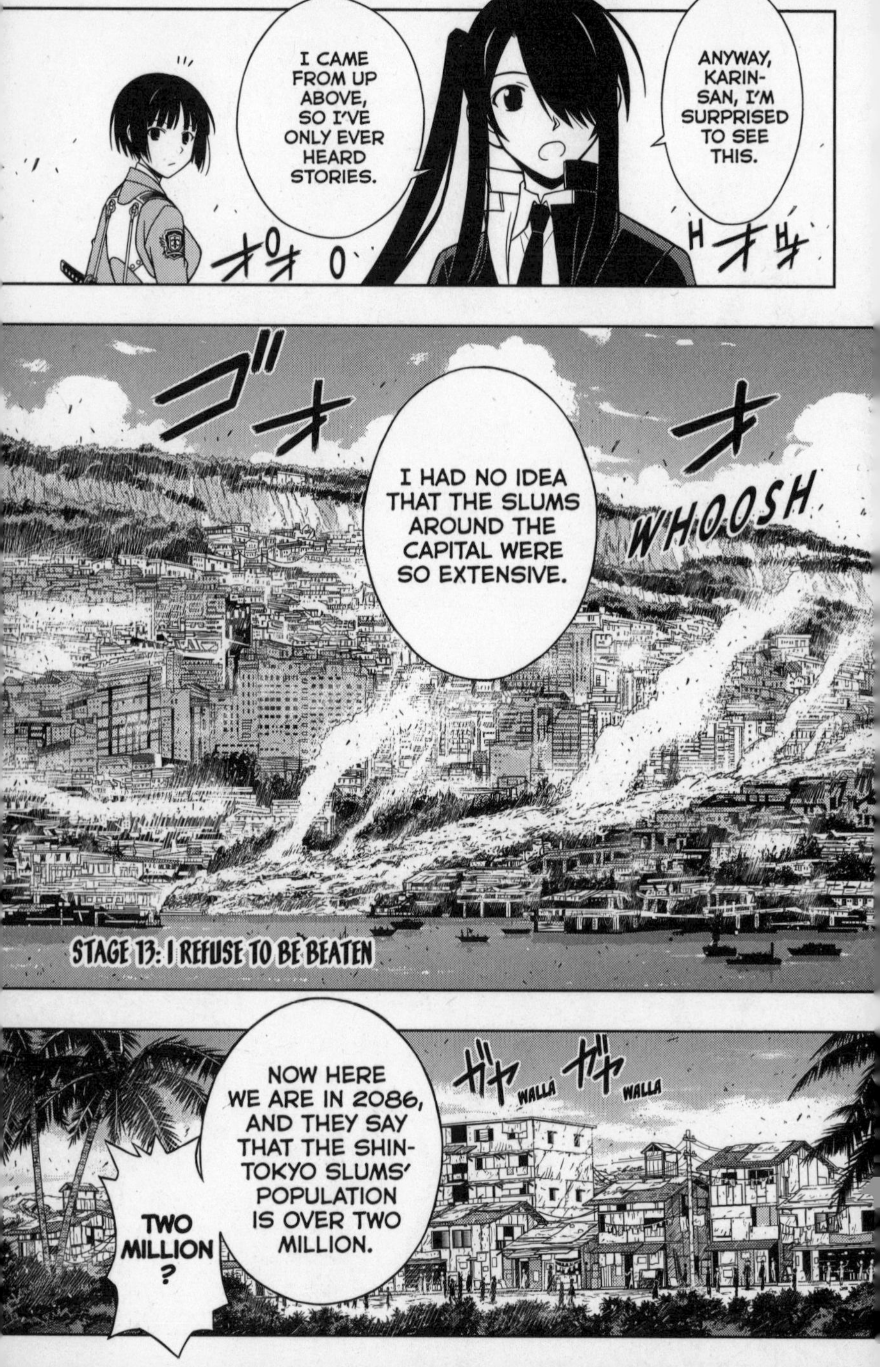
ANYWAY, KARIN-SAN, I'M SURPRISED TO SEE THIS.
I CAME FROM UP ABOVE, SO I'VE ONLY EVER HEARD STORIES.
I HAD NO IDEA THAT THE SLUMS AROUND THE CAPITAL WERE SO EXTENSIVE.
WHOOSH
STAGE 13: I REFUSE TO BE BEATEN
WALLA
WALLA
NOW HERE WE ARE IN 2086, AND THEY SAY THAT THE SHIN-TOKYO SLUMS' POPULATION IS OVER TWO MILLION.
TWO MILLION?

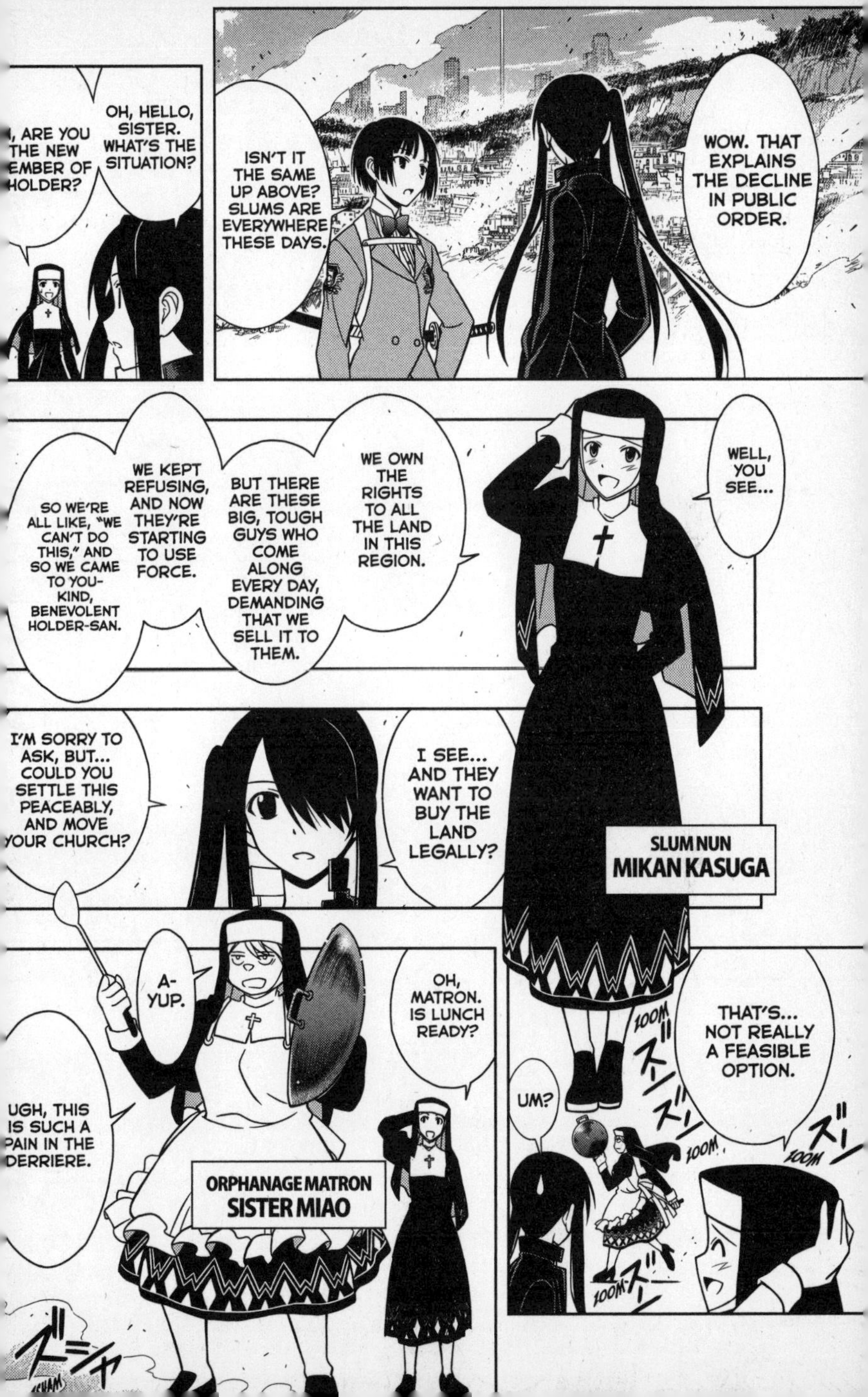
WOW. THAT EXPLAINS THE DECLINE IN PUBLIC ORDER.
ISN'T IT THE SAME UP ABOVE? SLUMS ARE EVERYWHERE THESE DAYS.
OH, HELLO, SISTER. WHAT'S THE SITUATION?
, ARE YOU THE NEW EMBER OF HOLDER?
WELL, YOU SEE...
WE OWN THE RIGHTS TO ALL THE LAND IN THIS REGION.
BUT THERE ARE THESE BIG, TOUGH GUYS WHO COME ALONG EVERY DAY, DEMANDING THAT WE SELL IT TO THEM.
WE KEPT REFUSING, AND NOW THEY'RE STARTING TO USE FORCE.
SO WE'RE ALL LIKE, "WE CAN'T DO THIS," AND SO WE CAME TO YOU-KIND, BENEVOLENT HOLDER-SAN.
SLUM NUN
MIKAN KASUGA
I SEE... AND THEY WANT TO BUY THE LAND LEGALLY?
I'M SORRY TO ASK, BUT... COULD YOU SETTLE THIS PEACEABLY, AND MOVE YOUR CHURCH?
THAT'S... NOT REALLY A FEASIBLE OPTION.
ZOOM
ZOOM
ZOOM
ZOOM
UM?
OH, MATRON. IS LUNCH READY?
A-YUP.
ORPHANAGE MATRON
SISTER MIAO
UGH, THIS IS SUCH A PAIN IN THE DERRIERE.

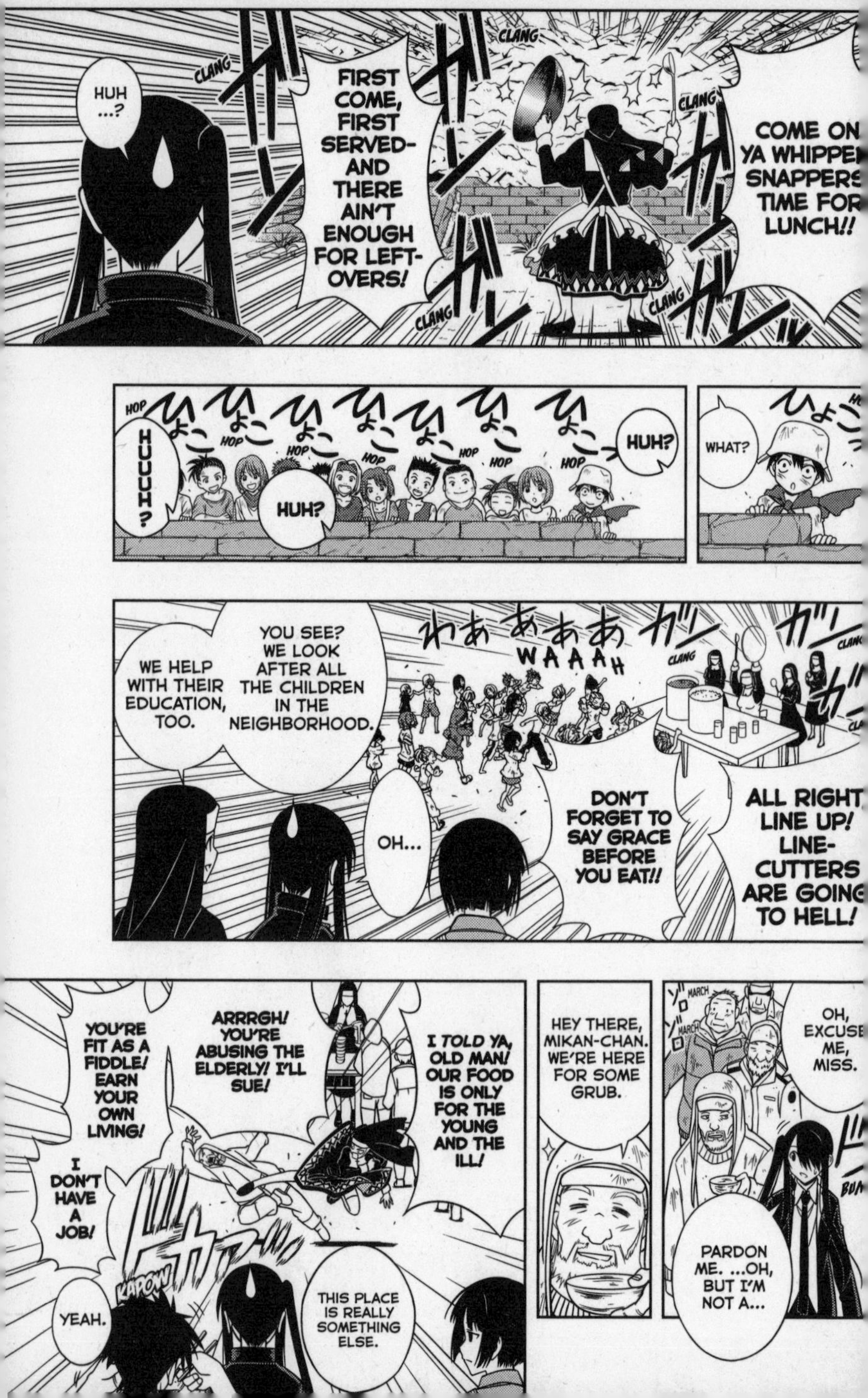
COME ON YA WHIPPER SNAPPERS TIME FOR LUNCH!!
CLANG
CLANG
CLANG
CLANG
CLANG
FIRST COME, FIRST SERVED- AND THERE AIN'T ENOUGH FOR LEFT-OVERS!
HUH ...?
WHAT?
HUH?
HOP
HOP
HOP
HOP
HOP
HUH?
HUUUH?
ALL RIGHT LINE UP! LINE-CUTTERS ARE GOING TO HELL!
CLANG
DON'T FORGET TO SAY GRACE BEFORE YOU EAT!!
WAAAH
YOU SEE? WE LOOK AFTER ALL THE CHILDREN IN THE NEIGHBORHOOD.
WE HELP WITH THEIR EDUCATION, TOO.
OH...
OH, EXCUSE ME, MISS.
MARCH
MARCH
PARDON ME. ...OH, BUT I'M NOT A...
HEY THERE, MIKAN-CHAN. WE'RE HERE FOR SOME GRUB.
I *TOLD* YA, OLD MAN! OUR FOOD IS ONLY FOR THE YOUNG AND THE ILL!
ARRRGH! YOU'RE ABUSING THE ELDERLY! I'LL SUE!
YOU'RE FIT AS A FIDDLE! EARN YOUR OWN LIVING!
I DON'T HAVE A JOB!
KAPOW
THIS PLACE IS REALLY SOMETHING ELSE.
YEAH.

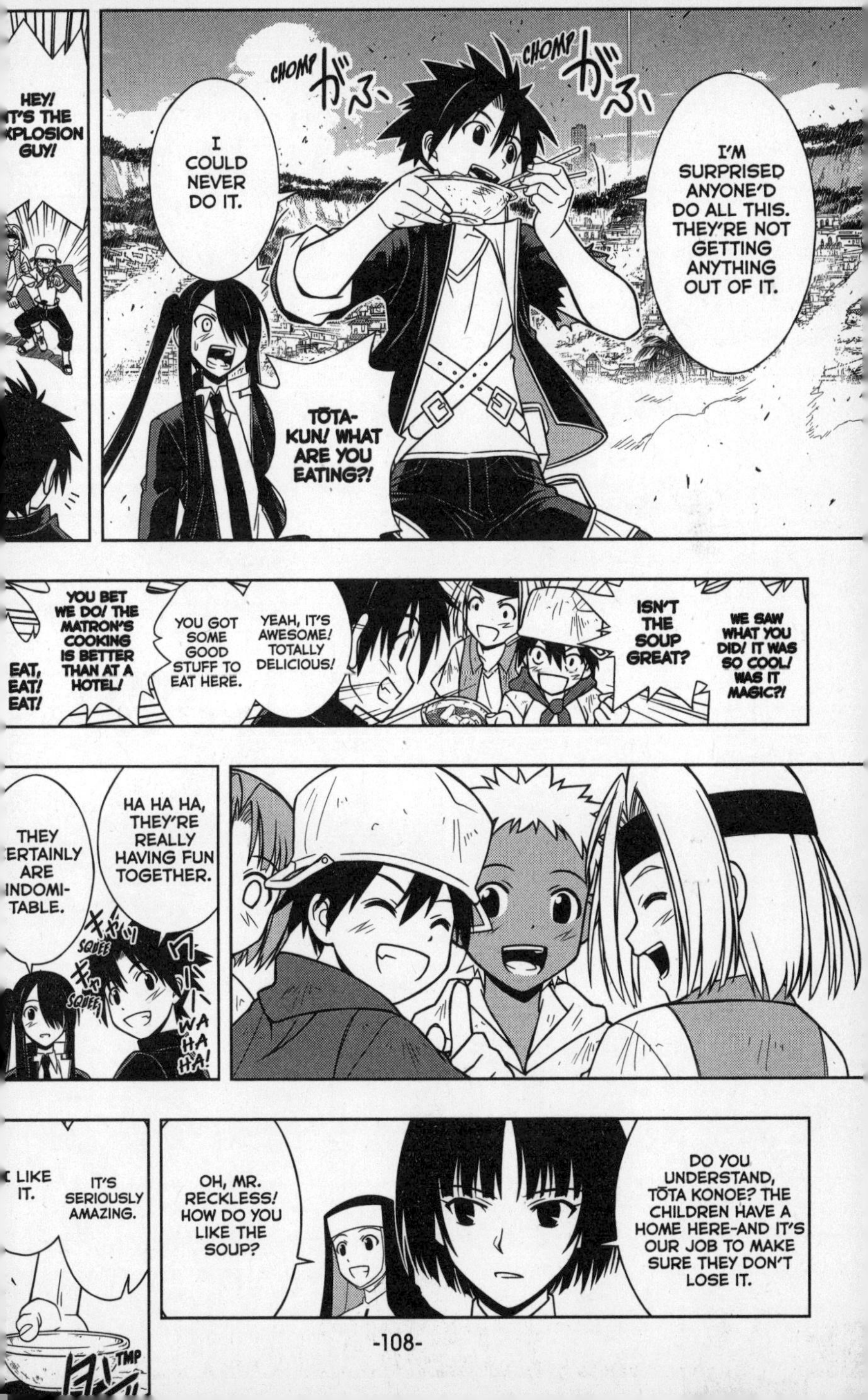
I'M SURPRISED ANYONE'D DO ALL THIS. THEY'RE NOT GETTING ANYTHING OUT OF IT.
CHOMP がふ
CHOMP がふ
I COULD NEVER DO IT.
TŌTA-KUN! WHAT ARE YOU EATING?!
HEY! T'S THE XPLOSION GUY!
WE SAW WHAT YOU DID! IT WAS SO COOL! WAS IT MAGIC?!
ISN'T THE SOUP GREAT?
YEAH, IT'S AWESOME! TOTALLY DELICIOUS!
YOU GOT SOME GOOD STUFF TO EAT HERE.
YOU BET WE DO! THE MATRON'S COOKING IS BETTER THAN AT A HOTEL!
EAT, EAT! EAT!
HA HA HA, THEY'RE REALLY HAVING FUN TOGETHER.
WA HA HA HA!
SQUEE
SQUEE
THEY ERTAINLY ARE INDOMI-TABLE.
DO YOU UNDERSTAND, TŌTA KONOE? THE CHILDREN HAVE A HOME HERE-AND IT'S OUR JOB TO MAKE SURE THEY DON'T LOSE IT.
OH, MR. RECKLESS! HOW DO YOU LIKE THE SOUP?
IT'S SERIOUSLY AMAZING.
LIKE IT.
TMP

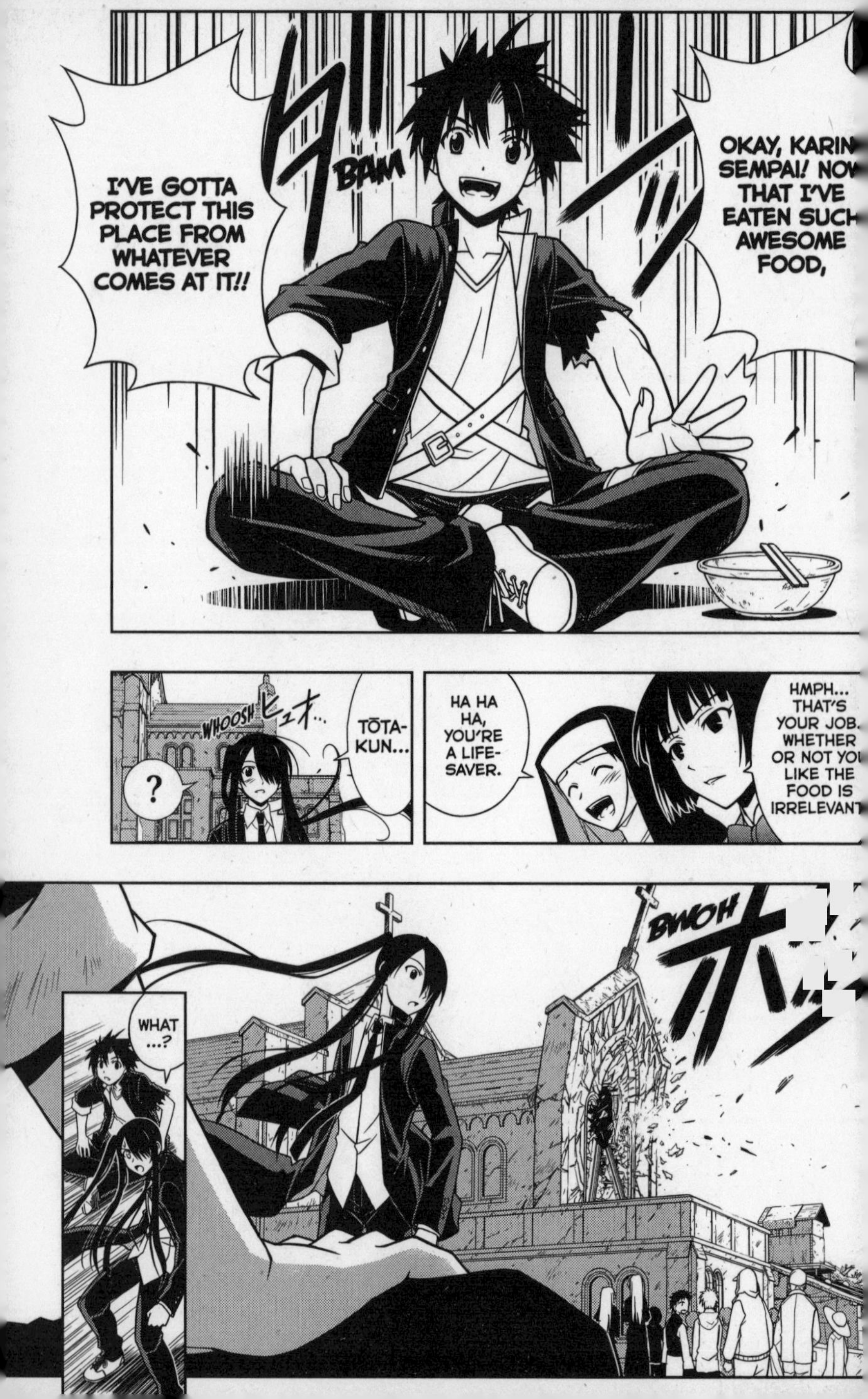
OKAY, KARIN SEMPAI! NOW THAT I'VE EATEN SUCH AWESOME FOOD,
BAM
I'VE GOTTA PROTECT THIS PLACE FROM WHATEVER COMES AT IT!!
HMPH... THAT'S YOUR JOB. WHETHER OR NOT YOU LIKE THE FOOD IS IRRELEVANT
HA HA HA, YOU'RE A LIFE-SAVER.
WHOOSH
TŌTA-KUN...
?
BWOH
WHAT ...?

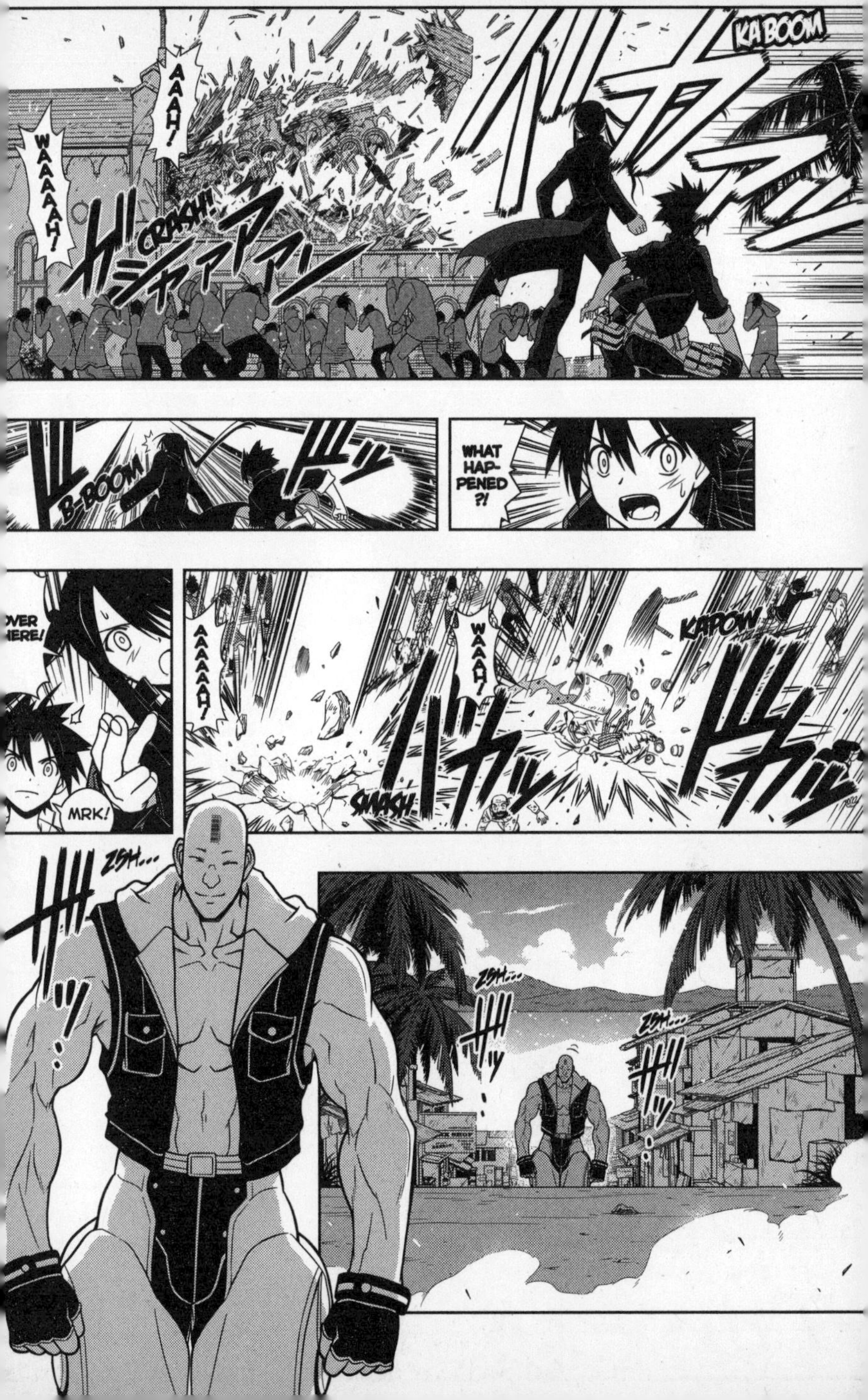
KA BOOM
AAAH!
WAAAAAAH!
CRASH!
WHAT HAP-PENED?!
B-BOOM
KAPOW
WAAAH!
AAAAAAH!
SMASH
OVER HERE!
MRK!
ZSH...
ZSH...
ZSH...

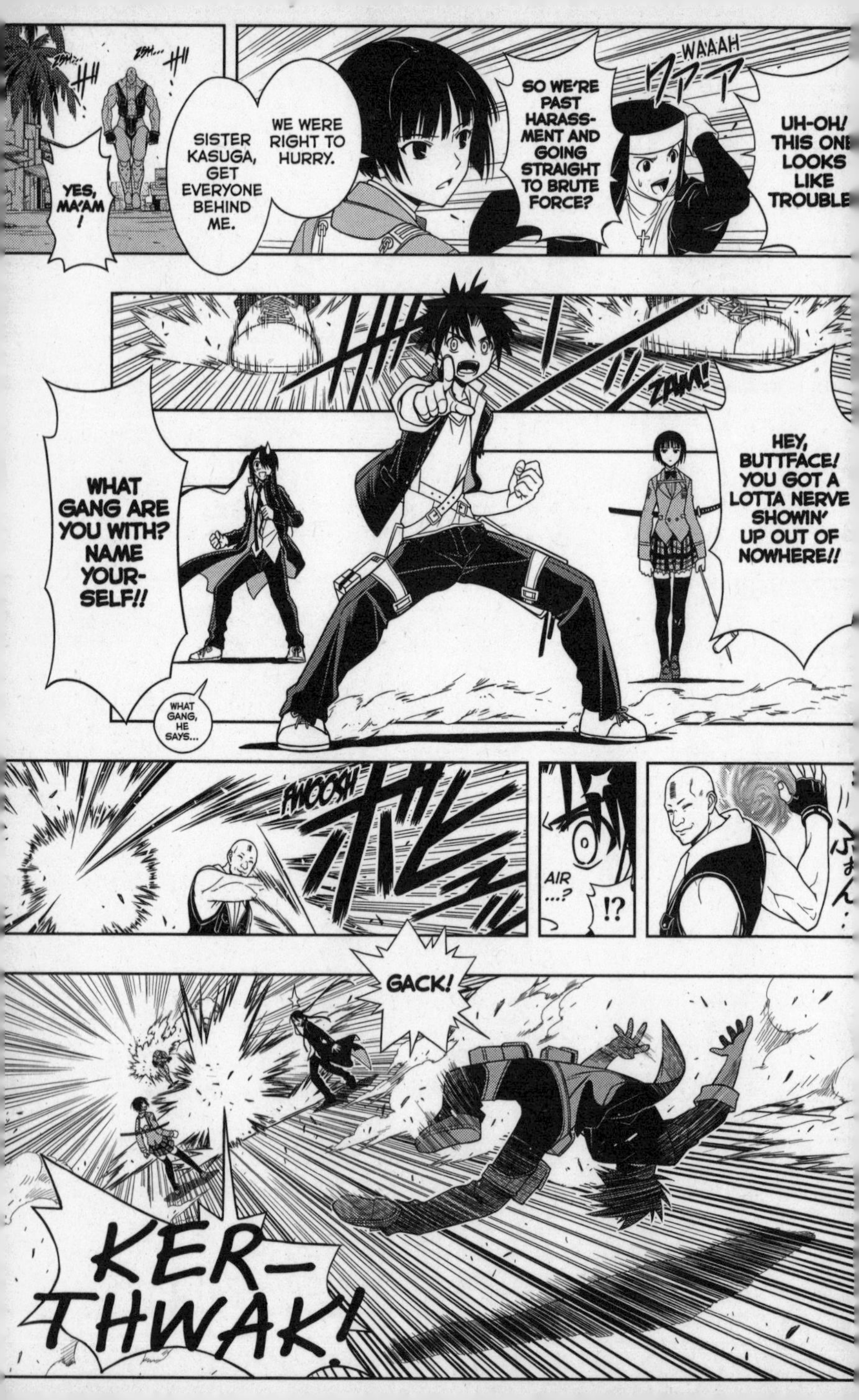

WAAAH
UH-OH! THIS ONE LOOKS LIKE TROUBLE
SO WE'RE PAST HARASS-MENT AND GOING STRAIGHT TO BRUTE FORCE?
WE WERE RIGHT TO HURRY.
SISTER KASUGA, GET EVERYONE BEHIND ME.
ZSH...
YES, MA'AM!
ZAM!
HEY, BUTTFACE! YOU GOT A LOTTA NERVE SHOWIN' UP OUT OF NOWHERE!!
WHAT GANG ARE YOU WITH? NAME YOUR-SELF!!
WHAT GANG, HE SAYS...
!?
AIR ...?
FWOOSH
GACK!
KER-THWAK!

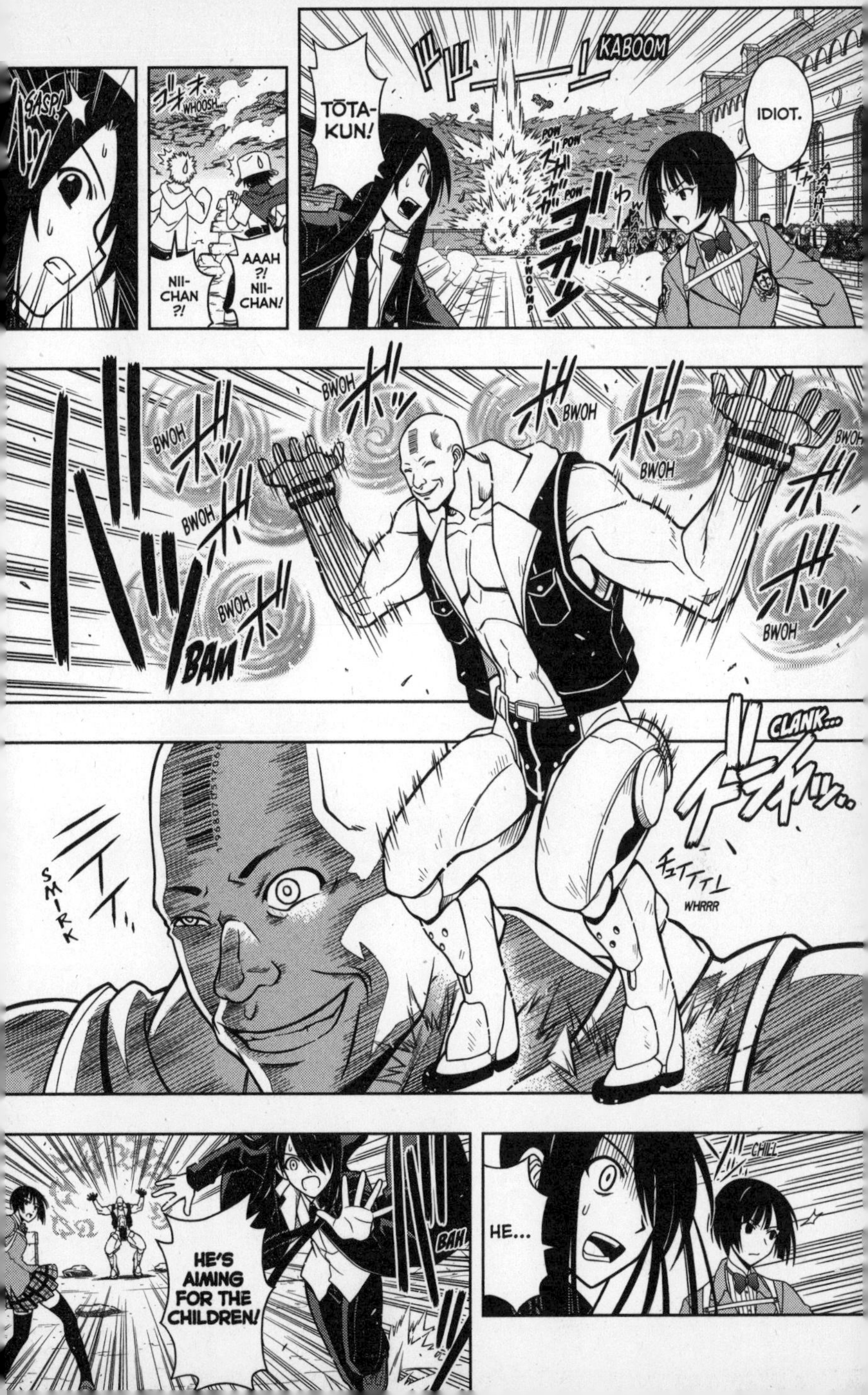
KABOOM
IDIOT.
WAAAH!
POW POW
POW
TŌTA-KUN!
FWOOMP
WHOOSH...
AAAH ?! NII-CHAN!
NII-CHAN ?!
GASP!
BWOH
BWOH
BWOH
BWOH
BWOH
BWOH
BWOH
BWOH
BAM
CLANK...
WHRRR
SMIRK
CHILL
HE...
BAH
HE'S AIMING FOR THE CHILDREN!

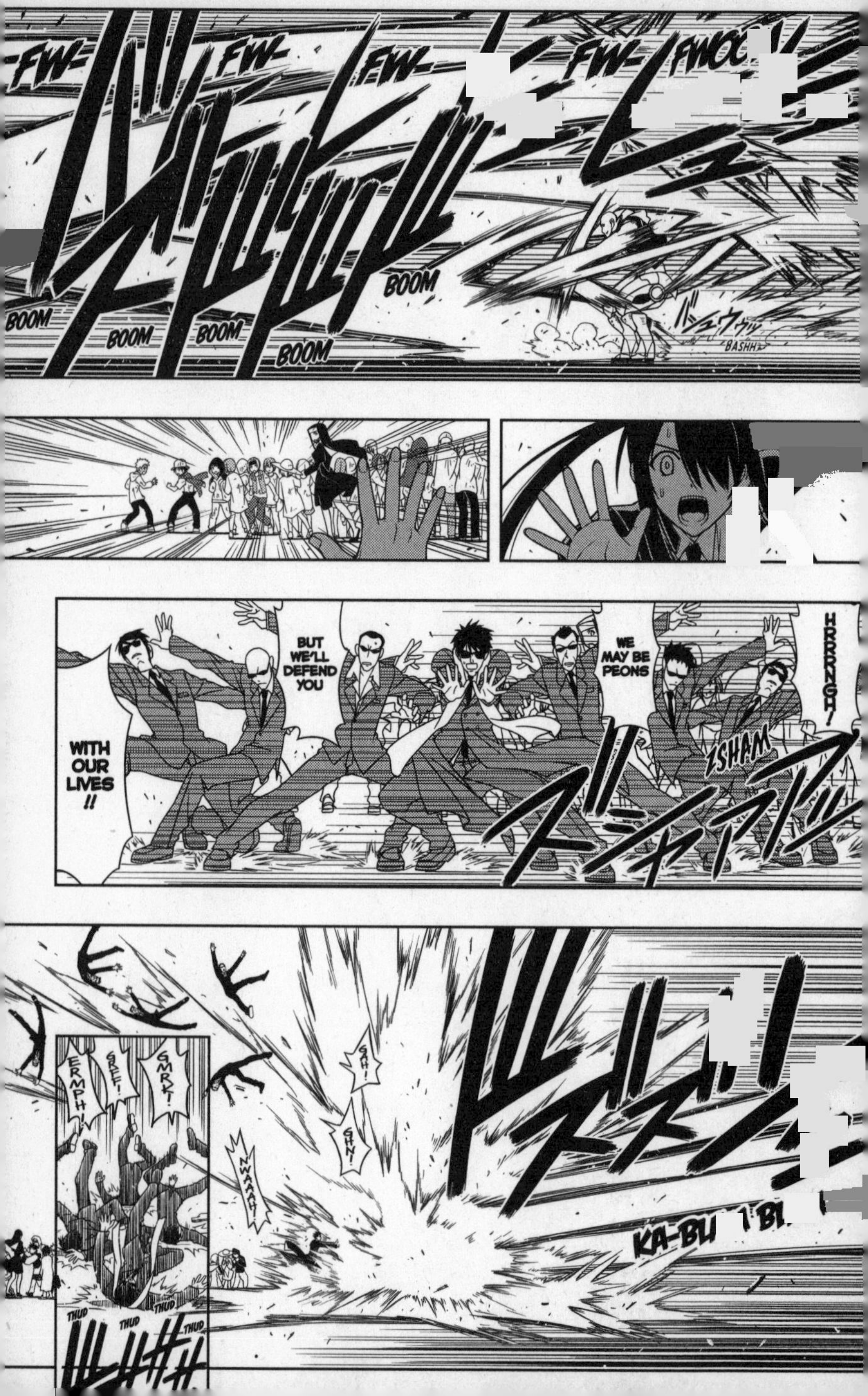

FWOO
FW-
FW-
FW-
FW-
BASHH
BOOM
BOOM
BOOM
BOOM
BOOM
HRRRNGH!
ZSHAM
WE MAY BE PEONS
BUT WE'LL DEFEND YOU
WITH OUR LIVES!!
GAH!
GHN!
NWAAAH!
GMRK!
GREF!
ERMPH!
THUD
THUD
THUD
THUD

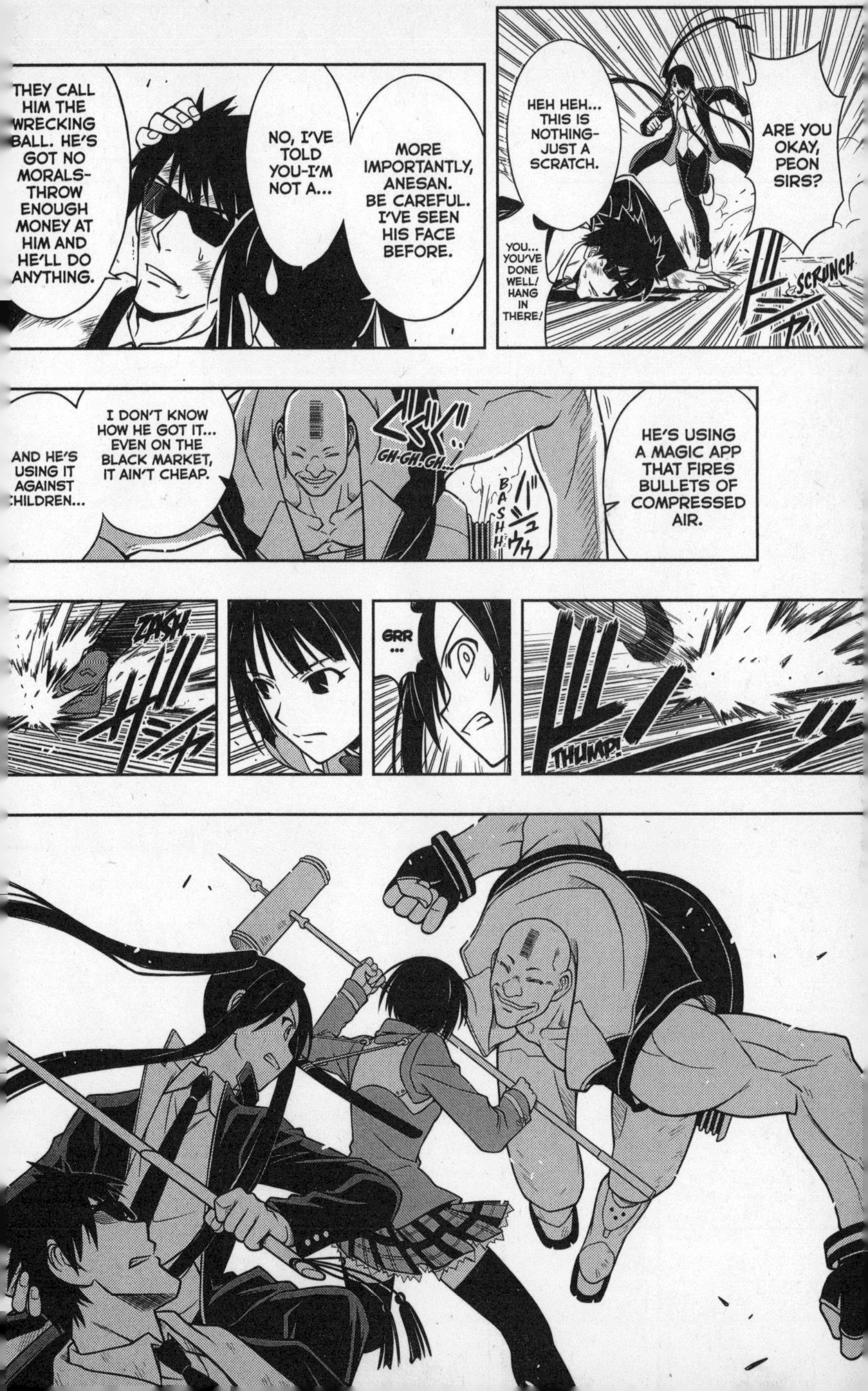
ARE YOU OKAY, PEON SIRS?
HEH HEH... THIS IS NOTHING–JUST A SCRATCH.
YOU... YOU'VE DONE WELL! HANG IN THERE!
SCRUNCH
MORE IMPORTANTLY, ANESAN. BE CAREFUL. I'VE SEEN HIS FACE BEFORE.
NO, I'VE TOLD YOU–I'M NOT A...
THEY CALL HIM THE WRECKING BALL. HE'S GOT NO MORALS–THROW ENOUGH MONEY AT HIM AND HE'LL DO ANYTHING.
HE'S USING A MAGIC APP THAT FIRES BULLETS OF COMPRESSED AIR.
BASHH
GH-GH-GH...
I DON'T KNOW HOW HE GOT IT... EVEN ON THE BLACK MARKET, IT AIN'T CHEAP.
AND HE'S USING IT AGAINST CHILDREN...
THUMP!
GRR...
ZASH

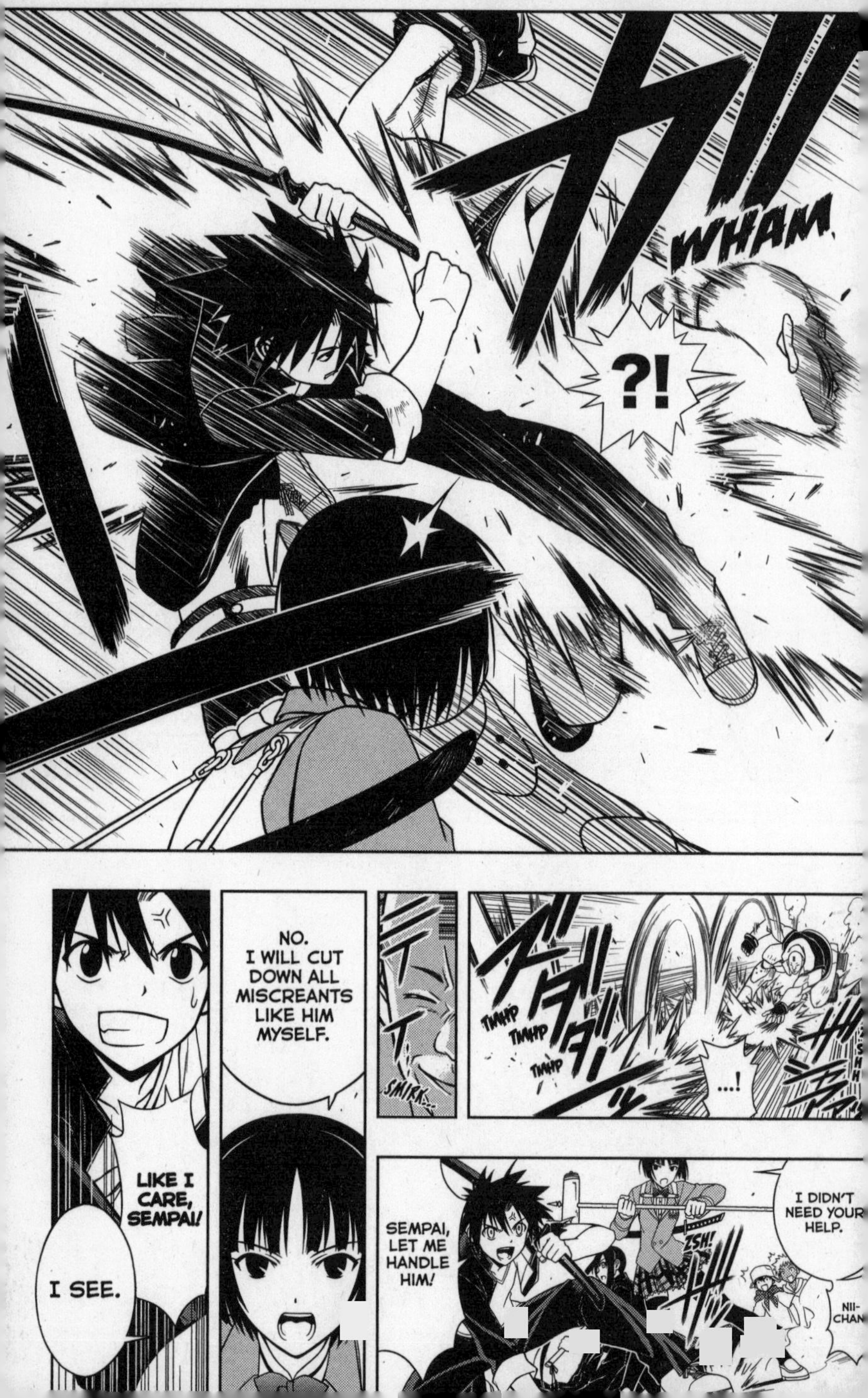

WHAM
?!
TWHP
TWHP
TWHP
...!
SMIRK...
NO. I WILL CUT DOWN ALL MISCREANTS LIKE HIM MYSELF.
I DIDN'T NEED YOUR HELP.
NII-CHAN
SEMPAI, LET ME HANDLE HIM!
ZSH!
I SEE.
LIKE I CARE, SEMPAI!

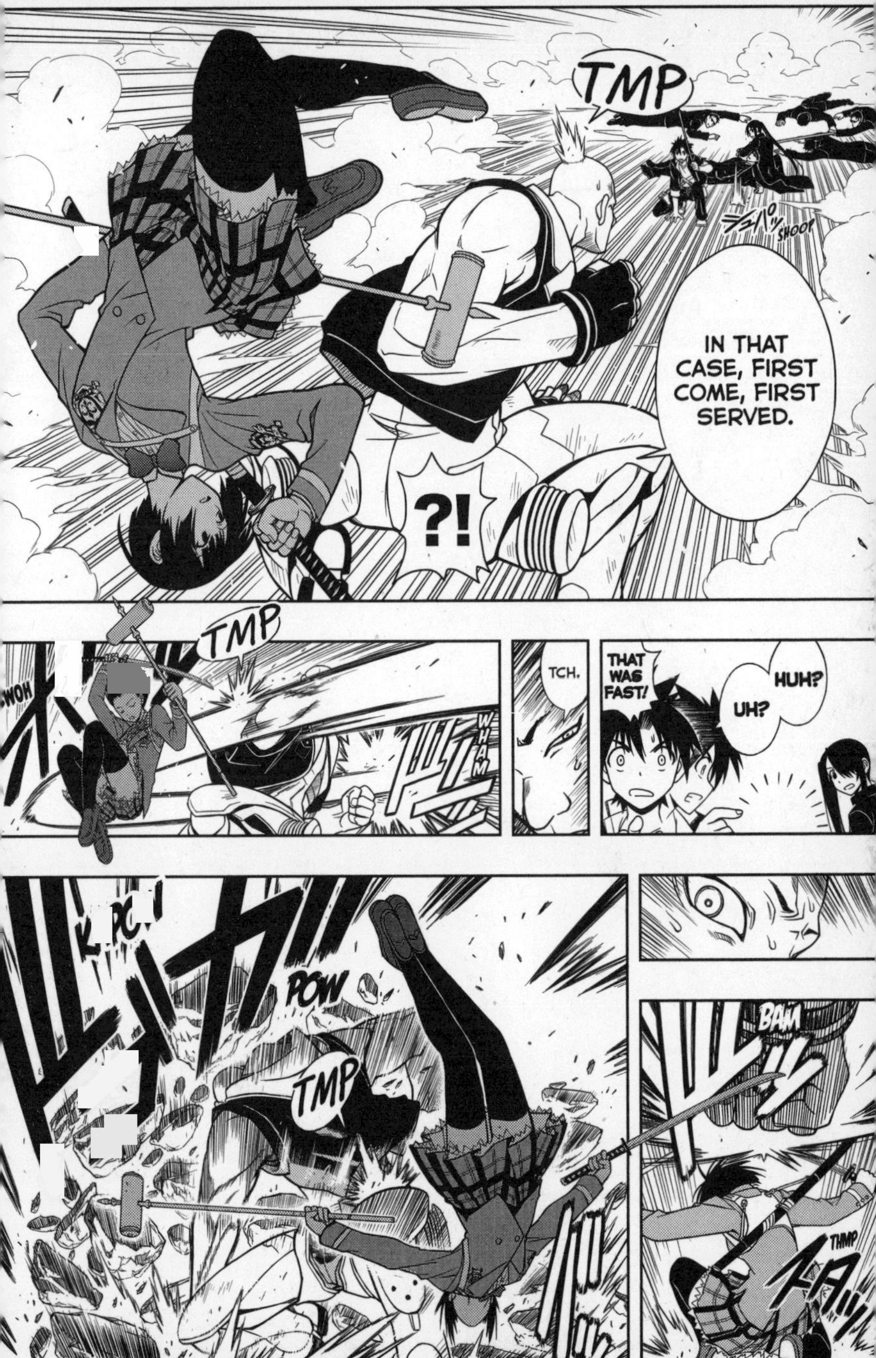
TMP
SHOOP
IN THAT CASE, FIRST COME, FIRST SERVED.
?!
HUH?
UH?
THAT WAS FAST!
TCH.
TMP
WHAM
BAM
THMP
POW
TMP
BAH

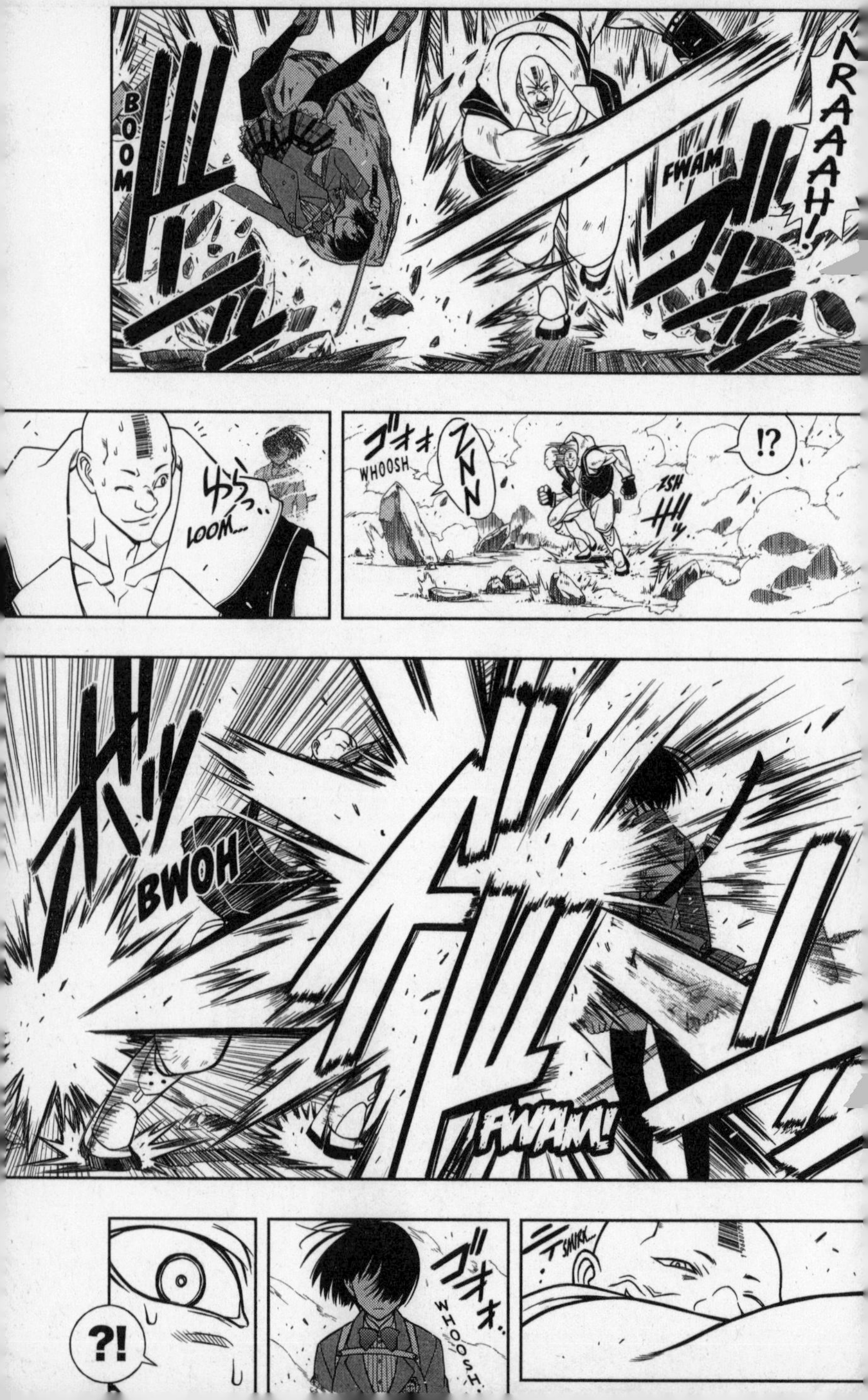
NRAAAAH!
FWAM
BOOM
!?
ZNN
WHOOSH
ZSH
LOOM...
BWOH
FWAM!
SNIKK...
WHOOSH...
?!

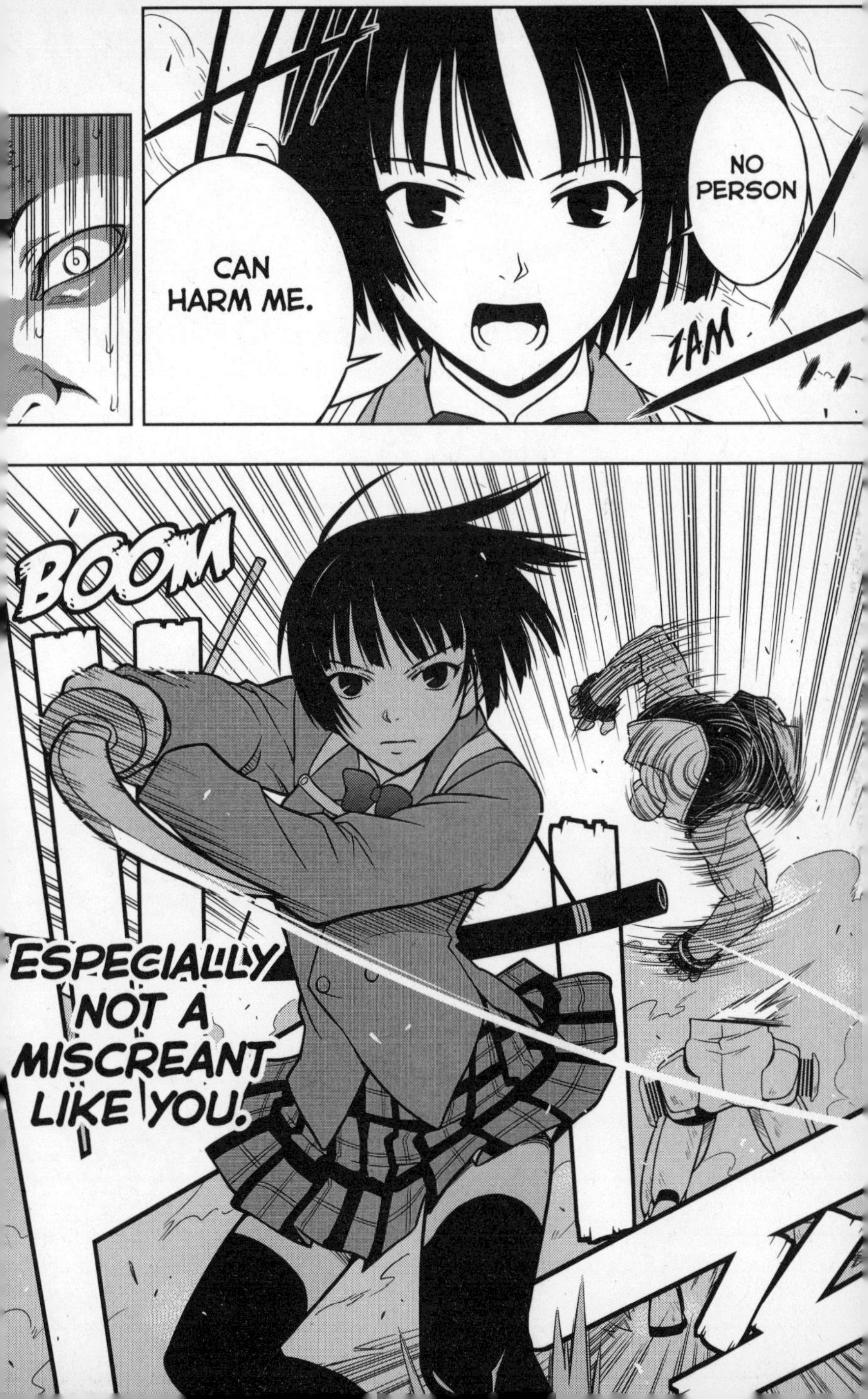
NO PERSON
CAN HARM ME.
ZAM
BOOM
ESPECIALLY NOT A MISCREANT LIKE YOU.

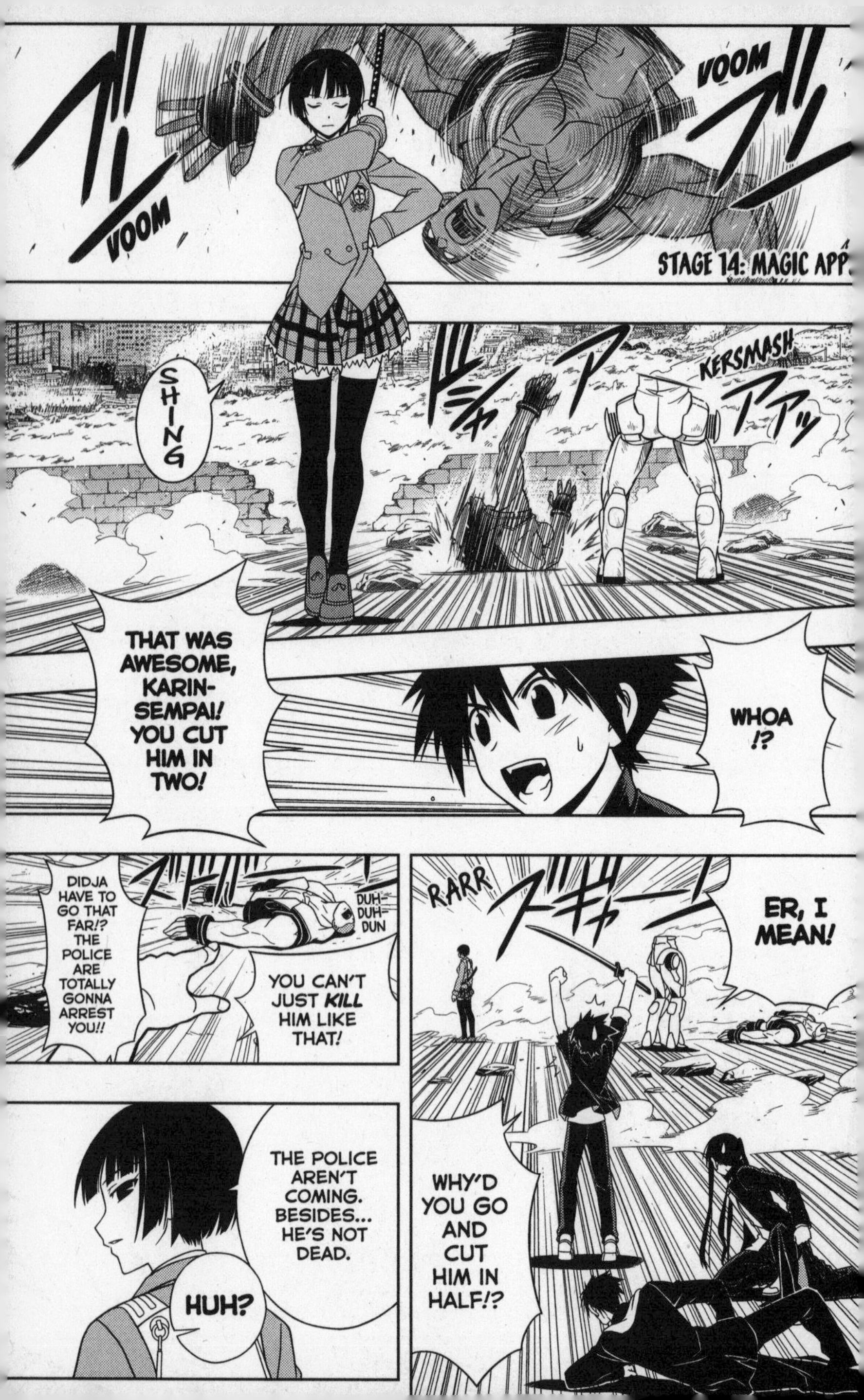
VOOM
VOOM
STAGE 14: MAGIC APP
KERSMASH
SHING
WHOA!?
THAT WAS AWESOME, KARIN-SEMPAI! YOU CUT HIM IN TWO!
RARR
ER, I MEAN!
WHY'D YOU GO AND CUT HIM IN HALF!?
DUH-DUH-DUN
YOU CAN'T JUST *KILL* HIM LIKE THAT!
DIDJA HAVE TO GO THAT FAR!? THE POLICE ARE TOTALLY GONNA ARREST YOU!!
THE POLICE AREN'T COMING. BESIDES... HE'S NOT DEAD.
HUH?

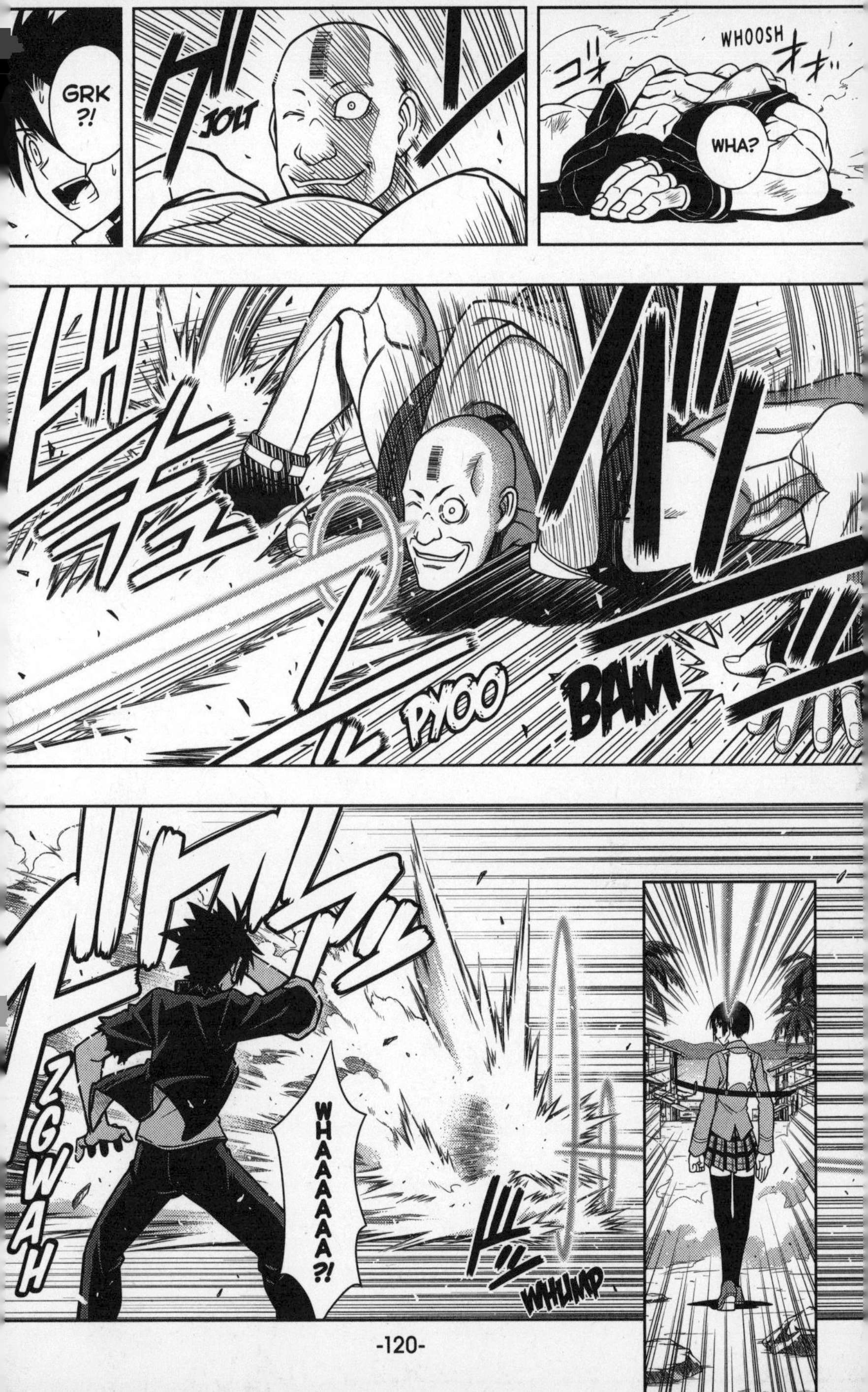
WHOOSH
WHA?
JOLT
GRK ?!
BAM
PYOO
WHUMP
WHAAAAAAA?!
ZGWAH

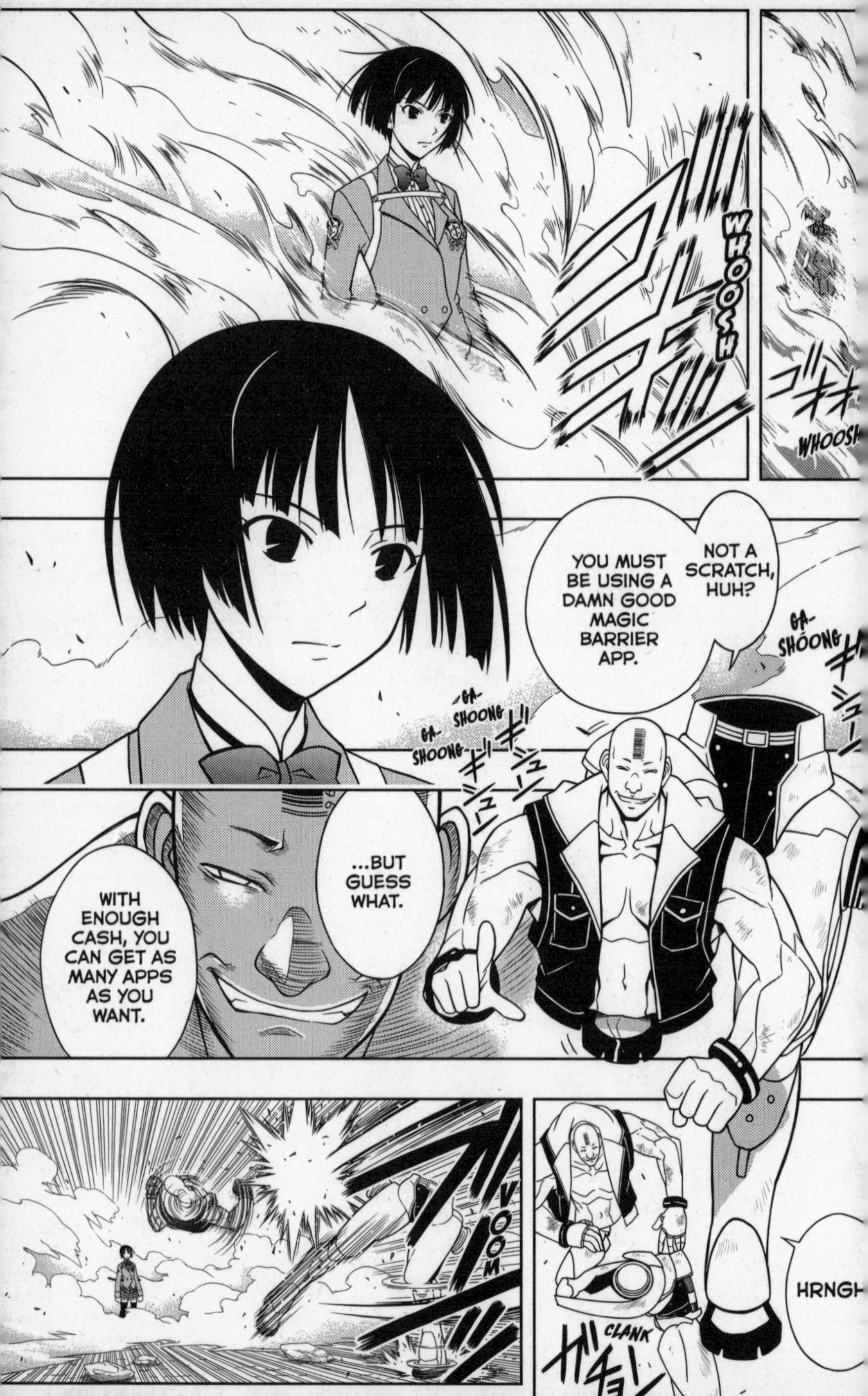
WHOOSH
WHOOSH
NOT A SCRATCH, HUH?
YOU MUST BE USING A DAMN GOOD MAGIC BARRIER APP.
GA-SHOONG
GA-SHOONG
GA-SHOONG
...BUT GUESS WHAT.
WITH ENOUGH CASH, YOU CAN GET AS MANY APPS AS YOU WANT.
HRNGH
CLANK
VOOM

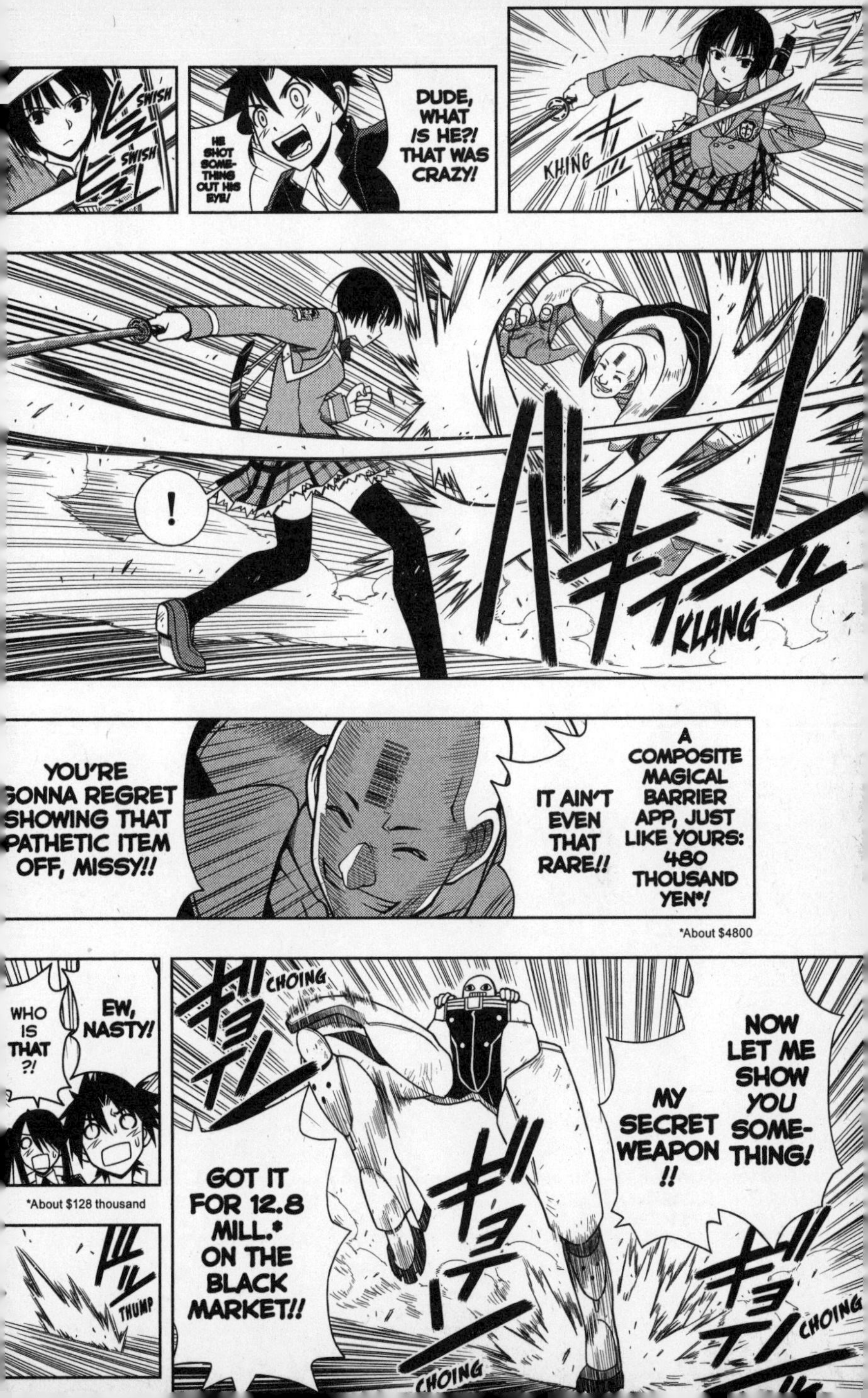
KHING
DUDE, WHAT IS HE?! THAT WAS CRAZY!
HE SHOT SOME-THING OUT HIS EYE!
SWISH
SWISH
KLANG
!
A COMPOSITE MAGICAL BARRIER APP, JUST LIKE YOURS: 480 THOUSAND YEN*!
IT AIN'T EVEN THAT RARE!!
YOU'RE GONNA REGRET SHOWING THAT PATHETIC ITEM OFF, MISSY!!
*About $4800
NOW LET ME SHOW YOU SOME-THING!
MY SECRET WEAPON!!
GOT IT FOR 12.8 MILL.* ON THE BLACK MARKET!!
CHOING
CHOING
CHOING
EW, NASTY!
WHO IS THAT?!
*About $128 thousand
THUMP

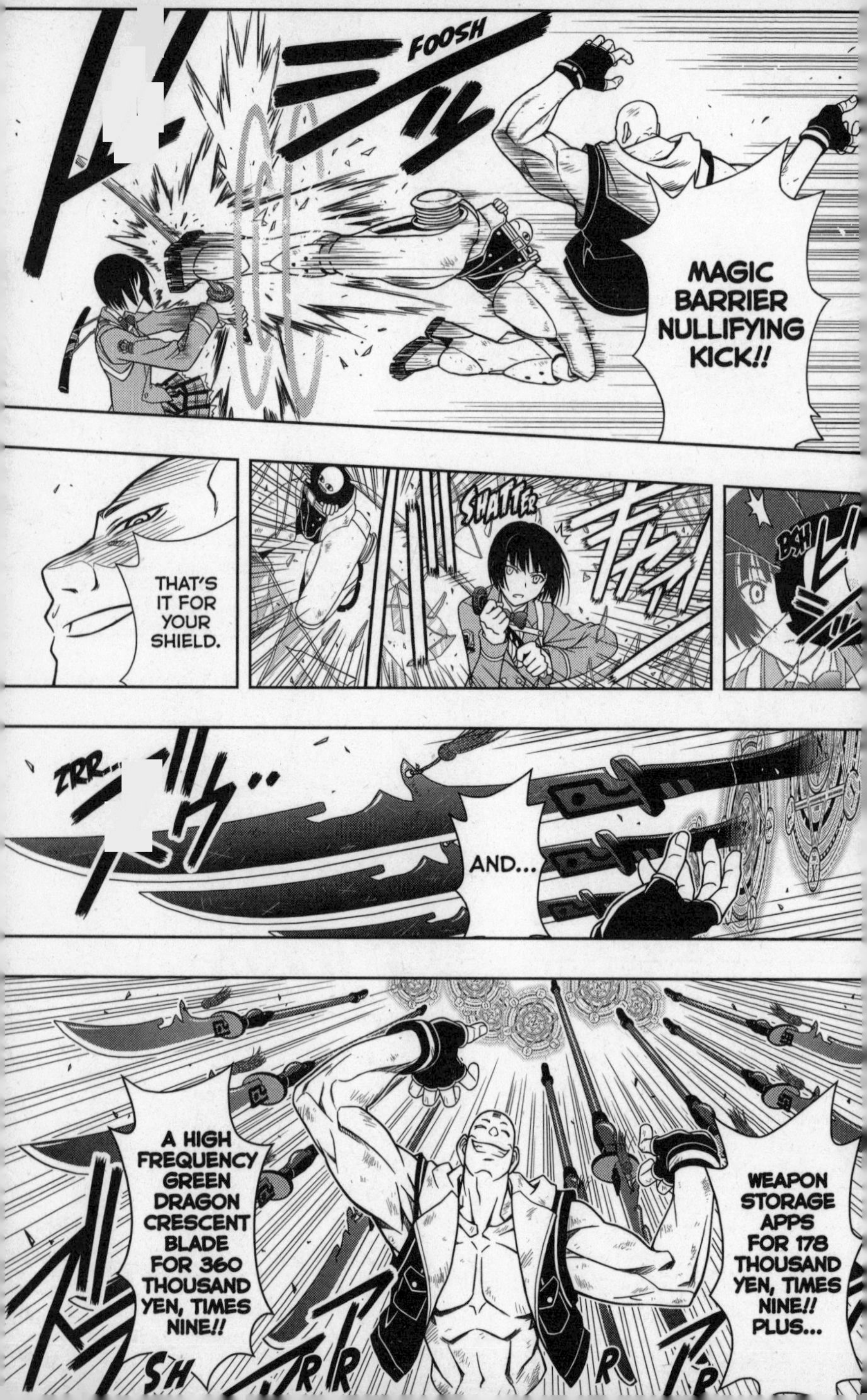
FOOSH
MAGIC BARRIER NULLIFYING KICK!!
BSH
SHATTER
THAT'S IT FOR YOUR SHIELD.
AND...
ZRR...
WEAPON STORAGE APPS FOR 178 THOUSAND YEN, TIMES NINE!! PLUS...
A HIGH FREQUENCY GREEN DRAGON CRESCENT BLADE FOR 360 THOUSAND YEN, TIMES NINE!!

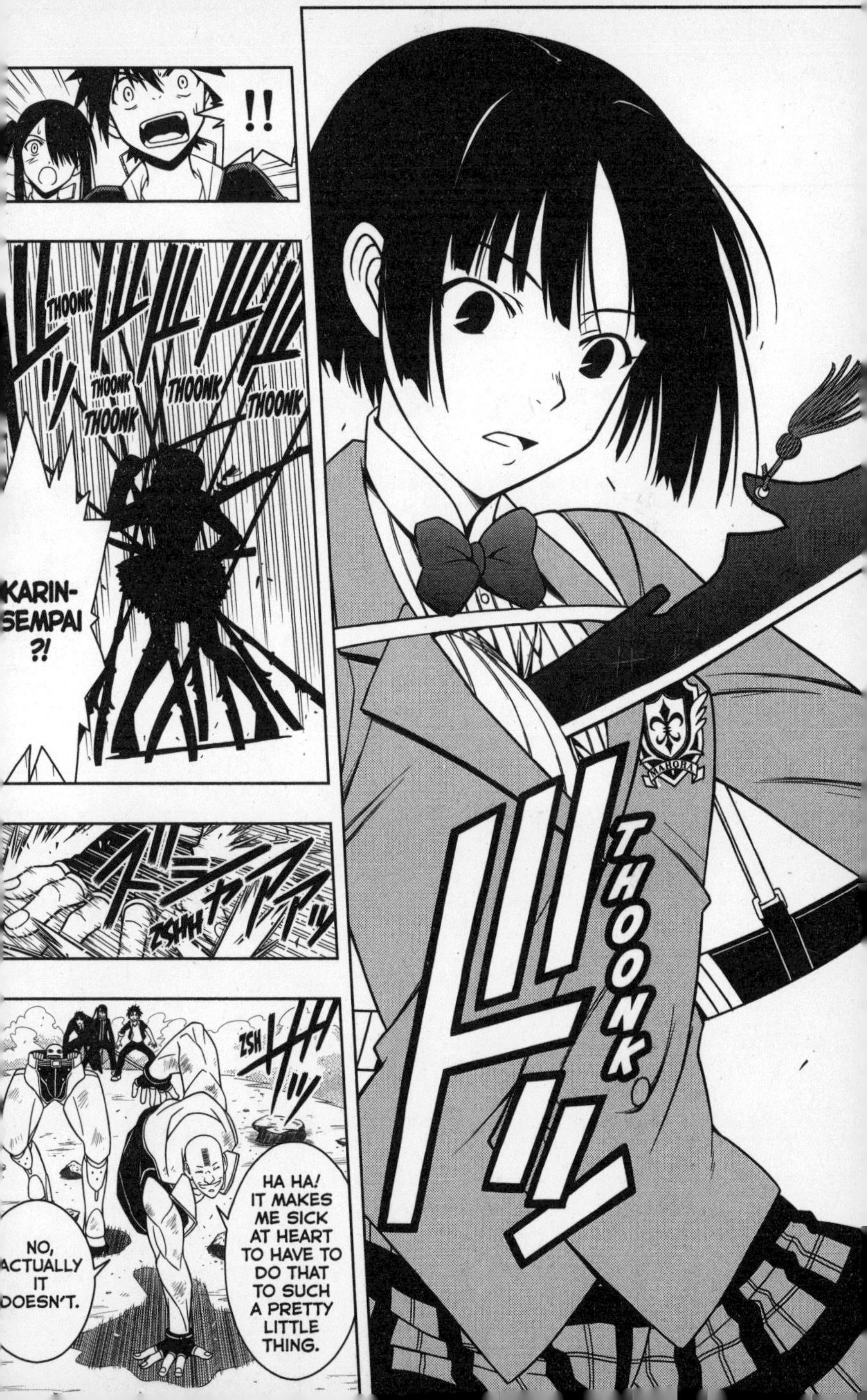
THOONK
!!
THOONK
THOONK
THOONK
THOONK
THOONK
KARIN-SEMPAI ?!
ZSHH
ZSH
HA HA! IT MAKES ME SICK AT HEART TO HAVE TO DO THAT TO SUCH A PRETTY LITTLE THING.
NO, ACTUALLY IT DOESN'T.

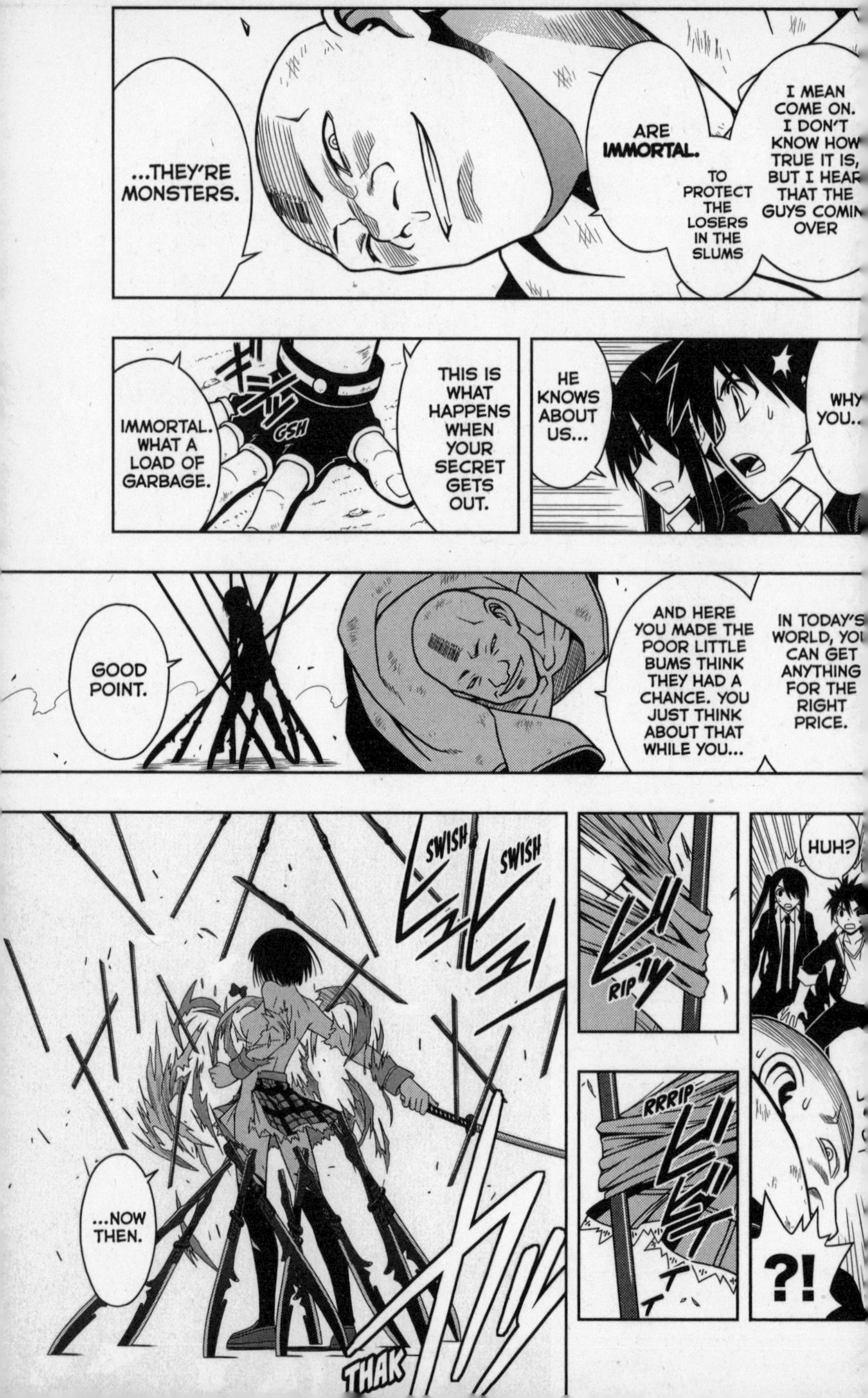
I MEAN COME ON. I DON'T KNOW HOW TRUE IT IS, BUT I HEAR THAT THE GUYS COMIN OVER
TO PROTECT THE LOSERS IN THE SLUMS
ARE **IMMORTAL.**
...THEY'RE MONSTERS.
WHY YOU...
HE KNOWS ABOUT US...
THIS IS WHAT HAPPENS WHEN YOUR SECRET GETS OUT.
GSH
IMMORTAL. WHAT A LOAD OF GARBAGE.
IN TODAY'S WORLD, YOU CAN GET ANYTHING FOR THE RIGHT PRICE.
AND HERE YOU MADE THE POOR LITTLE BUMS THINK THEY HAD A CHANCE. YOU JUST THINK ABOUT THAT WHILE YOU...
GOOD POINT.
HUH?
?!
RIP
RRRIP
SWISH
SWISH
...NOW THEN.
THAK

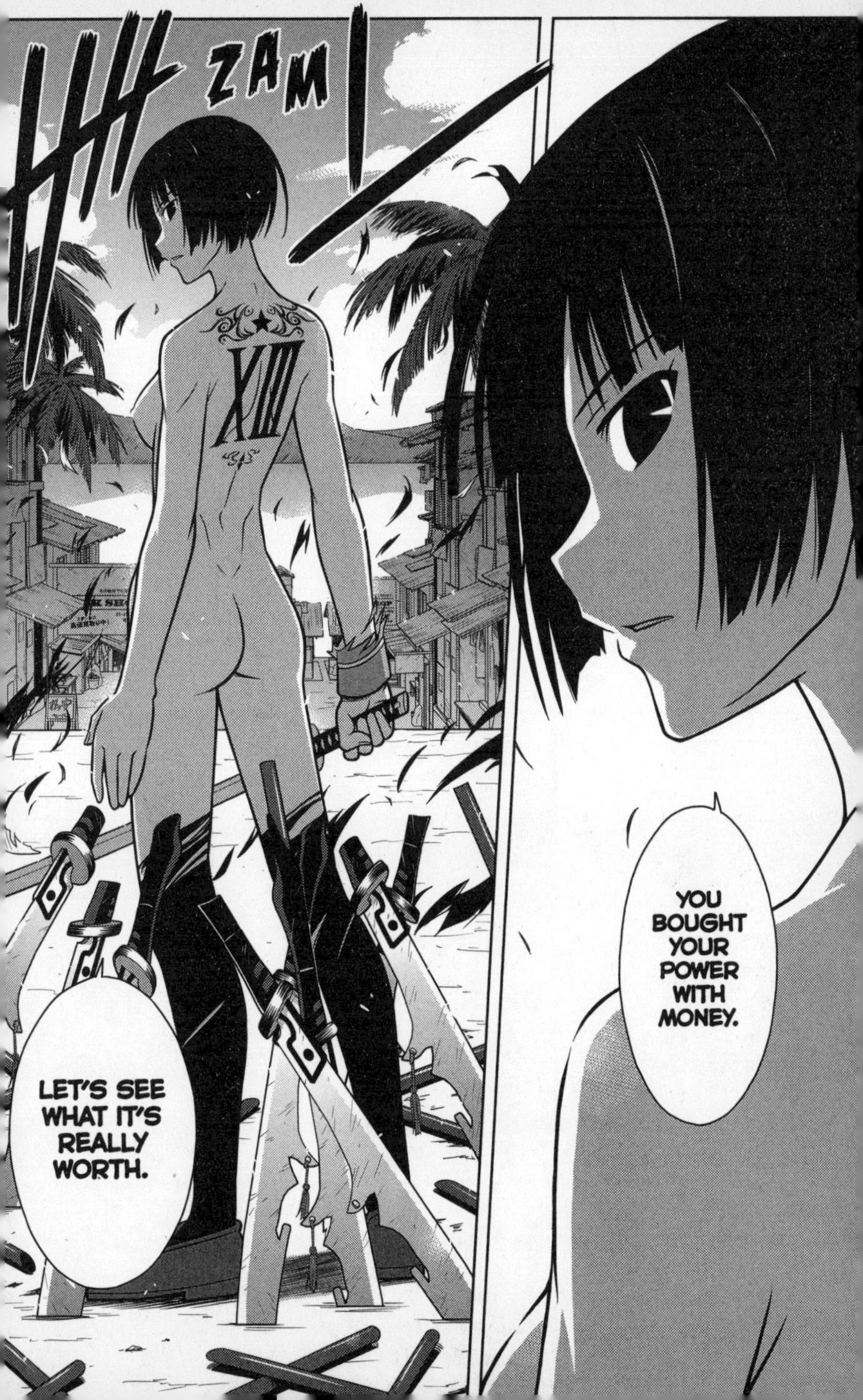
YOU BOUGHT YOUR POWER WITH MONEY.
ZAM
LET'S SEE WHAT IT'S REALLY WORTH.

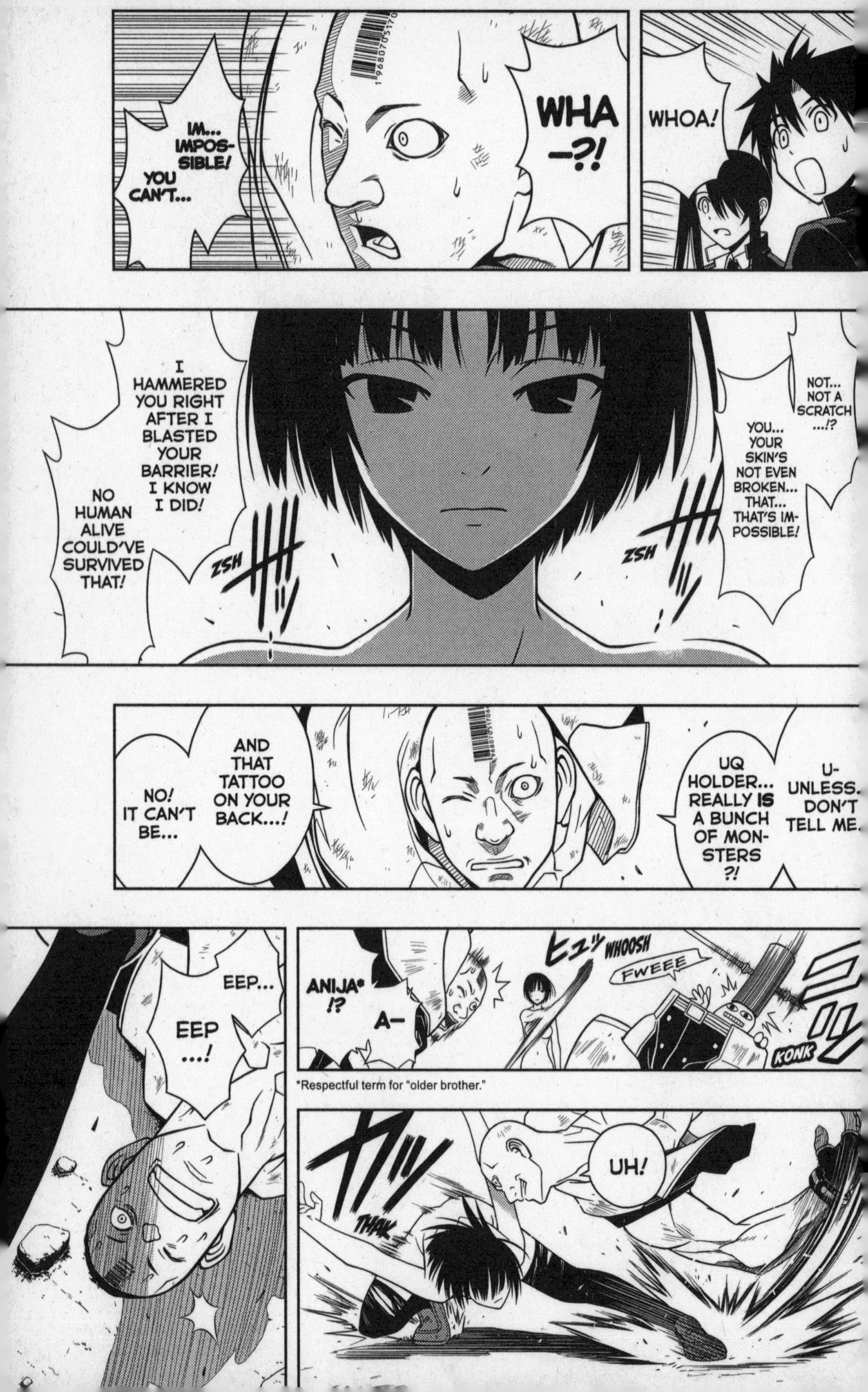
WHOA!
WHA—?!
IM... IMPOSSIBLE! YOU CAN'T...
NOT... NOT A SCRATCH ...!?
YOU... YOUR SKIN'S NOT EVEN BROKEN... THAT... THAT'S IMPOSSIBLE!
ZSH
I HAMMERED YOU RIGHT AFTER I BLASTED YOUR BARRIER! I KNOW I DID!
ZSH
NO HUMAN ALIVE COULD'VE SURVIVED THAT!
U-UNLESS. DON'T TELL ME.
UQ HOLDER... REALLY IS A BUNCH OF MONSTERS ?!
AND THAT TATTOO ON YOUR BACK...!
NO! IT CAN'T BE...
KONK
FWEEE
WHOOSH
A-
ANIJA* !?
UH!
THAK
EEP...
EEP ...!
*Respectful term for "older brother."

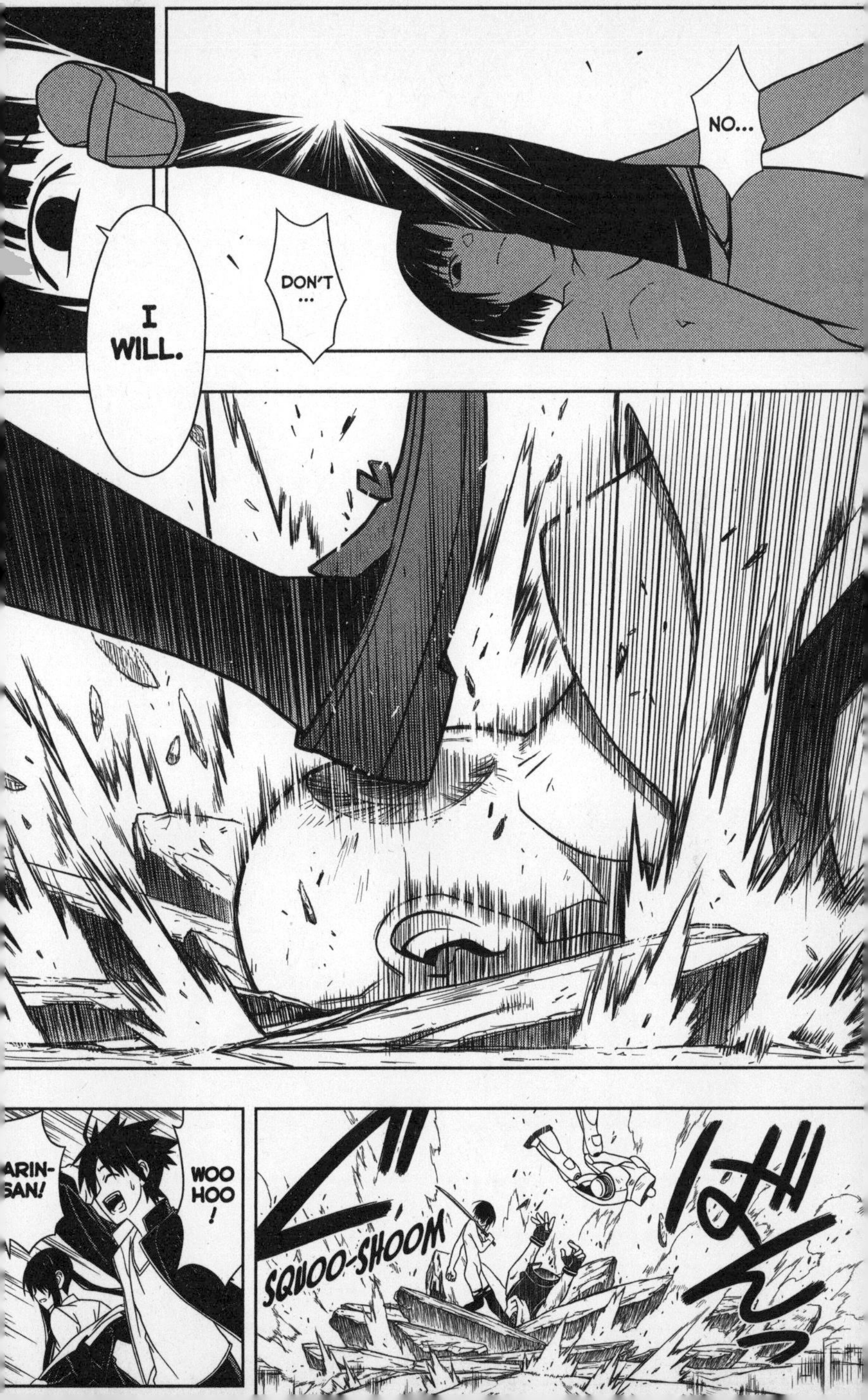
NO...
DON'T ...
I WILL.
SQUOO-SHOOM
WOO HOO !
ARIN- SAN!

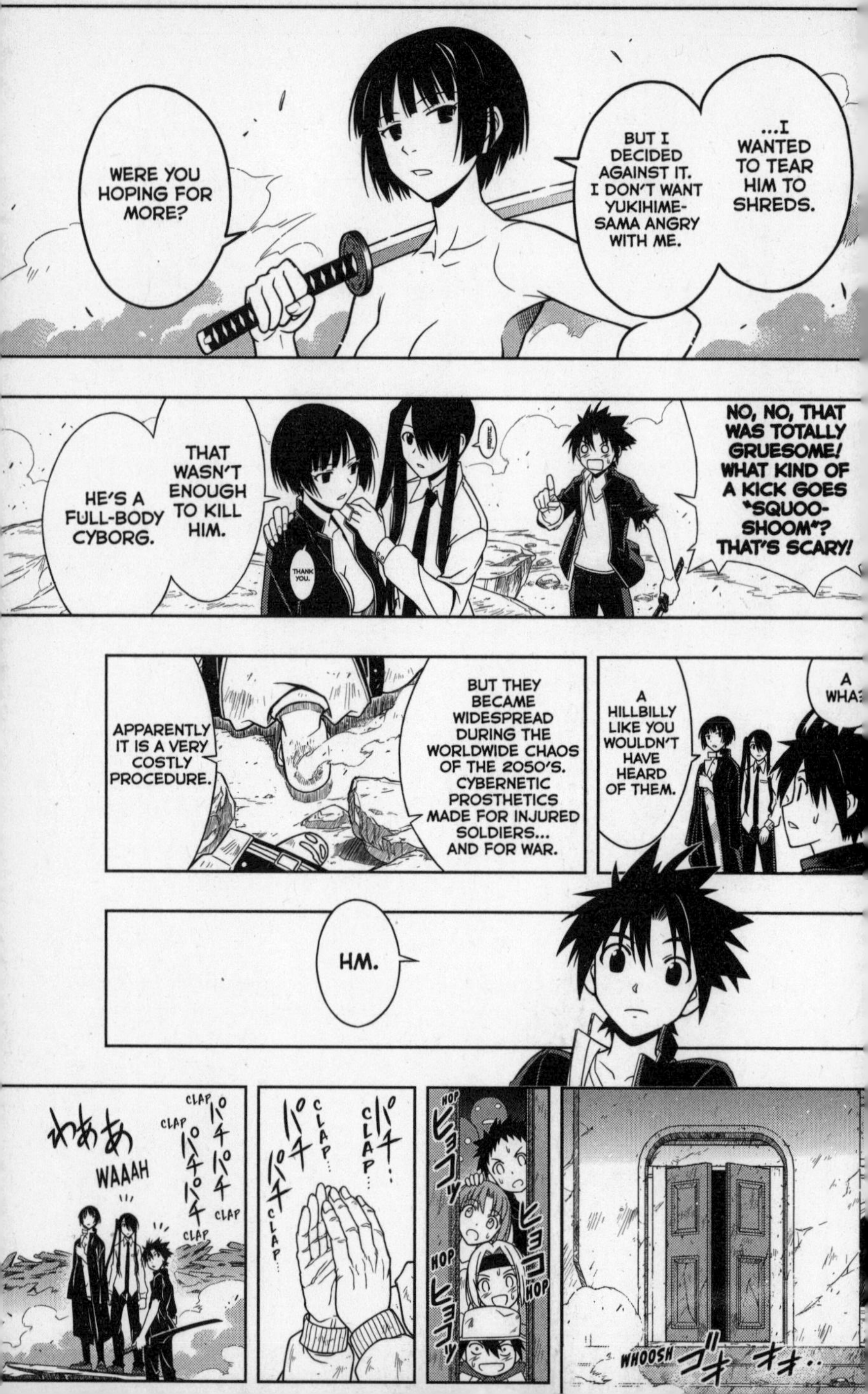
...I WANTED TO TEAR HIM TO SHREDS.
BUT I DECIDED AGAINST IT. I DON'T WANT YUKIHIME-SAMA ANGRY WITH ME.
WERE YOU HOPING FOR MORE?
NO, NO, THAT WAS TOTALLY GRUESOME! WHAT KIND OF A KICK GOES "SQUOO-SHOOM"? THAT'S SCARY!
THAT WASN'T ENOUGH TO KILL HIM.
HE'S A FULL-BODY CYBORG.
THANK YOU.
A WHA?
A HILLBILLY LIKE YOU WOULDN'T HAVE HEARD OF THEM.
BUT THEY BECAME WIDESPREAD DURING THE WORLDWIDE CHAOS OF THE 2050'S. CYBERNETIC PROSTHETICS MADE FOR INJURED SOLDIERS... AND FOR WAR.
APPARENTLY IT IS A VERY COSTLY PROCEDURE.
HM.
ゴオ オオ…
WHOOSH
ヒョコッ
HOP
ヒョコッ
HOP
ヒョコッ
HOP
パチ…
CLAP…
パチ
CLAP…
パチ
CLAP…
パチパチ
CLAP
パチパチ
CLAP
CLAP
CLAP
わあああ
WAAAH

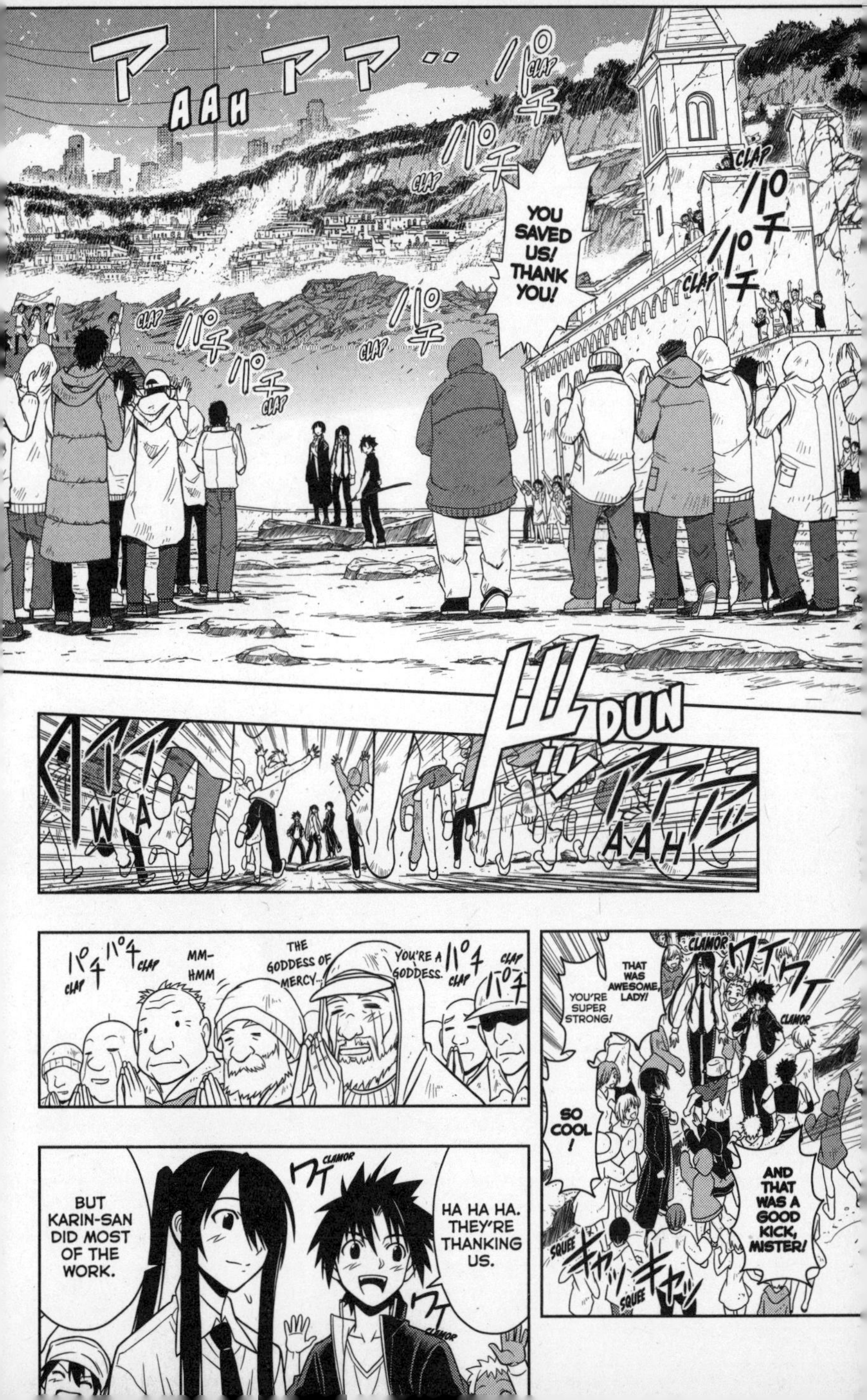
CLAP
パチ
パチ
CLAP
YOU SAVED US! THANK YOU!
パチ
CLAP
パチ
CLAP
パチ
CLAP
パチ
CLAP
パチ
CLAP
アア…
AAH
ア
ド
DUN
アアッ
AAH
ワーイ
WA
ワイワイ
CLAMOR
THAT WAS AWESOME, LADY!
YOU'RE SUPER STRONG!
CLAMOR
SO COOL!
AND THAT WAS A GOOD KICK, MISTER!
キャッ
SQUEE
キャッ
SQUEE
パチ
CLAP
パチ
CLAP
YOU'RE A GODDESS.
THE GODDESS OF MERCY...
MM-HMM
パチ
CLAP
パチ
CLAP
ワイ
CLAMOR
HA HA HA. THEY'RE THANKING US.
ワイ
CLAMOR
BUT KARIN-SAN DID MOST OF THE WORK.

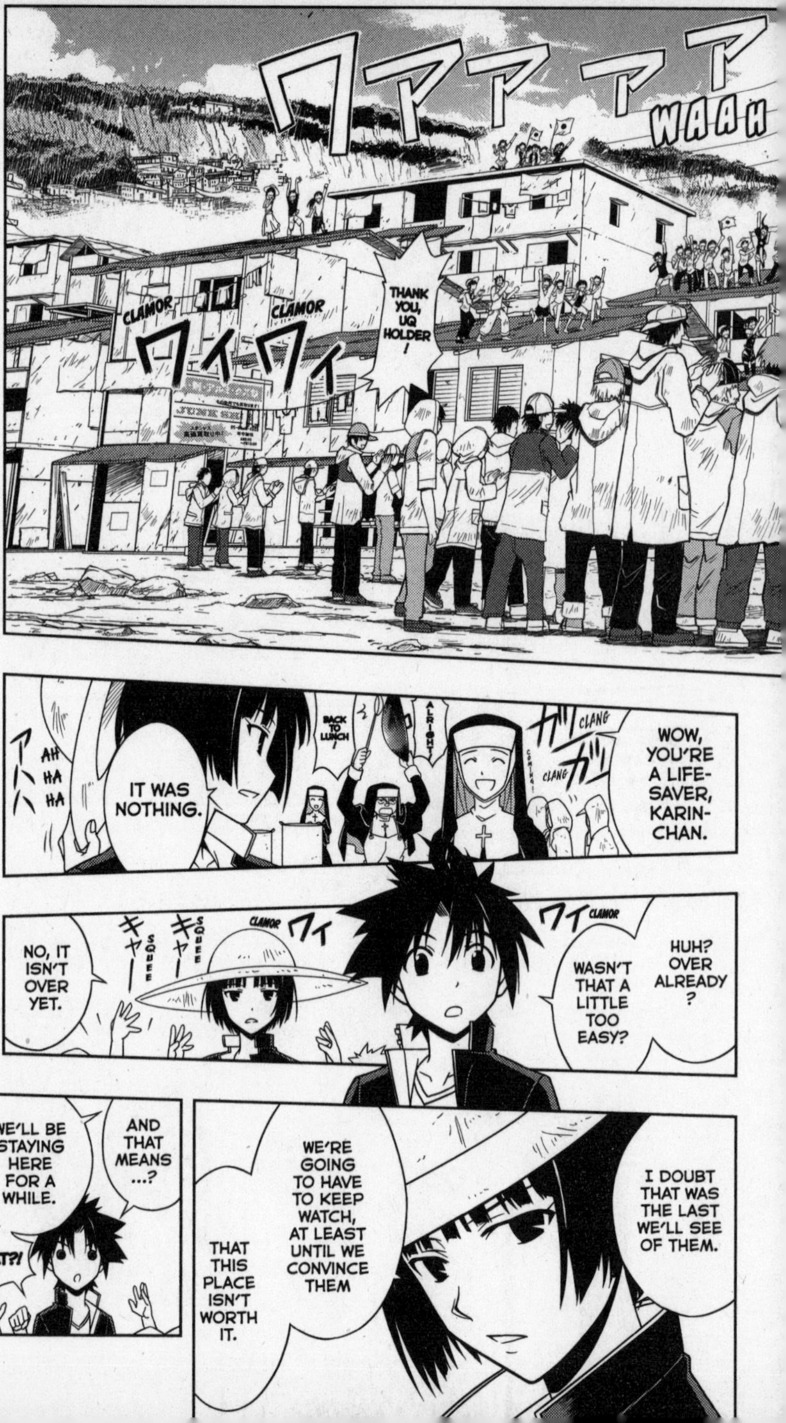
ワァァァア
WAAH
THANK YOU, UQ HOLDER!
CLAMOR
ワイワイ
CLAMOR
WOW, YOU'RE A LIFE-SAVER, KARIN-CHAN.
ガン CLANG
ガン CLANG
ALRIGHT!
BACK TO LUNCH!
IT WAS NOTHING.
アハハ
AH HA HA
HUH? OVER ALREADY?
WASN'T THAT A LITTLE TOO EASY?
ワイ CLAMOR
ワイ CLAMOR
キャー SQUEE
キャー SQUEE
NO, IT ISN'T OVER YET.
I DOUBT THAT WAS THE LAST WE'LL SEE OF THEM.
WE'RE GOING TO HAVE TO KEEP WATCH, AT LEAST UNTIL WE CONVINCE THEM
THAT THIS PLACE ISN'T WORTH IT.
AND THAT MEANS...?
WE'LL BE STAYING HERE FOR A WHILE.
WHAAAT?!

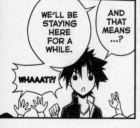

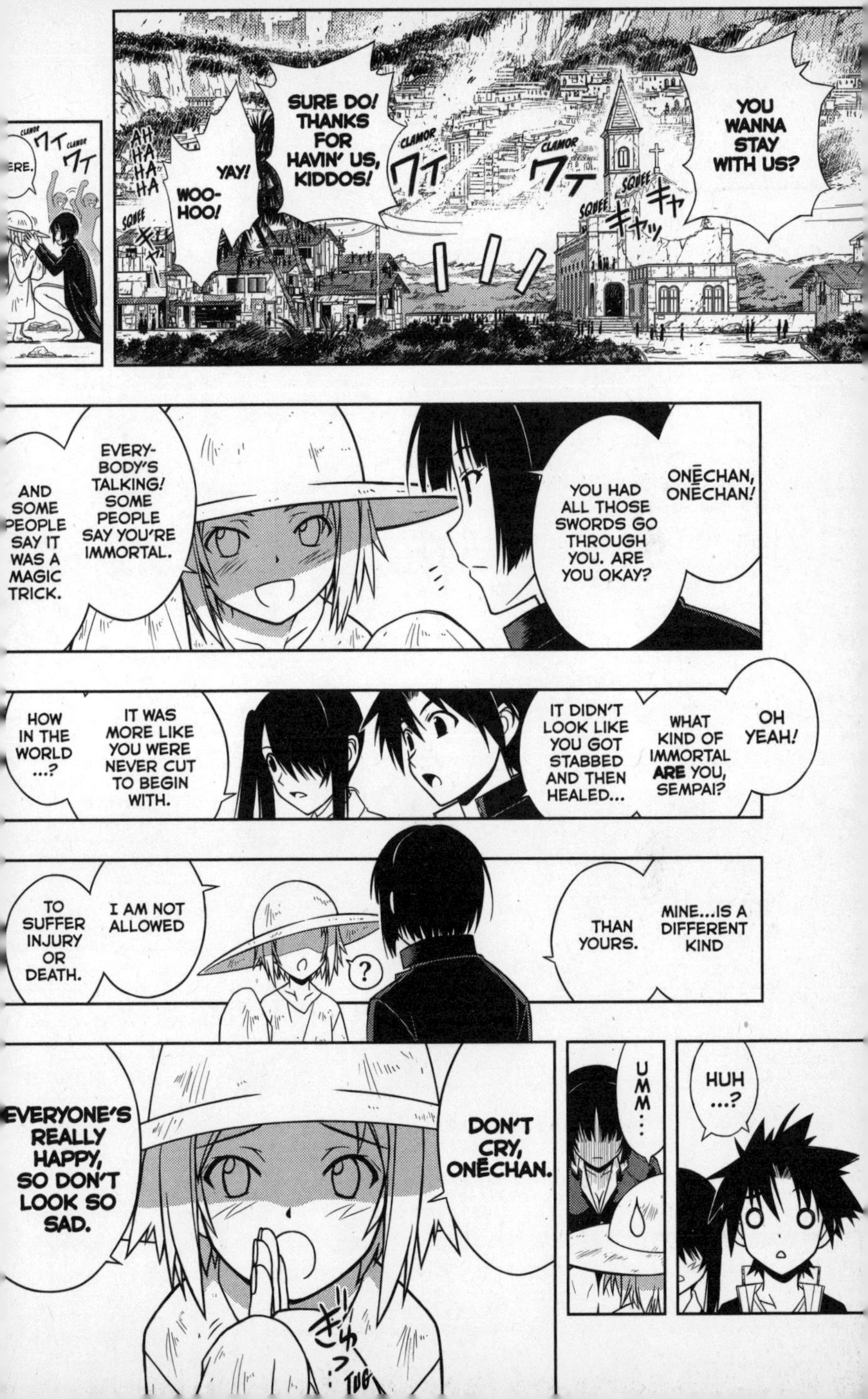
YOU WANNA STAY WITH US?
SQUEE ギャ
SQUEE ギャッ
CLAMOR ワァ
CLAMOR ワァ
SURE DO! THANKS FOR HAVIN' US, KIDDOS!
YAY!
WOO-HOO!
AH HA HA HA
SQUEE キャ
CLAMOR ワァ CLAMOR ワァ
ERE.
ONĒCHAN, ONĒCHAN!
YOU HAD ALL THOSE SWORDS GO THROUGH YOU. ARE YOU OKAY?
EVERY-BODY'S TALKING! SOME PEOPLE SAY YOU'RE IMMORTAL.
AND SOME PEOPLE SAY IT WAS A MAGIC TRICK.
OH YEAH!
WHAT KIND OF IMMORTAL ARE YOU, SEMPAI?
IT DIDN'T LOOK LIKE YOU GOT STABBED AND THEN HEALED...
IT WAS MORE LIKE YOU WERE NEVER CUT TO BEGIN WITH.
HOW IN THE WORLD ...?
MINE...IS A DIFFERENT KIND
THAN YOURS.
?
I AM NOT ALLOWED
TO SUFFER INJURY OR DEATH.
HUH ...?
UMM...
DON'T CRY, ONĒCHAN.
EVERYONE'S REALLY HAPPY, SO DON'T LOOK SO SAD.
ぎゅっ TUG

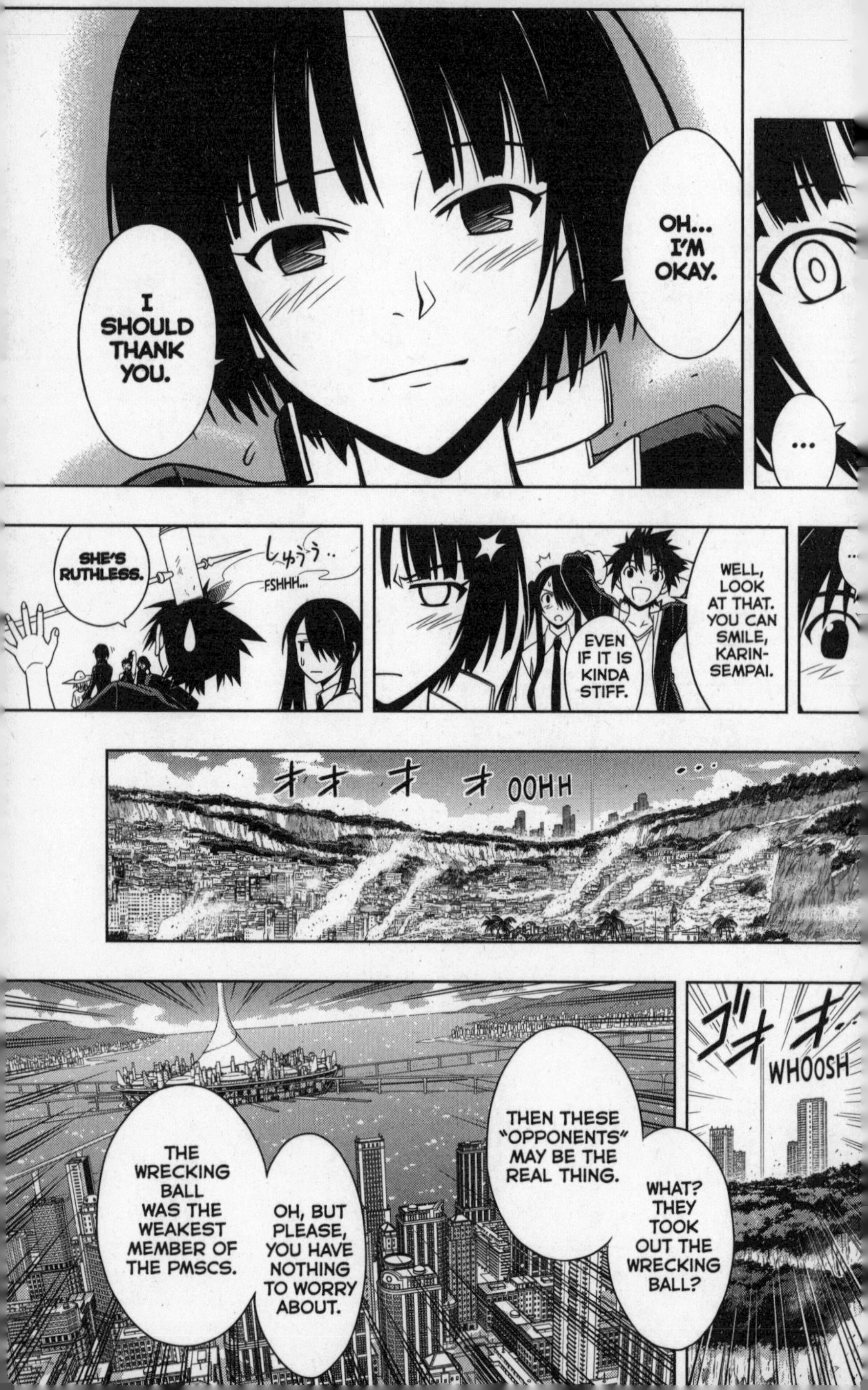
...
OH... I'M OKAY.
I SHOULD THANK YOU.
...
WELL, LOOK AT THAT. YOU CAN SMILE, KARIN-SEMPAI.
EVEN IF IT IS KINDA STIFF.
しゅううう‥
FSHHH...
SHE'S RUTHLESS.
...
オオオオ
OOHH
ゴオオ‥
WHOOSH
WHAT? THEY TOOK OUT THE WRECKING BALL?
THEN THESE "OPPONENTS" MAY BE THE REAL THING.
OH, BUT PLEASE, YOU HAVE NOTHING TO WORRY ABOUT.
THE WRECKING BALL WAS THE WEAKEST MEMBER OF THE PMSCS.

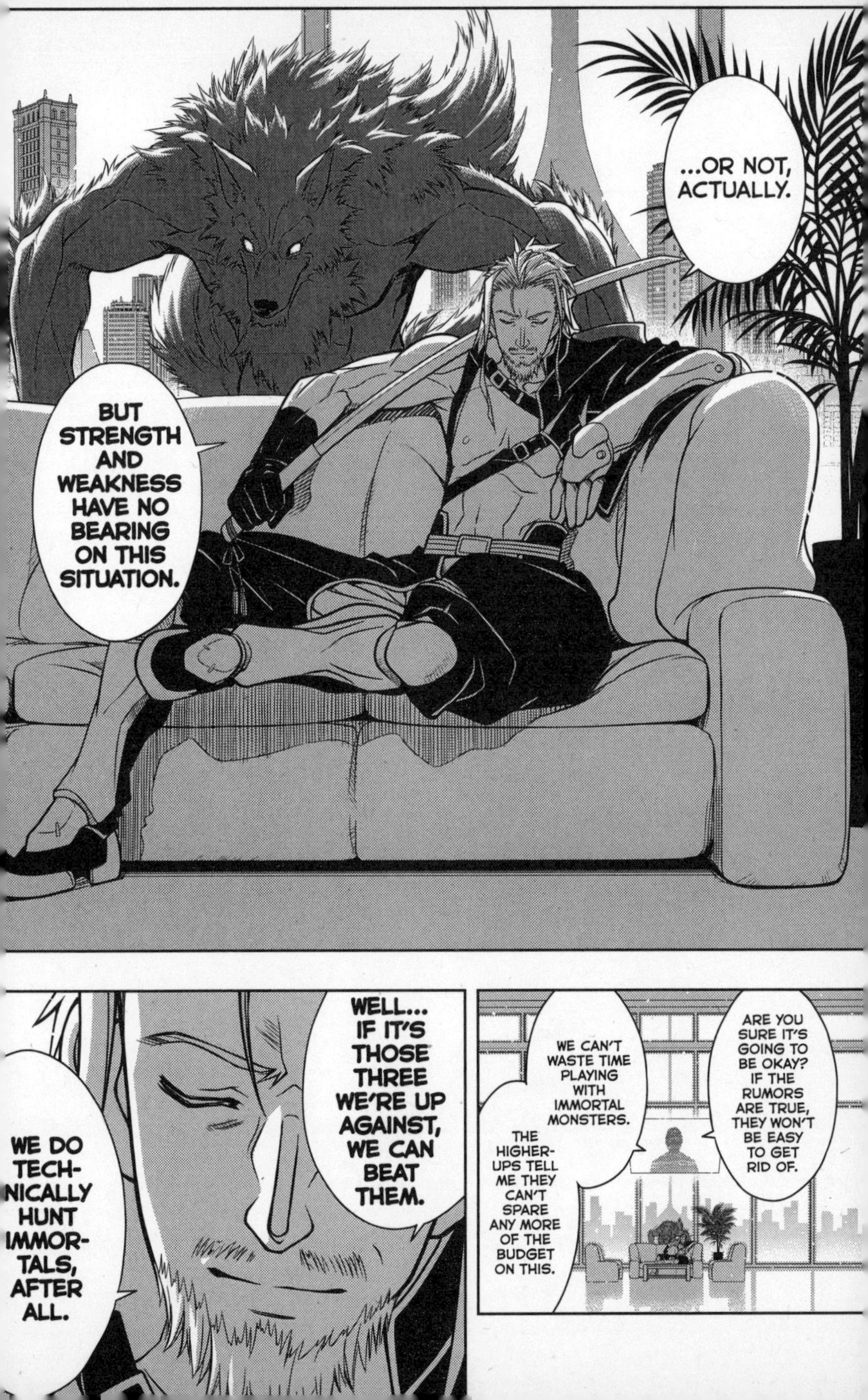
...OR NOT, ACTUALLY.
BUT STRENGTH AND WEAKNESS HAVE NO BEARING ON THIS SITUATION.
ARE YOU SURE IT'S GOING TO BE OKAY? IF THE RUMORS ARE TRUE, THEY WON'T BE EASY TO GET RID OF.
WE CAN'T WASTE TIME PLAYING WITH IMMORTAL MONSTERS.
THE HIGHER-UPS TELL ME THEY CAN'T SPARE ANY MORE OF THE BUDGET ON THIS.
WELL... IF IT'S THOSE THREE WE'RE UP AGAINST, WE CAN BEAT THEM.
WE DO TECHNICALLY HUNT IMMORTALS, AFTER ALL.

UQ HOLDER!

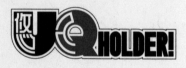

UQ
HOLDER!
ユーキューホルダー！

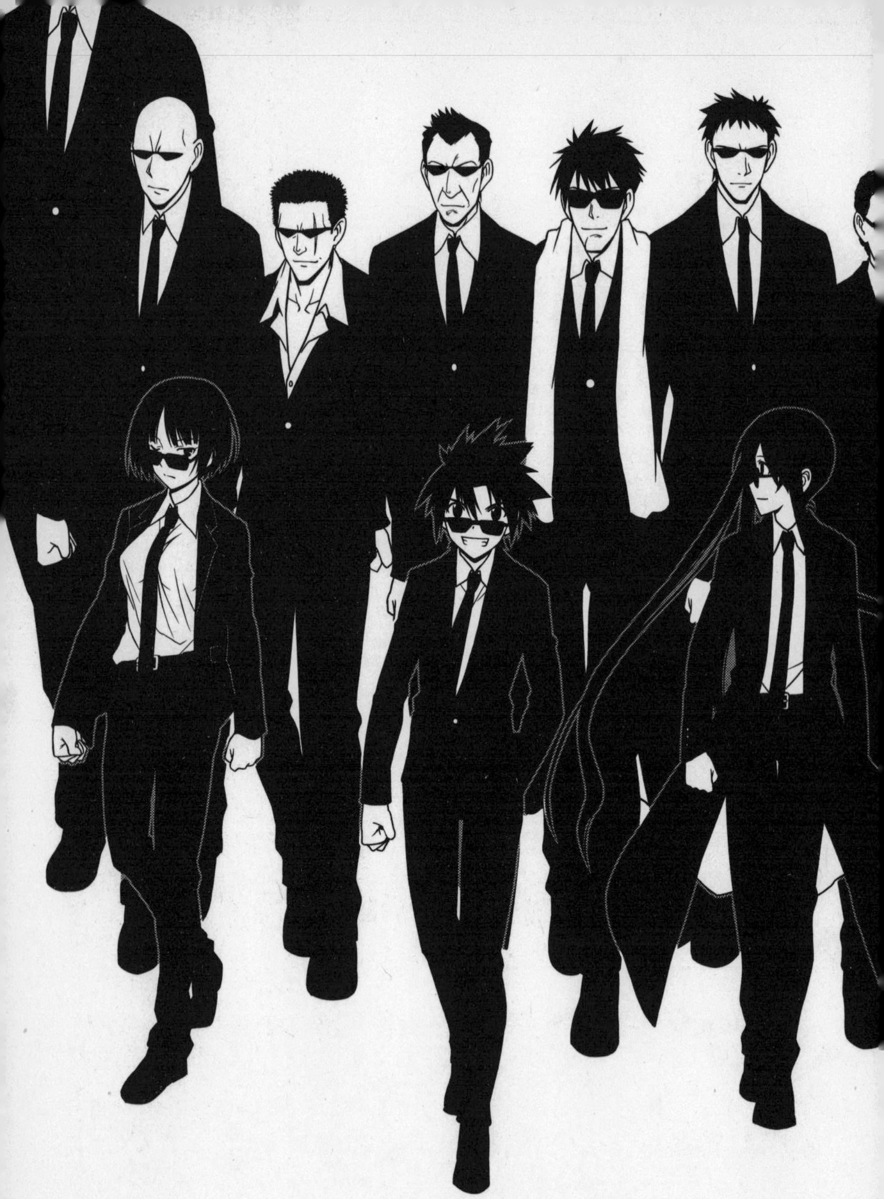

STAGE 15: THE FRUITS OF TRAINING

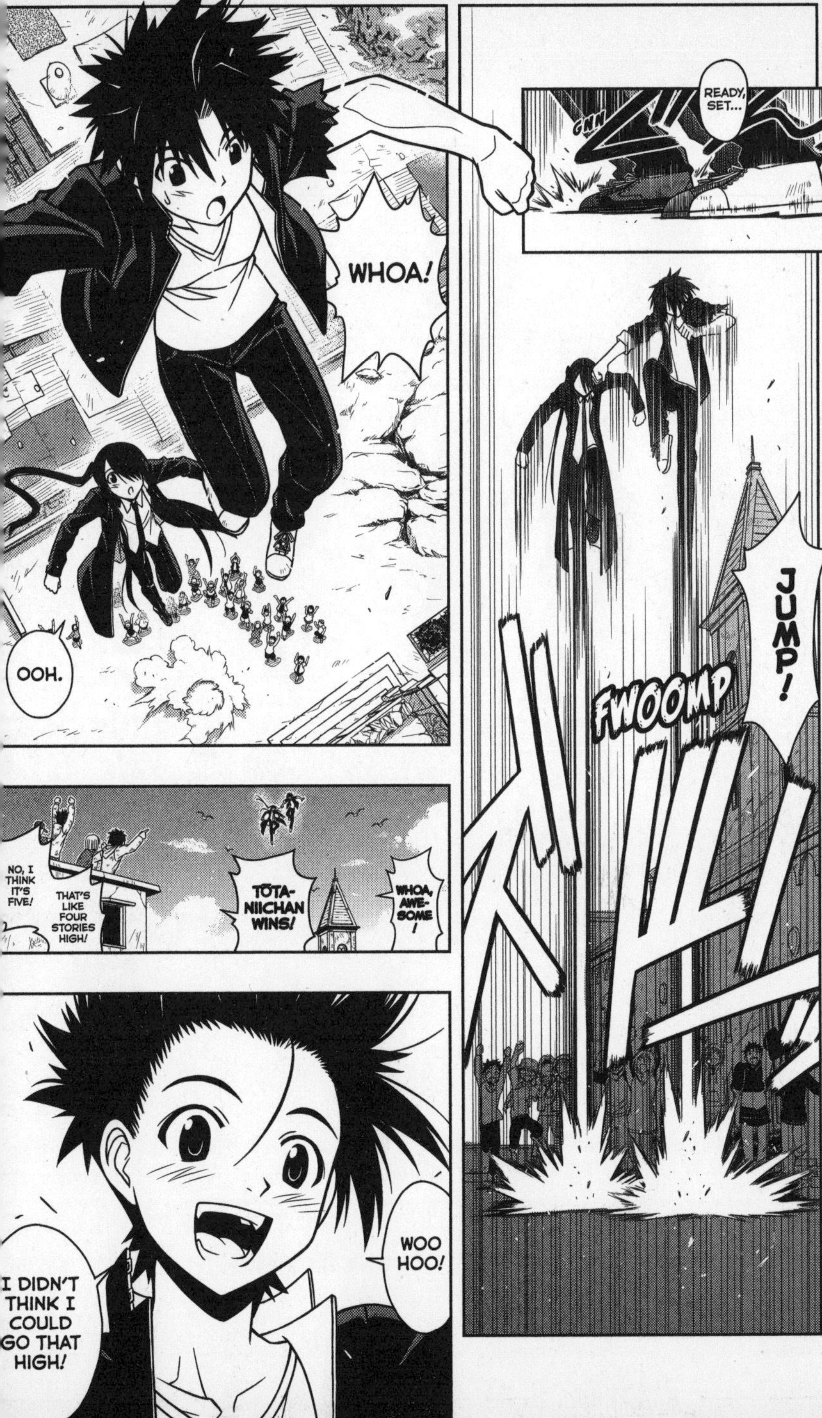
READY, SET...
GNN
JUMP!
FWOOMP
WHOA!
OOH.
WHOA, AWESOME!
TŌTA-NIICHAN WINS!
THAT'S LIKE FOUR STORIES HIGH!
NO, I THINK IT'S FIVE!
WOO HOO!
I DIDN'T THINK I COULD GO THAT HIGH!

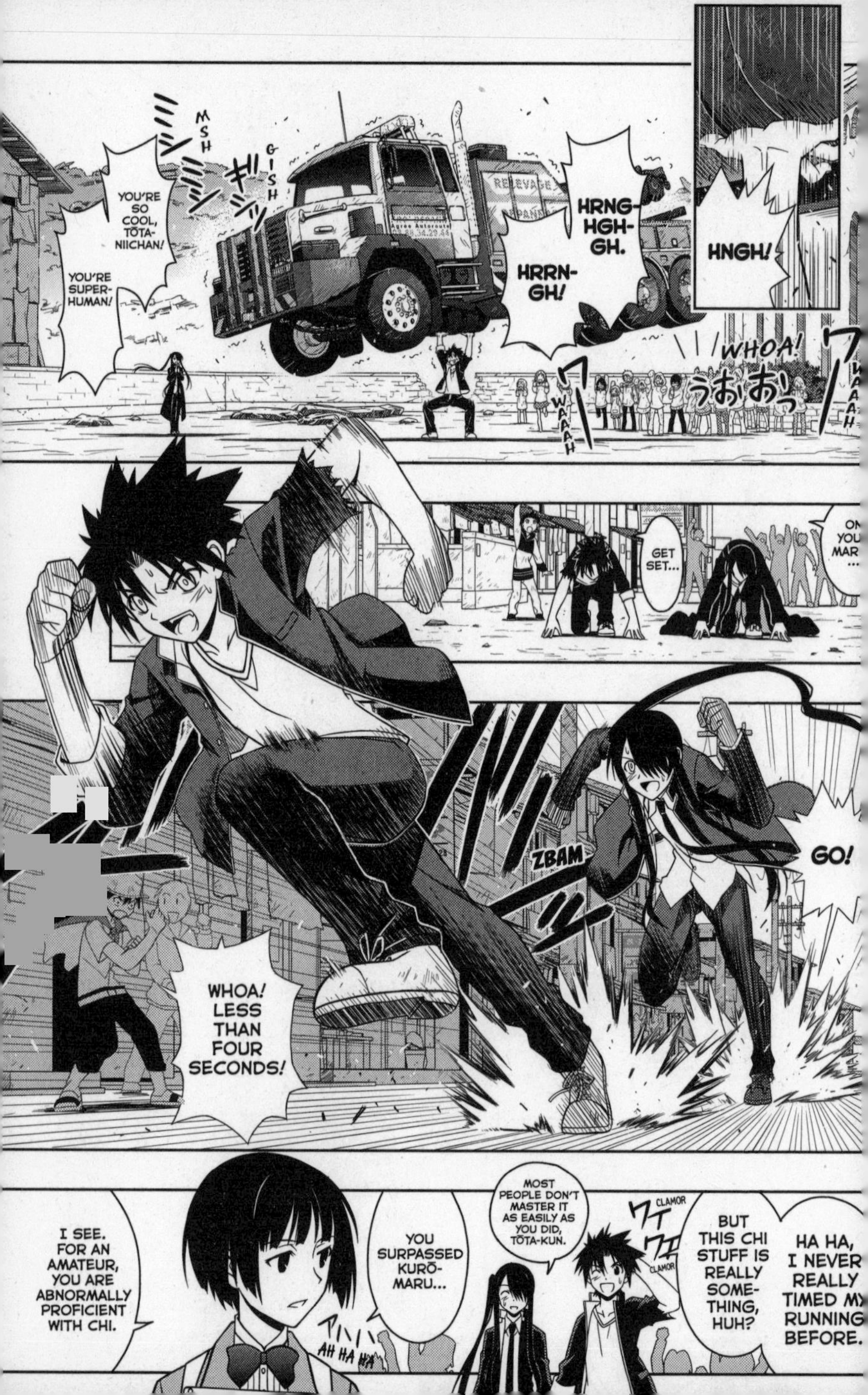
HNGH!
HRNG-HGH-GH.
HRRN-GH!
GISH
ギシッ
MSH
ミシミシ
YOU'RE SO COOL, TŌTA-NIICHAN!
YOU'RE SUPER-HUMAN!
ワー
WAAAH
うおおっ
WHOA!
ワー
WAAAH
ON YOU MAR...
GET SET...
GO!
ZBAM
WHOA! LESS THAN FOUR SECONDS!
HA HA, I NEVER REALLY TIMED MY RUNNING BEFORE.
BUT THIS CHI STUFF IS REALLY SOME-THING, HUH?
ワイワイ
CLAMOR
CLAMOR
MOST PEOPLE DON'T MASTER IT AS EASILY AS YOU DID, TŌTA-KUN.
YOU SURPASSED KURŌ-MARU...
アハハ
AH HA HA
I SEE. FOR AN AMATEUR, YOU ARE ABNORMALLY PROFICIENT WITH CHI.

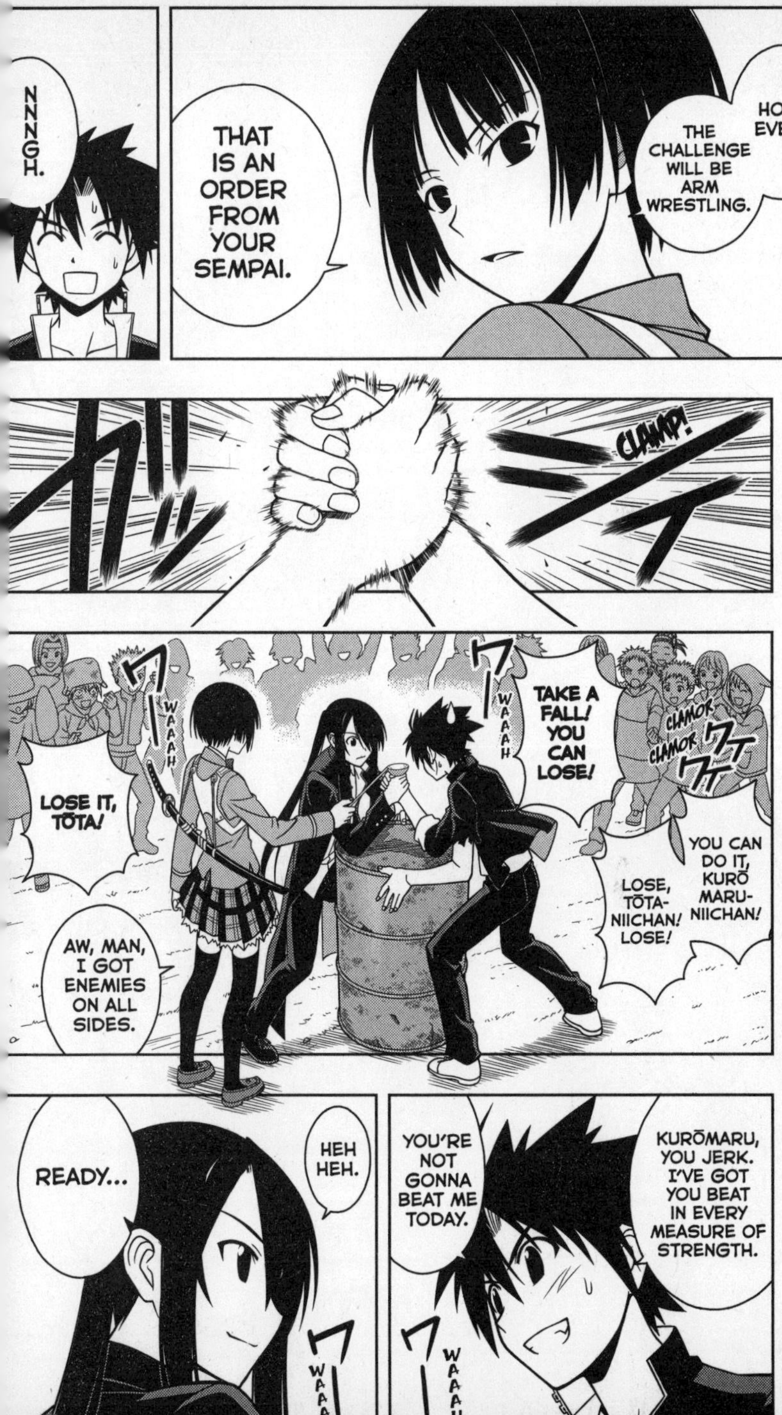
HOW-EVER. THE CHALLENGE WILL BE ARM WRESTLING.
THAT IS AN ORDER FROM YOUR SEMPAI.
NNNGH.
CLAMP!
YOU CAN DO IT, KURŌ MARU-NIICHAN!
LOSE, TŌTA-NIICHAN! LOSE!
CLAMOR
CLAMOR
TAKE A FALL! YOU CAN LOSE!
WAAAH
WAAAH
LOSE IT, TŌTA!
AW, MAN, I GOT ENEMIES ON ALL SIDES.
KURŌMARU, YOU JERK. I'VE GOT YOU BEAT IN EVERY MEASURE OF STRENGTH.
YOU'RE NOT GONNA BEAT ME TODAY.
WAAAH
HEH HEH.
READY...
WAAA

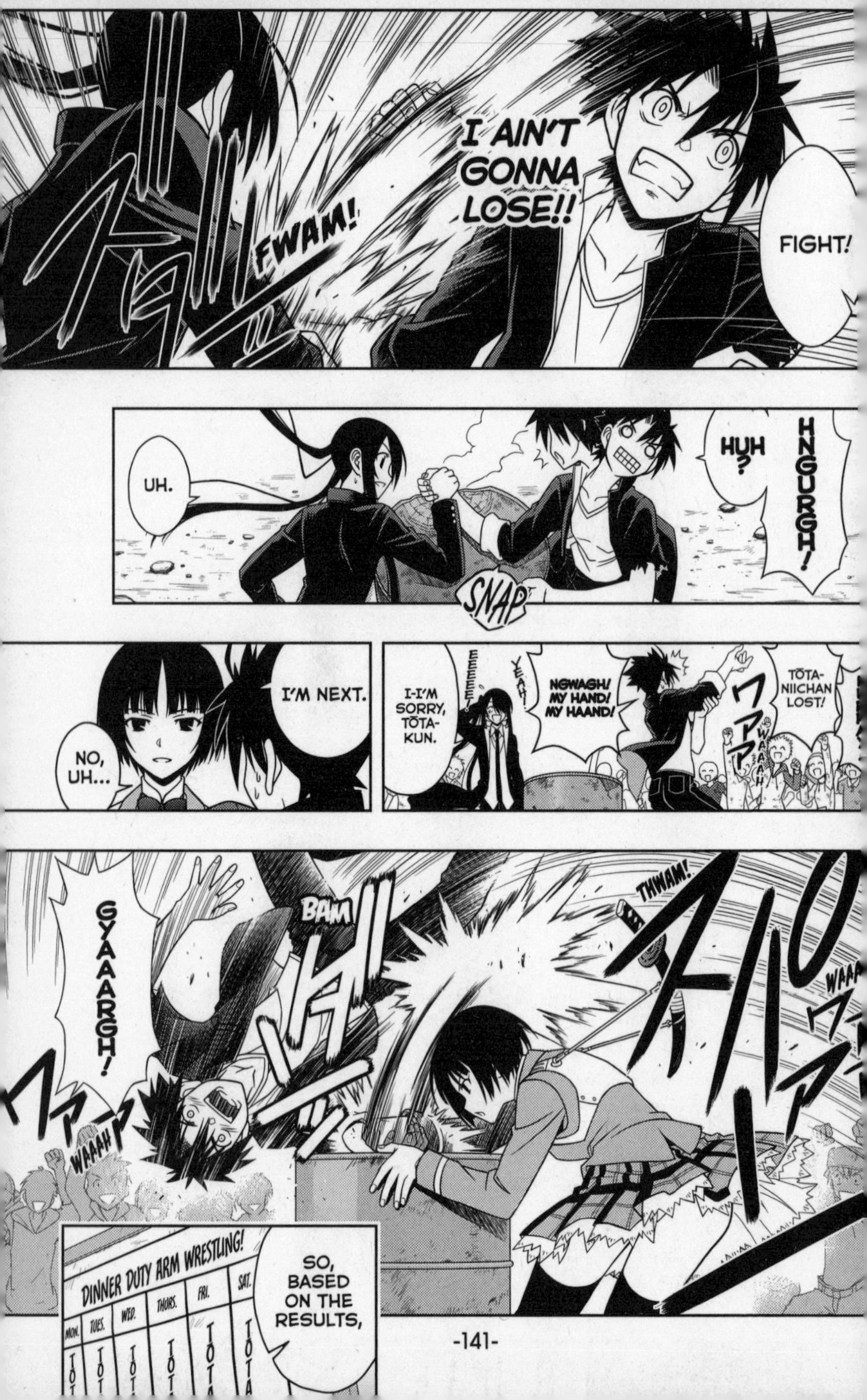
FIGHT!
I AIN'T GONNA LOSE!!
FWAM!
HNGURGH!
HUH?
UH.
SNAP
TŌTA-NIICHAN LOST!
WAAAH
NGWAGH! MY HAND! MY HAAND!
YEAH!
EEEEE!
I-I'M SORRY, TŌTA-KUN.
I'M NEXT.
NO, UH...
THWAM!
WAAA
BAM
GYAAAARGH!
WAAAH
SO, BASED ON THE RESULTS,
DINNER DUTY ARM WRESTLING!
MON.
TUES.
WED.
THURS.
FRI.
SAT.

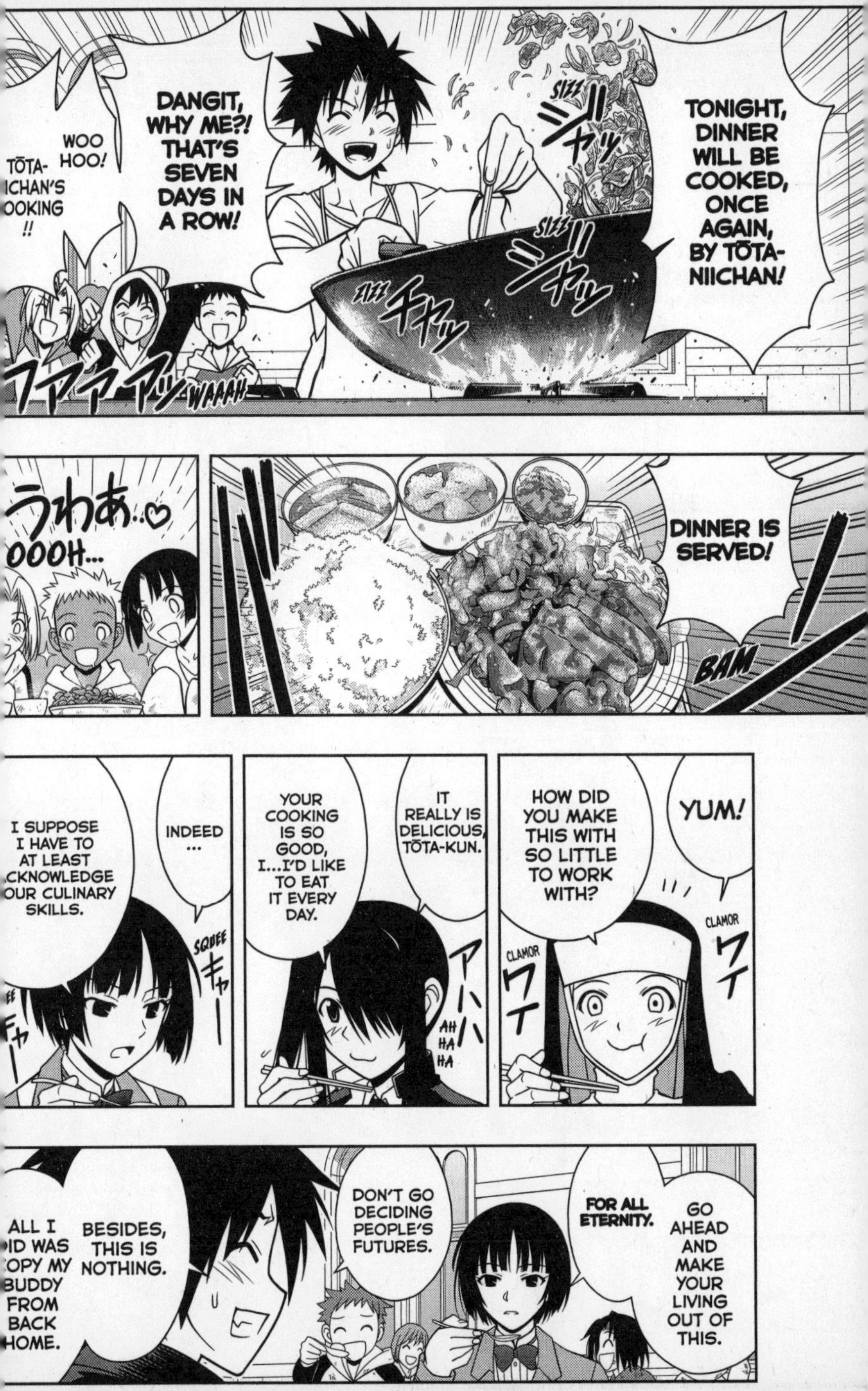
TONIGHT, DINNER WILL BE COOKED, ONCE AGAIN, BY TŌTA-NIICHAN!
SIZZ
SIZZ
DANGIT, WHY ME?! THAT'S SEVEN DAYS IN A ROW!
SIZZ
WOO HOO!
TŌTA- ICHAN'S OOKING !!
WAAAH
DINNER IS SERVED!
BAM
うわあ‥♡
OOOH...
YUM!
HOW DID YOU MAKE THIS WITH SO LITTLE TO WORK WITH?
CLAMOR
CLAMOR
IT REALLY IS DELICIOUS, TŌTA-KUN.
YOUR COOKING IS SO GOOD, I...I'D LIKE TO EAT IT EVERY DAY.
AH HA HA HA
INDEED...
I SUPPOSE I HAVE TO AT LEAST CKNOWLEDGE OUR CULINARY SKILLS.
SQUEE
GO AHEAD AND MAKE YOUR LIVING OUT OF THIS.
FOR ALL ETERNITY.
DON'T GO DECIDING PEOPLE'S FUTURES.
BESIDES, THIS IS NOTHING.
ALL I ID WAS OPY MY BUDDY FROM BACK HOME.

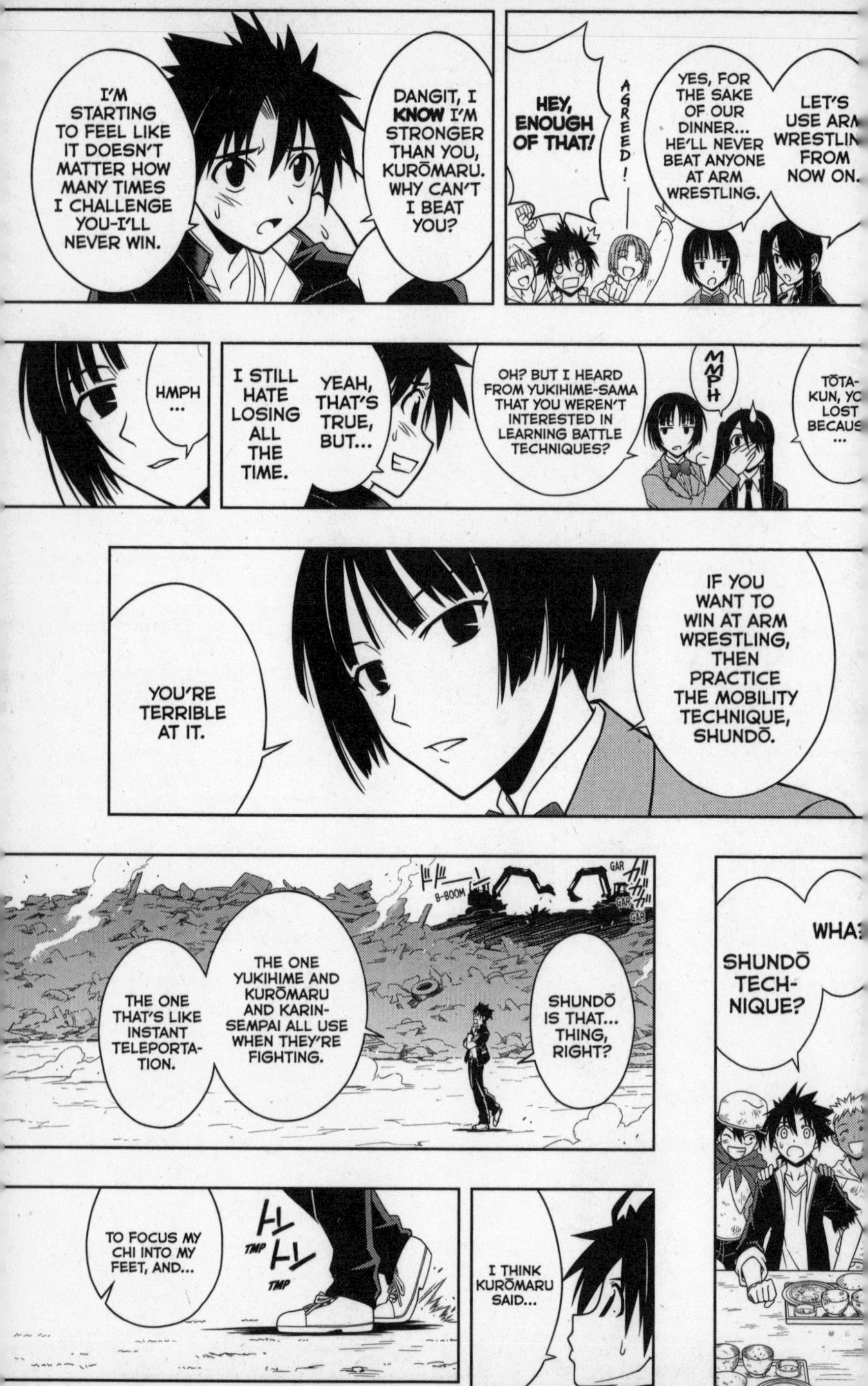
LET'S USE ARM WRESTLIN FROM NOW ON.
YES, FOR THE SAKE OF OUR DINNER... HE'LL NEVER BEAT ANYONE AT ARM WRESTLING.
AGREED!
HEY, ENOUGH OF THAT!
DANGIT, I KNOW I'M STRONGER THAN YOU, KURŌMARU. WHY CAN'T I BEAT YOU?
I'M STARTING TO FEEL LIKE IT DOESN'T MATTER HOW MANY TIMES I CHALLENGE YOU-I'LL NEVER WIN.
TŌTA-KUN, YO LOST BECAUS ...
MMPH
OH? BUT I HEARD FROM YUKIHIME-SAMA THAT YOU WEREN'T INTERESTED IN LEARNING BATTLE TECHNIQUES?
YEAH, THAT'S TRUE, BUT...
I STILL HATE LOSING ALL THE TIME.
HMPH ...
IF YOU WANT TO WIN AT ARM WRESTLING, THEN PRACTICE THE MOBILITY TECHNIQUE, SHUNDŌ.
YOU'RE TERRIBLE AT IT.
WHA
SHUNDŌ TECH-NIQUE?
B-BOOM
GAR
GAR
GAR
SHUNDŌ IS THAT... THING, RIGHT?
THE ONE YUKIHIME AND KURŌMARU AND KARIN-SEMPAI ALL USE WHEN THEY'RE FIGHTING.
THE ONE THAT'S LIKE INSTANT TELEPORTA-TION.
I THINK KURŌMARU SAID...
TMP
TMP
TO FOCUS MY CHI INTO MY FEET, AND...

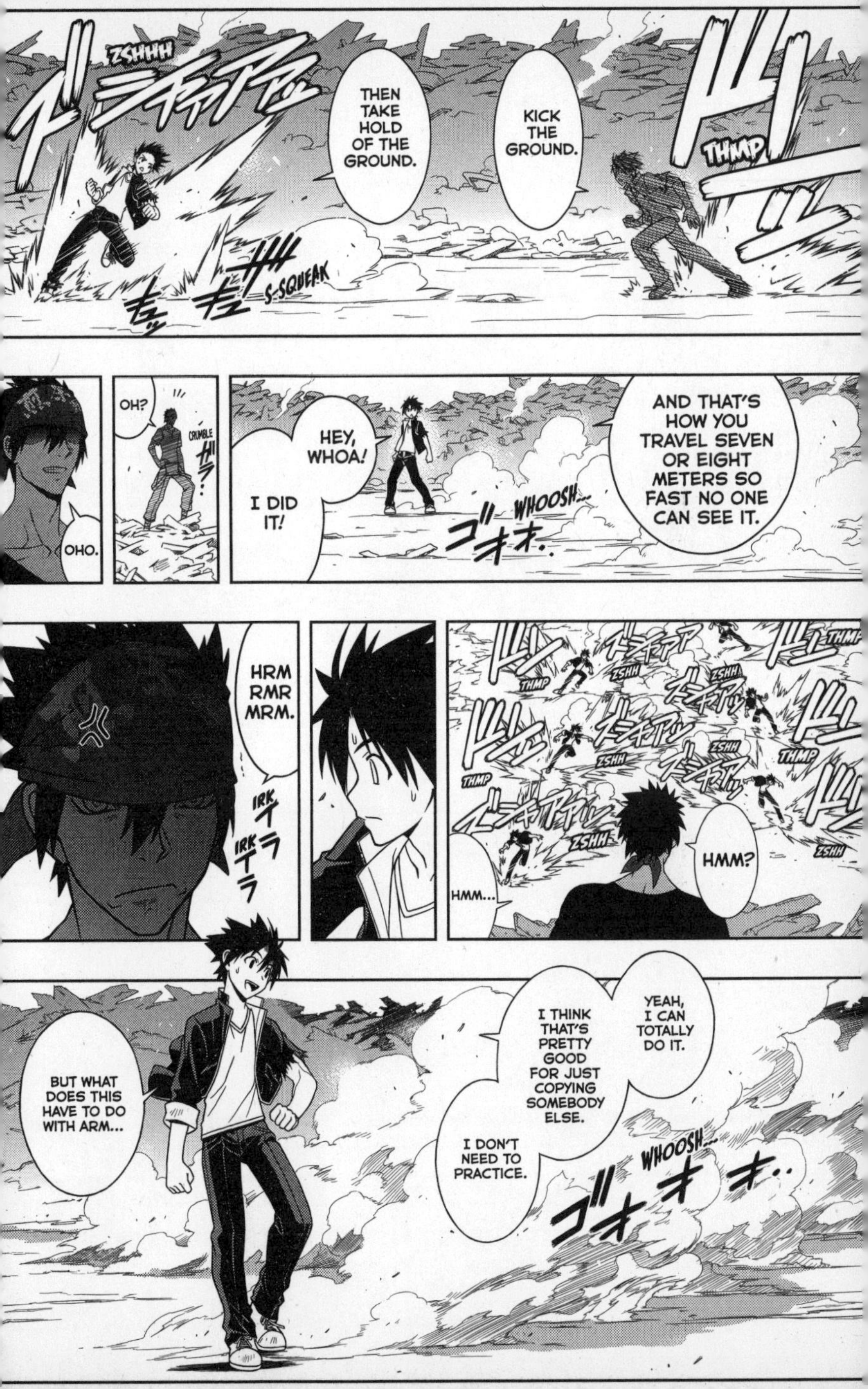
THMP
KICK THE GROUND.
THEN TAKE HOLD OF THE GROUND.
ZSHHH
S-SQUEAK
AND THAT'S HOW YOU TRAVEL SEVEN OR EIGHT METERS SO FAST NO ONE CAN SEE IT.
WHOOSH...
HEY, WHOA!
I DID IT!
OH?
CRUMBLE
OHO.
THMP
ZSHH
THMP
ZSHH
ZSHH
THMP
ZSHH
THMP
ZSHH
ZSHH
HMM?
HMM...
HRM RMR MRM.
IRK
IRK
YEAH, I CAN TOTALLY DO IT.
I THINK THAT'S PRETTY GOOD FOR JUST COPYING SOMEBODY ELSE.
I DON'T NEED TO PRACTICE.
WHOOSH...
BUT WHAT DOES THIS HAVE TO DO WITH ARM...

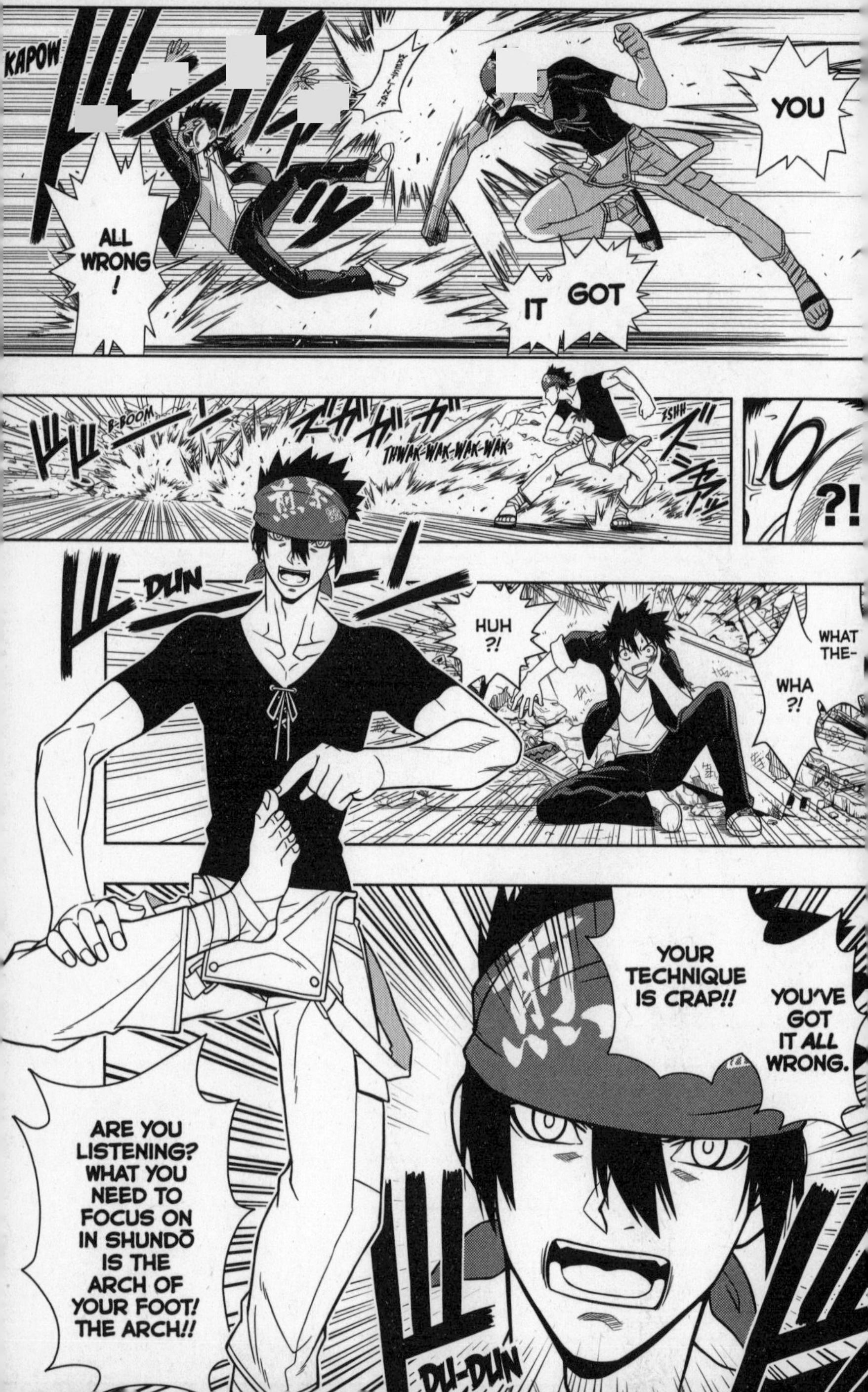
YOU
GOT IT
ALL WRONG!
KAPOW
?!
ZSHH
THWAK-WAK-WAK-WAK
B-BOOM
WHAT THE-
WHA ?!
HUH ?!
YOU'VE GOT IT ALL WRONG.
YOUR TECHNIQUE IS CRAP!!
DU-DUN
DUN
ARE YOU LISTENING? WHAT YOU NEED TO FOCUS ON IN SHUNDŌ IS THE ARCH OF YOUR FOOT! THE ARCH!!

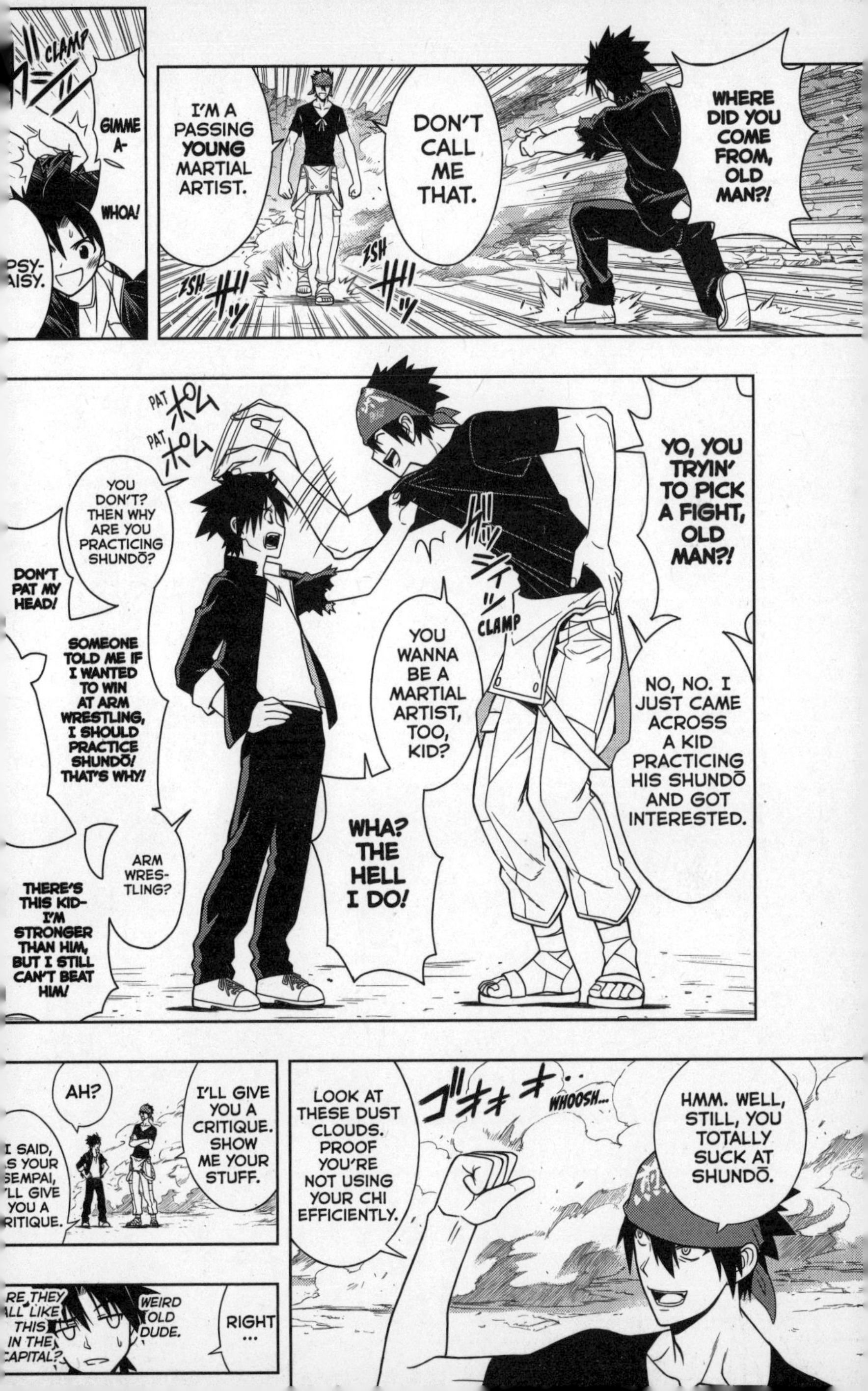
WHERE DID YOU COME FROM, OLD MAN?!
DON'T CALL ME THAT.
I'M A PASSING YOUNG MARTIAL ARTIST.
ZSH
ZSH
CLAMP
GIMME A-
WHOA!
PSY- AISY.
YO, YOU TRYIN' TO PICK A FIGHT, OLD MAN?!
CLAMP
NO, NO. I JUST CAME ACROSS A KID PRACTICING HIS SHUNDŌ AND GOT INTERESTED.
YOU WANNA BE A MARTIAL ARTIST, TOO, KID?
WHA? THE HELL I DO!
PAT
PAT
YOU DON'T? THEN WHY ARE YOU PRACTICING SHUNDŌ?
DON'T PAT MY HEAD!
SOMEONE TOLD ME IF I WANTED TO WIN AT ARM WRESTLING, I SHOULD PRACTICE SHUNDŌ! THAT'S WHY!
ARM WRES- TLING?
THERE'S THIS KID- I'M STRONGER THAN HIM, BUT I STILL CAN'T BEAT HIM!
HMM. WELL, STILL, YOU TOTALLY SUCK AT SHUNDŌ.
WHOOSH...
LOOK AT THESE DUST CLOUDS. PROOF YOU'RE NOT USING YOUR CHI EFFICIENTLY.
I'LL GIVE YOU A CRITIQUE. SHOW ME YOUR STUFF.
AH?
I SAID, S YOUR EMPAI, 'LL GIVE YOU A RITIQUE.
RIGHT...
WEIRD OLD DUDE.
RE THEY LL LIKE THIS IN THE CAPITAL?

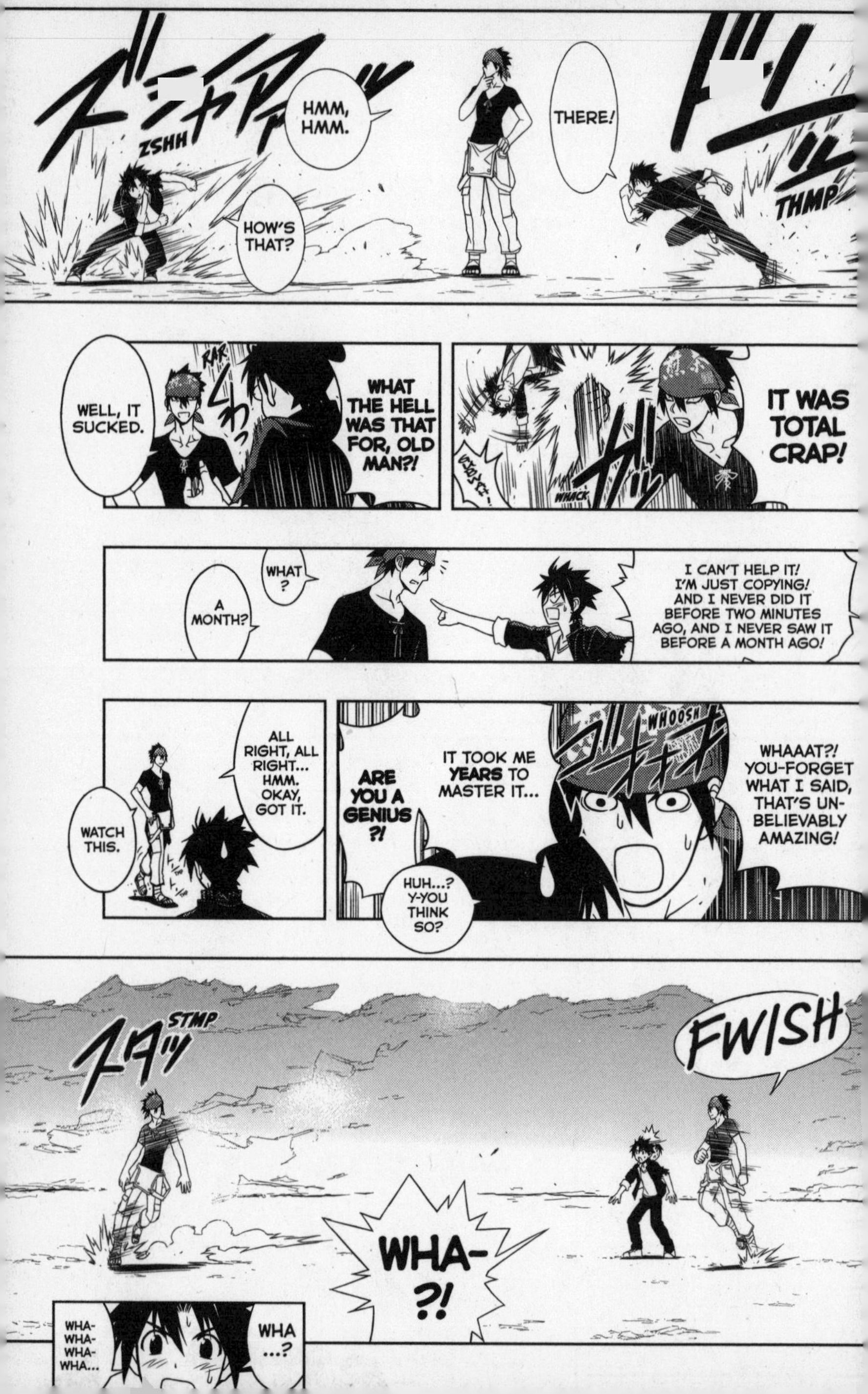
THMP
THERE!
HMM, HMM.
ZSHH
HOW'S THAT?
IT WAS TOTAL CRAP!
WHACK
WHAT THE HELL WAS THAT FOR, OLD MAN?!
RAR
WELL, IT SUCKED.
I CAN'T HELP IT! I'M JUST COPYING! AND I NEVER DID IT BEFORE TWO MINUTES AGO, AND I NEVER SAW IT BEFORE A MONTH AGO!
WHAT?
A MONTH?
WHAAAT?! YOU-FORGET WHAT I SAID, THAT'S UN-BELIEVABLY AMAZING!
WHOOSH
IT TOOK ME YEARS TO MASTER IT...
ARE YOU A GENIUS?!
HUH...? Y-YOU THINK SO?
ALL RIGHT, ALL RIGHT... HMM. OKAY, GOT IT.
WATCH THIS.
FWISH
STMP
WHA-?!
WHA...?
WHA-WHA-WHA-WHA...

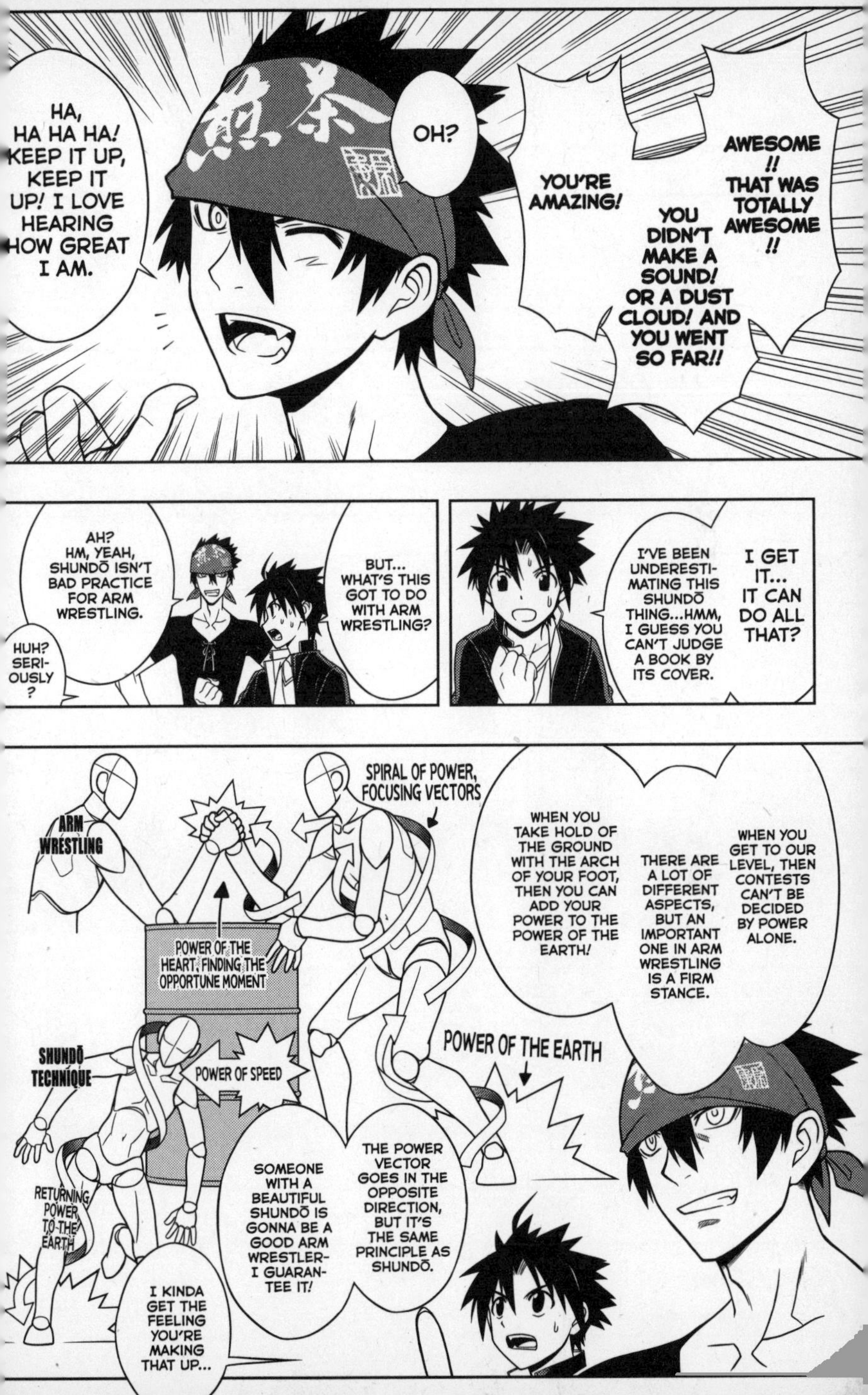
AWESOME!! THAT WAS TOTALLY AWESOME!!
YOU DIDN'T MAKE A SOUND! OR A DUST CLOUD! AND YOU WENT SO FAR!!
YOU'RE AMAZING!
OH?
HA, HA HA HA! KEEP IT UP, KEEP IT UP! I LOVE HEARING HOW GREAT I AM.
I GET IT... IT CAN DO ALL THAT?
I'VE BEEN UNDERESTI-MATING THIS SHUNDŌ THING...HMM, I GUESS YOU CAN'T JUDGE A BOOK BY ITS COVER.
BUT... WHAT'S THIS GOT TO DO WITH ARM WRESTLING?
AH? HM, YEAH, SHUNDŌ ISN'T BAD PRACTICE FOR ARM WRESTLING.
HUH? SERI-OUSLY?
WHEN YOU GET TO OUR LEVEL, THEN CONTESTS CAN'T BE DECIDED BY POWER ALONE.
THERE ARE A LOT OF DIFFERENT ASPECTS, BUT AN IMPORTANT ONE IN ARM WRESTLING IS A FIRM STANCE.
WHEN YOU TAKE HOLD OF THE GROUND WITH THE ARCH OF YOUR FOOT, THEN YOU CAN ADD YOUR POWER TO THE POWER OF THE EARTH!
SPIRAL OF POWER, FOCUSING VECTORS
ARM WRESTLING
POWER OF THE HEART, FINDING THE OPPORTUNE MOMENT
POWER OF THE EARTH
SHUNDŌ TECHNIQUE
POWER OF SPEED
RETURNING POWER TO THE EARTH
THE POWER VECTOR GOES IN THE OPPOSITE DIRECTION, BUT IT'S THE SAME PRINCIPLE AS SHUNDŌ.
SOMEONE WITH A BEAUTIFUL SHUNDŌ IS GONNA BE A GOOD ARM WRESTLER-I GUARAN-TEE IT!
I KINDA GET THE FEELING YOU'RE MAKING THAT UP...

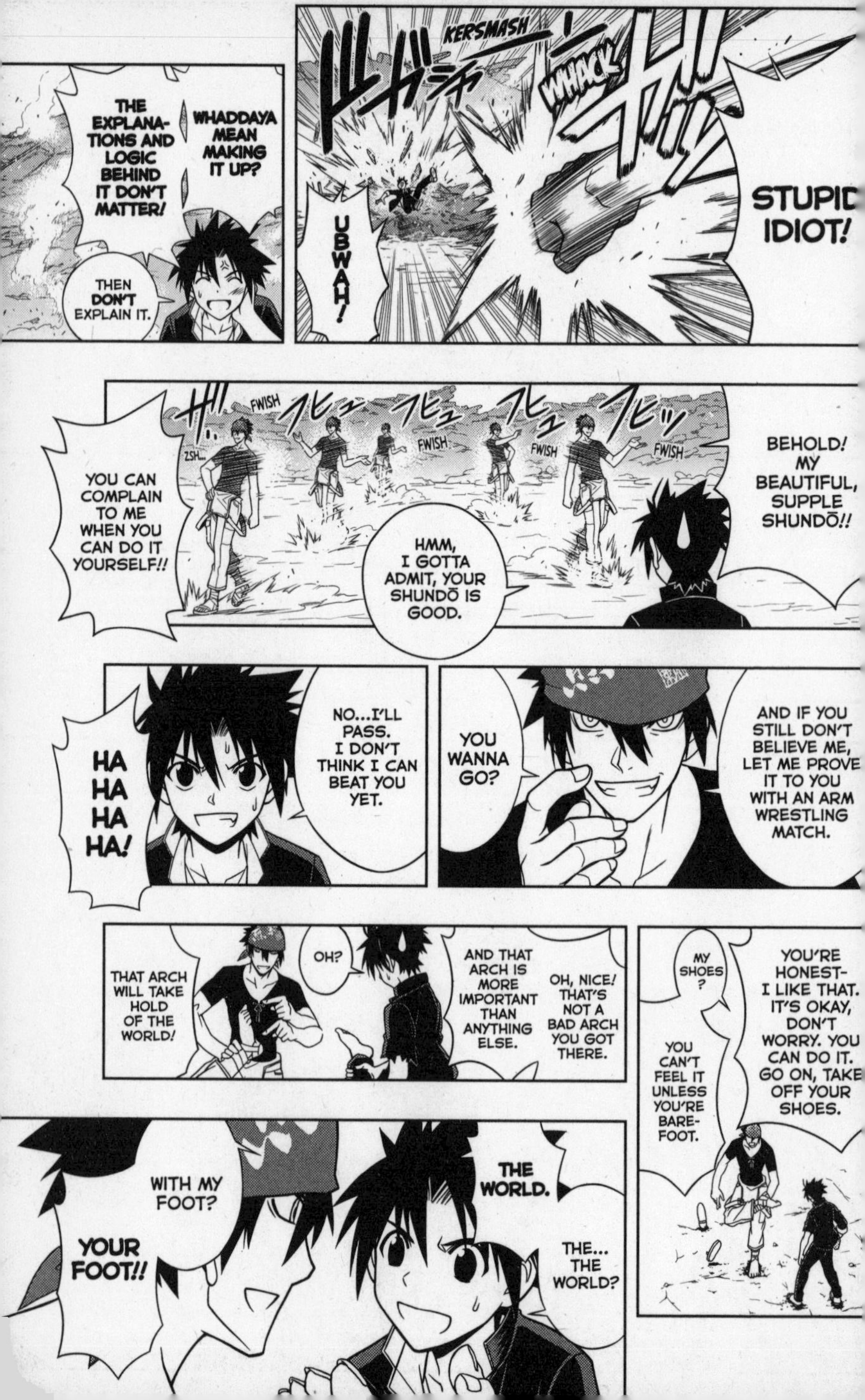
KERSMASH
WHACK
STUPID IDIOT!
UBWAH!
WHADDAYA MEAN MAKING IT UP?
THE EXPLANATIONS AND LOGIC BEHIND IT DON'T MATTER!
THEN DON'T EXPLAIN IT.
BEHOLD! MY BEAUTIFUL, SUPPLE SHUNDŌ!!
FWISH
FWISH
FWISH
FWISH
ZSH...
HMM, I GOTTA ADMIT, YOUR SHUNDŌ IS GOOD.
YOU CAN COMPLAIN TO ME WHEN YOU CAN DO IT YOURSELF!!
AND IF YOU STILL DON'T BELIEVE ME, LET ME PROVE IT TO YOU WITH AN ARM WRESTLING MATCH.
YOU WANNA GO?
NO...I'LL PASS. I DON'T THINK I CAN BEAT YOU YET.
HA HA HA HA!
YOU'RE HONEST- I LIKE THAT. IT'S OKAY, DON'T WORRY. YOU CAN DO IT. GO ON, TAKE OFF YOUR SHOES.
MY SHOES?
YOU CAN'T FEEL IT UNLESS YOU'RE BARE-FOOT.
OH, NICE! THAT'S NOT A BAD ARCH YOU GOT THERE.
AND THAT ARCH IS MORE IMPORTANT THAN ANYTHING ELSE.
OH?
THAT ARCH WILL TAKE HOLD OF THE WORLD!
THE WORLD.
THE... THE WORLD?
WITH MY FOOT?
YOUR FOOT!!

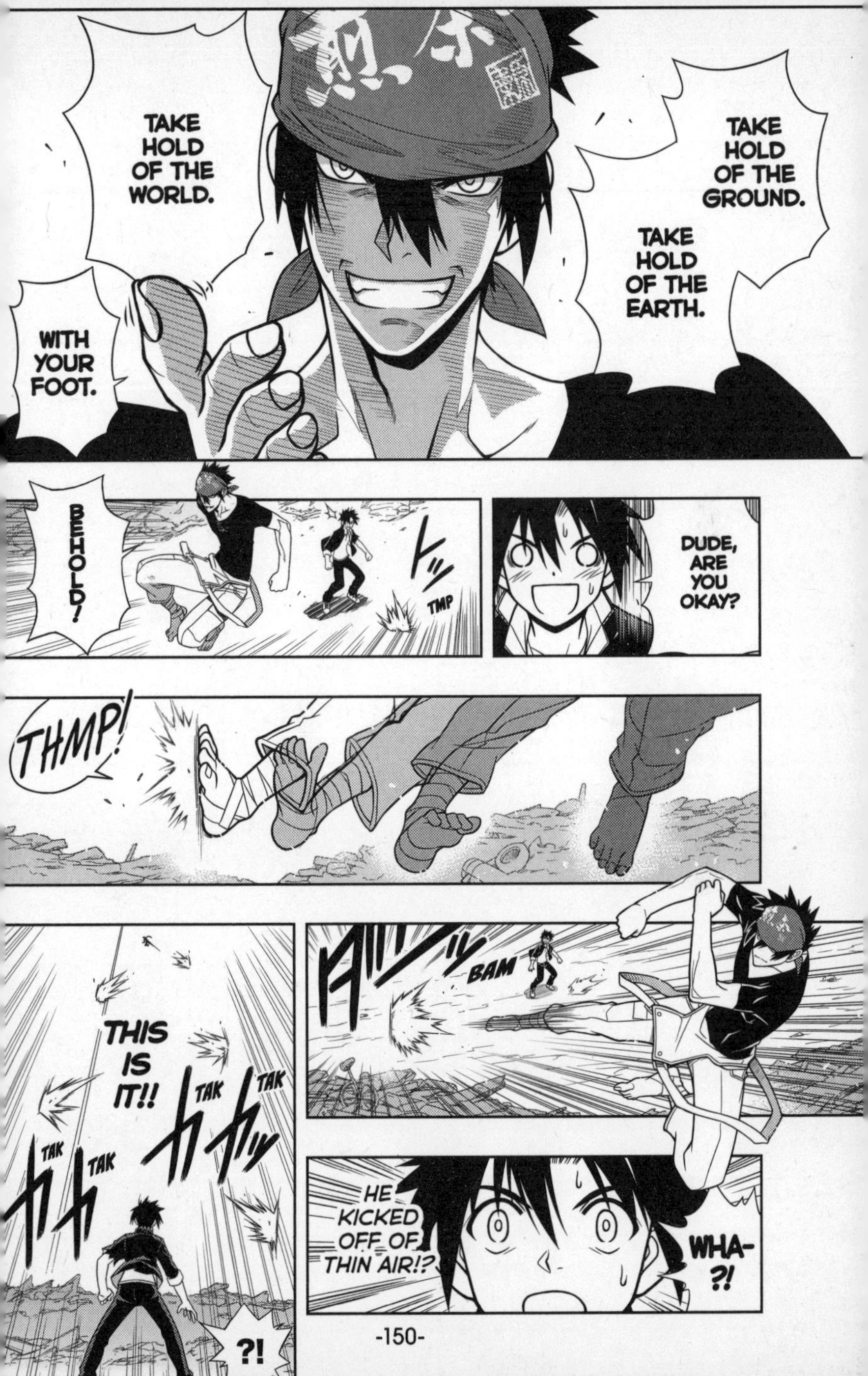

TAKE HOLD OF THE GROUND.
TAKE HOLD OF THE EARTH.
TAKE HOLD OF THE WORLD.
WITH YOUR FOOT.
DUDE, ARE YOU OKAY?
TMP
BEHOLD!
THMP!
BAM
THIS IS IT!!
TAK
TAK
TAK
TAK
?!
WHA-?!
HE KICKED OFF OF THIN AIR!?

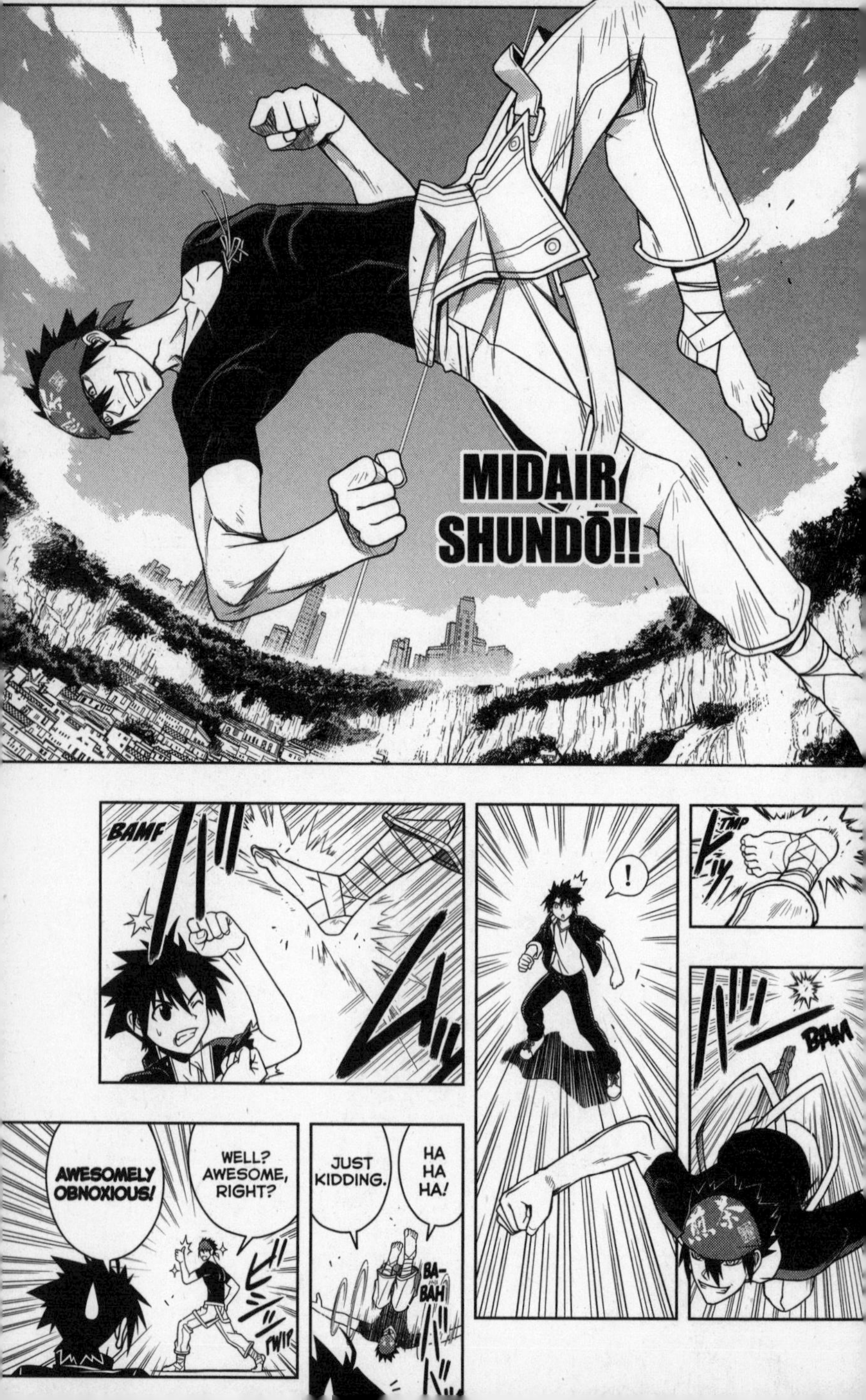
MIDAIR SHUNDŌ!!
TMP
BAM
!
BAMF
HA HA HA!
JUST KIDDING.
BA-BAH
WELL? AWESOME, RIGHT?
AWESOMELY OBNOXIOUS!
FWIP

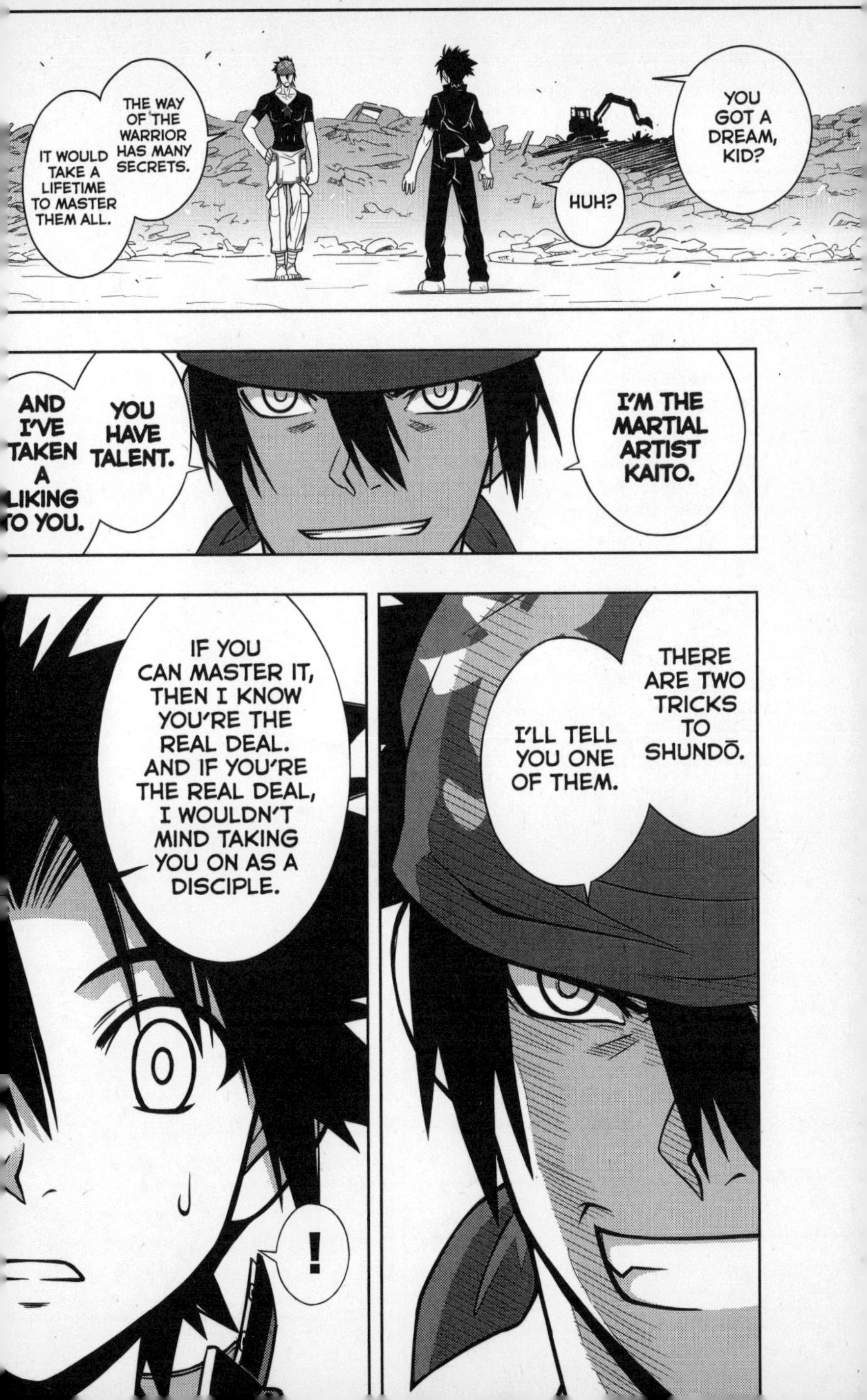
YOU GOT A DREAM, KID?
HUH?
THE WAY OF THE WARRIOR HAS MANY SECRETS.
IT WOULD TAKE A LIFETIME TO MASTER THEM ALL.
I'M THE MARTIAL ARTIST KAITO.
YOU HAVE TALENT.
AND I'VE TAKEN A LIKING TO YOU.
THERE ARE TWO TRICKS TO SHUNDŌ.
I'LL TELL YOU ONE OF THEM.
IF YOU CAN MASTER IT, THEN I KNOW YOU'RE THE REAL DEAL. AND IF YOU'RE THE REAL DEAL, I WOULDN'T MIND TAKING YOU ON AS A DISCIPLE.
!

UQ HOLDER!

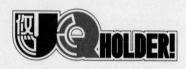

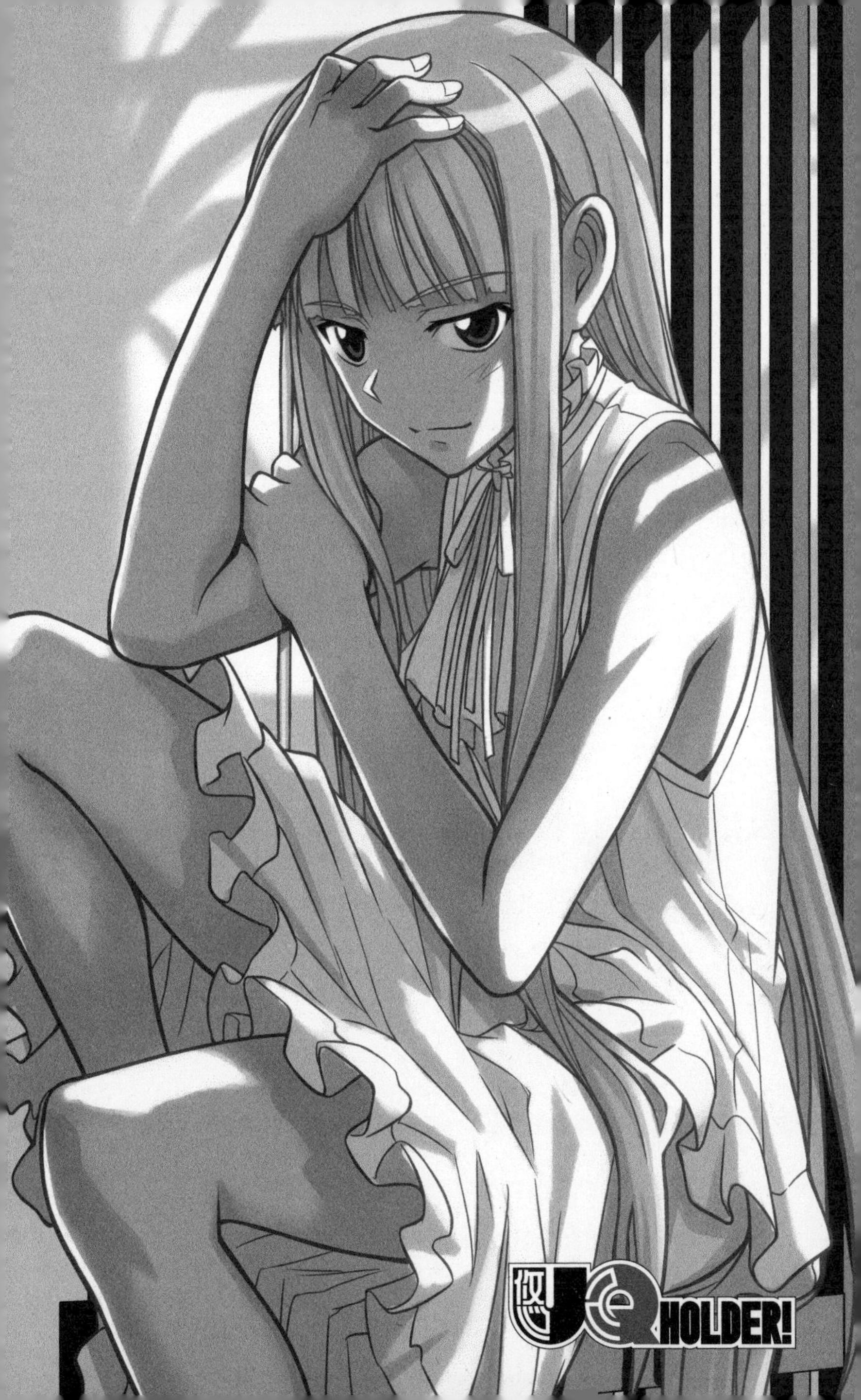
UQ HOLDER!

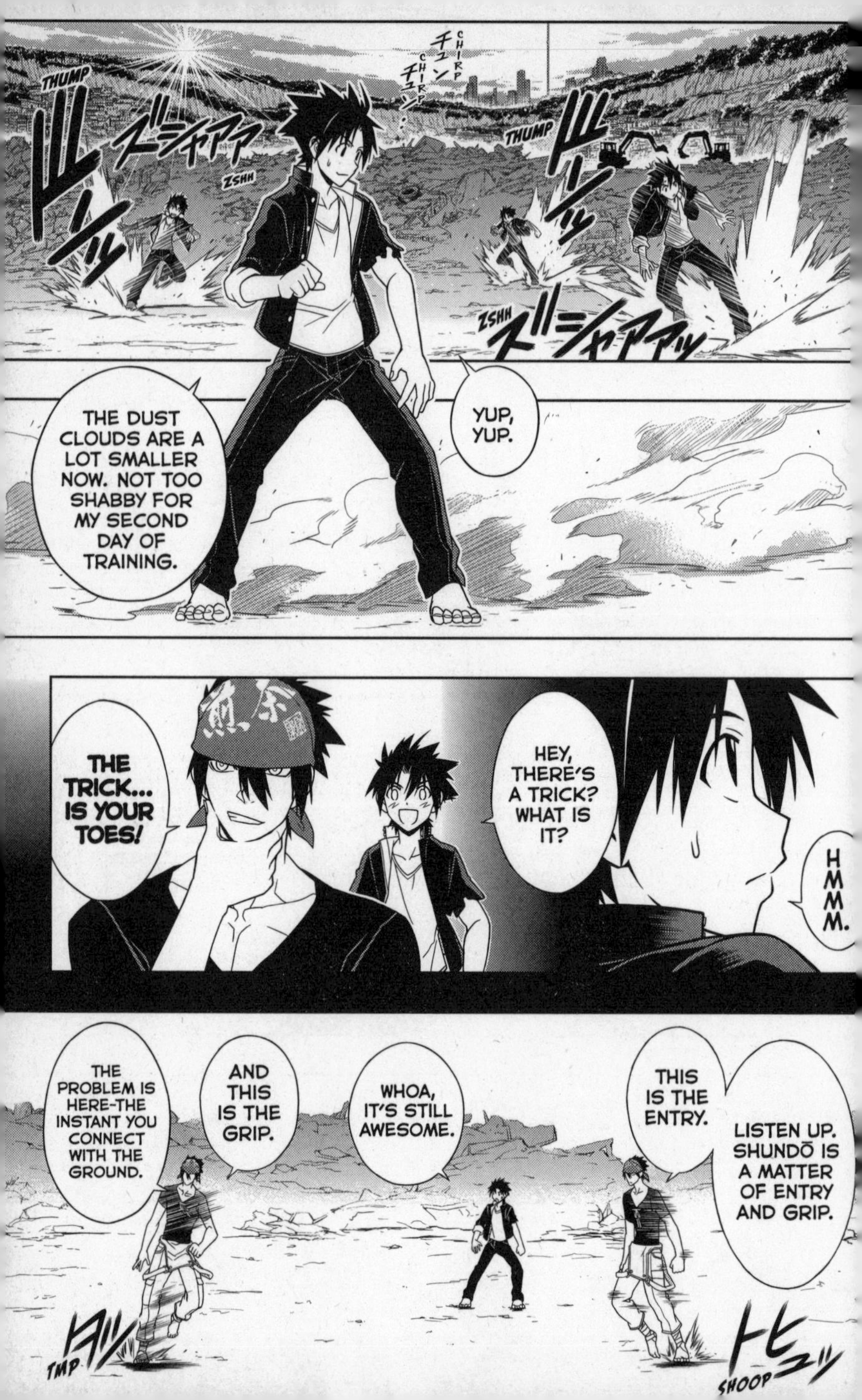

THUMP ドンッ
ZSHH ズシャアアッ
CHIRP チュン
CHIRP チュン…
THUMP ドンッ
ズシャアア ZSHH
YUP, YUP.
THE DUST CLOUDS ARE A LOT SMALLER NOW. NOT TOO SHABBY FOR MY SECOND DAY OF TRAINING.
HMMM.
HEY, THERE'S A TRICK? WHAT IS IT?
THE TRICK... IS YOUR TOES!
LISTEN UP. SHUNDŌ IS A MATTER OF ENTRY AND GRIP.
THIS IS THE ENTRY.
SHOOP
WHOA, IT'S STILL AWESOME.
AND THIS IS THE GRIP.
THE PROBLEM IS HERE-THE INSTANT YOU CONNECT WITH THE GROUND.
TMP

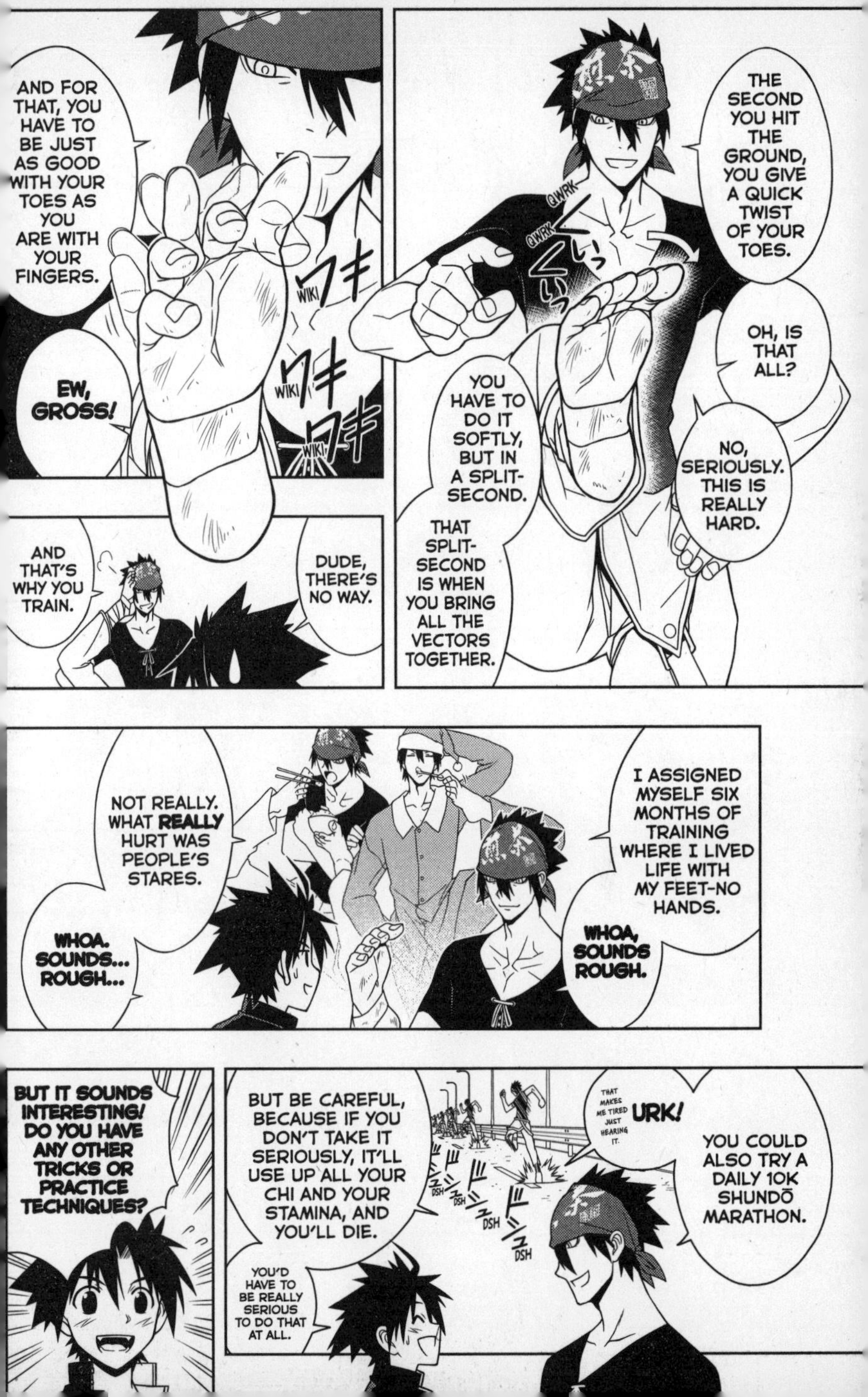
THE SECOND YOU HIT THE GROUND, YOU GIVE A QUICK TWIST OF YOUR TOES.
QWRK
QWRK
OH, IS THAT ALL?
NO, SERIOUSLY. THIS IS REALLY HARD.
YOU HAVE TO DO IT SOFTLY, BUT IN A SPLIT-SECOND.
THAT SPLIT-SECOND IS WHEN YOU BRING ALL THE VECTORS TOGETHER.
AND FOR THAT, YOU HAVE TO BE JUST AS GOOD WITH YOUR TOES AS YOU ARE WITH YOUR FINGERS.
WIKI
WIKI
WIKI
EW, GROSS!
DUDE, THERE'S NO WAY.
AND THAT'S WHY YOU TRAIN.
I ASSIGNED MYSELF SIX MONTHS OF TRAINING WHERE I LIVED LIFE WITH MY FEET-NO HANDS.
WHOA, SOUNDS ROUGH.
NOT REALLY. WHAT REALLY HURT WAS PEOPLE'S STARES.
WHOA. SOUNDS... ROUGH...
YOU COULD ALSO TRY A DAILY 10K SHUNDŌ MARATHON.
URK!
THAT MAKES ME TIRED JUST HEARING IT.
BUT BE CAREFUL, BECAUSE IF YOU DON'T TAKE IT SERIOUSLY, IT'LL USE UP ALL YOUR CHI AND YOUR STAMINA, AND YOU'LL DIE.
DSH
DSH
DSH
DSH
YOU'D HAVE TO BE REALLY SERIOUS TO DO THAT AT ALL.
BUT IT SOUNDS INTERESTING! DO YOU HAVE ANY OTHER TRICKS OR PRACTICE TECHNIQUES?

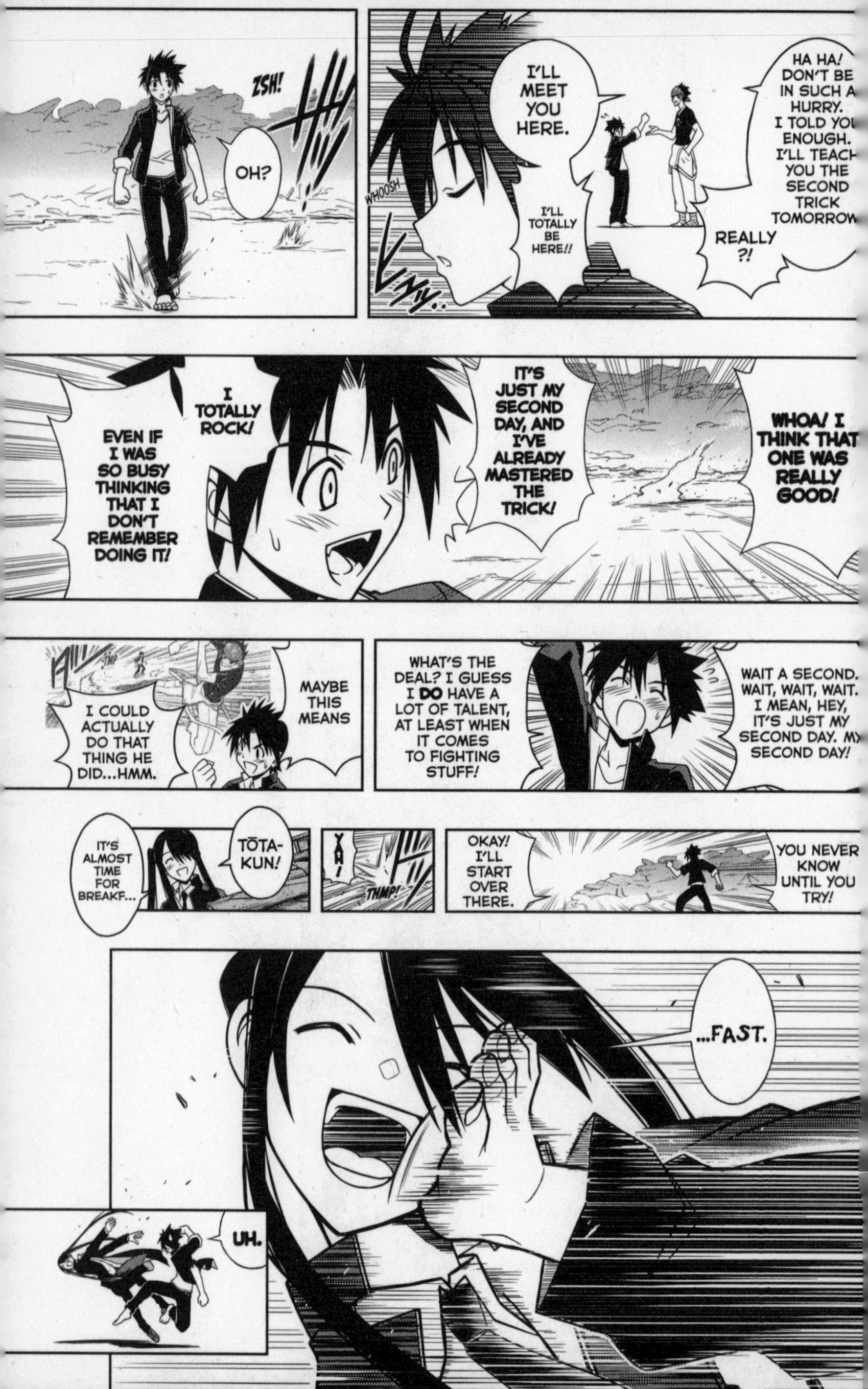

HA HA! DON'T BE IN SUCH A HURRY. I TOLD YOU ENOUGH. I'LL TEACH YOU THE SECOND TRICK TOMORROW
I'LL MEET YOU HERE.
REALLY?!
I'LL TOTALLY BE HERE!!
WHOOSH
ZSH!
OH?
WHOA! I THINK THAT ONE WAS REALLY GOOD!
IT'S JUST MY SECOND DAY, AND I'VE ALREADY MASTERED THE TRICK!
I TOTALLY ROCK!
EVEN IF I WAS SO BUSY THINKING THAT I DON'T REMEMBER DOING IT!
WAIT A SECOND. WAIT, WAIT, WAIT. I MEAN, HEY, IT'S JUST MY SECOND DAY. MY SECOND DAY!
WHAT'S THE DEAL? I GUESS I **DO** HAVE A LOT OF TALENT, AT LEAST WHEN IT COMES TO FIGHTING STUFF!
MAYBE THIS MEANS
I COULD ACTUALLY DO THAT THING HE DID...HMM.
YOU NEVER KNOW UNTIL YOU TRY!
OKAY! I'LL START OVER THERE.
YAH!
THMP!
TŌTA-KUN!
IT'S ALMOST TIME FOR BREAKF...
...FAST.
UH.

STAGE 16: THE BLIND IMMORTAL HUNTER

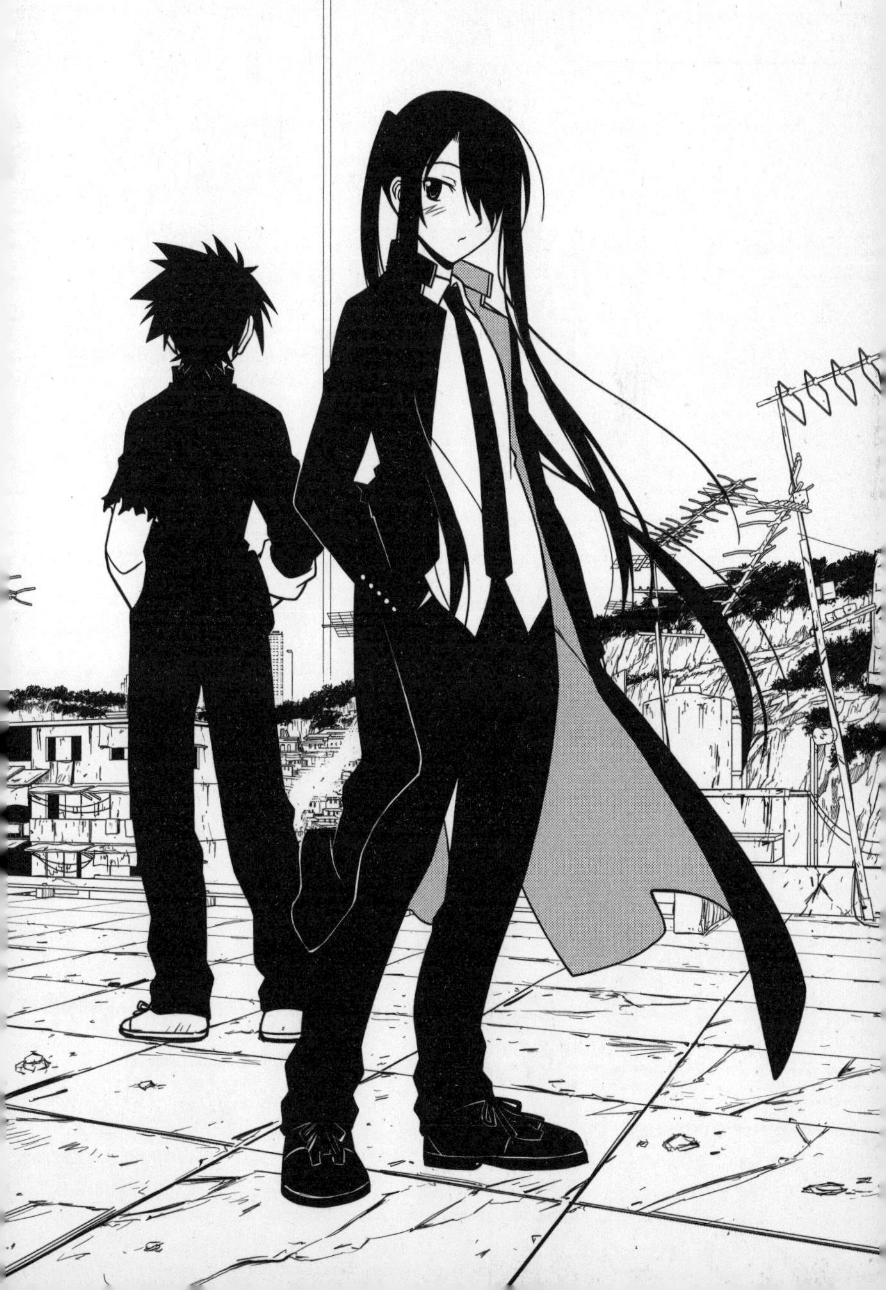

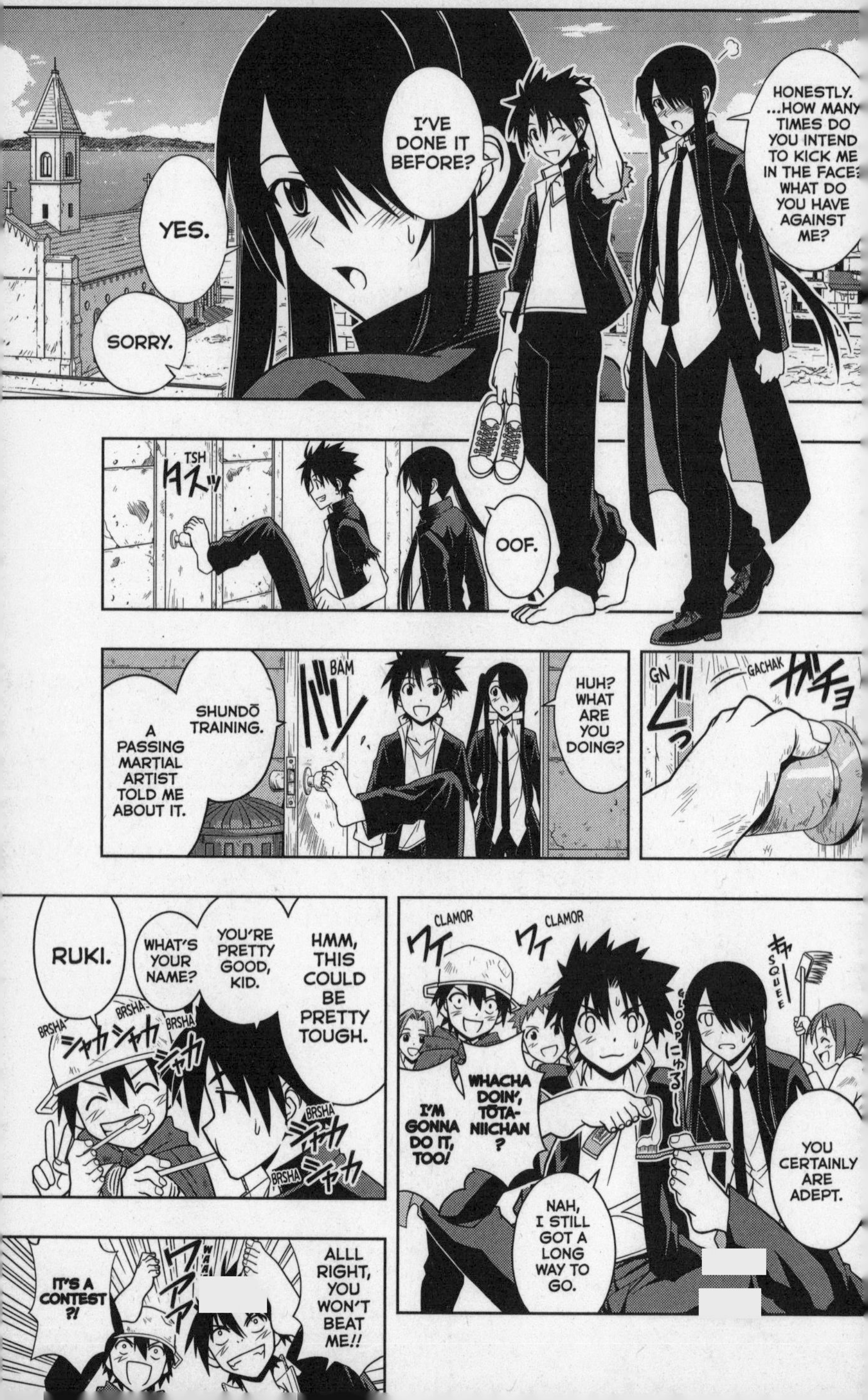
HONESTLY. ...HOW MANY TIMES DO YOU INTEND TO KICK ME IN THE FACE? WHAT DO YOU HAVE AGAINST ME?
I'VE DONE IT BEFORE?
YES.
SORRY.
OOF.
TSH
GACHAK
GN
HUH? WHAT ARE YOU DOING?
BAM
SHUNDŌ TRAINING.
A PASSING MARTIAL ARTIST TOLD ME ABOUT IT.
CLAMOR
CLAMOR
SQUEE
GLOOP
YOU CERTAINLY ARE ADEPT.
WHACHA DOIN', TŌTA-NIICHAN?
I'M GONNA DO IT, TOO!
NAH, I STILL GOT A LONG WAY TO GO.
HMM, THIS COULD BE PRETTY TOUGH.
YOU'RE PRETTY GOOD, KID.
WHAT'S YOUR NAME?
RUKI.
BRSHA
BRSHA
BRSHA
BRSHA
BRSHA
ALLL RIGHT, YOU WON'T BEAT ME!!
WAAA
IT'S A CONTEST?!

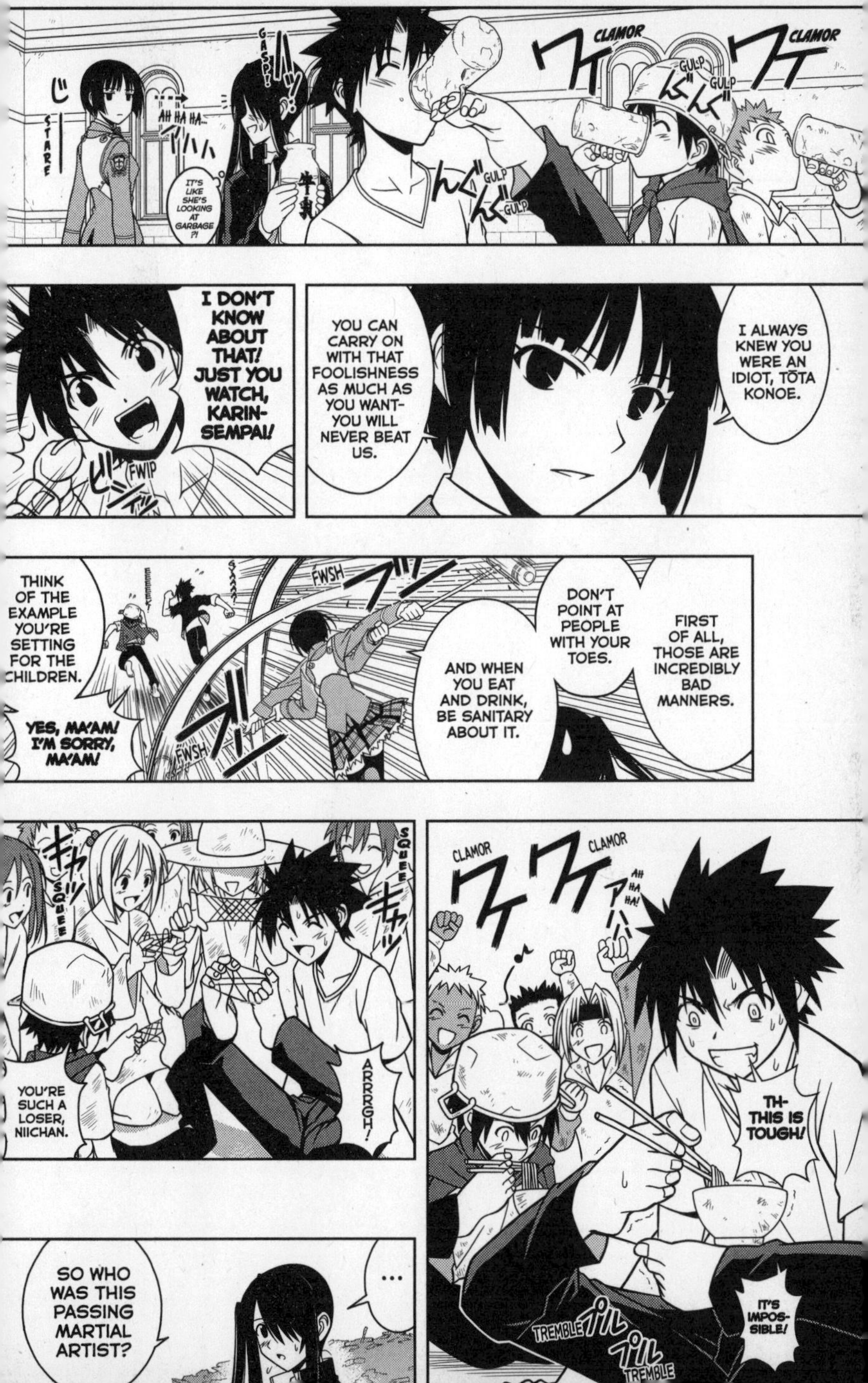
CLAMOR
CLAMOR
GULP GULP
GULP GULP
GASP!
AH HA HA...
IT'S LIKE SHE'S LOOKING AT GARBAGE?!
STARE
I ALWAYS KNEW YOU WERE AN IDIOT, TŌTA KONOE.
YOU CAN CARRY ON WITH THAT FOOLISHNESS AS MUCH AS YOU WANT- YOU WILL NEVER BEAT US.
I DON'T KNOW ABOUT THAT! JUST YOU WATCH, KARIN-SEMPAI!
FWIP
FIRST OF ALL, THOSE ARE INCREDIBLY BAD MANNERS.
DON'T POINT AT PEOPLE WITH YOUR TOES.
AND WHEN YOU EAT AND DRINK, BE SANITARY ABOUT IT.
FWSH
THINK OF THE EXAMPLE YOU'RE SETTING FOR THE CHILDREN.
YES, MA'AM! I'M SORRY, MA'AM!
FWSH
CLAMOR
CLAMOR
AH HA HA!
TH- THIS IS TOUGH!
IT'S IMPOSSIBLE!
TREMBLE
TREMBLE
SQUEE
SQUEE
ARRRGH!
YOU'RE SUCH A LOSER, NIICHAN.
...
SO WHO WAS THIS PASSING MARTIAL ARTIST?

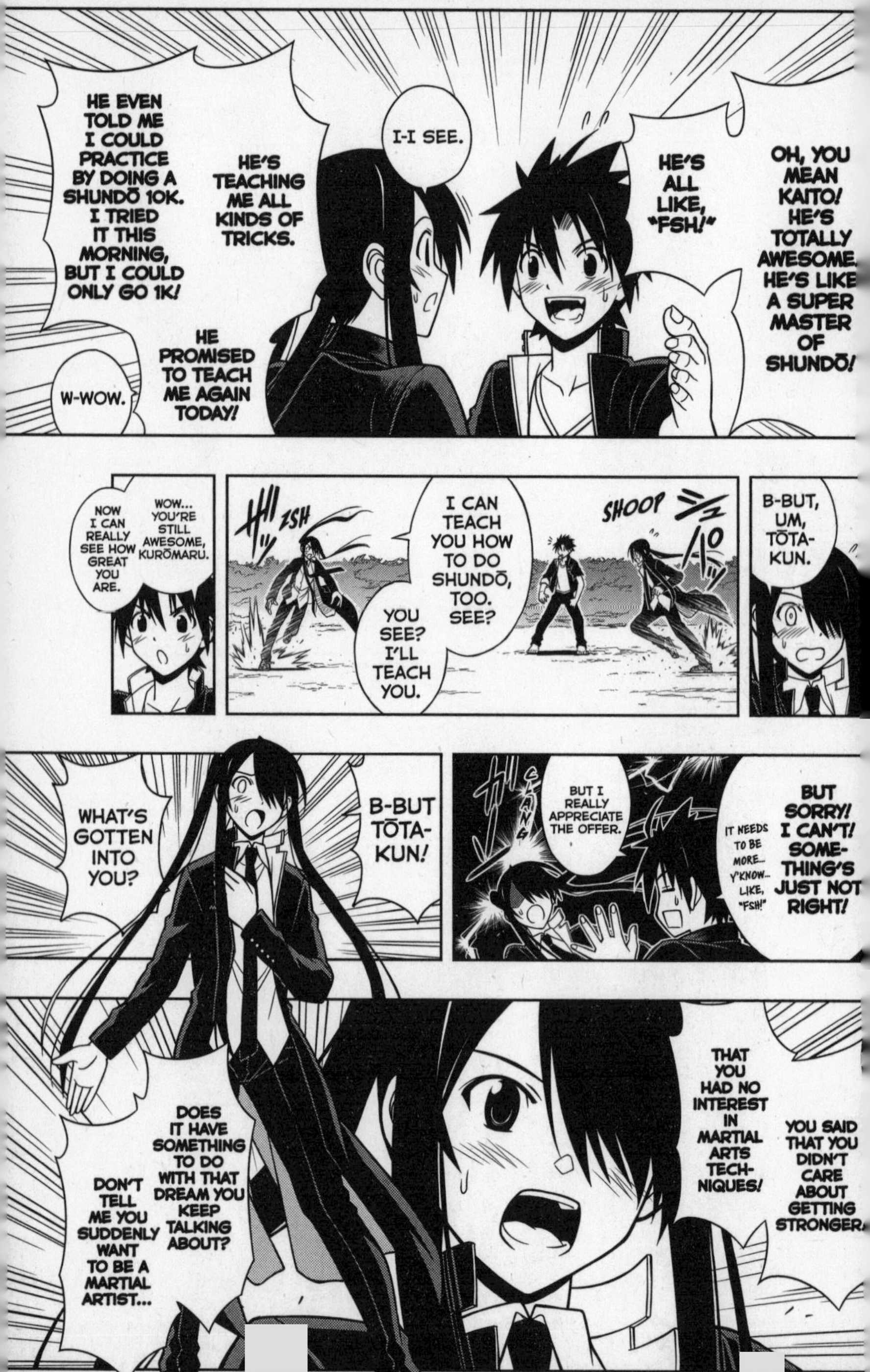
OH, YOU MEAN KAITO! HE'S TOTALLY AWESOME. HE'S LIKE A SUPER MASTER OF SHUNDŌ!
HE'S ALL LIKE, "FSH!"
I-I SEE.
HE'S TEACHING ME ALL KINDS OF TRICKS.
HE EVEN TOLD ME I COULD PRACTICE BY DOING A SHUNDŌ 10K. I TRIED IT THIS MORNING, BUT I COULD ONLY GO 1K!
HE PROMISED TO TEACH ME AGAIN TODAY!
W-WOW.
B-BUT, UM, TŌTA-KUN.
SHOOP
I CAN TEACH YOU HOW TO DO SHUNDŌ, TOO. SEE?
ZSH
YOU SEE? I'LL TEACH YOU.
WOW... YOU'RE STILL AWESOME, KURŌMARU.
NOW I CAN REALLY SEE HOW GREAT YOU ARE.
BUT SORRY! I CAN'T! SOME-THING'S JUST NOT RIGHT!
IT NEEDS TO BE MORE... Y'KNOW... LIKE, "FSH!"
BUT I REALLY APPRECIATE THE OFFER.
SHANG
B-BUT TŌTA-KUN!
WHAT'S GOTTEN INTO YOU?
YOU SAID THAT YOU DIDN'T CARE ABOUT GETTING STRONGER.
THAT YOU HAD NO INTEREST IN MARTIAL ARTS TECH-NIQUES!
DOES IT HAVE SOMETHING TO DO WITH THAT DREAM YOU KEEP TALKING ABOUT?
DON'T TELL ME YOU SUDDENLY WANT TO BE A MARTIAL ARTIST...

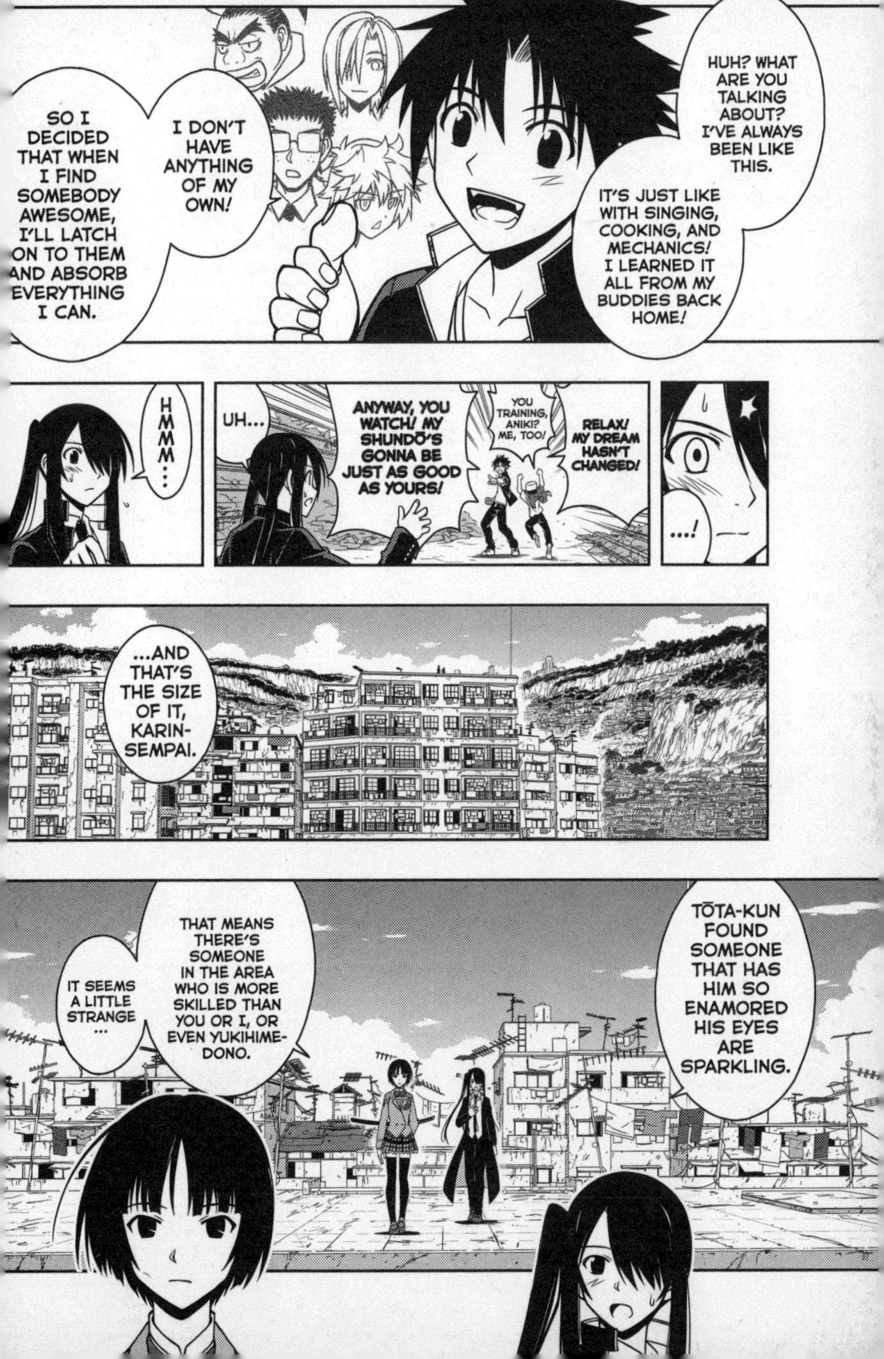
HUH? WHAT ARE YOU TALKING ABOUT? I'VE ALWAYS BEEN LIKE THIS.
IT'S JUST LIKE WITH SINGING, COOKING, AND MECHANICS! I LEARNED IT ALL FROM MY BUDDIES BACK HOME!
I DON'T HAVE ANYTHING OF MY OWN!
SO I DECIDED THAT WHEN I FIND SOMEBODY AWESOME, I'LL LATCH ON TO THEM AND ABSORB EVERYTHING I CAN.
...!
RELAX! MY DREAM HASN'T CHANGED!
YOU TRAINING, ANIKI? ME, TOO!
ANYWAY, YOU WATCH! MY SHUNDŌ'S GONNA BE JUST AS GOOD AS YOURS!
UH...
HMMM...
...AND THAT'S THE SIZE OF IT, KARIN-SEMPAI.
TŌTA-KUN FOUND SOMEONE THAT HAS HIM SO ENAMORED HIS EYES ARE SPARKLING.
THAT MEANS THERE'S SOMEONE IN THE AREA WHO IS MORE SKILLED THAN YOU OR I, OR EVEN YUKIHIME-DONO.
IT SEEMS A LITTLE STRANGE ...

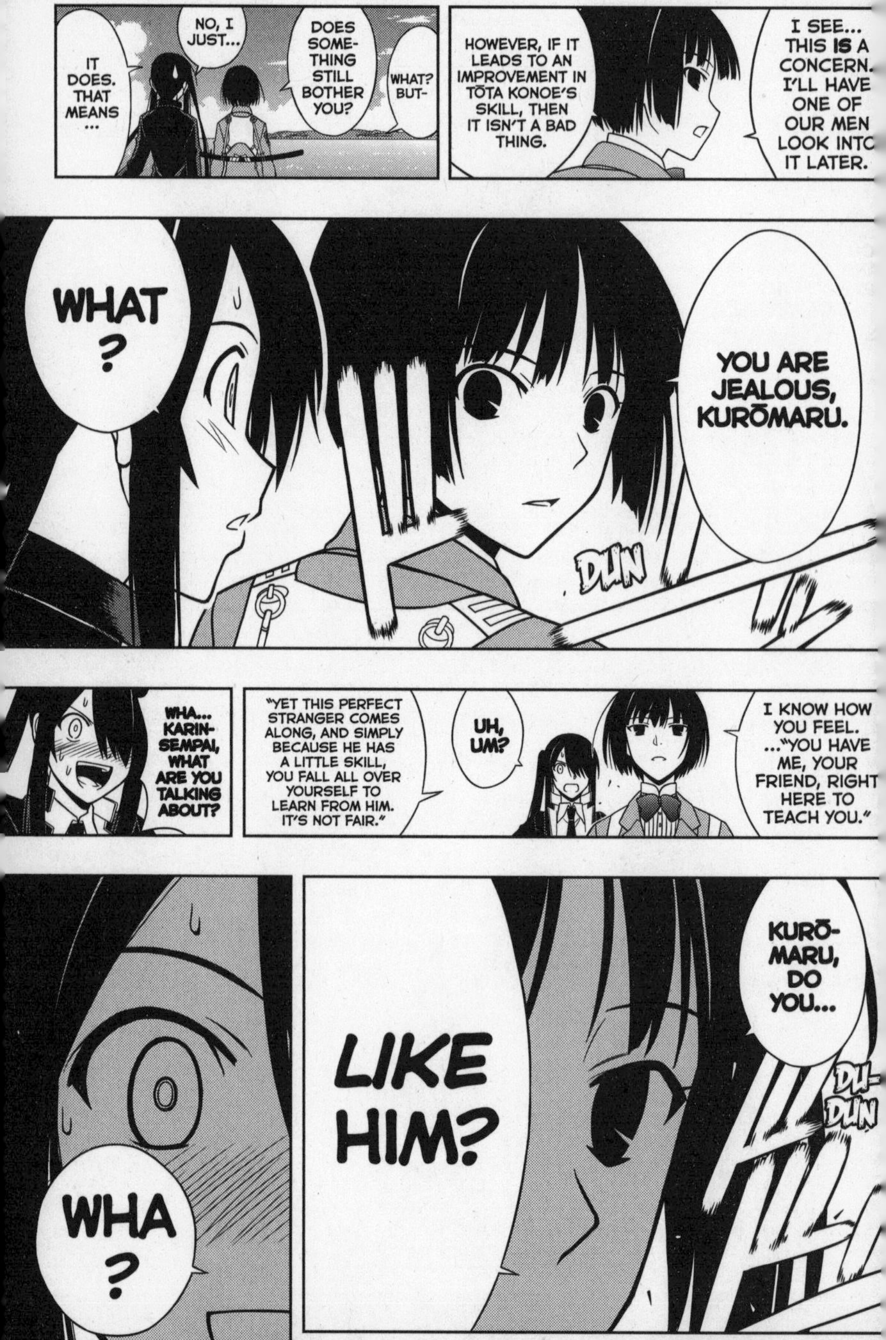
I SEE... THIS IS A CONCERN. I'LL HAVE ONE OF OUR MEN LOOK INTO IT LATER.
HOWEVER, IF IT LEADS TO AN IMPROVEMENT IN TŌTA KONOE'S SKILL, THEN IT ISN'T A BAD THING.
WHAT? BUT-
DOES SOMETHING STILL BOTHER YOU?
NO, I JUST...
IT DOES. THAT MEANS...
YOU ARE JEALOUS, KURŌMARU.
DUN
WHAT?
I KNOW HOW YOU FEEL. ..."YOU HAVE ME, YOUR FRIEND, RIGHT HERE TO TEACH YOU."
UH, UM?
"YET THIS PERFECT STRANGER COMES ALONG, AND SIMPLY BECAUSE HE HAS A LITTLE SKILL, YOU FALL ALL OVER YOURSELF TO LEARN FROM HIM. IT'S NOT FAIR."
WHA... KARIN-SEMPAI, WHAT ARE YOU TALKING ABOUT?
KURŌ-MARU, DO YOU...
DU-DUN
LIKE HIM?
WHA?

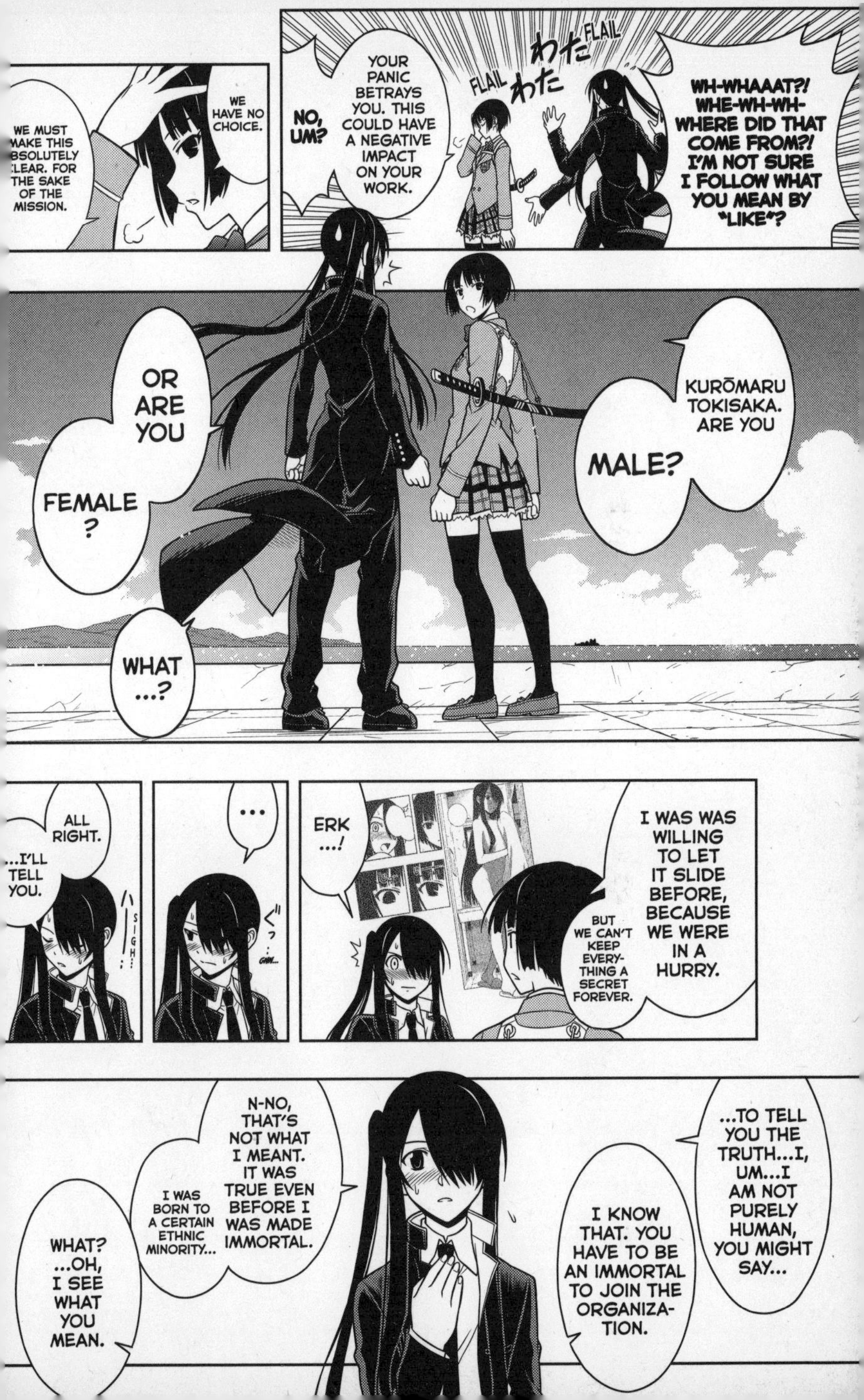

WH-WHAAAT?! WHE-WH-WH- WHERE DID THAT COME FROM?! I'M NOT SURE I FOLLOW WHAT YOU MEAN BY "LIKE"?
わた FLAIL
わた FLAIL
NO, UM?
YOUR PANIC BETRAYS YOU. THIS COULD HAVE A NEGATIVE IMPACT ON YOUR WORK.
WE HAVE NO CHOICE.
WE MUST MAKE THIS BSOLUTELY LEAR. FOR THE SAKE OF THE MISSION.
KURŌMARU TOKISAKA. ARE YOU
MALE?
OR ARE YOU
FEMALE?
WHAT...?
I WAS WAS WILLING TO LET IT SLIDE BEFORE, BECAUSE WE WERE IN A HURRY.
BUT WE CAN'T KEEP EVERYTHING A SECRET FOREVER.
ERK...!
...
ぐっ GAH...
ALL RIGHT.
...I'LL TELL YOU.
ハ… SIGH…
...TO TELL YOU THE TRUTH...I, UM...I AM NOT PURELY HUMAN, YOU MIGHT SAY...
I KNOW THAT. YOU HAVE TO BE AN IMMORTAL TO JOIN THE ORGANIZATION.
N-NO, THAT'S NOT WHAT I MEANT. IT WAS TRUE EVEN BEFORE I WAS MADE IMMORTAL.
I WAS BORN TO A CERTAIN ETHNIC MINORITY...
WHAT? ...OH, I SEE WHAT YOU MEAN.

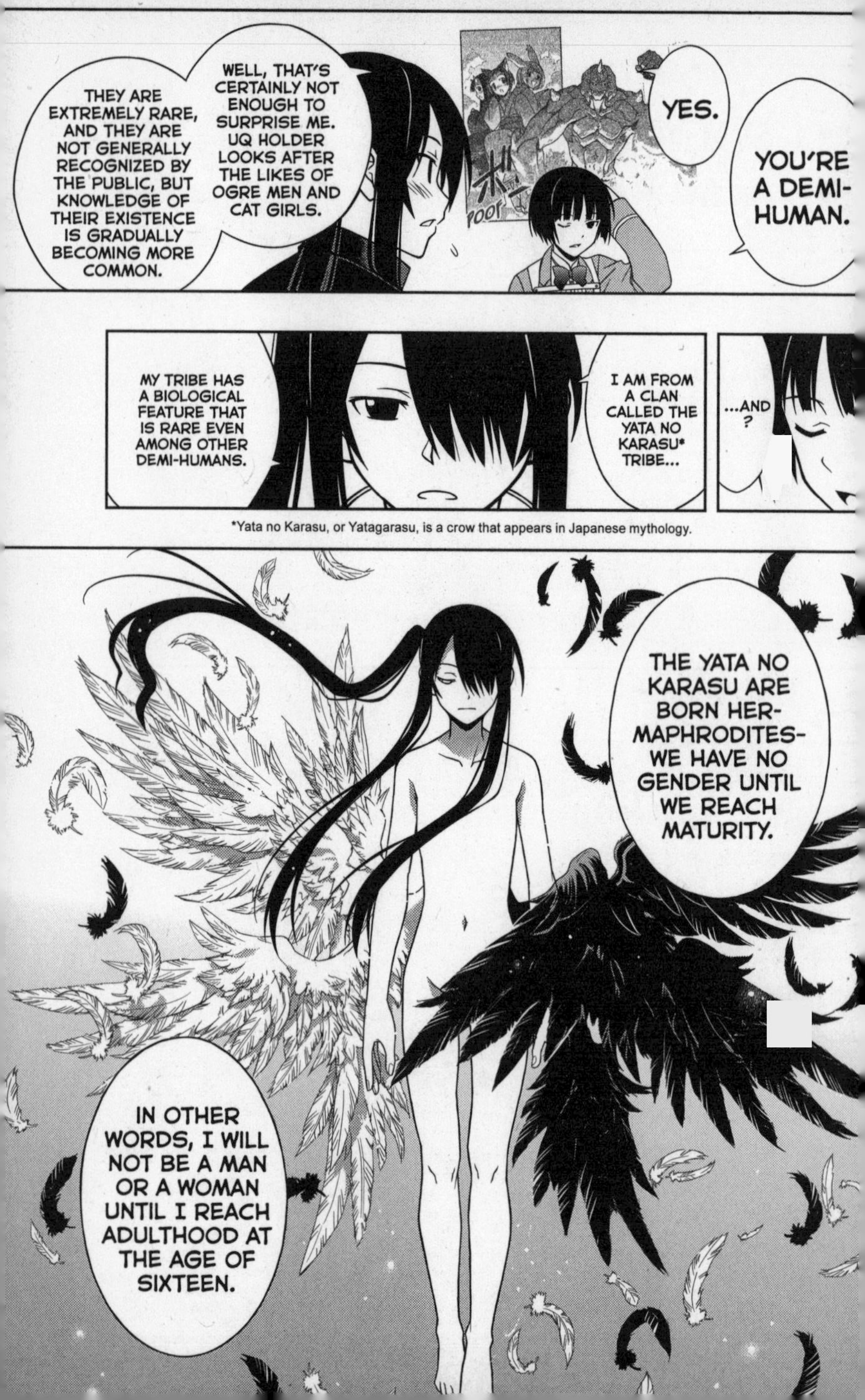
YOU'RE A DEMI-HUMAN.
YES.
POOF
WELL, THAT'S CERTAINLY NOT ENOUGH TO SURPRISE ME. UQ HOLDER LOOKS AFTER THE LIKES OF OGRE MEN AND CAT GIRLS.
THEY ARE EXTREMELY RARE, AND THEY ARE NOT GENERALLY RECOGNIZED BY THE PUBLIC, BUT KNOWLEDGE OF THEIR EXISTENCE IS GRADUALLY BECOMING MORE COMMON.
...AND ?
I AM FROM A CLAN CALLED THE YATA NO KARASU* TRIBE...
MY TRIBE HAS A BIOLOGICAL FEATURE THAT IS RARE EVEN AMONG OTHER DEMI-HUMANS.
*Yata no Karasu, or Yatagarasu, is a crow that appears in Japanese mythology.
THE YATA NO KARASU ARE BORN HER-MAPHRODITES-WE HAVE NO GENDER UNTIL WE REACH MATURITY.
IN OTHER WORDS, I WILL NOT BE A MAN OR A WOMAN UNTIL I REACH ADULTHOOD AT THE AGE OF SIXTEEN.

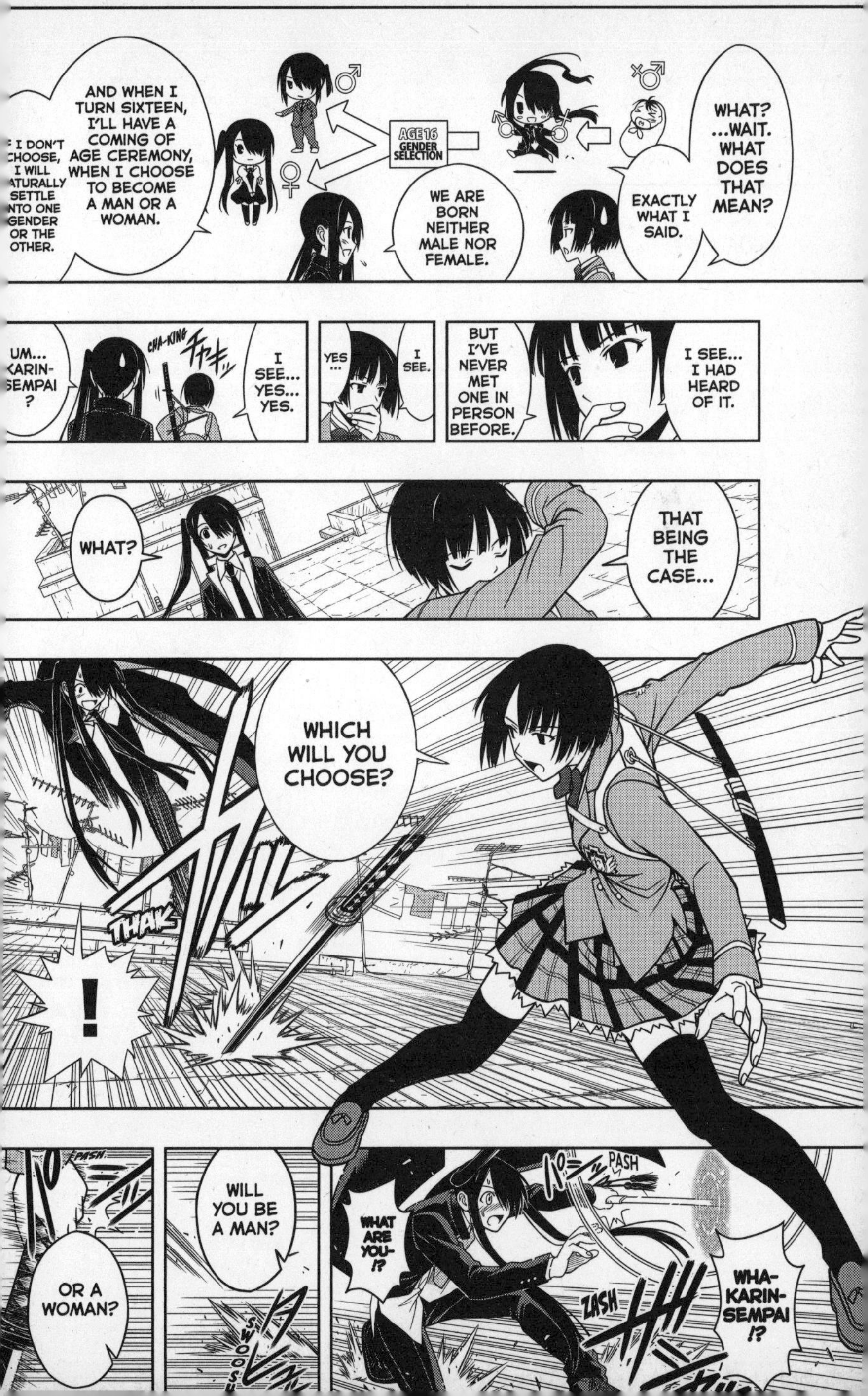
WHAT? ...WAIT. WHAT DOES THAT MEAN?
EXACTLY WHAT I SAID.
WE ARE BORN NEITHER MALE NOR FEMALE.
♂
♀
AGE16 GENDER SELECTION
♂
♀
AND WHEN I TURN SIXTEEN, I'LL HAVE A COMING OF AGE CEREMONY, WHEN I CHOOSE TO BECOME A MAN OR A WOMAN.
F I DON'T CHOOSE, I WILL ATURALLY SETTLE NTO ONE GENDER OR THE OTHER.
I SEE... I HAD HEARD OF IT.
BUT I'VE NEVER MET ONE IN PERSON BEFORE.
I SEE.
YES...
I SEE... YES... YES.
CHA-KING
UM... KARIN-SEMPAI?
THAT BEING THE CASE...
WHAT?
WHICH WILL YOU CHOOSE?
THAK
!
WHA- KARIN-SEMPAI!?
PASH
ZASH
WHAT ARE YOU-!?
SWOOSH
WILL YOU BE A MAN?
OR A WOMAN?
PASH

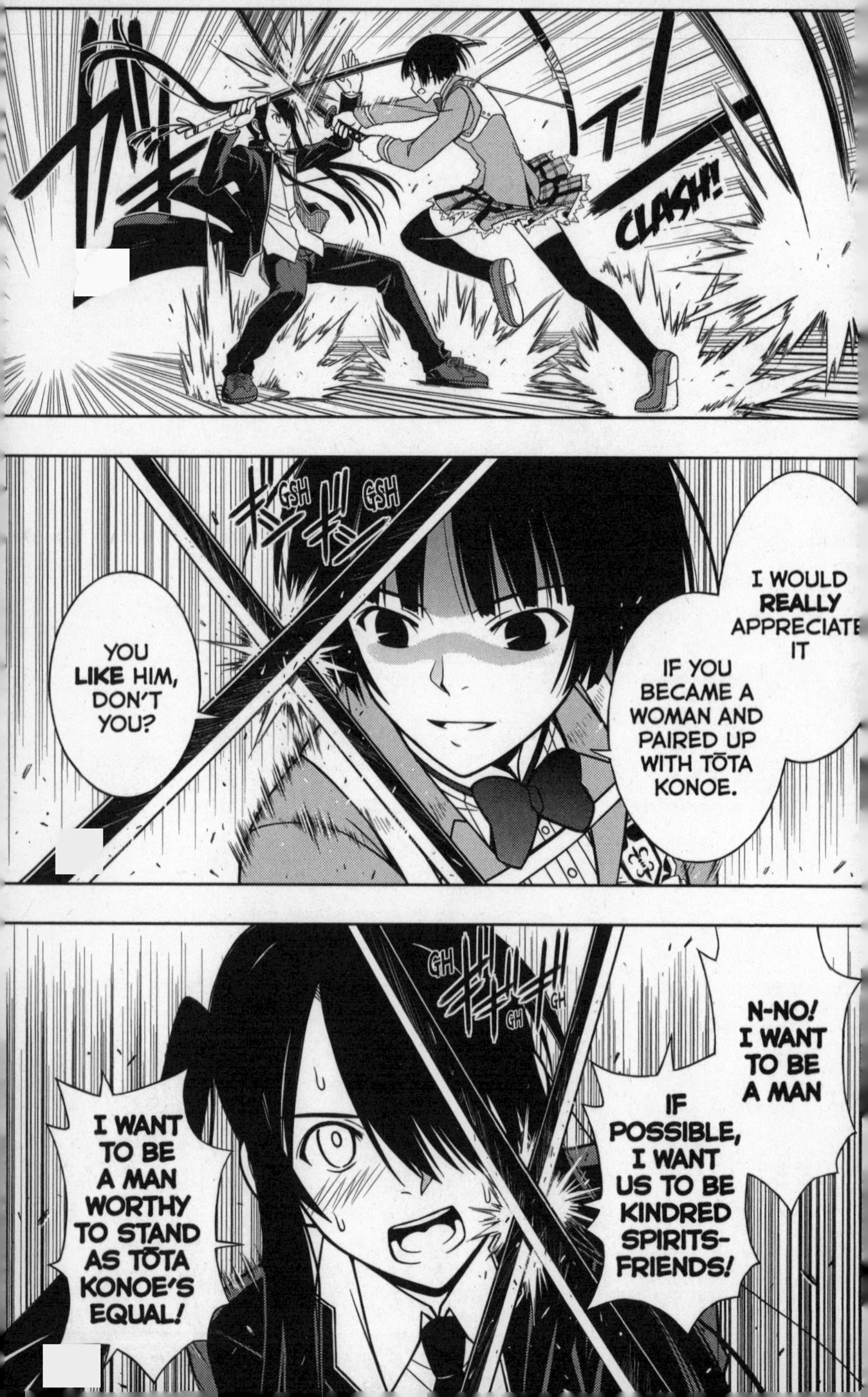

CLASH!!
I WOULD REALLY APPRECIATE IT
IF YOU BECAME A WOMAN AND PAIRED UP WITH TŌTA KONOE.
GSH GSH
YOU LIKE HIM, DON'T YOU?
GH GH GH
N-NO! I WANT TO BE A MAN
IF POSSIBLE, I WANT US TO BE KINDRED SPIRITS-FRIENDS!
I WANT TO BE A MAN WORTHY TO STAND AS TŌTA KONOE'S EQUAL!

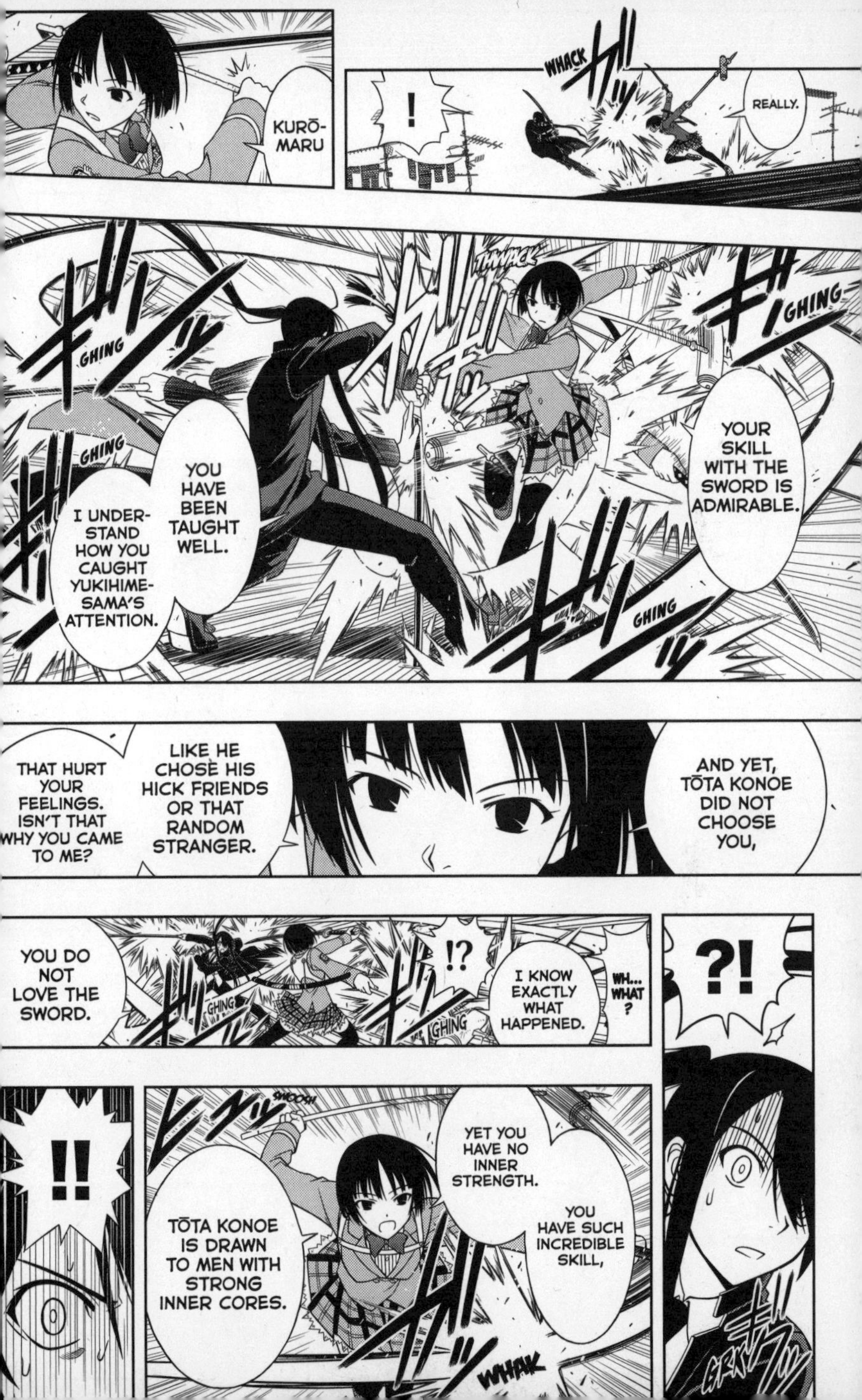
REALLY.
WHACK
!
KURŌ-MARU
THWACK
GHING
YOUR SKILL WITH THE SWORD IS ADMIRABLE.
YOU HAVE BEEN TAUGHT WELL.
I UNDER-STAND HOW YOU CAUGHT YUKIHIME-SAMA'S ATTENTION.
GHING
GHING
GHING
AND YET, TŌTA KONOE DID NOT CHOOSE YOU,
LIKE HE CHOSE HIS HICK FRIENDS OR THAT RANDOM STRANGER.
THAT HURT YOUR FEELINGS. ISN'T THAT WHY YOU CAME TO ME?
?!
WH... WHAT?
I KNOW EXACTLY WHAT HAPPENED.
!?
GHING
GHING
YOU DO NOT LOVE THE SWORD.
YOU HAVE SUCH INCREDIBLE SKILL,
YET YOU HAVE NO INNER STRENGTH.
SWOOSH
TŌTA KONOE IS DRAWN TO MEN WITH STRONG INNER CORES.
WHAK
!!

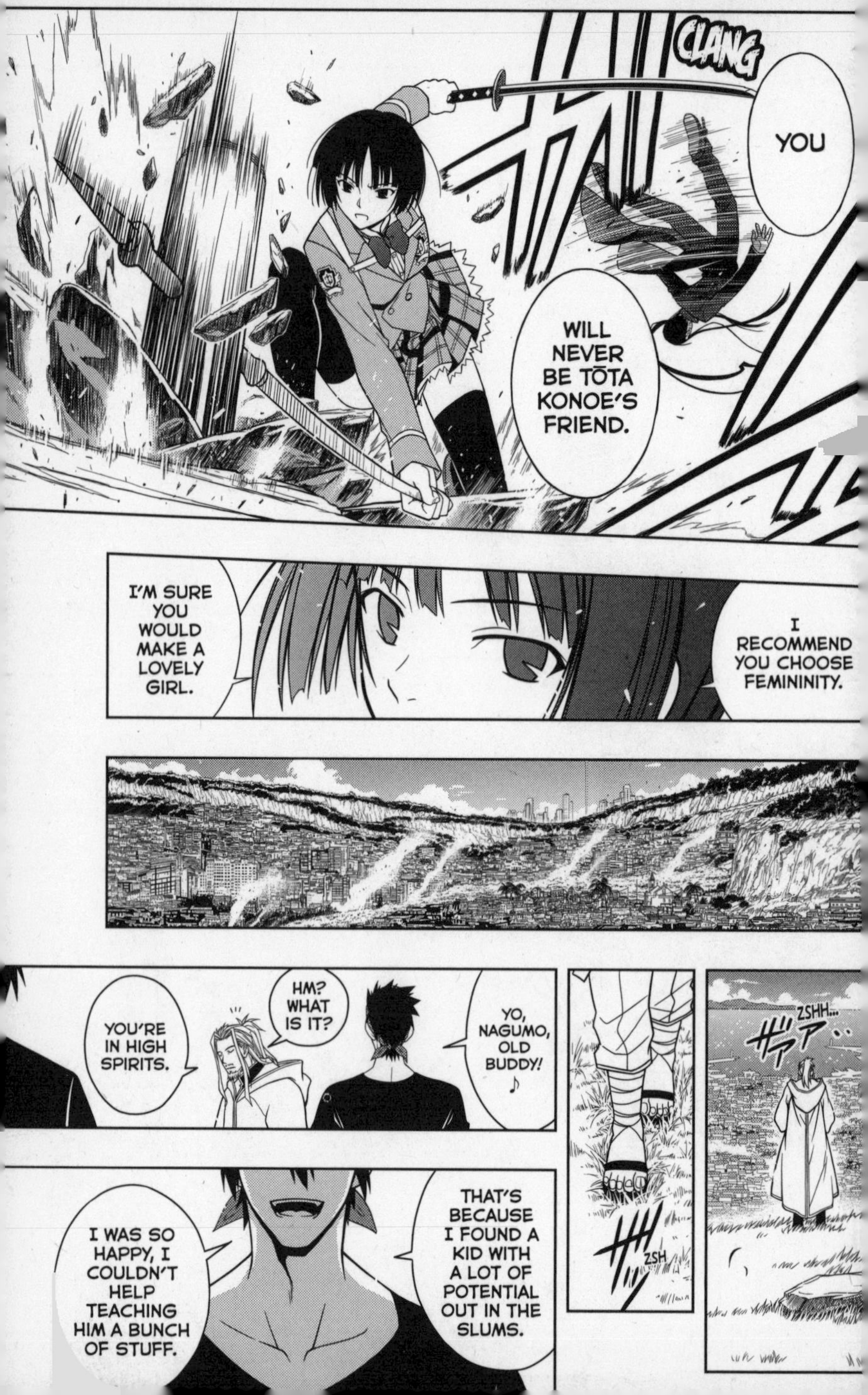
CLANG
YOU
WILL NEVER BE TŌTA KONOE'S FRIEND.
I RECOMMEND YOU CHOOSE FEMININITY.
I'M SURE YOU WOULD MAKE A LOVELY GIRL.
ZSHH...
ザァ
ZSH
YO, NAGUMO, OLD BUDDY! ♪
HM? WHAT IS IT?
YOU'RE IN HIGH SPIRITS.
THAT'S BECAUSE I FOUND A KID WITH A LOT OF POTENTIAL OUT IN THE SLUMS.
I WAS SO HAPPY, I COULDN'T HELP TEACHING HIM A BUNCH OF STUFF.

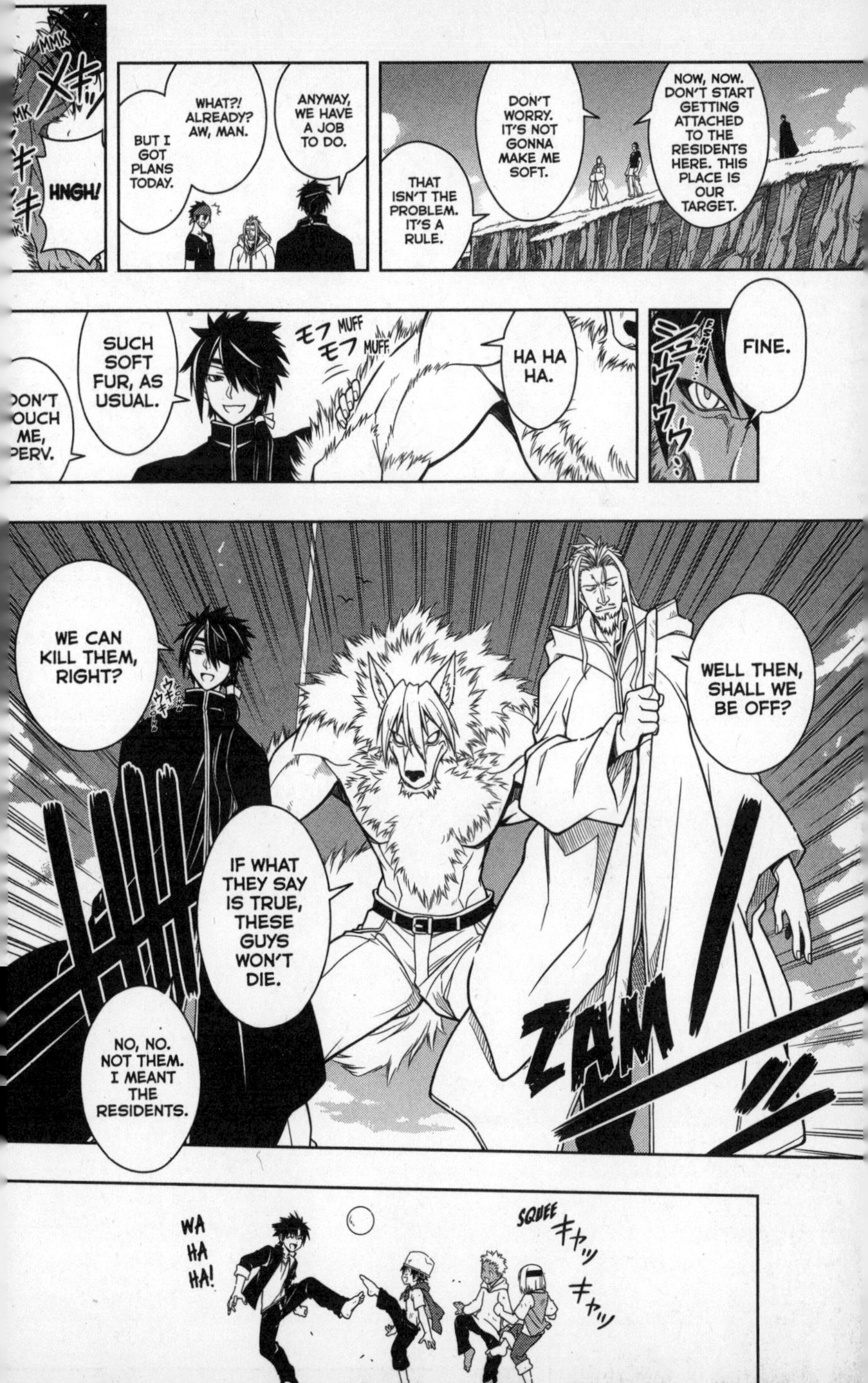
NOW, NOW. DON'T START GETTING ATTACHED TO THE RESIDENTS HERE. THIS PLACE IS OUR TARGET.
DON'T WORRY. IT'S NOT GONNA MAKE ME SOFT.
THAT ISN'T THE PROBLEM. IT'S A RULE.
ANYWAY, WE HAVE A JOB TO DO.
WHAT?! ALREADY? AW, MAN.
BUT I GOT PLANS TODAY.
MMK
HNGH!
FINE.
HA HA HA.
MUFF MUFF
SUCH SOFT FUR, AS USUAL.
DON'T OUCH ME, PERV.
WELL THEN, SHALL WE BE OFF?
WE CAN KILL THEM, RIGHT?
IF WHAT THEY SAY IS TRUE, THESE GUYS WON'T DIE.
NO, NO. NOT THEM. I MEANT THE RESIDENTS.
ZAM
SQUEE
WA HA HA!

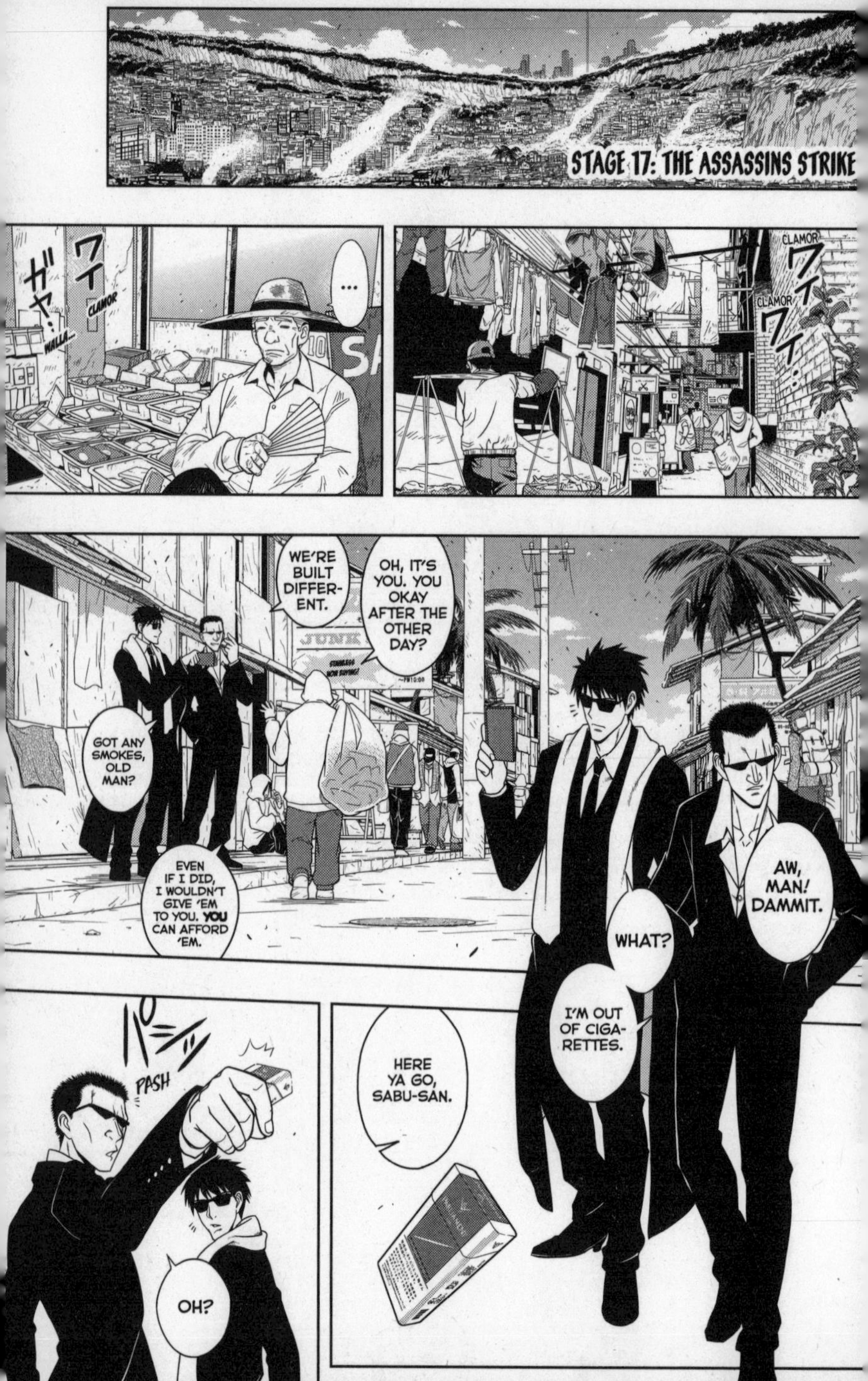
STAGE 17: THE ASSASSINS STRIKE
CLAMOR
ワイ
CLAMOR
ワイ
ガヤ
WALLA...
ワイ
CLAMOR
...
GOT ANY SMOKES, OLD MAN?
EVEN IF I DID, I WOULDN'T GIVE 'EM TO YOU. YOU CAN AFFORD 'EM.
OH, IT'S YOU. YOU OKAY AFTER THE OTHER DAY?
WE'RE BUILT DIFFER- ENT.
JUNK
AW, MAN! DAMMIT.
WHAT?
I'M OUT OF CIGA- RETTES.
HERE YA GO, SABU-SAN.
パ
PASH
OH?

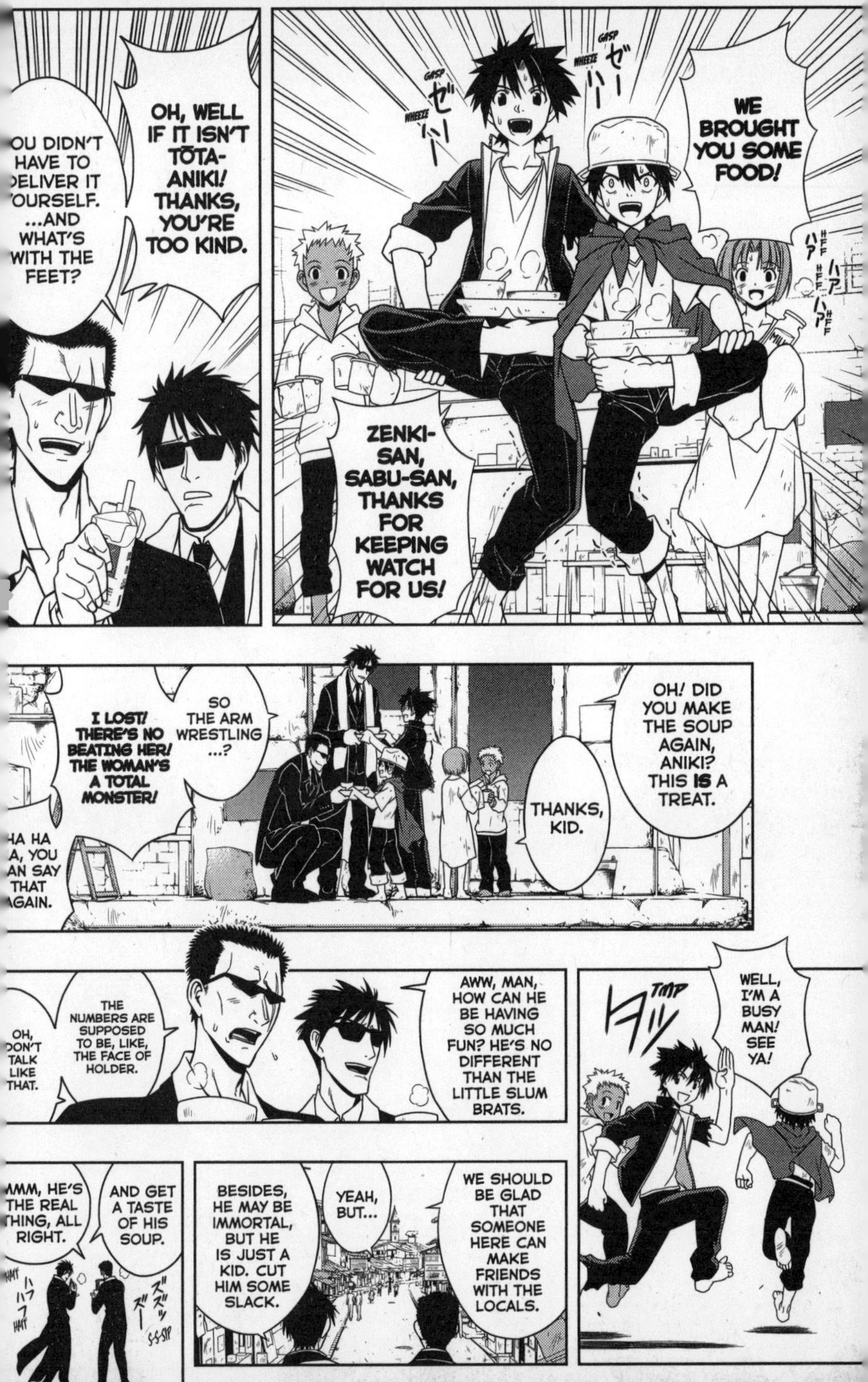
GASP
ゼー
WHEEZE
ハー
GASP
ゼー
WHEEZE
ハー
WE BROUGHT YOU SOME FOOD!
HFF ハァ
HFF ハァ
HFF ハァ
ZENKI-SAN, SABU-SAN, THANKS FOR KEEPING WATCH FOR US!
OH, WELL IF IT ISN'T TŌTA-ANIKI! THANKS, YOU'RE TOO KIND.
OU DIDN'T HAVE TO ELIVER IT OURSELF. ...AND WHAT'S WITH THE FEET?
OH! DID YOU MAKE THE SOUP AGAIN, ANIKI? THIS IS A TREAT.
THANKS, KID.
SO THE ARM WRESTLING ...?
I LOST! THERE'S NO BEATING HER! THE WOMAN'S A TOTAL MONSTER!
HA HA A, YOU AN SAY THAT AGAIN.
WELL, I'M A BUSY MAN! SEE YA!
TMP
タッ
AWW, MAN, HOW CAN HE BE HAVING SO MUCH FUN? HE'S NO DIFFERENT THAN THE LITTLE SLUM BRATS.
THE NUMBERS ARE SUPPOSED TO BE, LIKE, THE FACE OF HOLDER.
OH, ON'T TALK LIKE THAT.
WE SHOULD BE GLAD THAT SOMEONE HERE CAN MAKE FRIENDS WITH THE LOCALS.
YEAH, BUT...
BESIDES, HE MAY BE IMMORTAL, BUT HE IS JUST A KID. CUT HIM SOME SLACK.
AND GET A TASTE OF HIS SOUP.
MMM, HE'S THE REAL HING, ALL RIGHT.
ズズッ ズー
S-S-SIP
ハフ
HAFF
ハフ
HAFF

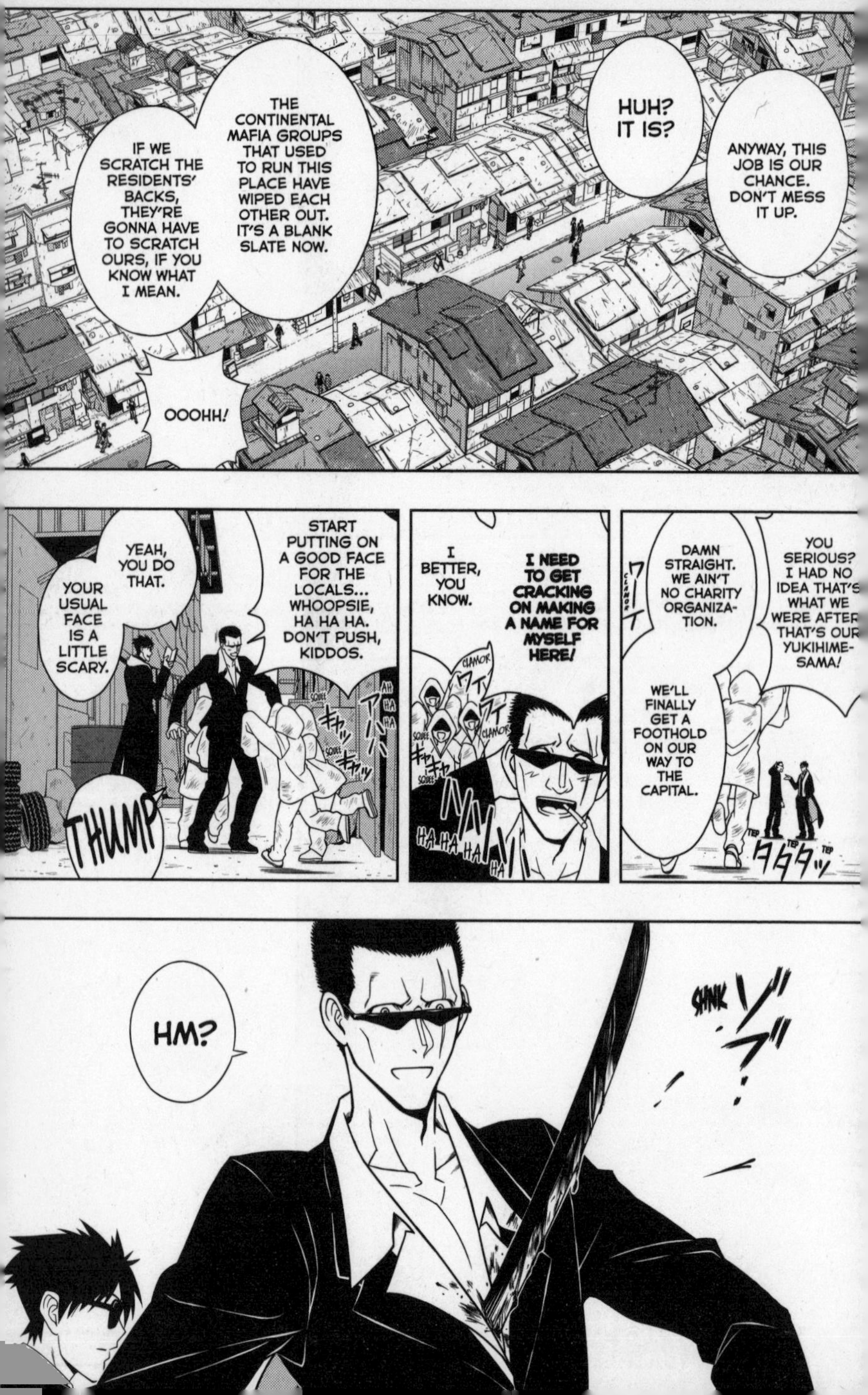
ANYWAY, THIS JOB IS OUR CHANCE. DON'T MESS IT UP.
HUH? IT IS?
THE CONTINENTAL MAFIA GROUPS THAT USED TO RUN THIS PLACE HAVE WIPED EACH OTHER OUT. IT'S A BLANK SLATE NOW.
IF WE SCRATCH THE RESIDENTS' BACKS, THEY'RE GONNA HAVE TO SCRATCH OURS, IF YOU KNOW WHAT I MEAN.
OOOHH!
YOU SERIOUS? I HAD NO IDEA THAT'S WHAT WE WERE AFTER THAT'S OUR YUKIHIME-SAMA!
DAMN STRAIGHT. WE AIN'T NO CHARITY ORGANIZA-TION.
CLAMOR
WE'LL FINALLY GET A FOOTHOLD ON OUR WAY TO THE CAPITAL.
TEP TEP TEP
I NEED TO GET CRACKING ON MAKING A NAME FOR MYSELF HERE!
I BETTER, YOU KNOW.
CLAMOR
CLAMOR
SQUEE
SQUEE
HA HA HA HA
START PUTTING ON A GOOD FACE FOR THE LOCALS... WHOOPSIE, HA HA HA. DON'T PUSH, KIDDOS.
YEAH, YOU DO THAT.
YOUR USUAL FACE IS A LITTLE SCARY.
AH HA HA
SQUEE
SQUEE
THUMP
SHNK
HM?

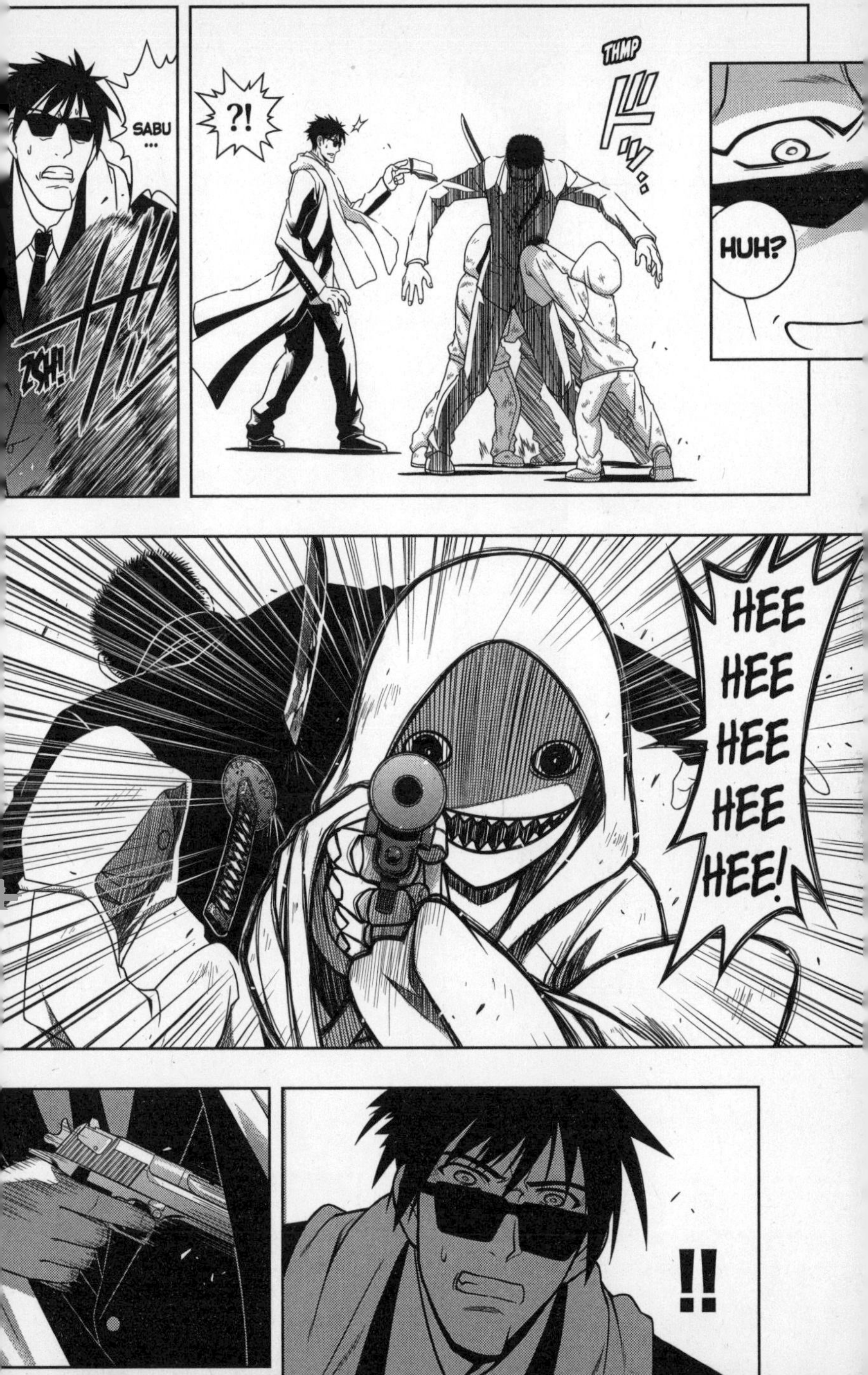
HUH?
THMP
?!
SABU…
ZSH!
HEE HEE HEE HEE HEE!
!!

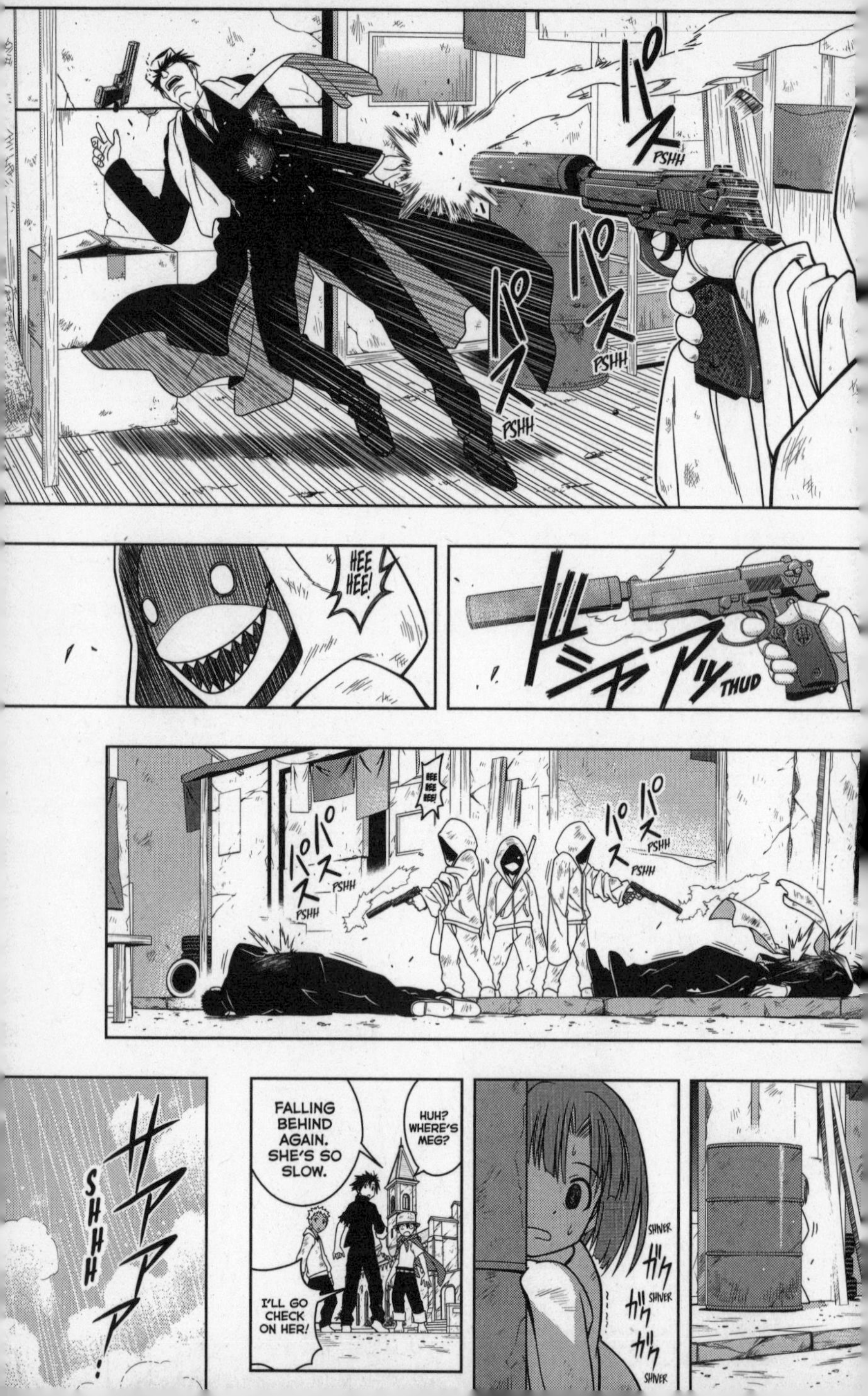
パス
PSHH
パス
PSHH
パス
PSHH
ドシャアッ
THUD
HEE HEE!
HEE HEE HEE!
パス
PSHH
パス
PSHH
パス
PSHH
パス
PSHH
SHIVER
ガク
SHIVER
ガク
ガク
SHIVER
HUH? WHERE'S MEG?
FALLING BEHIND AGAIN. SHE'S SO SLOW.
I'LL GO CHECK ON HER!
サァァァ…!
SHHH

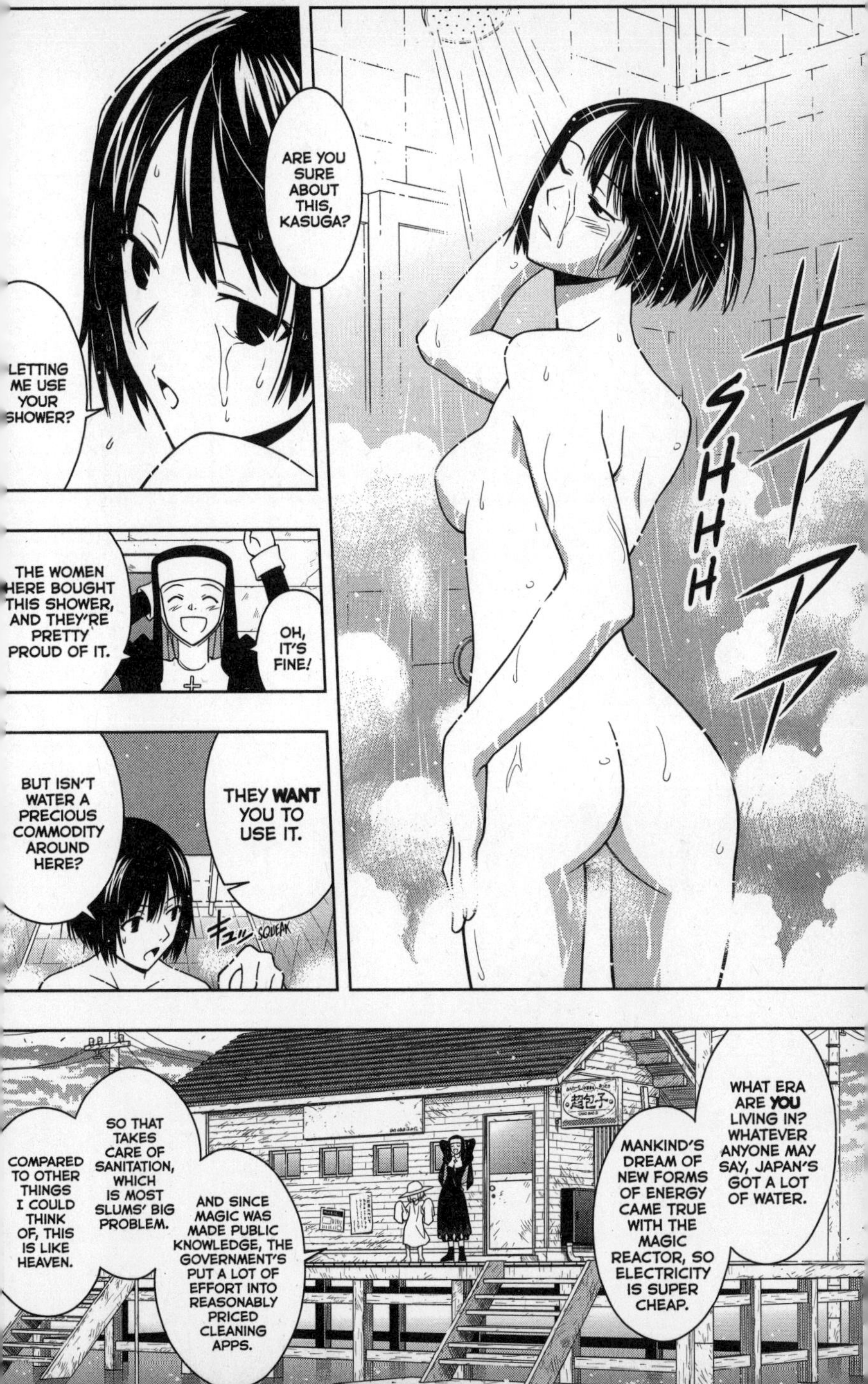
SHHH
ARE YOU SURE ABOUT THIS, KASUGA?
LETTING ME USE YOUR SHOWER?
OH, IT'S FINE!
THE WOMEN HERE BOUGHT THIS SHOWER, AND THEY'RE PRETTY PROUD OF IT.
THEY **WANT** YOU TO USE IT.
BUT ISN'T WATER A PRECIOUS COMMODITY AROUND HERE?
SQUEAK
WHAT ERA ARE **YOU** LIVING IN? WHATEVER ANYONE MAY SAY, JAPAN'S GOT A LOT OF WATER.
MANKIND'S DREAM OF NEW FORMS OF ENERGY CAME TRUE WITH THE MAGIC REACTOR, SO ELECTRICITY IS SUPER CHEAP.
AND SINCE MAGIC WAS MADE PUBLIC KNOWLEDGE, THE GOVERNMENT'S PUT A LOT OF EFFORT INTO REASONABLY PRICED CLEANING APPS.
SO THAT TAKES CARE OF SANITATION, WHICH IS MOST SLUMS' BIG PROBLEM.
COMPARED TO OTHER THINGS I COULD THINK OF, THIS IS LIKE HEAVEN.

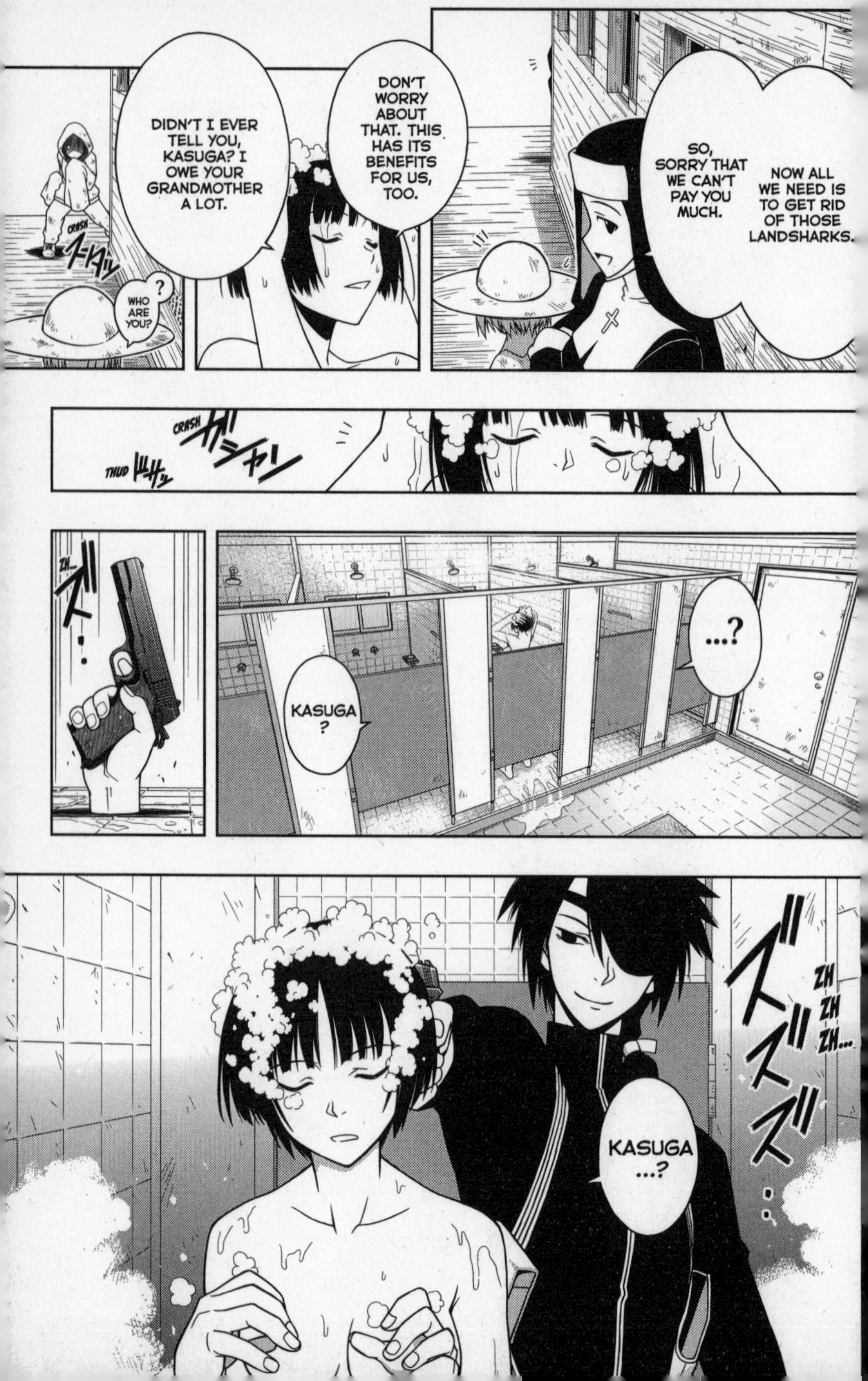
NOW ALL WE NEED IS TO GET RID OF THOSE LANDSHARKS.
SO, SORRY THAT WE CAN'T PAY YOU MUCH.
DON'T WORRY ABOUT THAT. THIS HAS ITS BENEFITS FOR US, TOO.
DIDN'T I EVER TELL YOU, KASUGA? I OWE YOUR GRANDMOTHER A LOT.
CRASH
?
WHO ARE YOU?
CRASH
THUD
...?
KASUGA?
ZH...
ZH ZH ZH...
KASUGA...?

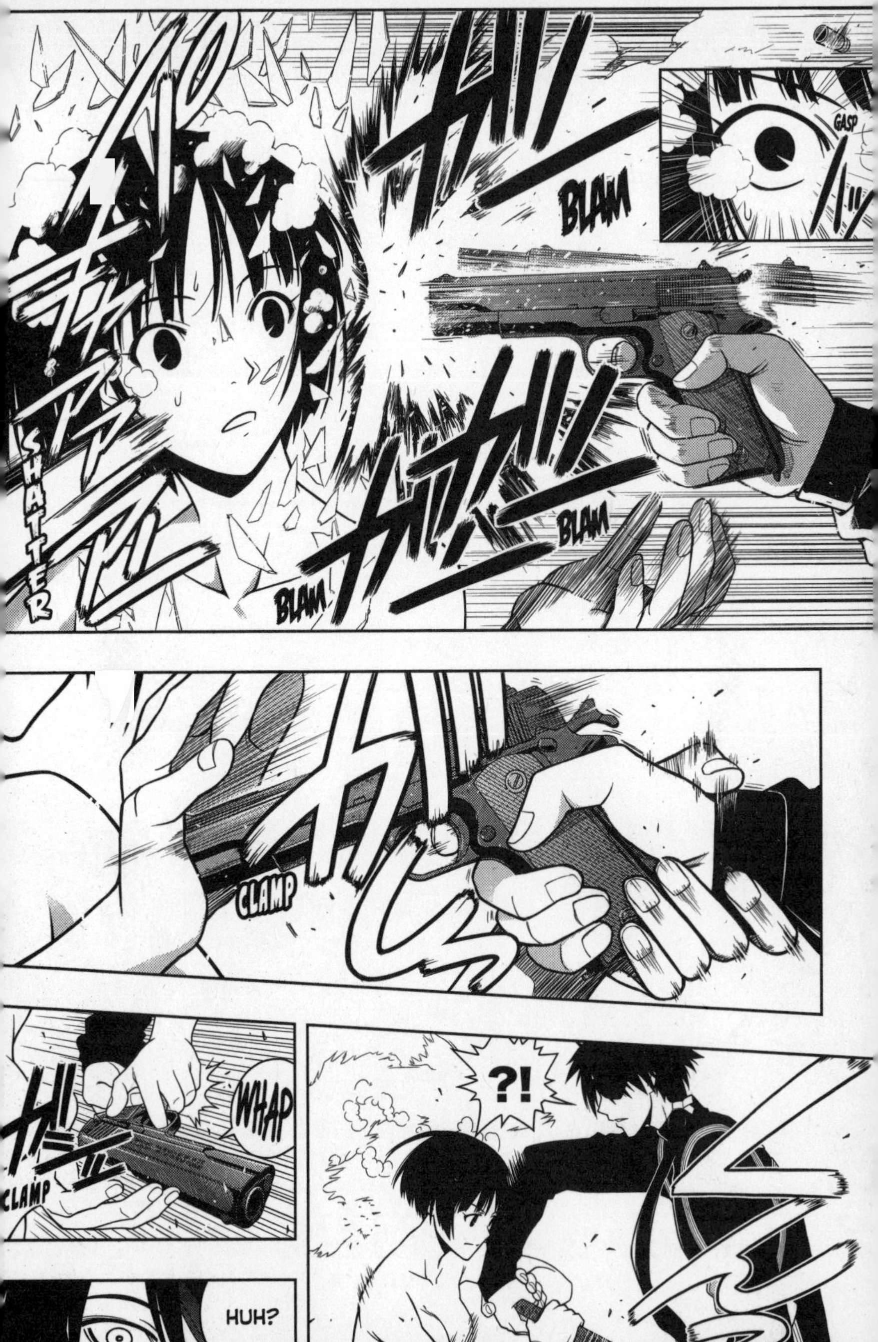
GASP
BLAM
BLAM
BLAM
SHATTER
CLAMP
?!
BLAM
WHAP
CLAMP
HUH?

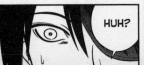

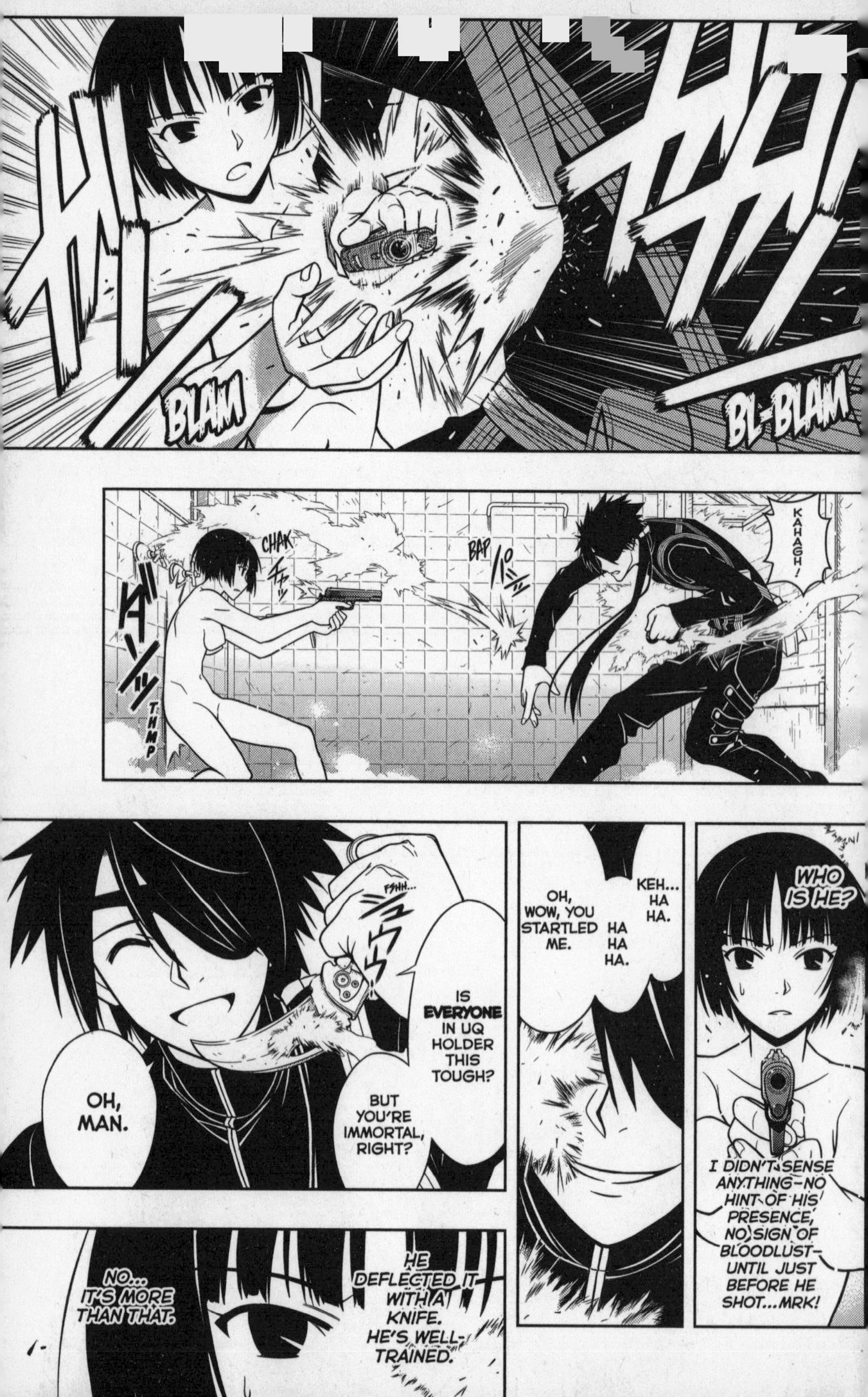
BL-BLAM
BLAM
KAHAGH!
BAP
CHAK
THMP
WHO IS HE?
I DIDN'T SENSE ANYTHING—NO HINT OF HIS PRESENCE, NO SIGN OF BLOODLUST—UNTIL JUST BEFORE HE SHOT...MRK!
KEH... HA HA.
OH, WOW, YOU STARTLED ME. HA HA HA.
FSHH...
IS EVERYONE IN UQ HOLDER THIS TOUGH?
BUT YOU'RE IMMORTAL, RIGHT?
OH, MAN.
HE DEFLECTED IT WITH A KNIFE. HE'S WELL-TRAINED.
NO... IT'S MORE THAN THAT.

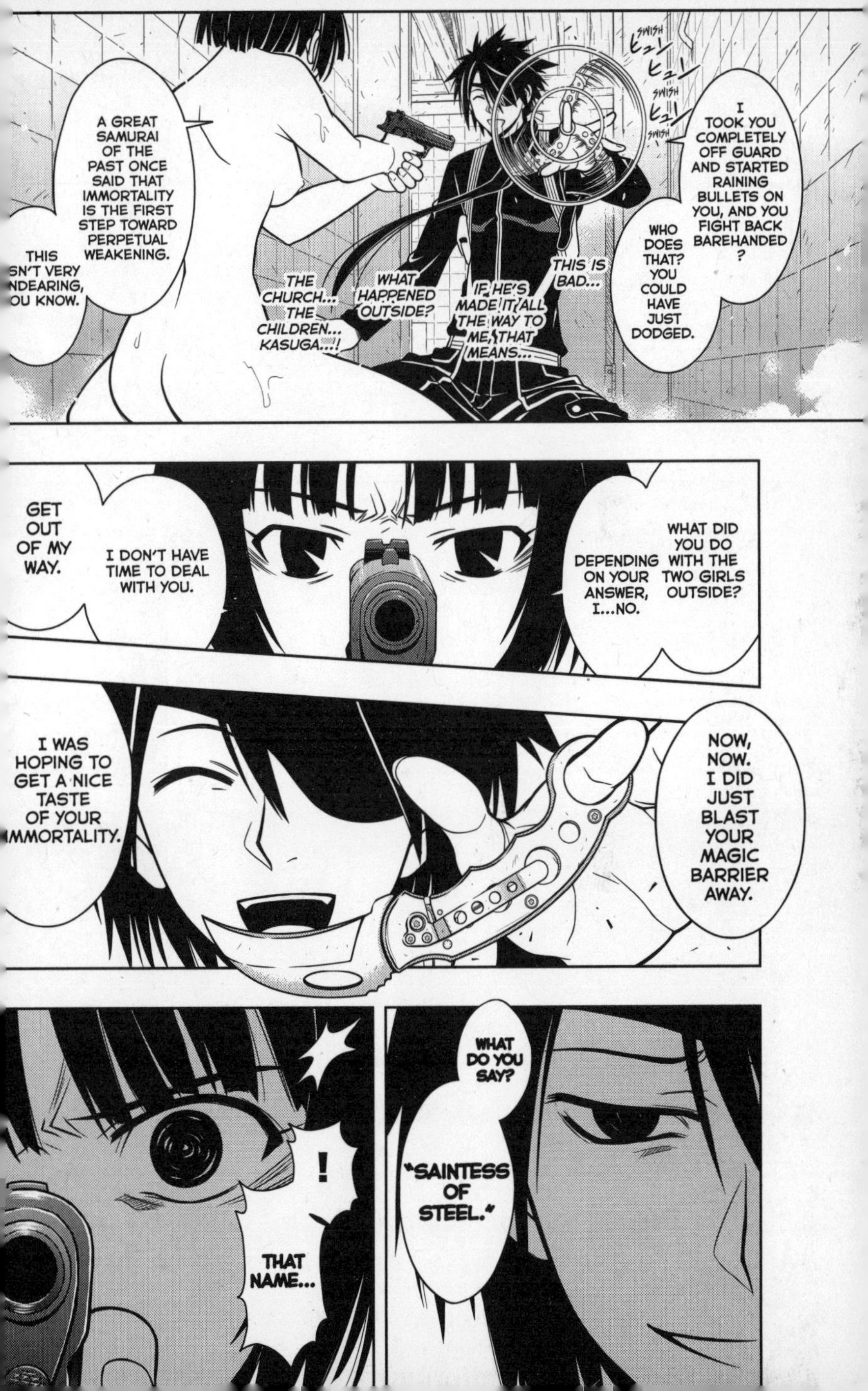
SWISH
SWISH
SWISH
I TOOK YOU COMPLETELY OFF GUARD AND STARTED RAINING BULLETS ON YOU, AND YOU FIGHT BACK BAREHANDED?
WHO DOES THAT? YOU COULD HAVE JUST DODGED.
THIS IS BAD...
IF HE'S MADE IT ALL THE WAY TO ME, THAT MEANS...
WHAT HAPPENED OUTSIDE?
THE CHURCH... THE CHILDREN... KASUGA...!
A GREAT SAMURAI OF THE PAST ONCE SAID THAT IMMORTALITY IS THE FIRST STEP TOWARD PERPETUAL WEAKENING.
THIS SN'T VERY NDEARING, OU KNOW.
WHAT DID YOU DO WITH THE TWO GIRLS OUTSIDE?
DEPENDING ON YOUR ANSWER, I...NO.
I DON'T HAVE TIME TO DEAL WITH YOU.
GET OUT OF MY WAY.
NOW, NOW. I DID JUST BLAST YOUR MAGIC BARRIER AWAY.
I WAS HOPING TO GET A NICE TASTE OF YOUR MMORTALITY.
WHAT DO YOU SAY?
"SAINTESS OF STEEL."
!
THAT NAME...

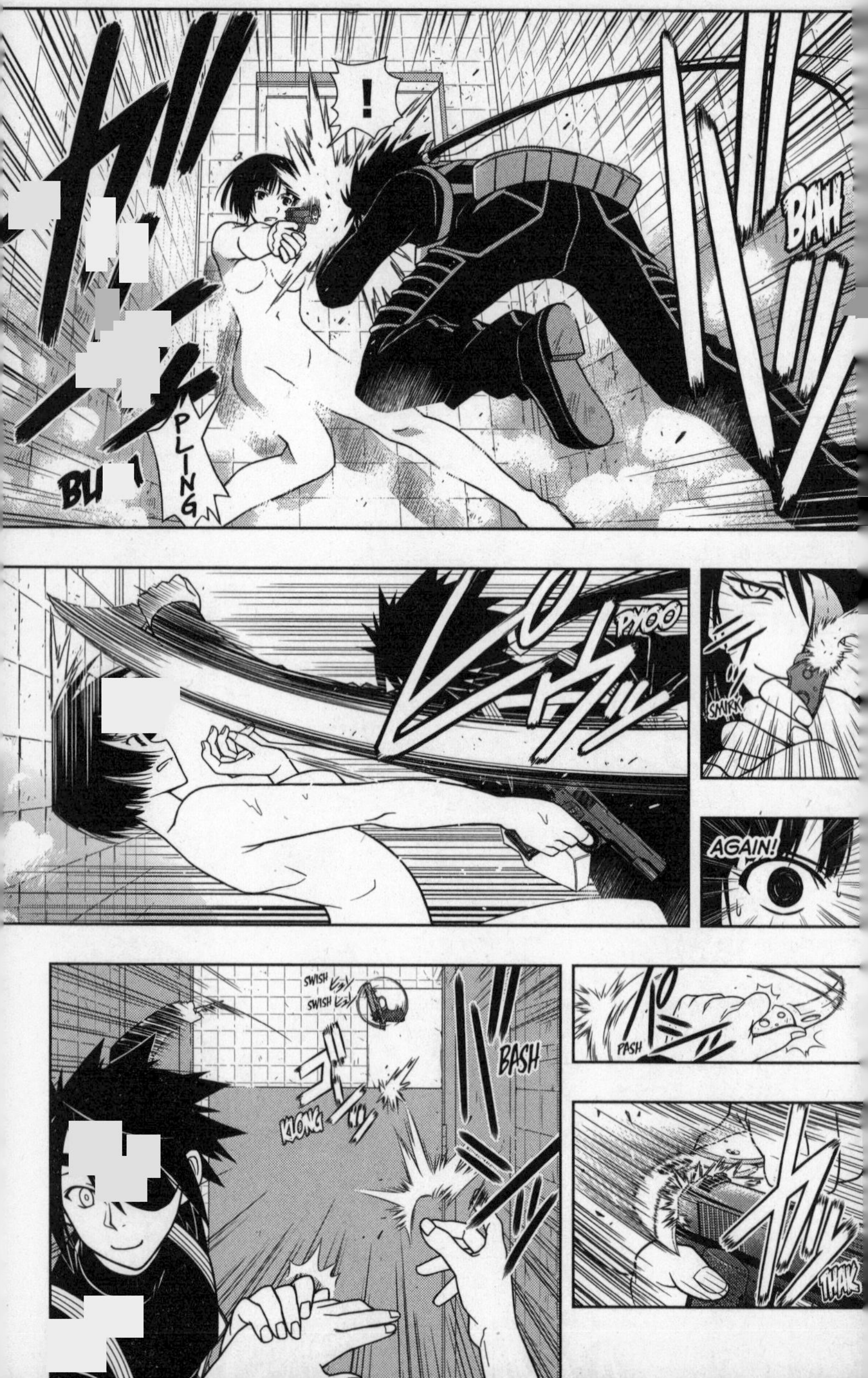
!
BAH
PLING
SMIRK
AGAIN!
PYOO
PASH
THAK
SWISH
SWISH
BASH
KLONG

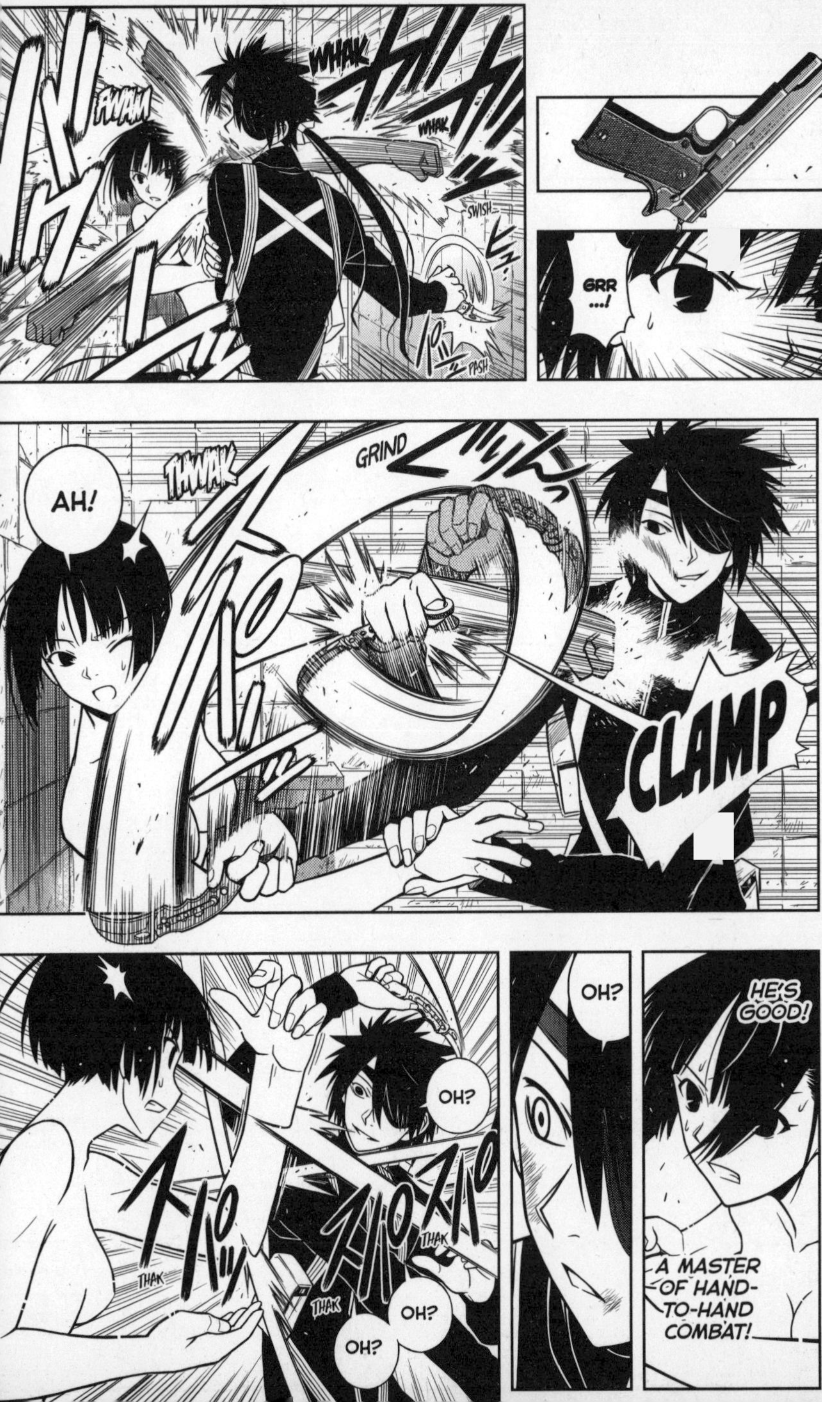
GRR ...!
WHAK
WHAK
FWAM
SWISH
PASH
GRIND
THWAK
AH!
CLAMP
HE'S GOOD!
A MASTER OF HAND-TO-HAND COMBAT!
OH?
OH?
THAK
THAK
OH?
OH?
THAK

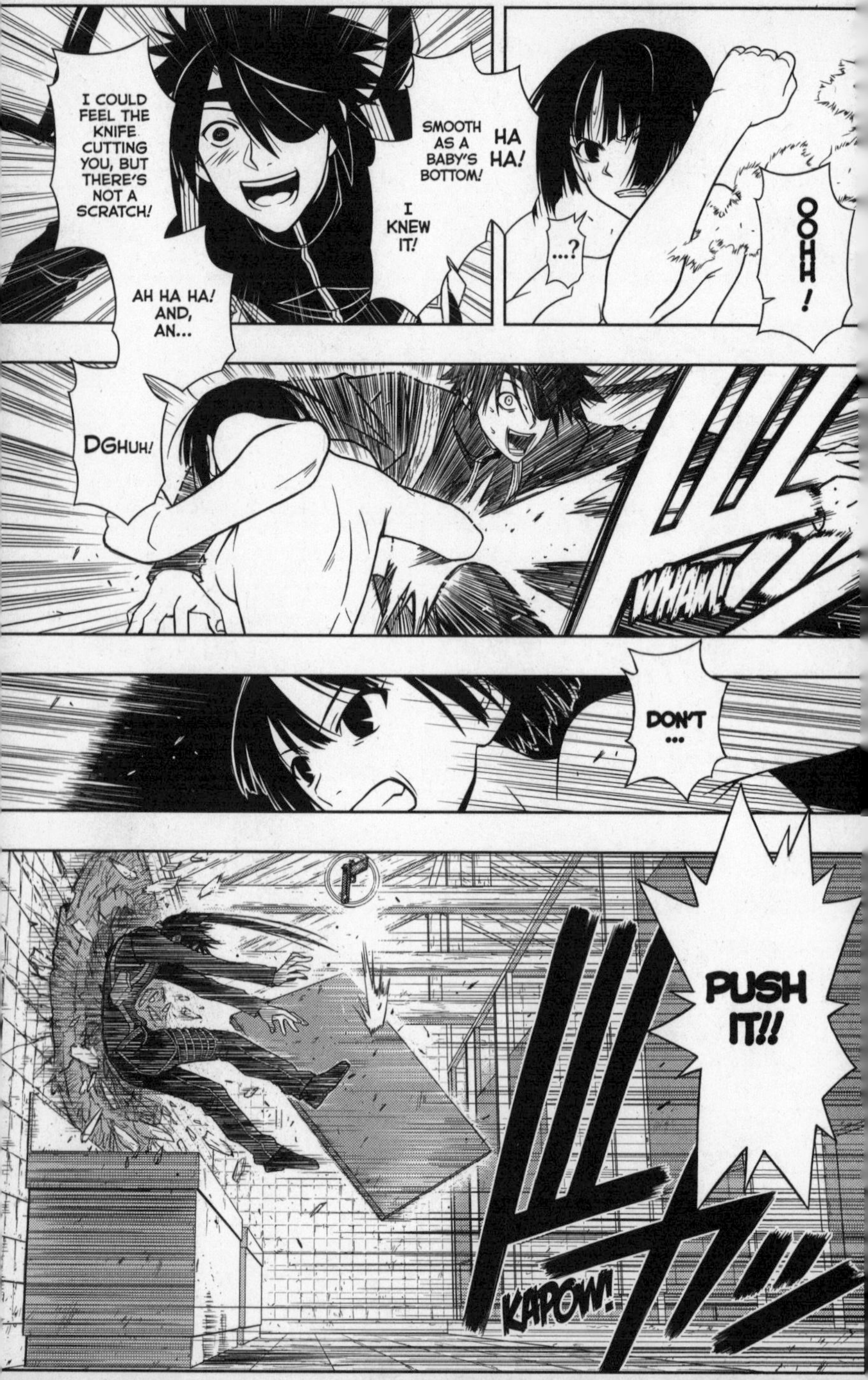
OOHH!
...?
HA HA!
SMOOTH AS A BABY'S BOTTOM!
I KNEW IT!
I COULD FEEL THE KNIFE CUTTING YOU, BUT THERE'S NOT A SCRATCH!
AH HA HA! AND, AN...
WHAM!
DGHUH!
DON'T ...
PUSH IT!!
KAPOW!

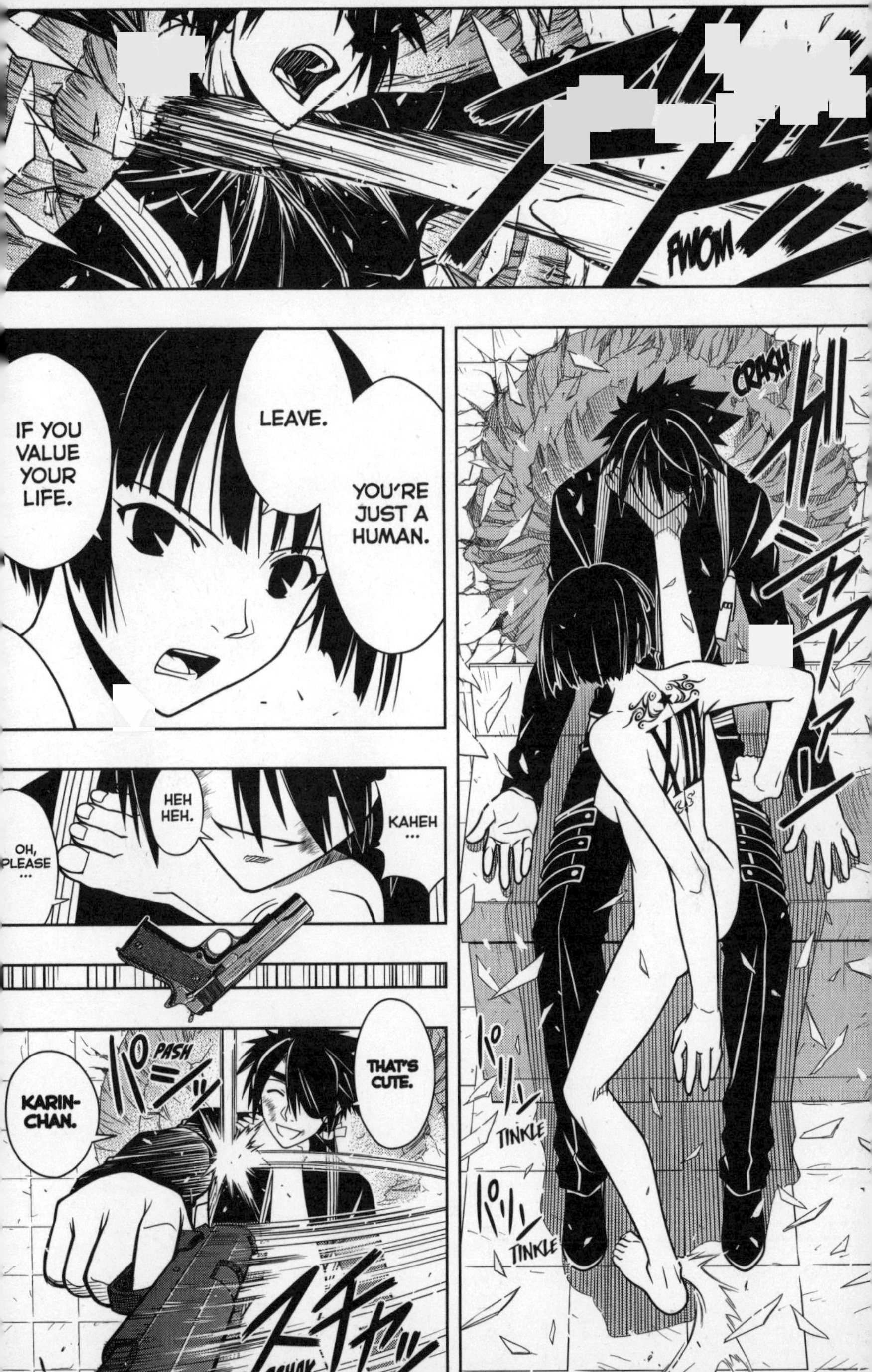
FWOM
CRASH
TINKLE
TINKLE
LEAVE.
YOU'RE JUST A HUMAN.
IF YOU VALUE YOUR LIFE.
KAHEH ...
HEH HEH.
OH, PLEASE ...
THAT'S CUTE.
PASH
KARIN-CHAN.
SCHAK

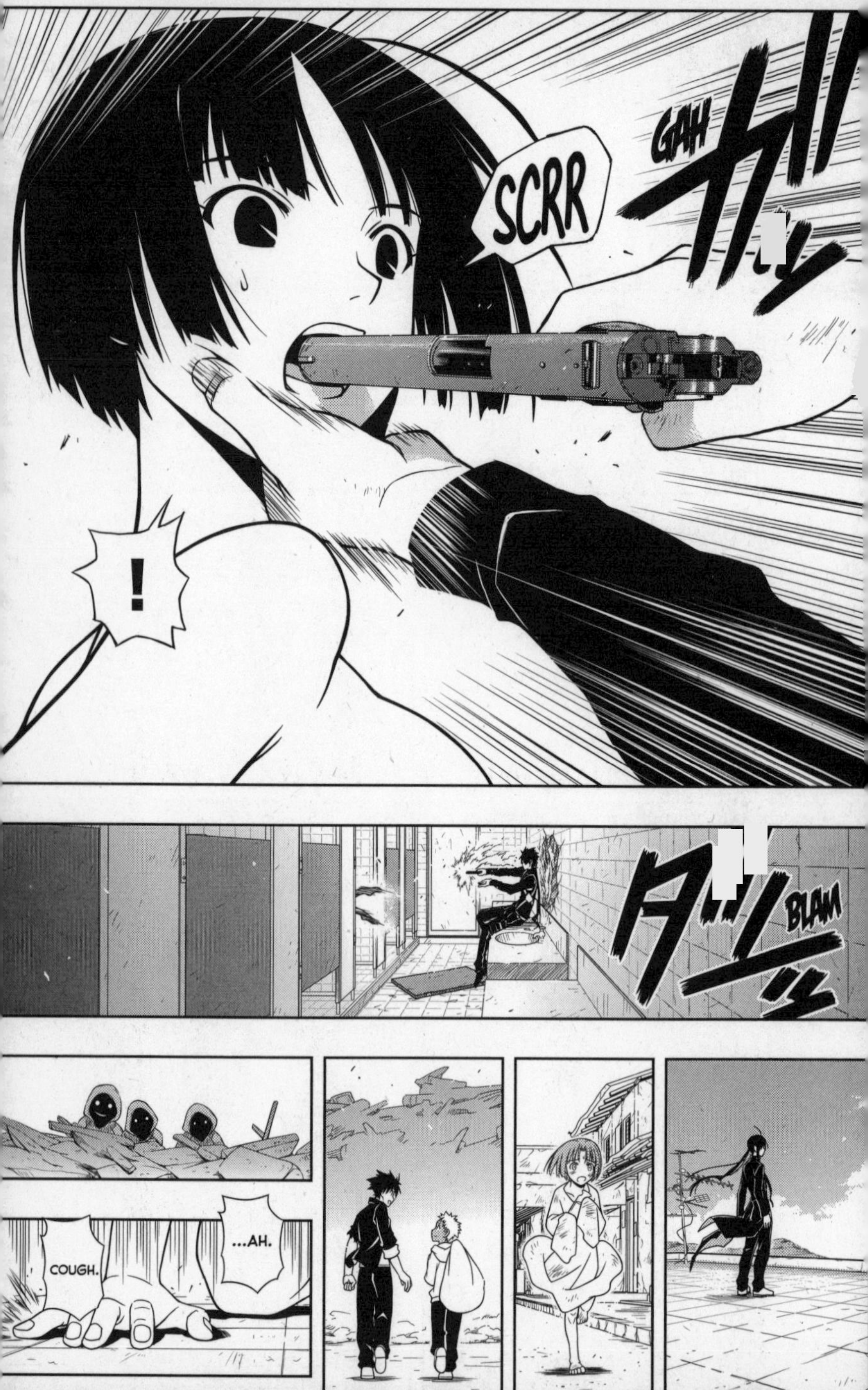
GAH
SCRR
!
BLAM
...AH.
COUGH.

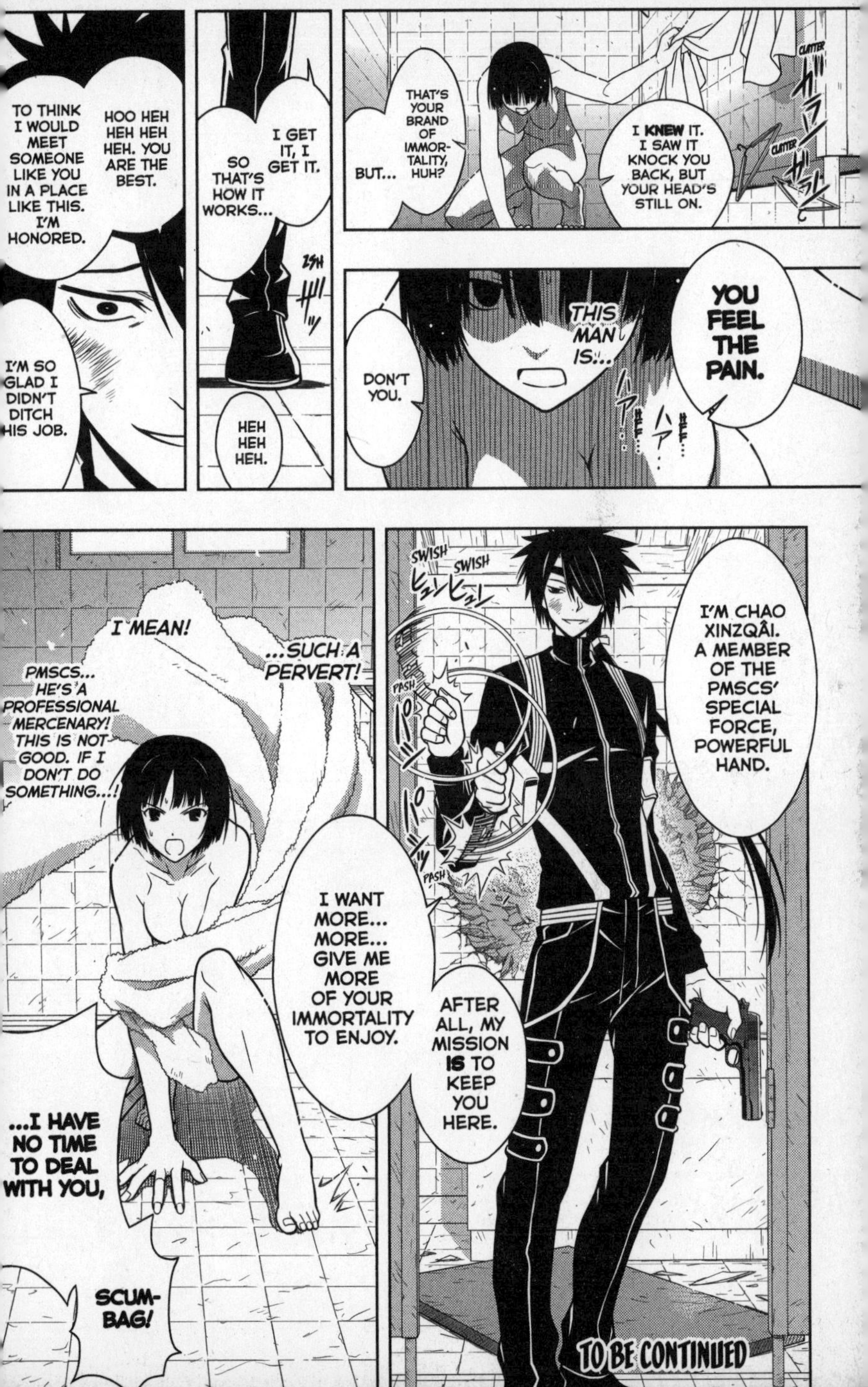
CLATTER
CLATTER
I KNEW IT. I SAW IT KNOCK YOU BACK, BUT YOUR HEAD'S STILL ON.
THAT'S YOUR BRAND OF IMMORTALITY, HUH?
BUT...
YOU FEEL THE PAIN.
DON'T YOU.
THIS MAN IS...!
HFF... HFF...
I GET IT, I GET IT.
SO THAT'S HOW IT WORKS...
ZSH
HEH HEH HEH.
HOO HEH HEH HEH HEH. YOU ARE THE BEST.
TO THINK I WOULD MEET SOMEONE LIKE YOU IN A PLACE LIKE THIS. I'M HONORED.
I'M SO GLAD I DIDN'T DITCH HIS JOB.
SWISH SWISH
PASH
PASH
I'M CHAO XINZQÂI. A MEMBER OF THE PMSCS' SPECIAL FORCE, POWERFUL HAND.
I WANT MORE... MORE... GIVE ME MORE OF YOUR IMMORTALITY TO ENJOY.
AFTER ALL, MY MISSION IS TO KEEP YOU HERE.
...SUCH A PERVERT!
I MEAN!
PMSCS... HE'S A PROFESSIONAL MERCENARY! THIS IS NOT GOOD. IF I DON'T DO SOMETHING...!
...I HAVE NO TIME TO DEAL WITH YOU,
SCUM-BAG!
TO BE CONTINUED

UQ HOLDER!

STAFF

Ken Akamatsu

Takashi Takemoto

Kenichi Nakamura

Keiichi Yamashita

Tohru Mitsuhashi

Susumu Kuwabara

Yuri Sasaki

Thanks to Ran Ayanaga

FROM HIRO MASHIMA, CREATOR OF RAVE MASTER

FAIRY TAIL

FAIRY TAIL
1
Hiro Mashima Creator of Rave Master

FAIRY TAIL
2
Hiro Mashima Creator of Rave Master

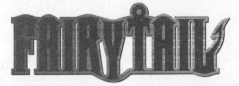

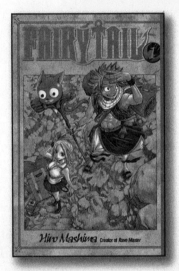

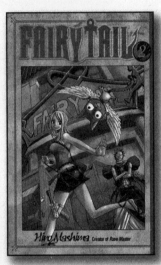

Lucy has always dreamed of joining the Fairy Tail, a club for the most powerful sorcerers in the land. But once she becomes a member, the fun really starts!

Special extras in each volume! Read them all!

RATING T AGES 13+

VISIT WWW.KODANSHACOMICS.COM TO:

- View release date calendars for upcoming volumes
- Find out the latest about new Kodansha Comics series

KC KODANSHA COMICS

NO.6

A PERFECT LIFE
IN A PERFECT CITY

For Shion, an elite student in the technologically sophisticated city No. 6, life is carefully choreographed. One fateful day, he takes a misstep, sheltering a fugitive his age from a typhoon. Helping this boy throws Shion's life down a path to discovering the appalling secrets behind the "perfection" of No. 6.

KC
KODANS
COMIC

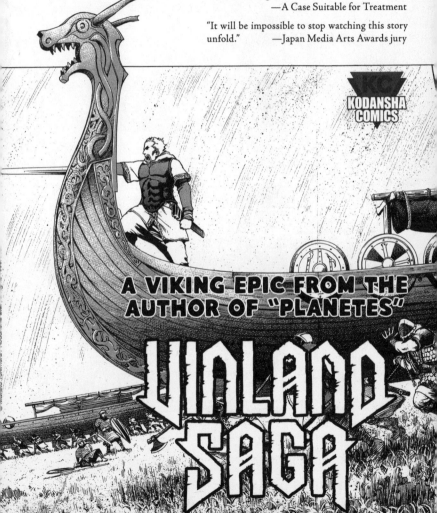

SHERLOCK BONES

DEDUCTIVE DOG DETECTIVE

When Takeru adopts a new pet, he's in for a surprise—the dog is none other than the reincarnation of Sherlock Holmes. With no one else able to communicate with Holmes, Takeru is roped into becoming Sherdog's assistant, John Watson. Using his sleuthing skills, Holmes uncovers clues to solve the trickiest crimes.

UQ HOLDER! VOLUME 2 IS A WORK OF FICTION. NAMES, CHARACTERS, PLACES, AND INCIDENTS ARE THE PRODUCTS OF THE AUTHOR'S IMAGINATION OR ARE USED FICTITIOUSLY. ANY RESEMBLANCE TO ACTUAL EVENTS, LOCALES, OR PERSONS, LIVING OR DEAD, IS ENTIRELY COINCIDENTAL.

A KODANSHA COMICS TRADE PAPERBACK ORIGINAL

PUBLISHED IN THE UNITED STATES BY KODANSHA COMICS, AN IMPRINT OF KODANSHA USA PUBLISHING, LLC, NEW YORK.

PUBLICATION RIGHTS FOR THIS ENGLISH EDITION ARRANGED THROUGH KODANSHA LTD., TOKYO.

FIRST PUBLISHED IN JAPAN IN 2014 BY KODANSHA LTD., TOKYO.

ISBN 978-1-61262-935-3

PRINTED IN THE UNITED STATES OF AMERICA.

WWW.KODANSHACOMICS.COM

9 8 7 6 5 4 3 2 1

TRANSLATOR: ALETHEA NIBLEY AND ATHENA NIBLEY
LETTERING: JAMES DASHIELL